The
Lies
We Hide

S.E. LYNES

bookouture

Published by Bookouture in 2019

An imprint of Storyfire Ltd.
Carmelite House
50 Victoria Embankment
London EC4Y 0DZ

www.bookouture.com

ISBN: 978-1-83888-187-0
eBook ISBN: 978-1-83888-186-3

For my dad, Stephen Ball, with love

PART ONE

CHAPTER ONE

Carol

Blackpool Pleasure Beach, 1968

They've only been there five minutes when Ted grabs her hand.

'Carol, look,' he says, tilting his head. 'The rockets! Come on!'

In front of them is the giant spider of Maxim's Flying Machine. Blackpool is famous for it. That and the bright pink rock that sticks your teeth together. Oh, and the illuminations, of course.

Carol shakes her head. 'No, Ted,' she says, pulling against him as he drags her towards the ride.

'Aw, come on! You can't come all this way and not go on Maxim's.' He's still pulling her forward; her stiletto soles slip on the grimy ground.

'You know I can't be doing with heights,' she says. 'You go on. Go on, go.'

He looks at her a moment before snatching a quick kiss. 'All right then,' he says, already backing away. 'Wait here for me.'

He lets go of her hand and she watches him, the cocksure way he walks, pulling his comb from the back pocket of his suit trousers, teasing the slick duck's arse to perfection, returning the comb with one deft hand.

She loses him then, in the crowd. Meanwhile, the torpedo-shaped cars fill with thrill-seekers. They're excited to be out on a Friday night, flush with a week's pay, armed with pastel clouds of candyfloss and filthy innuendos. Lads joke and flirt. Girls laugh and smooth out their miniskirts. Fleeting orange sparks of last-minute cigarettes flash to the ground.

Minutes later, there's Ted: last on, hooking one drainpiped leg into his capsule, grinning and mugging at her like a lunatic. From this distance, his bootlace tie is lost against his pale pink shirt, his black velvet lapels invisible against the milk-chocolate brown of his jacket.

No sooner is he in his seat than the rockets begin to chug, lurching along to the first slow, discordant notes of the organ. Smells of petrol, cigarettes and sugar syrup settle on Carol's new cream mohair cardie. The rockets climb; as Ted's capsule lifts, he half stands, wobbling, his body at a terrifying angle. The great metal spider extends its legs; the rockets climb higher. Ted is flying towards her now, coming up to eye level.

'Carol Green!' he shouts at the top of his voice as he glides past. 'Will you marry me?'

And then he's gone, the back end of his capsule circling away.

Her mouth is open in shock. She can hear Ted laughing madly, hidden inside his pod. He reappears then, further away. He's sitting down, thank heavens, but he's still larking about. His rocket floats lower, there on the other side of the ride; a couple of bumps and it begins to climb once more, heading back around to where Carol stands rooted to the wet tarmac.

He begins again to stand. Oh for pity's sake. Bloody idiot.

'Ted!' she cries out to him. 'Sit down, will you? You'll get yourself killed.'

Embarrassed, she stares at her feet, covers her forehead with her hand. But here he comes again, higher and higher, over her head.

'Carol Gree-een!' Only the round base of the rocket above her. Only his voice. 'Will you marry me? Oi! Carol! Can you hear me?'

Never mind me, she thinks. *The whole fairground can hear you.*

In the puddle by her feet, the crescent moon shines up at her: a white arc in a reflected navy sky – faceless, like the grin of the Cheshire Cat. The rockets revolve, faster now. Up and down, round and round on the ends of the spindly spider legs. The music reaches full speed: a heady, spinning waltz. She can't hear Ted anymore and it looks like he's sat down properly now, thank goodness. Oh, but he's still waving his arms about, still carrying on. He's always mucking about, is Ted. Always creating. But he's never shouted down at her like that before, never asked her *that*.

He was only joking, though.

Obviously he was.

She's not stupid.

Once he gets off, he'll not ask her again.

Not to her face.

Will he?

As if to get her attention, the funfair flashes its lights – rudely, she thinks. *It might have been pouring down since dawn*, they seem to say, *but the rain's stopped now, it's getting dark and we'll not be put out, so stop your brooding, Carol Green. This is a funfair. You're supposed to have fun.*

A hiss and a heavy, industrial clunk. The rockets slow, descend, stop. The laughing riders clamber out: squeals, shrieks, names lost on the sticky air. The turnstile gives out greasy squeaks as, one by one, the new crowd pushes through while the old is spewed, chattering, through the exit.

'Oi.' Ted appears in front of her, blows at his black quiff, smooths one side with the flat of his hand. 'Didn't you hear me?'

She nods at the puddle between them. 'Mind your shoes. Suede never comes right if you get it wet.'

He steps over in one stride and grabs her by the shoulders. His fingers are thick. He's hurting her a bit, but she doesn't say anything. In the blinking coloured lights, his dark eyes shine with something like mischief. She can smell Old Spice, whisky and cigarettes – things she's been told to avoid.

'Carol? Didn't you hear me, what I was shouting?' He hitches up a trouser leg, gets down on one knee.

'Ted! Your good suit!' Around them, people stall, stare, nudge each other's elbows, oh heavens above.

'Carol …'

'I did hear you,' she whispers. Her hand comes to rest on the swell of her belly, a bump it's getting harder to hide. 'But you don't have to, you know, just because …'

'Don't be daft. I'd've asked you anyway.' In his black eyes, the white sliver of moon – tiny and still grinning in a smaller, darker sky. He is so handsome. She can only bring herself to look at him for a couple of seconds at a time. Any longer and she begins to feel like her make-up needs fixing or her hair has gone wrong or something.

Ted doesn't flinch. He never flinches. 'Come on, Carol Green. You'd be a fool not to marry me.'

CHAPTER TWO

Nicola

Merseyside, 2019

That's how it starts, for me, the story of my mother. In Blackpool, that midsummer's night, with Ted Watson, a man I ceased to call father a long time ago. All that followed would never have occurred without his flamboyant proposal in that damp, defiant funfair. So yes, it starts there, but of course there is a before. There is always a before. My mother was pregnant, her parents had thrown her out, she was living, as she called it, in sin. Marriage was the only way out of shame, as far as she was concerned, and if I can remember every detail of that scene, if I can see those flying rockets and smell the oil and the candyfloss, it is only because, in sentimental mood, she would tell me that particular story over and over. For her, it still had a romance to it, even after everything he did to her.

It wasn't me in her belly. It was my older brother, Graham. Conceived if not in love, since I don't believe my father capable of it, then in passion – the furtive fumblings of late-sixties sex. Any swinging associated with the decade had not yet reached the small towns of Merseyside in anything other than music and fashion, jukeboxes and coffee bars; the pill, out of wedlock, was not something my mother ever would have dreamed of. Brought up on a Northern working-class diet of fear and gratitude, she would never have had the confidence to ask for such a thing. She would not have had the vocabulary.

The call came a week ago. I was on my way out of court. I was meeting Seb for a drink at Waterloo before we caught the train home together. It was Friday. We always try to meet at the station on Fridays after work. On average, we achieve this twice a month, if I'm honest, sometimes once. A shared bottled of Pinot Grigio in a busy station is what passes, what has to pass, for a date just at the moment. There's a bar called the Cabin on the upper level, where you can drink and talk and watch the train timetable on a television screen and we know we can make it to our platform in three minutes. It's our way of being together for as many minutes and seconds as we can, and that we still want to do this is, to me, romantic. The train ride also counts. Once home, domesticity will, we know, swamp us, and by the time we are alone again, our last remaining drops of energy will have been spent on the girls.

So when the call came, I was on the Strand. A GBH case had taken less time than I'd anticipated, and I was considering texting Seb to tell him I was heading back to chambers and that I'd see him later at home. I took my phone out of my coat pocket, and at the sight of my brother's name, my body tingled with presentiment. I just knew, as they say.

'Graham,' I said.

'All right.' The T hissed; my blood chilled.

'Is it Mum?'

'Yeah.'

You can prepare yourself for a moment you know is coming. You can make plans, even rehearse it in your mind. I knew my mother was dying. She had been transferred to the hospice a month earlier. I had travelled north the previous weekend, said goodbye just in case. I truly believed I'd made my peace with the inevitable. But now here was Graham telling me that he had held her hand and that she had taken 'this big breath, a big gasp, like', then closed her eyes, sending one tear trickling down each side of her face into her near-white hair.

'And then she let go,' he said, his voice cracking. 'And that was it, like. That was it.'

My brother doesn't say much, but he had known, without me asking, that I would need every detail, second by second, and he had given it his best shot. It was his way of including me in the immense and private privilege of our mother's last moments.

'Thanks for calling,' I said, which seems ridiculous to me now, like thanking someone for reminding me of a hair appointment or a delivery. 'I'll call you tomorrow.'

'Are you going to be all right?'

'Yes. I'm meeting Seb.'

'Good. Tell him I said all right.'

'OK. Talk to you tomorrow.'

I had prepared. But there is no preparation. Nothing can or will help. Any plans you make for yourself and how you will behave will be forgotten. You will be alone, not with loved ones, as planned. You will be alone on the street and you will be crying like you told yourself you would not, and you will descend into precisely the red, snotty mess of your fears, blowing loud sobs into a crowd of strangers, there in your suit and your high-heeled shoes – the armour you were foolish enough to think would protect you. And you will find the sight of so many people carrying on as if nothing has happened so surreal, so fucking offensive, frankly, that you will have to stagger into a side street and find a wall to lean on while you get yourself together enough to text your husband.

Mum's gone.

Seb would still be at work. I wasn't sure if he'd even have his phone with him; tried not to let that thought fill me with panic. But he rang immediately.

'Hey. Are you OK?'

'I'm fine,' I managed.

'Where are you?'

'The Strand.'

'All right. I can be there in half an hour, three quarters.' He paused, enough to sense that I couldn't speak. 'First one there gets the drinks. I'm on my way, Nick. I'll see you soon, all right? Walk there. Take the air, look at the beautiful city. Do you want me to stay on the phone?'

'No. No, I'm all right. I'll see you there.'

If you were walking across Jubilee Bridge that day, you would have seen a very smartly dressed woman with a great haircut weeping snottily into a shrivelled tissue. Perhaps you would have smiled your sympathy and looked away. But she would not have seen you. That day she didn't even remember to look at the view: the South Bank Centre, the London Eye, the glorious sweep of the capital's riverside. And when she arrived at the bar, she had no idea how she had got there.

Seb was already sitting on the red leather couch at the back. Bottle of white in a silver wine cooler. This didn't make sense; I'd been nearer to Waterloo than him, but now I think about it, I think I must have wandered about in a daze for a bit. I have a memory of looking at lipsticks in Boots that can only have been that afternoon, a shop assistant asking if she could help me. I never buy lipstick in Boots. The way Seb looked at me as I made my way through the bar was enough to make tears come again. I blinked them back and sank down beside him. He kissed the top of my head.

'Petes,' he said.

Story on that: my brother's nickname for me is posh twat. I'm not, not really, but everything's relative. When I first met Seb at a juvenile court case long ago, I told him this and it amused him. I don't know what you're laughing at, I said. You're a much posher twat than me. Posh twat became PT, which became Petey, which became Petes. There.

I let Seb hold me while I cried into the new cashmere jumper I'd bought him for Christmas, the one he said was too expensive for a social worker but which he'd not had off his back.

'Sorry,' I said.

'This jumper's dry-clean only,' Seb replied, which made me laugh while, with the discretion of a priest, a waiter slid a stack of white paper napkins onto the table.

I took one and pressed it to my face. 'It's all right, I cried most of my mascara off on the Strand.' I met his eye. 'Don't say anything kind.'

'All right. Shall I tell you I was called Shrek four times today?'

I laughed, tears spilling. Seb isn't ugly, but his ears stick out and his nose is, how can I put it … kind of rickety. Like a contraption that would straighten if you were to wiggle it. We have both broken our noses, actually, though mine was only a hairline fracture, with no lasting disfigurement. And of course Seb's was broken by a slope at St Anton whereas mine was broken by a fist. His eyes aren't all that fantastic either, to be honest. With Seb, it's all about the smile. Think ice caps melting. Think jelly legs. Think this is probably my subjective opinion.

He had filled my glass, was now topping up his own, saying nothing.

'I'll be all right in a minute,' I said.

'I know you will.' He moved closer along the couch until our thighs touched. He tightened his arm around me and kissed my hair, and I was more grateful for him in that moment than I had been in a while. He is so kind that I forget it. That he would only ever lay his hands on me in affection or desire is something I don't think about. But I gave silent thanks in that moment for the fact that I'd married a man so unfailingly kind that I have the luxury of letting it slip my mind.

We made short work of the bottle and the *just one more* large glass each for the road. Once home, once the nanny had left,

I was still tipsy enough to tell the girls that their grandma had died without making too much of a mess of it: normal, not scary, amounts of crying. We huddled together on the sofa and had what my mother would have called a right good weep. They didn't see their nan that much, but they loved her and spoke to her every week on the phone. Seb went for fish and chips. And that was how the immediate aftermath went: a good weep; fish and chips; Carol anecdotes and teary laughter. It was exactly what Mum would have wanted.

And now here I am a week later, at the pine table of my mother's kitchen, in the silent aftermath of her wake. Seb and the kids are at home in south London – we decided that the girls were too young to face a funeral – and so now, alone, prompted by more than a few drinks in her honour amidst cheap sharp suits and signet rings, set hair and firm bosoms, I find myself thinking about that night in Blackpool in 1968, the year my parents decided it was a good idea to get married. And remembering my mother – I have done little else since I heard – I feel an overwhelming, indescribable, almost *eerie* connection to her. Something not of the mind but of the body.

Stage one, stage two, stage whatever, grief is the same yet different for us all. Perhaps what I mean is that the specifics of grief are individual. For me, raw and new as I am to it, Carol is knocking at the doors, asking to be let in. My mother is a spirit – not bad for an atheist like myself, for a woman of reason, of the law – and I am the medium. She's here, she's everywhere, inside and out, in the air, in the water, in the things she left behind. In her spotless kitchen, I open a drawer at random and find the red-and-white-checked tea towels that she favoured, the cloth napkins she never used because they were too posh, and, here, a handkerchief, laundered, pressed, initialled in bright blue cotton: *TW*. Thomas Wilson. Tommy. I know this handkerchief. Its whiteness is marked with an old, old stain. How that stain came to be there is the story of the night she bundled a few scant belongings into bags and took me and my older brother with her out of the fear and violence that was her life.

And here, now, this night, my mother's bravery strikes me perhaps harder than ever. So much I witnessed as a child, only understanding its meaning many years later. So much I only knew on some foggy, intangible level. But now that she is irreversibly gone, I realise I want to piece the whole thing together. Because nothing brings home our adult status like the loss of both parents. I want to understand. Graham told me some of it, but only after the years we spent estranged from one another. My mother filled in other parts much, much later as we sat up together, two women talking – dry-roasted peanuts, cheap box of red, me cadging one of the cigarettes that ultimately killed her.

That I will never see her again, never feel the warmth of her next to me as we chat for hours on her soft old sofa, never hear her laugh when I say something clever or mimic someone we both know is as unbelievable to me as God. All that I have left of her, beyond the material remains, is this need to be with her, and to make final sense of her life. Call it survivor's guilt, some vague desire to make amends for my career, my lovely home, my kind, boxer-nosed husband and my two children: well dressed, well fed, safer than I ever was. Call it the familiar floral scent of this bloodstained handkerchief that I press to my nose; call it the maudlin after-effects of too much fizzy wine drunk in toasts to her; call it, quite simply, love – for my mother, Carol, who one night in 1984, with no qualifications, no possessions and no home, struck out alone with her children into the unknown.

CHAPTER THREE

Carol

Runcorn, 1984

Carol is in the hallway, putting on her make-up before Pauline and Tommy's wedding. It is the last day of her marriage, but she doesn't know that yet.

The bulb in the hall is dim. Carol Watson, née Green, has read in *Woman's Own* that you're supposed to have bright light when you apply make-up, but at this moment she can't for the life of her imagine why. You'd never go out again if you did that, she's thinking as she rubs a blob of foundation as thickly as she can over the bruise under her left eye. She pats at it with the ends of her fingers. In *Woman's Own* there are never any tips on how to cover a shiner – this is a technique she's invented all on her own. She tops the look off with her new red lipstick: Soldier Soldier by Avon.

'Ted,' she calls into the lounge. 'Better get off soon, eh, love.'

She ducks her head into the cupboard under the stairs. Her jacket is stuck under Nicola's anorak. Nicola, her princess, her too-clever-for-me girl. She lifts both coats, puts her daughter's back on the hook and pulls her own free. Behind her comes Ted's rattling cough. She steels herself and turns to face him, the war between dread and hope burning its usual hole in her chest.

His eyes go straight to her lips. Dread wins out. The lipstick. A mistake.

'It's only for the wedding.' She covers her mouth with her fingers.

He knocks her hand away and grabs her chin. His fingers press hard on her jaw. In the dining room, the kids fall silent – an alarm system in reverse.

'What is that?' he says in his low, quiet voice.

'It's only from the catalogue,' she says. 'I got it with my points.'

'Take it off.' He lets go and heads through to the kids, who are eating sandwiches at the table. 'Right, you lot, there's two Lion bars in the sideboard,' she hears him say as she wipes the lipstick from her mouth with a cotton wool ball and some of the Anne French cleansing milk she keeps on the phone table. 'They're not for you,' he jokes. 'Just keep an eye on them for us till we get home.'

'Aw, Dad!' The children laugh, and she tells herself that if the kids are laughing, then things must be normal. This is family life. Every household has its ups and downs. Women complain about their husbands' bad moods the same way men talk about football, don't they?

She steps out into the garden and lights a ciggie to calm her nerves. In the flower bed, the funny faces of her violet pansies shimmer in the breeze. Behind them, rooted by concrete posts, the green wire fence runs along the back of all the gardens, hemming everything in. If you were to lift it up, this fence, all the little strips of lawn, the wooden pickets and the gardens and the houses would dangle from it like washing on a line. On the other side of the fence, the field stretches away – out of the estate and beyond, to the railway track, to the expressway, to who knows where.

With no Pauline to talk to over the fence today, she smokes quickly and stubs her fag out on the wall. Inside, Ted is saying ta-ta to the kids. Once she's sure he's gone out to the car, she hurries back so she can say goodbye to them herself without him hovering over her.

The two of them are still in their pyjamas, watching *Saturday Superstore*, their weekend treat. It's nearly midday.

'Get dressed straight after, all right?' she says. They nod, blank-eyed, chewing. She picks up the empty squash jug. 'I'll just get you some more juice before I go. Your dad's waiting.' She turns to make her way out to the kitchen to find Ted filling the doorway of the dining room. 'Jesus.' She almost drops the jug on her foot.

He throws his arms up against the door frame. 'For Christ's sake, I live here, don't I?' He glares at her like she's mad, a fool to startle like that.

'Sorry. Thought you'd gone to the car, that's all. Do you want a sarnie? Don't know when the buffet'll be, do we?'

'I'm not hungry.'

'I've made boiled ham and salad cream. Or there's tongue.'

'I said I'm not hungry, didn't I?' He heads back into the hall, shaking his head. The chink of keys as he lifts them from the phone table, another phlegmy cough. She hopes he's not over the limit already. She smelled mint on his breath just now. He's checking himself in the mirror, turning his head this way and that. Finding himself marvellous. He has on his best shiny grey suit from C&A, the sky-blue shirt she ironed for him yesterday and a new paisley tie she picked up in Burton's in the Shopping City. The skin of his neck overlaps his collar in an oily fold. He's taken trouble over his hair for once, combed a duck's arse at the back. Usually he just does the quiff at the front and leaves the back flat, as if he's run out of energy halfway through, but today, with it being next-door's wedding, she guesses, he's made an effort. He looks like a ruddy throwback. It's 1984, for pity's sake. Thirty-three years old and he still thinks he's Elvis.

'Are we going then or what?' he calls to her.

'Yes, love. All set.' She bustles round the children, kissing both of them on the cheek. 'Be good now, kids, all right?'

'M-Mum, stop f-f-fussing.' Graham speaks with his mouth full.

'Graham Watson,' she says. 'Mouth. How many times?'

He makes a great show of swallowing. His hair is thick and black like his dad's. 'B-beautiful M-Mother, please may you stop f-f-fussing?' He opens his mouth wide, to show that it's empty, making Nicola giggle.

'Don't be cheeky.' Carol gives him a wink, lays her hand on her daughter's cheek and smiles at them both: her world, her two reasons to keep going. 'Nicky, be good for your big brother, all right? I don't want any nonsense.' Holding on to the door handle a moment, she charges the batteries of her heart with the sight of them. They're getting older, bigger, living proof of time passing. 'Right, troops,' she says. 'I'm off.'

'Carol,' Ted shouts from the front door.

'Coming!'

'Mum,' says Graham.

She turns back to her son. Quick, love, she wants to say, but she can't, of course – that'll only make him worse. 'What, love?'

He gives her an awkward smile; his eyelids hover, almost close with the effort of speaking. 'Y-you look really n-n-nice.'

The waiting room of the register office is packed, the smell of shoe leather and cigarettes just about held at bay by a medley of perfumes and aftershaves. Ted still hasn't come back. He said he needed the gents, but Carol knows better. He'll be outside, smoking, swigging, looking common.

Tommy and Pauline, the happy couple, are over on the far side, by the entrance to the wedding suite. Carol's brother, Johnny, is chatting to them, waving his hands about as he does. He hasn't brought anyone by the looks of things. Shame, Carol was hoping he might have a date. There's a chap she doesn't recognise next to a green plastic plant on a pillar, chatting to Trevor from Trev's Tyres. He's fair, very tall. He has to bend forward to hear what Trevor is saying.

From behind the closed door, music drifts into the foyer. The previous wedding finished, the newly married couple will be on their way out through the back. This place is a conveyor belt, she thinks, waiting for one couple to tie the knot before the next can go in – a sausage factory, twisting links.

For a few minutes then there's no music at all, only chatter bubbling in the air, before the far door opens and a song plays out: 'How 'Bout Us', Pauline's favourite. She and Tommy go ahead into the wedding suite, laughing. 'Some people are made for each other,' Carol whispers, allowing herself the smallest private moment of something like bitterness or regret.

The crowd follow the happy couple, surging in through the double doors. Still no sign of Ted. Carol has to go in with the others, she knows that. She's chief witness. But if she doesn't wait for Ted, that might make him cross, and his anger will write itself on her body later, invisible ink that reveals its black message by degrees. Where the heck is he, though, really? A frantic scan of the foyer, a quick look out onto the car park at the front – but nothing, no sign. Pauline will be waiting. It's not right to keep her hanging about, not after all she's done.

After another few seconds, Carol steels herself and goes alone into the wedding suite to find Pauline looking preoccupied at the front, standing next to a little table with a red ghetto blaster on it. Two silver-haired women fuss over paperwork. When she sees Carol, Pauline's frown breaks into a smile.

'Here she is,' she calls out, waving, and to Carol's horror, everyone turns to look at her.

A last glance over her shoulder in case Ted has returned, then she pulls at the shallow brim of her hat and makes her way over to her friend. In a cloud of Poison, Pauline throws an arm around her, presses her to her ample bosom and plants several kisses on her cheek. She's wearing the pillar-box-red suit with short sleeves that Carol helped her choose in John Lewis, and a small matching beret with black netting at the front and a little dove-grey feather.

'You look lovely.' It's true, she does. Carol glances down at her own flowery blouse, long-sleeved, elasticated wrists; her ancient blue skirt already creased across the tops of her thighs. 'Ted won't be a minute.'

'Never mind Ted.' Pauline takes Carol's hand and squeezes it. 'Bloody Tommy only forgot the money for the registrar. Can you believe it? I had to borrow twenty quid from me dad.'

'Pretty cheap to get rid of you once and for all, I'd say.'

'Cheeky cow.'

The two of them snigger, bump hats and snigger some more.

Pauline turns away then to fix Tommy's tie. Adrift, Carol searches for Ted along the rows, her stomach a fist. The tall, sandy-haired man is sitting at the back. At that moment, the woman in front of him bends down to fish something out of her handbag, and Carol sees that he's wearing a kilt. That explains the frilly white shirt. Scottish, then. Either that, or he's wearing the whole lot for a bet.

He meets her eye, gives her a broad smile. Without thinking, she smiles back and then, flustered, turns away and sits down next to Pauline. She's never seen a kilt in real life before. It makes him look hearty, she thinks, like he could carry a wench under each arm or something; tear the meat off a ham bone with his teeth.

Out of nowhere, in a pungent cloud of smoke, Old Spice and cold air, Ted slumps next to her. Whisky, not vodka; she can smell it on him now. How must he have looked standing outside, propped against the wall, his red face glistening, ripe. His hip flask pushes a square bulge in his pocket; his double chin presses on his chest. The bloody shame of him. Not that he's completely out of it yet, just dazed. But she knows that once they get to the reception, he'll be worse, much worse; that this is just the start.

CHAPTER FOUR

Nicola

2019

'Nick?'

'Seb! Hi, honey.' I pour the last dregs of a bottle of fizz into my flute.

'You OK? Funeral go all right?'

'God, yes. Graham did a great job. Seb, he made a speech.'

'Graham? You're joking! Wow. Good on him.'

'I know. He seemed to want to do it so I ... well, what could I say?'

'So did you do yours as well?'

'No! It's still in my bag. Don't tell him.'

'Of course not, why would I? It's great that he did it. That must have been a big deal.'

We both know what we're saying. Graham hardly stutters these days, but public speaking is another thing. With my confident barrister's rhetoric I would have walked it, but it was better that my brother did it. Sometimes the less polished speech is the more affecting. And by the time Graham had finished his halting, heartfelt tribute, there wasn't a dry eye in the house.

'Thanks for the bouquet, by the way,' I say. 'That was a lovely thing to do.'

'Oh good, you got it.' Down the line, I hear him sigh. I wish I could summon him to me. We could sit in the almost darkness, hold hands and say nothing at all.

'The others have gone to the pub. I didn't … I just needed to be on my own, you know? How are the girls?'

'Good, yeah. Took Phoebe to violin, and while we waited in the car, Rosa chatted me to near catatonia. Wow, that girl can talk.'

'She can.' I smile. My cheeks feel like they're under a fine face mask, which is cracking; the edges of my eyes are sticky.

'Then nothing much, really. We went to Pizza Express for dinner.'

'Tea, you mean.'

'Don't go all Northern on me,' he says mock-gravely. 'You've been there less than twenty-four hours.'

He has managed to make me laugh. Although, thinking about it, I have laughed a lot today. My family are very funny, their friends a hoot. To be perfectly honest, there have been moments when I wasn't sure whether I was laughing or crying. Eventually I just gave in and let my eyes leak.

I chat to Seb a little longer, let him soothe me until he yawns, making me yawn, and we say goodnight. He'll kiss the girls for me, tell them I love them, he won't forget Rosa has hockey practice in the morning, he loves me, he's with me in spirit. I ring off and think about what a lovely husband and father he is, how safe our girls are with him, how safe I am. I chose him through love, yes, but there was something else in there too, always, some seed of determination for history not to repeat itself. Like much of history, mine doesn't bear repeating. I needed a different kind of husband. And whatever children I had, I was going to make damn sure they had a different kind of father.

In our separate careers, Seb and I deal with people like my father all the time. It saddens me to say that we also deal with people like my brother. If you meet me in my professional capacity, it probably means you've made some poor choices. It will be a low point in your life. You will be sharing details with me that you wouldn't tell your closest friend. Grubby secrets, bloody facts. And regardless of whether I like you or not, whether I believe you or not, you have a right to a defence in a court of law. You will be relying on me to give you that to the best of my ability. What you will never know are my reasons for entering into this career and how utterly I give myself to it. I have made some poor choices too. But I try not to think about that. It isn't, as they say, helpful.

Another thing my clients will never find out is how deeply and personally I understand how grave the consequences of a guilty verdict are; how easily a beautiful soul can become a murderous mess. We have evolved from capital punishment, yes, but the loss of liberty to be with the people you love, to provide for your family, to experience your children's childhoods, your friends, your favourite places and even your parents' last days is for many a far greater torture than mere death. Those who go to prison suffer. Those who are left outside suffer too. My brother was guilty and served his time. My father was guilty but never made it as far as a court. His justice was of the poetic kind, as it turned out. As for myself, I am guilty too, but I use the law to try to make things right day to day. For the rest, my aim is to keep my daughters for as long as possible wrapped up in blissful ignorance.

As a child, I could have done with a little more ignorance. I didn't want to hear the things I heard, interpret the evidence I saw. Watching my mother leave for Tommy and Pauline's wedding that afternoon, I could never have known that the next time I saw her would be in the dead of that same night: eyes wide, words hissed into the dark.

I need you to keep quiet for me, love. Can you do that? Not a word, all right? Good girl.

Graham knew more than I did. He was sixteen. I was ten. I never witnessed my father's physical abuse at first hand. Through the walls of adjacent rooms, there were shouts, bangs, roars. Yelps too – like the sound my friend's dog would make if you stepped on its paw. The way my father spoke to my mother was, for me, normal, although I do remember that my stomach used to tighten sometimes when he was around. But I hadn't yet spent enough time in other people's houses to realise that other fathers spoke to other mothers differently. I could not have clarified the tone of his voice as that of withering disdain, nor perceive how anxious he made her, how her every word and move around him was tentative. My unease was loose, vague. Only later did I realise that she, Carol, spent our entire childhood living in dread, that she did that for us, every day, from some received notion that she should put up with it, and because she thought she had no choice.

Tommy and Pauline's wedding reception was held at the community centre on the housing estate where we lived. I knew the hall well, because as kids Graham and I spent every summer there at the volunteer-run play scheme while my mother worked on the till at Safeway. The centre was by turns a function room, theatre, dance studio, sports club, pub, church, youth club and disco. The storeroom was a cornucopia of equipment for every possible activity: badminton nets, boxes of Golden Wonder crisps, footballs in huge net bags, scenery from last year's Christmas play …

I have no trouble imagining the place kitted out for a wedding. The DJ has set up on the stage at the back – huge black speakers, those eighties red, amber and green disco lights, dog-eared boxes of vinyl. He talks between records, takes requests, wears his thin leather tie a little askew. Long trestle tables, fetched from the storeroom earlier in the day, most probably by my parents' friends and relatives, have been pushed together in rows. Paint splashes and chipped veneer are disguised with white paper cloths. The blue velvet chairs I would sit on later at weekly teenage discos fill now with chatting, smoking, drinking guests. Down by the long bar on the left, men lean in, heads fogged with smoke, hands tight around pints of brown and yellow.

And there's Ted, his back to Carol, a five-pound note folded between the middle and forefingers of his raised hand.

My mother is sitting as far from the action as she can, at the back, where the hall is a little darker. She is wearing long sleeves, as she always does. She will have refreshed her foundation in the mirror of the ladies, will have waited until no one else was looking to do this. All around her there is motion and noise. Joy. Some of the guests barely stop to put down their bags and coats before heading straight for the dance floor, laughing together, arms pumping, mock-disco moves.

They know how to have a good time.

CHAPTER FIVE

Carol

1984

Carol is watching Ted. He's back-slapping, pointing, downing a chaser before picking up their drinks. Now he's heading over, has her locked in his sights. When he gets to the table, he puts the cola she never asked for in front of her. He sits heavily, sups half his pint in one go. The urge to tell him to slow down still comes to her, but, knowing better now, she keeps her mouth shut. He pulls out his cigarette packet and shakes it.

'Fuck,' he mutters, his expression bitter. Without looking at her, digging in his pocket, he adds, 'Have you got fags?'

She scrambles in her bag, offers him her pack of B&H. 'Here y'are.'

Eyes screwed up, he holds up his own cigarettes, pushes the packet close to her face. 'I don't mean *now*. I've got one *now*, but it's my last one, i'n't it?'

She nods, takes one of her own and lights first his then hers.

After a bit, and without a word, he shambles back to the bar, disappears into the group of men.

While some people dance, at other tables groups of women exchange stories and laughter. If any of them do look her way, she doesn't see them. That Scottish chap likes to dance, though. He's the life and soul, by the looks of things. Under the table, she taps her foot to the beat, sings the odd line under her breath, wonders if this will be *a night to remember*.

After a while, Ted brings her another cola and takes two of her ciggies. One she lights for him, the other goes behind his ear. Common. Common as muck. There's a buffet, which she doesn't eat much of, and Ted doesn't eat at all. At the speeches, Tommy scans the room, seems to look at every one of them.

'I might have found my Pauline late in life,' he says. 'But I tell you all something. She was worth every bloody day of the wait.'

Pauline catches Carol's eye and winks, making her well up. Pauline has been a bloody rock all these years. Not that Carol has said a word to her. She's never had to. When she lifts her glass for the toast – *The bride and groom!* – her throat thickens. If she can't be happy, then perhaps Pauline can. She deserves it.

The disco starts up again. The upended traffic lights flash; sixties hits replace seventies disco: the Beatles, the Kinks, the Rolling Stones. Ted, who she didn't see coming over, stumbles into the table and just about gets his bum onto the seat next to her.

'You're not dancing,' he says, without looking at her. It strikes her as a strange thing to say; she hasn't danced for the last ten years.

'I'm not. I'm sitting down.'

'Are you being funny?'

Her chest flares with heat. 'No. I'm just saying, that's all.'

His eyes are half closed. Two fingers swear at her for a cigarette. She lights one and passes it to him. He sups his pint, mumbles something she doesn't catch. His ciggie drops onto the table. She picks it up and puts it out before it sets light to the paper cloth. He appears not to notice any of this. After a moment, he opens his mouth as if to say something but falls against her, his forehead hot and clammy on her neck. Hands to her chest, he pushes back, eyes straining to focus, then keels backwards into his chair. His head lolls. Another beat and he slides to the floor.

Christ, she thinks, eyes darting all about her to see if anyone's looking. If they were, they've turned away now. She crouches beneath the table and tries to pull him up by his arms. He's half propped against the chair leg, his chin crushed into his neck, his legs spread wide apart. It's no good; she's not strong enough to move him. Tommy would usually help, always helps on a Friday. But Pauline and Tommy are staying at the Holiday Inn before they drive up to the Lake District for their honeymoon. They can't come back with her tonight. She's not thought it through. Maybe Johnny will help, if he doesn't get lucky. If not, she'll have to somehow get Ted into the car and go and wake Graham.

She leaves him sprawled asleep on the abrasive blue carpet.

'… nine, ten,' she whispers, sitting back in her chair. 'Out for the count.'

Something close to relief allows her shoulders to lower an inch. He won't wake up now, not till tomorrow. He is at least reliable in this one thing.

She remembers her lipstick. She finds it in her bag, together with her compact. She flips the mirror open and carefully paints her lips red. She smiles, checks her teeth, rubs her lips together. There in the reflection is a girl she remembers, though they lost touch many years ago now. Lighting another fag, she wonders whether she could get half a lager and lime now that Ted's passed out; maybe a Bacardi for her Coke. Only she'd have to get Ted's wallet from his trouser pocket.

So no.

Pretending, even to herself, that she needs something else from her bag, she bends down to the floor to check again on Ted. His mouth is open, his lips wet and slack. She clenches her teeth against rising disgust and swallows hard. At least the crotch of his trousers is dry, for now. Beyond Ted's body, she sees a movement. On the other side of the table, planted on the floor, are two enormous black shoes, a cross between brogues and ballet pumps. Out of them rise two ankles in cream woollen socks.

The Scotsman.

She sits up, too quickly, cracks the back of her head on the edge of the table. 'Ow!'

'Ah, Christ.' The Scotsman claps his hand over his mouth, but she can see he's trying not to laugh. He's a few years older than her, she thinks, now that she can see him better. Maybe late thirties. His eyes crinkle at the edges. 'Are you OK?' His accent is so Scottish it sounds like he's putting it on.

'You're all right, love, I'm fine.' She rubs her head. *I've taken much worse cracks than that.*

'I'm Jim MacKay,' he says after a moment. 'Tommy's cousin? Listen, are you sure you're OK? Can I get you some ice?'

She scrutinises his face to see if he's serious. Not about the ice; about the name. 'Jim MacKay?' she says. 'Jimmy Mac? Are you having me on?'

'Not at all.' He grins and bows, places one hand to his chest. 'Not so ridiculous, is it?'

'No, it's just … I don't know … I just didn't realise anyone was actually called that.'

He grins. 'Jim's all the rage where I come from. Plenty of Jims, plenty of MacKays.'

'And do you all wear kilts all the time?'

'Aye. And we have haggis for breakfast. So's we have the strength for the pipes, you know?' He winks at her. 'Actually, the kilt's only for weddings and such. Parties, like, you know? Anyway, I was just coming over to ask you to dance – you cannae be sitting here on your own all night.' His hands are on his hips now, his spiky hair the colour of wet sand. He's just asked her to dance. Of course, he's not local.

From under the table, Ted's arm sticks out. She lifts it with her toe and pushes it out of sight, takes another drag on her cigarette and stares back through the smoke at Jim MacKay.

He glances towards the dance floor, back at her. 'So, do you want to dance then? Carol, isn't it?'

'I've got a gammy leg.'

'Aye, of course you have. We've all got gammy legs. Come on, you can dance with your good one.'

He tips his head to one side and holds out a hand. She presses the tip of her shoe into Ted's ribs. He's as still as a slug. Once he's out like this, he never wakes. But still …

She'll never get away with a dance. The lipstick alone is a risk; a drink would be reckless, a dance suicide. It's barely a year since she spoke in passing to a chap in the chippy. He'd only asked her for the time, but she paid for it with two cracked ribs when she got home. No. It's not worth it. She'd show this Jim chap her husband under the table, to explain, but for the shame of it.

'I can't.' She gives a little shrug, hoping he'll understand that when she says she can't, she really can't.

But he doesn't understand.

'Just one.' He holds up a finger. 'A wee one. A tiny one.'

Ted is very still. As if dead. *If only* is the thought she catches and puts out. One record. To dance, in public, after so long … If she makes sure she stays over the far side, she could say she's been to the toilet or something if Ted does, for any reason, wake up.

Jim is waiting for her. Seeing her hesitate has been enough for him. Perhaps he has understood after all. Perhaps he knows. She drives her cigarette into the ashtray.

'Just the one, then.' She stands up, but almost collapses. 'Oops,' she says, and laughs it off. 'I've been sitting for so long my legs have gone to sleep.' She leans her hands on the table a moment while her shakes die down. 'I'll be hopeless, by the way. I haven't danced for ten years.'

'Ach, you'll be fine. It's like riding a bike.'

He walks ahead of her down the length of the tables. His back is thick, his waist about three times the width of her own. They meet at the end and he leads her into the group with the lightest touch on her elbow.

'Return of the Mac!' Tommy punches the air, laughs at his own joke and almost falls over.

'Good for you, love,' Pauline murmurs into her ear. She means well, but the words are terrifying. Before Carol can bolt, though, the group has closed her in its embrace.

Jim is already organising everyone into doing something called an eightsome reel to 'Baby Love'. He grabs Carol's crossed hands, whirls her round so fast she fears she might fall over but for his strong and steady grip. It's a mess, a riot. It's funny, funnier than anything she can remember. After the song has finished, men rest their hands on their knees, panting. Carol wipes her eyes and shakes her head at the other women. For a moment, she feels like one of them, if only for as long as it takes her to catch the thought, to remember that she is not. She cranes her neck to check her table, but there is no sign of Ted, no commotion.

'Thanks, Jim,' she says as the next song – 'Lola' by the Kinks – starts up.

But Jim grabs her hand. 'One more, come on.'

'I can't.' Her chest tightens. The saliva dries up in her mouth. She looks back towards her table, sees only her drink, Ted's empty pint glass.

Jim pulls her towards him and puts his hand on her waist. 'Who is he? I'll beat him up for you.'

How little he knows. 'I can't.'

'You can. It's OK'

It isn't OK. She lets Jim push her away and pull her back – a gentle slow jive. She glances back to her table. Nothing. She checks the bar. Ted isn't there.

Jim bends to speak into her ear. 'Your hair's so shiny and dark.' His breath tickles. 'It's like Chinese hair.'

'Is it now?'

'Is there any Chinese in you, like?'

She stands on tiptoe and replies into his ear. 'No, and there never has been.'

He throws back his head and laughs. A thrill passes through her. She has made a man laugh, a man like him. His hand on her hip has warmed its own place. She doesn't want him to move it away. But he does, to send her spinning, holding on to the ends of her fingers. She closes her eyes, refusing to see the table, hoping this will be enough to push what lies beneath it out of her mind. It isn't of course. Oh, if Ted could only die, slip into oblivion there, now, on the sticky floor. It would be painless. And she would be free.

The first few notes of 'Stairway to Heaven' clear the floor by half to reveal Tommy and Pauline necking in the middle of the dance floor. Some of the guests are cheering them on. Carol steps back, unsure where to rest her gaze. Jim is looking straight at her. His eyes are blue. She thinks of Wedgwood pottery and a satin dress she loved as a teenager.

'Thanks,' she says. 'That was really—'

'Oh no you don't.' He reaches for her, but she dodges his hand and waves awkwardly.

'I can't. Really. I'm sorry.' She turns away.

Her half-empty Coke is still on the table, watery with melted ice. Against her foot, Ted's ribs open out and close, open and close. Thoughts of smothering him come to her. She pushes them aside, but they insist: herself, ducking under this table. Her hands on his neck. Quiet, no fuss. She could go to the ladies and come back and say, *Has anyone seen Ted?*

On the dance floor, Jim holds out his arms to her, cocks his head to one side.

'Come on,' he mouths.

Hand to her chest, she mimes a puff of tiredness. She has never felt less tired in her life. She sits down, but still she watches. Jim disappears in the crowd. A second later, he's jumping up and down and waving his hand above his head. She realises he's holding a small dagger. Curious, she stands up and moves closer, close enough to see, through heads, shoulders and arms, Jim making lassos in the air with the knife. What on earth is he doing? As if he's heard her, he looks her way and grins. She shakes her head at him and returns his smile.

The crowd thins. Jim is wiping the sweat from his face with both shirtsleeves. To more shrieks of delight, he does a comedy stagger, feigning a heart attack.

Against her foot, Ted twitches, then stills.

'OK, folks.' The DJ's voice is muffled through the microphone. 'Time for some old-school rock 'n' roll.'

Someone thumps into her back. She almost falls. It's Tommy – he's running towards the dance floor.

'Jimmy!' he yells, pointing wildly. 'Jim, mate. You're bleeding.'

Shouts. The music dips. Chatter fills its place. The main lights flicker on, throwing whiteness into the hall. Carol follows the line of Tommy's finger down to where everyone is looking, to Jim, to his sock, to a great red stain spreading in the cream wool.

Jim is bleeding.

His eyes find hers.

'I've sheathed the bloody skean-dhu in my leg,' he says, as if she's the only one who'll understand what he means. But she has no idea what he's on about. 'The wee dagger,' he adds, only to her. 'I've sheathed the dagger in my leg. Bloody thing was so sharp I didna notice.'

'Nothing to do with the six pints of lager, I suppose?' Tommy crouches in front of Jim and gingerly peels the sock away. At the sight of the wound, there is a collective gasp. Carol wants to hold back the crowd but does not, cannot move. Tommy presses a cotton handkerchief to the gash, then lifts it. A red sliver appears, thin, then oozing, like a strange red blossoming flower. 'Right, who's going to give this pillock a lift to casualty?'

'I will,' she hears herself say. 'I think there's only me sober.'

CHAPTER SIX

Nicola

2019

I return Tommy's old handkerchief to the drawer and think of my mother taking that terrible chance with a man she had only that moment met but who, she told me later, she felt she knew straight away.

'Outside it was that fine rain,' I hear her say. 'You know, when you don't think it's raining at all but next minute you're soaked through.'

I can hear her say it, the exact turn of phrase, as if she were here. I can feel that drizzle, the air cold after the heat of the party. Which is the point, I suppose. I want her. That's what, that's *all* grief is: wanting someone who is no longer there. It isn't that I have anything important to say. I'd only say *Hello, how's tricks? Shall I put the kettle on?* The last time I saw her, I told her about an armed robbery case. I told her about having my kitchen done, showed her the colour samples for my units. Enough to bore anyone to tears, but still, despite the oxygen tube up her nose, her body little more than a bag of bones, her once shiny black hair now thin and bleached with age, still she listened as if every word from my lips were gold.

If she were here right now, she'd probably tell me about her latest trip with Pauline into Liverpool: how she picked up a bargain, what diet Pauline was on, something outrageous Pauline said to the waiter in the Casa Italia, where they had taken to going for lunch these last ten years or so. Whatever. Normal stuff, quiet stuff, the day-to-day stuff of love. But we can't talk about anything anymore. And I can't have back the time I didn't spend with her when I was establishing my career, having a family, living in London. I'm still busy. An early night home is eight p.m.; a later night sees me waking up on the camp bed in chambers, scuttling out to M&S for new knickers and shirt if I've neglected to bring spares. Time I cannot get back. It's not that I regret it, not quite. Just that, right now, I'd happily shove a knife into my own leg if I thought it would buy me one more minute, one more second with her.

CHAPTER SEVEN

Carol

1984

Tommy hoists Jim's arm around his shoulders and limps with him across the car park to Carol's rusty old Cortina.

'Tommy,' she says, scurrying alongside. 'What about Ted? If I don't get back in time, like? It's your wedding. You can't be—'

'Leave it with us, Carol. Not like we're blushing brides, is it, me and Pauline? This has happened now. Your Johnny can help us later. We'll put Ted on the settee as per, OK? Johnny can stay at yours till you get back, eh?'

'Are you sure? Only—'

'Carol. Listen to me. It's fine. Ted'll be none the wiser. Why change the habit, eh?'

'But he might wake up.'

'Aye, and pigs might fly. Now open this car door before my arm breaks off.'

She laughs nervously, unlocks the door. Tommy helps Jim into the passenger seat.

'Hey, Jim,' he says. 'D'you want to borrow some undies? You know what them nurses are like.'

'Get back to your wife,' says Jim.

'Tell you what, you can borrow Pauline's knickers, can't you? Not like she'll be needing them much longer.'

The men laugh. Tommy bangs on the roof of the car, winks at Carol and runs back to the community centre. She bites her lip and watches him go inside, rubbing the rain out of his hair. Through the brick, the steady bass of the music throbs.

In the car, condensation fogs the windows. The interior is a state: the vinyl trim is hanging off the doors, yellow tongues of foam loll out, honeycomb where the kids have picked at it. These things don't bother her normally, but she's mortified now.

'It's wetter than you think,' says Jim.

'It is, yeah.' She runs her hand across her own hair. It's stuck together in a sheet. She looks a mess, she knows it. Jim's shirt is transparent on his shoulders; his blazer lies across his lap.

Start the car, Carol. Start the ruddy car and drive.

'Right then,' she says, nails digging into the palms of her hands. What if Ted wakes up? This will be the one time; it would be just like him. He'll wake up, she won't be home, he'll know. It's madness to take Jim to the hospital. But it's too late to go back to the wedding.

'You OK?' Jim asks.

'Fine,' she manages. 'What's with the knife anyway?' Her voice is too loud; it ricochets around the inside of the car like cowboy bullets on *The High Chaparral*. Out of the corner of her eye she sees him make a book with his hands.

'Worn by the menfolk,' he says, pretending to read, 'the small dagger or skean-dhu is a vital part of traditional Highland dress.'

She chuckles, a release of nerves, glad that he, like her, is keeping up the jokes now they've left the safety of other people.

'So are you supposed to stab yourself with it?'

'That's all part of it, aye. Actually no, you're supposed to put it into the sheath. Whoops, eh?'

Her jitters die down a little. 'Better get you to the hospital then. Don't want you bleeding to death. Make a right mess of the upholstery.'

'Well we wouldn't want that, would we?'

She dares herself to glance at him. He's grinning widely at her. She stabs at the ignition with the key. So many teeth. Surely he has more than most people. She wipes her cheeks, hopes her mascara hasn't run. Finally the key finds the ignition and she pulls the shuddering car forward. Ahead, gateposts stand sentry at the exit to the car park, a big white arrow on the tarmac and the words *WAY OUT*.

They have fallen silent. Her eyes hold the road but she can feel he's turned to look at her; can smell wet wool from his kilt as it dries in the heat of the car. She makes herself speak.

'So where're you from, then?'

He tells her that he lives in Perth, that he works on an oil rig. *I work the rigs, y'know?* is how he says it, and she has to ask him to explain.

'What's that like?' she says.

'It's OK. Plenty of time off and it's a good enough laugh, y'know? Christmas is shite, though. It's like an old folk's home, all these trapped fellas in paper hats blowing blowers, drinking alcohol-free lager. Tragic.'

It's raining harder. She tries the wipers on the faster speed, but the frantic swipe of them puts her even more on edge. She changes them back. The car fills with their intermittent frog croak. Up ahead, the slip road looms grey through the spattered windscreen.

Jim asks her about herself. She keeps to the facts. Two kids. Yes, her husband had a few too many tonight. Yes, it's lovely to see Tommy and Pauline so happy, tying the knot after all these years. She wonders how much Tommy has told him. He probably knows exactly what her life is. So why ask? Perhaps he's trying to give her back her privacy, covering her as you might throw a blanket over a naked troubled soul in the street.

'You married, then?' Heat climbs up her face. Honestly. Her and her stupid gob.

'Divorced,' he says simply. 'My marriage died the day she called me up on the rig. "It's Saturday night, Jim," she said.' He imitates a woman's voice like all men do: stupidly high-pitched, not like a woman at all. '"And there's gonna be some shagging in this house tonight whether you're here or not." That's what she said. Charming, eh?'

Shock courses through her. A thrill follows. 'She never said that?'

'She did. Put in an emergency call. I was beside myself.'

'God help us. What was her name?'

'Moira. She was bad news, but it was a long time ago.'

They have reached the hospital. She parks and pulls up the handbrake. He's not mentioned kids, she thinks. He's not mentioned a girlfriend.

In the waiting room, Carol checks her watch every five minutes. Almost midnight. The wedding will be wrapping up soon. Tommy and Johnny will be bundling Ted into the back of a cab within the next hour or so. Poor Tommy. Poor Pauline. They shouldn't have to get involved with her and Ted, not on their wedding day. Still, at least Tommy isn't here, waiting for the nurse.

'Mr MacKay?'

Carol startles. A stout nurse is standing in front of them, hands on hips. Her name tag says *Elsie Bryers*. She sighs with relief, realising only in that moment that it could have been someone she knew.

Jim is already on his feet. Carol jumps up too, and together they follow the nurse, who is already striding ahead down the shiny corridor.

'Elsie Bryers?' Jim whispers. 'Isn't she from *Coronation Street*?'

Carol whispers back, 'Shush! She might hear you! Anyway that's Elsie Tanner, you nutter.'

Suppressing giggles, they follow the nurse into a treatment room. Under the harsh lights, she cuts away Jim's sock, stitches his shin and straps it up with lint and tape. She is deft, gruff and kind.

'The stitches'll take about a week to dissolve,' she says, shaking her head at Carol, including her in some imaginary club of women and their loveable-rogue husbands. She hands her four painkillers in a paper strip and turns back to Jim. 'Your wife can help you to the car, all right?' She gives Carol a last smile and heads off down the corridor.

Carol pulls at her wedding ring. The nurse will have seen it and jumped to conclusions. But what can anyone ever tell from the outside? What does anyone ever know about what goes on in another person's life? The ring is stuck fast behind her knuckle. Jim is standing up, leaning on her shoulder for support.

At the hospital door, they stop and look out into the night.

'I'll get a cab from here,' says Jim.

She knows she should say that it's been nice to meet him, that she'll see him again. There are any number of things she should say.

But she doesn't say any of them.

'I've driven you this far,' is what she says. 'May as well take you to the hotel now.'

CHAPTER EIGHT

Carol

The lanterns outside the Holiday Inn put Carol in mind of a deserted street party – everyone home in bed and here they are, still shining. Ted will have been thrown onto the sofa by now. If he has woken up, he'll know she's not there. Her chest rises and falls. But there is some small relief in the knowledge that it's too late to go back now. She didn't mean to come this far. Only wanted to chat to Jim a bit longer. Jim, who doesn't make her feel mad or stupid or wrong in everything she says.

She switches off the engine. There is, strictly speaking, no need to do this. The rain has eased off, the car windows have cleared. Jim's seat creaks. She feels his hand, warm and rough, under her hair.

'I must look a right state,' she says, without glancing at him.

His hand traces round to her cheek. He guides her face towards his, leans towards her and kisses her on the mouth. It is no more than a couple of seconds, but unmistakably it is the kiss a man gives to a woman late at night in a deserted car park. She presses her forehead to his shoulder.

'Come on,' he says.

He limps around the back of the car. She holds her handbag on her knees. Three big breaths, Carol. One for the Father, one for the Holy Ghost and one for whatsisname, oh God, she can't remember. The car door opens. As she unclips her seat belt, a sigh shudders out of her.

'Come on,' he says again, softly, holding out his hand.

She throws her feet out of the car and stands up into him. He kisses her again, more firmly, his mouth opening, taking hers with it. The air is chilly now that the night is here and she finds she is shivering, glad of his arms wrapped so tightly around her, like cords on a life jacket.

Through the empty lobby, they hold hands.

At his room, he takes the key from his sporran.

'So that's what that is,' she says, giggling, trembling.

'It's my wee purse.' He shows her through the door first. 'Let me take your coat. Sit down. Sit on the bed.'

She makes her way into the dim room, trying not to look at the bed. 'You're the one who needs to sit down.'

Jim switches on a lamp by the portable telly and the tea-making things. He sits down on the end of the bed, pats the space beside him. The lamp throws a dim orange glow. She checks her watch. Quarter to one. She shouldn't be here.

'I better check that dressing.' There is no need to do this. She sits on the floor by his feet, takes his shoe in her hand and unpicks the laces. Jim is still and quiet, save for the soft rush of his breath.

She loosens the complicated shoes. 'Wouldn't want to put these on in a hurry.'

'I can do that.'

'It's all right, I don't mind.' She slides the brogues from his feet and rolls his remaining sock down and off. Her teeth chatter. She closes her mouth, but they won't stop.

'Should I make you a hot drink?' she asks, her stomach rolling over.

'I'm fine. Unless you want one? You're shaking; are you cold?'

'No. No, I'm fine.'

Ted will be on the sofa, dead to the world. Or not. Her brother in the armchair. Or calming Ted down, telling him … telling him what?

'I better go,' she says, kneeling up, gathering herself to stand. 'Look at me.'

She can only look at the floor. 'Jim, I'm a car crash.'

'You're not.'

'You must know something. Tommy must've said.'

'Come here.' His voice is thick, different. He tips her head, runs his thumbs from her nose out to her ears, pushes back her hair. She kisses the insides of his wrists, aware of herself as if from above. She lays her hands on his knees, pushes her splayed fingers up his thighs. Under the kilt, movement. She draws back and laughs, her hand clapped to her mouth.

'You think that's funny, do you?' He takes her hand from her mouth and holds it in his. 'That's the haggis.'

'Give over.'

They giggle, relieved to know they are both still themselves, that they can go back to these selves at any time if they need to.

Jim reaches forward and pulls her onto the bed, onto him. He kisses her with an open, unhesitating mouth. There is no hiding in a kiss like that, and after years without, it almost sends her running from the room. She rolls off him, aware of her heart beating. He props himself up on one elbow to look at her. She watches him watching her, wonders what he sees. Between his thumb and forefinger he holds a button of her blouse. He slides it open and her breath catches. He meets her gaze and opens another button.

'Jim.' She makes to raise herself up.

'It's OK.'

She watches him pull the blouse down to her waist and away, watches to see if he'll flinch at the sight of her, but his face is unchanged and tender. He kisses her left shoulder with no more than an eyelash's pressure, returns his lips to her skin, over and over, sending little electrical currents through her as he makes his way to the bruise on her arm, which time has paled to grey. On her thigh, she knows he'll find the thunder cloud, yellow at the edges like a halo of sunshine trying to break through. He spots it when he pulls her skirt from her hips, and then, yes, she sees something – in the tightening of his mouth, the quick flare of his nostrils.

'Jim, stop.' She sits up.

'It's OK.'

She shakes her head, willing herself not to cry. 'It's not.' She shifts to the end of the bed, pulls on her skirt. 'I'm sorry.' She picks up her blouse and puts it back on.

'There's nothing to be sorry for.' Jim grips both her hands in his, pulls her towards him and kisses her again. He doesn't let go, as if content to stay like that, kissing like young things in a park. He runs his lips down her neck.

'Jim, I can't. Did Tommy tell you?'

He nods. 'And I have eyes,' he says. 'You don't deserve that. No one deserves it. I'm not much, Carol, but I'm a good man, y'know? I would never hurt you, never. You're so … you're just so fucking lovely.'

'I was.' Tears run down her face. 'You're lovely too. You really are. But I have to go.'

For the first time since leaving the wedding, she is afraid; whatever madness has protected her until now, whatever spell, began to fade when she watched this lovely man see and pretend not to see the marks of her life. She was able until that point to forget it all, that other life, her life, that it was real, that it had happened, happened, would happen again. But now she is not able. She must get home now, while she still has a chance.

At the car, Jim lays his rough hand on her cheek and smiles at her with such softness in his eyes that she has to look away.

'Tommy's got my number,' he says. 'You know, if things … if things change or you need … Well, just give us a call, eh? Let me know how you're getting on. Please.'

CHAPTER NINE

Carol

It is half past one. She watches her home for signs of life. After a few minutes she gets out of the car and walks towards the house. She'd been expecting Ted to come running out, she realises. To come running out, open the car door and drag her inside by her hair. To drag her inside and knock seven bells out of her until he exhausts himself and passes out. Silently she slides her key into the lock and edges open the door. The house stinks of stale alcohol but is, at least, still. Ted is asleep under a blanket on the sofa. She eases the front door closed, creeps as far as the living room door and sees … not Ted, but Johnny.

Not Ted.

Ted must be upstairs. Nausea lurches in her belly. Somehow Johnny has got him upstairs. Unless he got there himself. In which case, he must have woken up. Oh God. A shuddering breath escapes her. In the cave of her chest, her heart thumps.

In the kitchen, she drinks a pint of water. She leans her hands on the counter, breathes in and out, in and out. She is aware of herself, of her hands on the counter, her breath, the prickling rise of sweat on her forehead.

She tiptoes back into the living room and shakes Johnny's shoulder.

'Johnny,' she whispers.

He opens first one eye, then the other. 'All right?'

She nods. 'They stitched him up. I dropped him off at his hotel.'

Johnny is blinking, coming round. With a thick smacking sound, his tongue unsticks from the roof of his mouth. His hair is standing up at the back, his crisp white shirt all crumpled, his bottle-green satin tie off to one side. It's funny to see him so dishevelled; he's usually not got a hair out of place. 'All right. I'll get off.'

A flame flares in her chest. Tommy and Pauline will be back at the Holiday Inn by now, the place she's just left. Honeymoon suite. Rose petals on the bed. She won't be able to call on them tonight.

'Stay if you like,' she whispers to her brother.

He sits up, yawns. 'I'll get out of your hair.'

'It's no bother. I can make up a bed on the couch.'

He doesn't reply, starts putting on his shoes.

'Ted upstairs then, is he?' she asks, like he could be anywhere else.

Johnny is on his feet now, pulling his suit jacket from the armchair, slipping his arms into the sleeves. Thirty seconds more and he'll be gone.

'He was out of it, don't worry.'

'Was he?' She manages a fake laugh, as if that's unusual. But why would her brother tell her not to worry unless he knows more than he's ever let on? Eight years younger than Carol, Johnny's not part of their social life, hasn't seen that this is what Ted is like week in week out. Maybe he's seen something. Heard a bit of gossip. 'Did he say anything?'

Johnny shrugs. 'Gibberish mostly, daft prick.'

She follows him to the door. He's right to go, of course he is. Bachelor Boy keeps himself to himself, always has. Can't be getting dragged into this lot.

'See you then,' she whispers as he steps out. She leans over, kisses him on the cheek, pats his shoulder. 'Thanks, eh. Safe home.'

'I'm sure I'll manage.'

She breaks his gaze, scared that she might crack, fall to her knees and beg him to stay.

The darkness swallows him – the last she sees of him is his head tipping forward as he lights a cigarette, shoulders hunched against the chill of the night. She closes the door behind him, bites her lip against the tiny click of the latch.

On the stairs, her legs ache. Her heart starts its battering once again.

In Nicola's room, the kids sleep. Graham is on the floor with his covers over him, as he often is. They must have been chatting or playing some game, bless them. Sometimes they play Name That Tune to get themselves to sleep, not that Graham would ever admit it.

She kisses their foreheads. She has left them alone tonight. She has thought only of herself, of her own delight. She has betrayed them, really. Put herself in danger when she is all they have. Never, ever will she let that happen again.

She steals across the landing to hers and Ted's room. On the bed, on top of the covers, Ted lies face down in last night's shirt, his pants and one black sock. Ugly and snoring, a stink that catches in the back of her throat. Johnny must have helped him up here. Must have. Who took off his trousers otherwise? Who put the glass of water on the bedside table?

She stares at the spare pillow; not for the first time wonders how easy or difficult it would be to suffocate him. The thought is stronger now than it has been in the past, almost overwhelming, but she'd have to be sure of finishing the job. It isn't something she'd want to get wrong.

The digital alarm clock reads 2.15. She stands over him. He might be pretending to be asleep. He grunts, rolls onto his side. The snoring stops a moment, resumes. She steps back, a blunt pain in her chest.

She will not, cannot get into that bed. It'll be her on the couch tonight.

Unable to tear her eyes from the rise and fall of his chest, she takes off her clothes. The sight of him has made her feel dirty. Dirty, yes, that's what she feels. Skin thick with filth that no brush or soap could ever scrub away. She tiptoes into the bathroom and closes the door. Sits on the loo long after she's finished peeing, staring at nothing. The rubber shower attachment is still wedged onto the bath taps where she rinsed the shampoo out of her hair this morning.

This morning, so long ago.

Jim.

She'd almost …

Through the wall comes the beast-like rumble of Ted. She finds that she's taken off the shower hose and is running a bath, though she can't remember deciding to do this. She's turned the taps to slow so as not to wake him – a habit. She pours in her favourite peach bath foam. Once in the hot water, she closes her eyes and pushes her head under the bubbles. The world fades, the repulsive pig noise of her husband all but gone. The heat eases her shoulders, slackens the tendons in her neck. Memories of Jim return in flashes: his hand on her waist, the crinkles at the corners of his eyes – *you cannae be sitting here on your own all night.* His voice. His touch.

Tommy's got my number … Give us a call, eh?

She sits up a little and draws up her knees. The bathroom light splits into hundreds of little stars, reflected tiny in each soap bubble as it slides down her legs. She crosses her arms and runs her fingers over her shoulders, down to her elbows. But her hands are too small to feel like Jim's.

A creak on the landing. She curls up. The water swishes loud in the tub; she cringes at the noise. Ted. He's woken up. He's woken up and he's—

The bathroom door flies open. Ted. Eyes bloodshot and wild, blind but seeing, a look full of hate aimed only at her. His nose wrinkles, his hand shoots out in front of him, a starfish of fingers. She shrieks, folds herself smaller still, arms over her head, eyes closed. The smell of whisky goes up her nose, whisky and smoke, sweat and pubs. This is it. She has not got away with it. The punishment is now.

She opens one eye. 'Ted—'

His pink hand blurs in her face; she closes her eyes. Here it comes.

A pressure on her forehead. The heel of his hand on her nose. 'Ted—'

Holding her fast, he pushes her down, down under the water.

The back of her head jams against the bottom of the bath. Her mouth and nostrils are under … under … under the water. Her arms flail, find his. Up again, out of the water. She gasps. Another splash, a white roar in her ears. His hand on her face. Underwater, underwater. Her nose … the heel of his hand on her nose … pain, so much pain. She can't breathe. Her throat throbs. She gulps, chokes. She's suffocating. She can't move her … can't move her head. She can't … He's too strong he's too strong he's too …

The weight of Ted's hand pushes, pushes on her face, pain in her nose, pain in the back of her head. Her own hands are loose in the water. The life is draining from her. The life is … Jim's hand on her waist. *I'm a car crash. You're not …* The kids … the kids standing by a hole in the ground, a coffin being lowered into the earth … It's her in the coffin … The kids have no mother, they don't understand, they'll never understand … The kids, alone with Ted … She's dead, she's dead and she can never tell them she'd never leave them … never … Some woman, some other woman in their lives, never able to love them like she does … Her kids are walking away. *Come back*, she calls after them. They're walking away. The beach is white sand. Their backs, their little hooded coats

… They're little again, they're only small, they're only children … *I'm coming.* She's running. *Wait. Hang on.* She's running … running after her children on the white sand. The sand sucks at her feet, won't let her run, but she has to reach her kids … *Wait. I'm coming. Mummy's coming. Hang on. Hang on, I'm …*

The weight of Ted's hand. Hands loose in the water. The weight, the weight …

The weight lifts.

She's up, she's out of the water. A gasp. Her own.

Ted crashes against the door frame. He lurches, goes growling down the landing.

She coughs. Grips the side of the bath. Not enough air – her mouth widens and sucks. Sucks. Filling her lungs. Gasping. Air. Air. Her head is light. It's heavy. She rests it on the hard edge of the bath. Her nose throbs, the back of her head burns. She gathers up handfuls of foam and rubs her face. The smell of him is on her hands: cigarettes, whisky. Snivelling, she grabs the nailbrush. The nailbrush is in her hand. She stares at it.

A crash from the stairs. The picture. He's knocked it off the wall. The picture of the kids, smashed.

'Fuck.' Ted. His shambling steps quieter now. She listens, holds her breath, hears the creaking thud as he hits the settee.

Forehead back on the side of the bath, she lets out a quiet, high wail. After a moment, she pulls her ragged bones out of the water, dries herself, throws on some clothes and ties back her wet hair. By the light of the bathroom, she scurries about. Into two sports bags, Graham's rucksack, anything she can lay her hands on in the dark, she stuffs hers and the kids' clothes. She creeps downstairs and puts the bags by the door. Ted is on the couch, snoring, on his back, mouth open. Her finger shivers in the dial as she calls a taxi: treble six treble nine. The dial tone is so loud, the number wheel crawls back from the nine so slowly she almost throws the whole lot at the wall. Into the handset she hisses her address, eyes fixed on Ted.

'Ask him just to wait,' she tells the cab lady. 'Ask him to wait at the end of the drive, please. He mustn't knock. Tell him to wait in the cab. We'll be out. It might take us a few minutes, but we'll be there.'

She cuts the line but doesn't let go of the receiver. In the phone table are bills, scraps of paper and, bingo, the piece of card with a picture of a robin on a snowy branch. She turns it over, reads the number that Pauline gave her, makes the call she never thought she'd make.

Back upstairs, she wakes Graham and switches on Nicky's bedside lamp. He screws up his eyes against the dull amber light.

'Graham, love. We're going now. This is it.'

'What?' He's confused, still asleep, rubbing his eyes.

'Your dad, love. We're leaving him. Can you do it? Only it needs to be now. I need you to help me.'

Now he's awake, awake and understanding everything. 'Oh. Y-yeah. Y-yeah. OK.'

The sound of Nicky's bed creaking, the sour-sweet smell of sleepy children. Nicky's arms thread through the sleeves of her T-shirt, thin as strands of white wool. *We're going on a trip*, Carol tells her. *But it's a secret trip.* Nicola's still half asleep. She's only ten – doesn't know if this is a dream or what. Ten. To be fleeing like this, to be homeless. Years later, when Carol thinks about this moment, she will wonder what she was thinking, what the hell she was thinking, and remember that she wasn't thinking at all. There was no thought, only a kind of heat in her body, and this, this whispered, frantic movement in the fraught, electric darkness.

She puts her finger to her lips, pulls the two of them into a huddle and shuts the bedroom door. Their eyes shine, their clothes lumpy over their pyjamas. She tries to keep her voice steady, to guide the ship of it over the roaring waves.

'We mustn't wake your dad. We can't wake him, all right?'

They nod. Halfway down the stairs, they pass the broken picture frame. She turns and puts her finger to her lips again.

'Shh.' She widens her eyes at them, gesticulates for them to be careful of the smashed glass. Mouths clamped shut, they give tight little nods. On the next step down, Ted cries out – a half-eaten protest. Graham's teeth are clenched. His eyelids flutter, hover, almost close.

'Don't …' Ted shouts. The rest collapses away to nothing. Silence.

There are eight more stairs to the front door. Then the catch. The catch will make a noise; she will have to tease it. The bags might knock against the door frame, the wall. They should leave them here and just go with what they have on. She can hear them all breathing in the dark. She can see them, as from above, halfway down the stairs. She makes a stop sign with her hand.

Ted gives a loud snore. Another beat; he snores again. She looks back to the front door and waits for a third snore, to be sure. When it comes, she turns back to the kids.

'OK,' she mouths. She gives a thumbs-up and creeps ahead down the stairs.

The latch makes a dull clunk as she pulls the lever. Her heart batters against her ribs. Sweat runs down the sides of her face. Slowly, slowly she pulls the door open and ushers the kids outside. For the last time, she glances at her husband, the father of her children. His jokes, his brown eyes, the lock of black hair that falls over one eye, his cocky way. His face red in hers, his spit in flecks on her cheek, his sickening words in her ears, the vice of his thick fingers on her arms, the unseen and sudden blow to the side of her head.

His mouth is open. His leg hangs off the sofa.

'Goodbye, Ted,' she whispers, and closes the door.

CHAPTER TEN

Carol

Huddled together in the taxi, stunned into silence, the kids stare out: round black eyes, knees pressed together. She has no right to drag them from their home. She has no right to ask them to stay. Through the dark, Graham smiles doubtfully at her and she knows then how worried he is, how scared. She should tell the driver to turn around and go back, she thinks. There was no time to tell Pauline. What on earth will she think when she gets back from her honeymoon? Will there even be a phone in this place? Is the place still a safe house?

Of course it is. Of course. She's just called them, hasn't she?

She realises she's left the number at home and immediately a new cloud of panic mushrooms in her chest. Ted might find the number and trace it. He might … but no, no. Pauline is the only other person who would recognise that scrap of card.

It was the only time Pauline ever let on about the bruises, about what she must have heard through the wall for years. 'It's one of them shelters.' She bit her bottom lip, unable to meet Carol's eyes. Carol didn't know what to say; simply stared at the card and let Pauline babble on. 'A safe house, like, a refuge. Where you go if … you know … if you need to, like.'

The figures went in and out of focus.

'It's not like you could come to ours,' Pauline went on. 'He wouldn't exactly have to be Sherlock Holmes, would he? I mean, we're next bloody door.' She laughed, though she still wasn't looking at Carol. 'I took a copy of it myself. Never know, I might come with you.'

All Carol could think was: *Pauline knows*. Of course she did; always had. That was friendship, wasn't it? All the things you knew about each other, both knew you knew, but never said in words.

Eventually the cab slows, the gears surge. Nicola has fallen asleep against her brother. They're driving through an estate, one Carol doesn't recognise. A shudder and the cab stops outside a house. She peers out of the window. The refuge is just a house – after all that. Just a house in a row of other houses, all of them built around an area of grass with what looks like a community centre or a church. How daft she is. She was expecting an air-raid shelter or a World War Two bunker or something.

'Here we are,' the driver says, smiling at her in the rear-view. His eyes are brown, like Ted's.

Nicola stretches. 'Are we there?'

'Yes, love.' Carol ducks out of the cab and helps her drowsy, blinking children down. The cab driver's dark, hairy forearm lies along the lowered window. He is humming softly.

'How much?' she asks.

He waves his hand. 'Don't worry about it.'

'Don't be daft. How much?' She meets his eyes, sees kindness. Pity. She takes out her purse, pulling out thirty pounds, all she has.

He shakes his head. 'Good luck to you, sweetheart, all right? God bless you.'

Before she can protest, he pulls away.

She calls her thanks but he doesn't hear. He's reversing around the kerb, stopping now at a distance, making sure she gets in safe. There are good men in the world, she thinks.

She knocks softly on the door. Within seconds, a pale woman with long, thin white-blonde hair and buck teeth answers.

'Come in, come in,' she whispers, reaches forward for their bags.

Carol turns to see the cab drive away, a big black crow eating up breadcrumbs from the road, leaving no link between the house she's left and the one she's about to enter. She should get back. If she goes back now, Ted will never even know she's been gone.

'Come in, love, it's cold.' The woman's accent is Northern, but Carol can't pin it to anywhere specific.

'I'm not sure I should …' she begins. 'I think I should …'

'Come in, love,' the woman says for the third time. 'Come on, out of the cold.'

Carol nods, steps into the house after her children.

The woman tells them she's Julie, the warden. She leads them upstairs. The carpet sinks under Carol's shoes. Words run around in her head, words she's trying out to make some sense of them, for herself, for the kids.

Your dad isn't well.

We have to let your dad be on his own for a while.

We had to leave while he was asleep because he would be too cross otherwise.

Perhaps these shadowy truths will be enough, for now.

'I won't keep you talking,' the warden whispers at the door of a room with a double bed and a put-me-up. 'Try to sleep if you can and I'll see you all in the morning, all right?'

Graham is quiet. Shell-shocked. Speaking is an effort for him at the best of times; no wonder silence is all he has just now. Nicky whispers constantly as Carol pulls the clothes from over her pyjamas.

Is this a hotel?

How long will we be here?

When are we going back home?

When is Daddy coming?

Carol bats her off as best she can. There are no ready answers, nothing concrete, only sand, slipping away as she picks it up.

I don't know how long we'll stay, love; we'll have to see.

This is a special place for women whose husbands aren't well.
Let's wait until morning, eh?
Sleep now.
Night, night.

They collapse, first in two beds, then one: three of them, holding on to each other.

Refugees.

CHAPTER ELEVEN

Nicola

2019

From the mantelpiece I pick up a photo of my mother, Graham and me. My mother smiles doubtfully in the way she always did, as if she can't trust her own happiness. It was taken on her sixtieth birthday, when we threw a party for her – a surprise; she would have panicked if we'd told her beforehand. It had to be held here, in her home – a posh hotel or restaurant would have had the same effect, plus she would have worried about the cost.

I drain my glass and think about that party, my mother's particular fragile happiness. I think about the night she left my father and try to imagine myself running out of my home in the dead of night with my two girls, not knowing what lies ahead, fearing for my life and for theirs. And for all that I have since dealt with women like my mother, with families like mine, I can't imagine it, not really, or if I can, it is but that: imagination. It is not real, not for me. I am forty-four years old, and only in the sudden silence of grief, of a house left empty, do I even have an inkling of what she went through, what it might be like to have to do what she did just to survive.

'Mum,' I whisper to the smiling image. 'Mum. What you … what you did.'

It's half past two in the morning, and here I stand, tired and tipsy, wet-eyed and sadder than I thought it possible to be. And something else. Proud. Yes. I am so proud of her. My packet of tissues long used up, I pull from my pocket a few sheets of loo roll I must have torn off at some point. I think tea would be better than wine at this hour. I have so much to do and only a few days to do it – Monday's case is a juvenile accused of assaulting a shopkeeper, whose leg was already broken from a fall, with his own crutch. The kid says he didn't do it. The evidence is circumstantial. His acquittal is my job.

I'm putting the kettle on when my mobile phone rings. It's Graham. Awake then, like me.

'Gray?'

'All right?' That's how Graham says hello, always has, always will. Such a Scouser; I tease him for it. 'Can't sleep,' he says.

'Nor me.' I answer the bleeding obvious with the bleeding obvious.

'Funeral was all right, wasn't it?'

'Except for you making everyone cry with your speech.' I hear him almost laugh. 'No, you did a great job. She had such a lot of friends in the end, didn't she?'

'She did, yeah.' I hear the suck and blow of his lips on a cigarette. At least it's only tobacco he's addicted to these days. 'What you up to?'

'Just … nothing. Looking through Mum's things. I found Tommy's handkerchief. You know, the one they used to bind Jim's leg? And that got me thinking about … you know. That night.'

'Wh-what do you want to think about that for?'

The merest hesitation over the *wh* of *what*. I smile to myself. If you didn't know him, you'd never know he stuttered as badly as he did. Neither of us says anything for a moment. We both know what happened after that wedding, how it changed all of our lives for ever, how it shaped us in such different ways.

'Don't know where to start,' I say, changing the subject. 'Or if I'm even supposed to touch anything.'

'Don't worry about it. I'll come over tomorrow. I was going to come over anyway. There's something … there's some stuff I need to tell you.'

'Sounds ominous.'

'Ominous.' He gives a derisive laugh. 'Posh twat.'

He tells me he'll come over at about nine in the morning. When he rings off, I realise that the hair is standing up on the back of my neck. Graham has always told me everything. Well, no, that's not true. There were years when he told me nothing. And later, I would visit him and we would exchange only small talk. The polite distance of it used to make me cry in the car afterwards. We had been so close. I idolised him when we were kids. And when he told me not to visit him anymore, my heart broke. All our childhood confidences, our reliance on each other counted for nothing, it seemed, at that time. We were strangers. After he got out, I understood that, having killed a man, it was too difficult for him to talk to me, his little sister; that an *actual* stranger was what he needed to help him finally find the words.

PART TWO

CHAPTER TWELVE

Richard

Lancaster, 1992

Outside the prison, Richard sits in his mother's car, listening to the volcanic rumbling of his guts. He should have eaten, but there was no food in the house. He could run into town and buy a sandwich, but no, he can't risk being late, not on his first day. Instead, taking hold of the steering wheel, he bows his head and offers a short, silent prayer.

Lord, give me the strength to help those you send to me today. Help me listen without judgement, help me to help them find their own way out of darkness. Amen.

Outside, a grey stream of cobbles bubbles down from the castle, whose purpose these days is less to keep people out than to keep them in. In front of the gatehouse, framed by the windscreen of his mother's old Ford Fiesta, clumps of people fidget, a motley tableau of tracksuits and cigarettes, hunched shoulders and screwed-up faces. On the bonnet of a rusted beige Astra, a cardboard tray of beer cans glistens with cellophane. In front of it, a man paces and smokes. Further down, a young woman in a tight skirt and high heels clutches an enormous bottle of champagne, the neck tied with pink ribbons that coil around her bony knuckles and fall away in shining ringlets.

Thursday is release day. That's right, Vivian did tell him over the phone, but there was so much to take in. He gets out of the car and locks it with care. The grass verge gleams with dew in the early-September sun. He hitches up his rucksack and clears the grass in one jump.

Ahead, Lancaster Castle looms. Rugged squares of saw teeth crawl across the top. Slowly he moves towards it, thinking about how no one, given the choice, would want to enter here. But it's too late to back out now.

He knocks on the black gate, turns and casts a last glance over the waiting crowd. Their faces have brightened with hope. But he has nothing to offer them.

In the internal courtyard, already the air feels thinner.

'I'm Richard Crown,' he says into the protective glass screen of the reception kiosk. 'I'm here to see Vivian Wolff. I'm the new chaplain.'

'Morning, Father.'

A glimpse of spectacles. He leans in closer to the glass. The spectacles belong to a slim-faced woman with dark brown hair.

'I'm not a priest,' he says gently. 'I'm just … y'know, ordinary.'

The woman says she'll take him up to the office this first time, to show him the ropes. Under her close supervision, he unlocks the first of the gates, closes it after himself and locks it again. This process he repeats a further four times, raising his eyes more than once to the curls of barbed wire that loop along the tops of the fences. Metal is everywhere – spun, meshed and moulded; hard, pale and grey.

'You'll get used to it.' She gives him a smile, for which he is grateful.

He follows her across the courtyard. She tells him that the walls here are six feet thick; that there is a back entrance for high-profile cases so as to avoid the press and *all that malarkey*. A small square of sunlight shines in the bottom corner of the yard; a bird of prey glides overhead. Another door waits at the base of a tower.

'This is B Wing,' the woman says, gesturing at the door, which Richard unlocks with the last of the keys and heaves open. 'The office is at the top of the stairs. Viv's expecting you. Good luck.'

'Oh. Yes. Thank you so much.'

He closes the door behind him, locks it, checks that he's done it correctly. The darkness is instantaneous. His eyes adjust, his nose twitching at the sour brew of trapped sweat, feet and hair. This, then, is the smell of enclosure, of institution. He wonders how long it will take him to get used to it; whether he ever will.

There are four flights of stairs. He is glad of his evening jogs; his fitness means he doesn't have to inhale too deeply. At each floor, the courtyard drops away, the square of sunlight shrinks. As the staircase darkens, Richard has the impression that he is not ascending but descending, into a basement.

The door of the education office is open. Inside are two women – one blonde, the other with long black hair, a lone purple stripe flashing at the front – and a rather nondescript man with grey hair and glasses. Unsure how to call attention to himself, Richard hesitates. But then the blonde woman looks up, sees him and stands.

'You must be Richard,' she says, smiling. She is what his mother would have called comely, with a wench-like quality he finds reassuring. 'I'm Viv. Nice to finally meet you. All set?'

'I think so.' He is still at the door.

'This is Richard Crown, folks. The new chaplain. He's going to be here Thursdays and Fridays, aren't you, love?'

Richard nods.

'Come in, come in,' continues Viv. 'Richard, this is Frank, Bernadette.' She holds him lightly at the elbow, giggling a little every time she speaks.

Richard says hello. Hello, hello. He is glad of his beard, hopes it's disguising the blush he can feel on his face and neck.

Viv gives him a copy of a pamphlet entitled *Clink*. 'That's the prison newsletter.' She hands him another note. 'Then that's an invite for Kevin's leaving drinks next Tuesday. He teaches decorating but he's moving to Chester.'

Richard tries to hold his face in a smile, and to look at no one in particular. He knows he will throw the invitation in the bin the moment he gets home, but there's no need to say that.

'Thank you,' he says, and, 'Great.'

On the desks and shelves are stained coffee mugs, overflowing pencil pots. Folders spew out sheets of paper. The musty smell of damp adds itself to the mix. Plaster bubbles on the walls. The wallpaper on the ceiling peels at the corners, as if at any moment it will come unstuck and fall on top of them all. The public sector, he thinks, crumbling; and then thinks of Andrew, who would have teased him for seeing the metaphor in everything. Really, though, how different this place would be if the rich ever found themselves at the bottom of society.

Viv squeezes between two desks and rifles through a pigeonhole before sidling her way back and handing him another piece of paper: a short list of names.

'It's pretty relaxed,' she says. 'They put in an app to come to chapel; I think I said. Anyway, we give them the OK to get out of woodwork or maths or whatever it is. They might stay a few minutes, sometimes a lot longer, but if it gets towards lockdown, the guard will take them back. They're unlocked at nine, so you'll see them between ten and twelve, if they turn up, then they go back to their pads and are unlocked again at two for their afternoon sessions. They're expecting a new chaplain, so they'll be prepared.'

'Great.' He scans the list, apprehension blooming in his chest. These are the men who will come to him for spiritual support, for guidance, or just to talk. He wonders how many, if any, he can lead into the light.

Viv shows him to the chapel. Up and down yet more stone steps. Men in matching grey jogging suits file along the corridors, close-cropped hair, tattooed forearms, subdued expressions.

Richard keeps his smile as neutral as he can. Viv makes a quick detour to the cells – the pads, as she calls them – to let him have a look. When they reach the block, Richard feels his breath hold in his chest. On long landings, blue door after blue door stands open. It is, of course, recognisable from programmes he's seen on television. But the stark reality of it takes him aback, the smell so strong here that it is only politeness that keeps him from covering his nose with his sleeve.

'The lads are in their classes just now,' she explains. 'They get paid to attend, in the hope that they'll fill their time usefully while they're here and learn, well, various things, as well as how to structure their days better.' She waits, indicating that he should look inside one of the pads.

The door is thick, metal. He imagines it closing for the night, the bang it must make, the clunk of the key as it is locked from the outside. There are two thin bunks against a wall, a small desk and chair, screwed down, a tiny white sink and an open loo. There is no seat, no lid.

'The toilet is inside their cell?' he asks stupidly.

Viv nods, her lips pressed into a tight line.

'So, they have to … in front of …'

'In front of their pad-mate – yes, love, that's right.' A brief chuckle escapes her. 'The Hilton this is not.'

A guard nods as they pass. Viv leads Richard back down more stairs, along a corridor, up yet more stairs. He is glad of his new trainers. She told him to make sure he had comfortable footwear, warning him over the phone that the floors were 'a right pig'.

'Here we are,' she says, standing outside a door much like any other in a corridor much like any other in what feels increasingly like a concrete warren. 'This is your manor.'

He steps inside.

The chapel is not the dim Norman crypt he envisaged. It is more like a classroom. It *is* a classroom: impersonal, with blue plastic chairs arranged in a circle. No wooden pews, no ancient confessionals, no thick slabs of stone. And the smell, the stale, closed-up damp stench that permeates every room. As he looks in dismay at the grim moulded seats, the cheap veneer tables and pallid green walls, he becomes conscious of his own romanticised notions of what form his new role might take. Books on self-help and spirituality line the dark shelves. But apart from the makeshift altar – a burgundy cloth thrown over a small square table – the only thing to distinguish the place as a chapel is one discreet cross on the wall.

In Mexico, there were crucifixes in the bars. Those eight months with Andrew were the best of his life. Would he still be with Andrew now, he wonders, if he hadn't had to leave? Probably not. Andrew was too brave, too witty, too extraordinary not to get tired one day of Richard and his hesitations. Richard tried not to let show his conviction that sooner or later he would not be enough for a man like that. But even so, he thinks now, they might have had a little longer …

Viv taps his arm. 'I'll leave you here then, love, all right? Patrick, the last chaplain, used to run a little choir, if that's of interest, and a mindfulness workshop; *be at one with the moment* type thing. Anyway, you've got Him upstairs for company, haven't you, so I'd better skedaddle.' She restrains herself from giggling and gives only a crazy smirk. 'Toddle back to the office at lunch, all right? Will you find your way?'

'Of course,' he says, though he is unsure if he will. 'Thank you.'

Viv makes her way out with the jolly gait of a baton twirler in a brass band. Once she has gone, the space fills with stillness and silence. All around is noise and movement – footsteps in other rooms, on the floor above, voices, the banging of doors. Walls are everywhere. Every window is sealed, of course; why had he not thought of that before? Every surface is hard. Sound has nothing to sink into, smell has nowhere to dissipate.

He picks up two of the plastic chairs and places them in a separate arrangement. He sits on one and, satisfied that it is the right distance from the other, wedges his Bible under his left thigh. It is 9.55. His eyes wander back to the crucifix, his mind to the bar in San Cristóbal de las Casas, to Andrew. Andrew, again, always, inevitably.

'Just tell her,' he is saying, his pale neck no less long in Richard's looping memory, the desire to put his lips to that neck no less strong. '*Mum, I'm gay*. It's three words.'

'Four. One's an abbreviation of two.'

'Pedant. Just tell her, for God's sake. Live your life.'

'It's not as simple as that,' Richard hears himself reply, and even in his memory his voice sounds weak. 'I'm not like you, Andrew. I'm not … confident. And I wasn't blessed with liberal parents.' A flash of guilt – then, and now. He should not have criticised his mother and father, should not have compared them and found them wanting. He hadn't meant to. No one can help what they are. If he'd ever had the courage to tell them, wouldn't that have been the first argument in his own defence?

Andrew is swigging from the green glass bottle, his eyes half closing for a second. He puts the bottle down on the table, takes a handful of sunflower seeds, splits the husk of one with his teeth and spits it into the sawdust. A beggar girl of no more than six sidles up, eyes like chocolate buttons. Andrew gives her a coin, waves her away. '*Vete. Fuera.*' Returns his gaze to Richard. 'You regretted not telling your dad, didn't you?'

'She's just ill,' he replies, the words landing in the present like a cruel taunt. 'It's not like she's dying or anything.'

A cough breaks the silence. A young man with the merest shadow of a black crew cut stands in the doorway. His shoulders are wide; his sweatshirt hangs from them as from a coat hanger. The rest of his body barely troubles his clothes. But most of all, it's his eyes that Richard notices. They are those of an animal: deep brown pools of fear.

'Come in.' Richard checks his list, stands up, offers his hand. 'Graham Watson, isn't it?'

The lad blinks, once, and is gone.

CHAPTER THIRTEEN

Nicola

2019

I barely remember the refuge. There were other women, other kids, but to my childish eyes they were all scary, mad, ugly. Now, of course, I see that they were afraid, anxious, damaged. We all were. I remember the volunteers helping my mother with the emergency benefit forms, her complaining that she needed a ruddy degree to understand the ruddy things. I remember asking for money to go to the shop to buy a packet of shortbread biscuits and my mother telling me that she only had ten pence in her purse; that I'd have to wait until the next day. I remember how silent the place was, despite being full. It was only later, dealing with these families in my professional life, that it dawned on me: these women, these children had been conditioned to be quiet. My clients helped me understand my own extremes of perfectionism and diligence, and of course my brother's stutter. His silence.

I remember the school a little more clearly. Our new surname, Morrison – the strangeness of that. I remember the kid that threw a desk at one of the teachers, the death list in the girls' toilets detailing all those who would be killed after school, the lads who sniffed glue on the far side of the school field, and the daily scraps, when all the kids would go running to watch some boy – or girl – knock seven bells out of another before the teacher came running, blowing hard into a metal whistle. Sometimes, when I recount things like that to my colleagues, I can see the blankness in their faces. They have no idea what I'm talking about. They have no idea what it's like to grow up in a world where violence is as constant and normal as air.

I remember my brother withdrawing into himself. His stutter made it hard for him. He constructed a new identity: silent, since speaking was difficult; violent, since no one speaks out against a fist; mean, since kindness got you nowhere. I, meanwhile, kept my head down, worked hard, drew no attention. We developed what I have come to see as our own individual coping strategies. What else were we to do? Here finally is a leveller: in a different way perhaps to my legal peers and the particular cruelties of their privileged educations, at our school, personality wasn't just about fitting in; it was about survival.

Graham told me later that we were in the shelter for over a year; that he finished his woeful education at that school. In my mind, the time frame is mere weeks. Funny how childhood shrinks and inflates memory where it chooses. Whatever, all I know is that by the time we left that place, Graham was not the same brother I had grown up with. Something inside him had shifted, hardened. I know from my experience dealing with people like us, like we were, that the moment of leaving an abusive partner and its immediate aftermath is the most dangerous. For the woman who leaves, it is then that she is most tempted to return. For the children, it is at best utterly confusing, at worst devastatingly traumatic. For Graham, it was then that he began to lose his way, of that I have no doubt. I wish I could have saved him. But he was my big brother. He had always looked after me. It never occurred to me to look after him.

In my mother's room, I sit at her dressing table, rest my mug of tea on the cloth doily alongside her perfumes, her face powder, her little pot of Nivea. She loved this table and its matching upholstered stool. As a girl, I would watch her put on her make-up here, wrapped in her towelling dressing gown on the stool, me on the bed, behind her in the three mirrors. I would watch her angle her face to apply eyeshadow, make an O with her mouth while she painted her lips, pluck a tissue from the box to blot them. She would study herself, serious for a second, before winking at me in the mirror.

'What d'you think?' she would ask. 'Knockout, eh?'

'Beautiful,' I would answer, meaning it so much it hurt, thrilled to find myself included in her private feminine ritual.

In the drawer, I find her lipsticks: Guerlain, Dior, Lancôme – all gifts from me, perks of a barrister's salary. They are all untouched. I always knew that she only ever wore, would only ever wear, her trusty Avon. The others she kept, along with the perfumes I gave her, for a best that would never come. I have no idea what she thought best was – a trip to Buckingham Palace, perhaps, though she would never have coped with that. She was a bag of nerves when I graduated, convinced she was dressed wrongly; the same when I finished my pupillage and took her for dinner at Quaglino's.

'You choose for me,' she said, confronted with the menu. And then, when the food arrived, she could not eat it.

Next to her lipsticks, in its own velvet-lined compartment, is a cassette tape. *Woman's Hour* is written on the label in black felt-tip pen. That's weird. As far as I know, she only ever listened to Radio 2; loved Jimmy Young, thought Terry Wogan was hilarious.

There's a portable radio cassette player on her bedside table. It makes me smile, because I don't know another living soul who still owns one. At home, our music is all digital, unless Seb is in the mood to listen to his vintage vinyl. We can choose to listen to whichever song we want, by whoever we want, wherever we want, and it will come to us through speakers in the ceiling. We control the sound through our mobile phones. If she'd ever had the nerve to visit me in London, my mum would have shaken her head. *Heavens*, she might have said. *Whatever next?* As for Seb's record player in the sitting room, it's a statement piece, apparently, though to me, it's a pretentious attempt to somehow channel the perceived authenticity of anything old – sorry, vintage. *Vintage, my arse,* my brother would say, and I tend to agree. As far as I'm concerned, the past can stay where it is.

To distract myself, I slide the tape into the deck and press play. The presenter is talking about a show called *Girls' Talk* opening in the West End. None the wiser, I rewind, play.

'Of course, what you have to realise is that by that time, the woman has no self-esteem left …' An educated voice. An expert of some sort.

'What?' I mutter. Stop, rewind, play.

'I had to break the cycle,' a different woman says. The voice is deeper, slower than my mother's. But the vowels are hers.

Stop, rewind, play.

'… held my head under the water.'

My mother. Disguised. But that phrase gives her away, at least to me.

Stop, rewind, play.

The bright enunciation of the presenter: '… with the daily threat of violence. Reporter Laura Budd spoke to some of these women and heard their stories …'

I feel behind me for the edge of the bed, sit down slowly.

'I suppose I didn't realise it was his problem.' My mother's artificially slow voice speaks to me through the tinny speakers. 'I thought it was my fault, like. I mean, the first time I made him cross. It was after our first was born. I was tired, I suppose, and I said something out of turn. I said something I shouldn't've. He'd been to the pub and he'd said he'd be back, like, and then, when he came in so late I asked him where he'd been, you know, why he'd not come home, and that was it.'

I pull three tissues from the box on my mother's bedside table and wipe my eyes.

'But he was so sorry afterwards. He was on his knees. Crying, he was. Begging and that, like, you know? He told me it'd never happen again, he'd never hit a woman before ... and I believed him. He said he loved me. He couldn't live without me. And we were married. We had our ... we had a child. Then we had two children. We were a family, like, you know? That's not something you can just walk away from.'

Another woman's voice speaks. Different story, same underlying theme. Women broken over years by abusive men. It is impossible to listen to, but I can't stop myself listening. Another woman, who had to have corrective surgery on her nose, then Carol again – that night under the bathwater.

'I thought I was dying. I could feel myself dying, like, you know? And I thought, if I live, I go tonight.' A suck, a blow – my mother, pulling on her B&H. 'I did live, God knows how. And I did get them out. I wanted to go back, but the social worker here told me that's common ... She's helping me understand things, like. I'm determined not to go back. I don't want my kids growing up thinking it's normal, do you know what I mean? It's no way to behave, is it? No way to treat people.'

'Did anyone know?' The reporter's voice, well spoken, soft.

'My neighbours knew what they heard. I never said owt, like. They knew I di'n't want any police or owt like that. But none of them knew the half of it, not really.'

The piece ends. A short, respectful silence ensues before the expert starts in.

'Of course, what you have to remember, in terms of these women staying, is that it's a question of—'

I press stop. I am shaking all over, the sharp edges of my fingernails cutting into the palms of my hands. I put my fists to my cheeks. My skin is hot, clammy. I eject the cassette. Withdraw it slowly from the slot. My head throbs. My chest rises and falls. With a roar, I pull at the tape, wrenching out great fistfuls of thin brown ribbon, which slithers and pools on my mother's floral bedspread. I bite at the cassette, madly, feel the pushback into my gums. Another roar and I've thrown the damn thing against the wall; the ribbon flies after in a frenzy of flickering loops.

My chest heaves. I burst into tears. Before I'm wholly aware of it, I'm on my feet, punching the bed, the pillows, grabbing the pillows and beating them against the mattress, hauling up the duvet and fighting with it, wrapping it around me, screaming at it. I collapse onto it. I am crying. I am laughing. I am insane. I am all over the place. I lie back in the whipped-up bedding and stare at the ceiling. I want her back. I want her back now. I want my mum. It's not fair, what she had to go through. How dare how fucking DARE ANYONE how dare he how DARE HE do that to her, to us? Years wasted, wasted, my poor beautiful brother, my mother, all I want is to lie next to her here and look up at the ceiling with her and tell her … oh, things. Just … just stuff. All I want is a few more minutes, that's all. That's all.

'Mum.' Tears fall fat and wet, slide down my neck into my top. Surely if I say it enough times she'll hear.

She never told me she'd been on the radio. She must have recorded this interview in the shelter. That must have taken guts, days or weeks after she left, terrified as she was that my father would find us. One more brave thing she did to add to the pile, this woman who in her later years was so nervous about the smallest things, as if she had used up all her mettle on her family's survival.

I wonder what else she did there, at the refuge, how she spent her days, whether she went out. She must have done, must have gone to the shops for food, but we never talked about that. All I know is that several months after that interview, we were housed, and that, as a kid, I was excited at first, until we pitched up in that terrible place. If I sound like a snob, well, I'm sorry. I lived there and it was terrible. You kept your head down and you stayed indoors at night, avoided the lost souls who shuffled like wraiths in their baggy, filthy clothes. They put us there so that I wouldn't have to change schools again. Ironic, since I'd only just moved up and certainly had no desire to stay. But we were all of us in a system run by forces outside our control. As for my mother, she was above all terrified that my dad would find us, worried sick that her son had become a stranger, and wondering how the hell she would ever pull herself free. The house she was offered was the safest choice she had. It was the only choice.

CHAPTER FOURTEEN

Carol

Rochdale, 1985

Carol pushes open her new front door, tries to keep her heart afloat. Junk mail shushes on the brown carpet and a gust of musty air hits her. At least Pauline is here. And the kids.

Keys in hand, she walks down the hallway into the kitchen. It's a little brighter in here, at least – big windows, another window in the back door, all in need of a damn good clean. The whole place smells of damp. She runs her fingers along the worktop. Wipes her sticky fingertips on her jeans. There's a dark line where the worktop meets the wall – she didn't notice that when she came here before with the social worker, who told her that this was the best she would get. Three small burn holes scar the Formica surface – fags, she thinks. Who would put out a ciggie on a worktop?

She digs into her bag for a tissue and wipes her hand. Looks about her, tries not to think of the home she left, of Ted sitting in what seems to her now to be the lap of luxury while she is here, facing this, this place, where she has to live now because of him. This, all of it, is the price of safety.

So why doesn't she feel safe?

The kids run ahead, clatter up the wooden slatted stairs, arguing over who's getting which room. *Don't get too excited*, she wants to shout. *They're both grim.*

'It's a bloody palace is this, Caz,' Pauline shouts from the lounge.

'Told you,' Carol shouts back, grateful for Pauline's sense of humour, lifting herself to meet it, heading back out the kitchen. 'Windsor Castle's got nothing on this place.'

There's no flap on the letter box. Cold air comes through in icy gusts.

Pauline has her back to her. She's looking out of the front window. At least in here the carpet isn't too bad, looking at it properly: brown shag pile, cream swirls like the Coffee Mate advert. Not Carol's taste, but it'll go well enough with her fawn three-piece. It makes sense to have the settee along the wall on the right. The television can go in the corner by the window.

'Lovely view,' says Pauline sarcastically.

Carol remembers she no longer owns a settee or armchairs, or a telly for that matter. She owns nothing, nothing at all. The carpet might as well be sky-blue pink with a finny addy border, as her mum used to say. She shivers. It's colder in here than outside. This frozen, closed-up air is seeping into her bones.

'I think the heating panel's in the kitchen,' she says, pulling her coat tight around her.

Pauline's shoulders make black curves against the light. Carol feels a rush of love for these shoulders, for this woman who's taken a day off work and driven nearly two hours just to help her. She joins her friend at the window and nods to the stretch of paving stones, the painted metal fence that runs between the block and the chicaned dead-end road. Opposite, there is an abandoned supermarket trolley.

'There's always a broken trolley in these places, isn't there?' she says. 'It's like shithole rules or something. Like carrots in sick.'

'Now, now.' Pauline fumbles in her bag for what Carol hopes is a packet of fags. She's too tired, all of a sudden, to go and get her own. Pauline lights two cigarettes and hands one to her. 'If we smoke, it might make the place smell a bit better.'

Carol laughs, despite everything. 'Thanks.'

There are no trees, no little grass verges, no green at all. A few of the front yards are neat enough, she supposes; others seem to be dumping grounds for heavy rubbish. Some of the windows have curtains, some are boarded up. There's a radiator in next door's garden.

On the far side of the street, a group of kids huddle in the gutter. Tatty coats hang off their shoulders and not one of them has a scarf or gloves or a hat. Their bare heads bend over whatever it is they're up to – drugs, most probably. A couple of them stand up, and she sees that they're playing marbles, rolling them along the drainage grid from one gap to the next. Her body relaxes a bit.

Pauline opens the window so they can flick their ash outside. Above them, Graham and Nicola are still bickering. Normally Carol would've chucked them outside, told them to go exploring, sent them to the shop. But maybe it's better if they stay in today.

She and Pauline finish their cigarettes, crush the butts on the outer wall and throw them to the ground.

'Pauline?'

'Yes, love?'

'What am I going to do?'

Pauline rubs Carol's arm briskly. 'We'll soon have it fixed up. They're bringing you some furniture, aren't they? Tommy's coming later with quilts and that. And wait till we go through them boxes – there's all sorts in there.'

'Have you seen our Johnny?'

'Not recently. Why, do you want me to tell him where you are?'

She shakes her head. 'Not just yet. In a bit.'

'All right, love. No rush, is there?'

Carol sighs. 'Of course, Ted's got all my pans and I don't think he can even boil an egg. His mother waited on him hand and foot, you know, until I took over – like a bloody idiot.' She looks Pauline in the eye. 'Do you see him at all?'

'He's been over a couple of times but he's not come in. Seems to think we know where you are, but Tommy told him to let us know if he finds you 'cos we're worried sick. That do?'

Carol nods, wipes her face with her hand. 'How is he in himself, like?'

Pauline grimaces, shakes her head. She opens her mouth to speak but appears to think better of it. It's no more than a moment, then she says, 'You don't need to think about that any more, love.'

'I'm not. It's just that now I'm here … now I'm not in the shelter like, I … I mean, what if he finds us, P? What if he followed you here today?'

'Well he won't … he didn't, all right? Forget about him, Caz. Honest to God, you'll give yourself an ulcer.' She looks about her. 'You need to think about this place now. Lick of paint, bit of Shake 'n' Vac on them carpets, honestly, it'll be smashing. And it's not for ever, is it? It's only tempor— Oh, come on, love. Don't cry.'

'I'm not.' Carol feels herself being pulled into a cloud of Poison perfume. She lets her head rest on her friend's soft bosom, lets herself be held. There's no difference between a happy hug and a sad one, she thinks, between a hug that says *hello* or *goodbye* or *you're in the shit but here I am*. 'Do you think I should go back? I mean, he might've learned his lesson.'

Pauline pulls away, holds on to the tops of Carol's arms, as if to make her stand up straight. 'No, you should bloody not go back. No way, José. I'll batter you myself if you do, d'you hear me?'

Carol laughs, sniffs, wipes her tears into her hair. 'Shall we go and get them boxes?'

'That's the ticket, my love. Tell you what, I've collected some right treats. Ornaments, would you believe, and bad taste isn't the word. Honest to God, you're going to wet your knickers.'

They make their way out to Pauline's car. On the street, there's no sign of their rusty old Cortina, no one waiting at the corner, at least no one that looks like Ted. Ted she'd recognise anywhere, from a mile away.

They load box after box into the house. Pauline has managed to get her hands on all sorts: tea towels, matches, things Carol wouldn't have thought of. They're able to make a brew with an old kettle that goes on the hob.

'Hey, look – pans.' Carol noses in one of the boxes. 'Oh, and plates … oh, and look, there's cutlery too. I'll be able to cook the tea. Where the heck did you find all this?'

Pauline holds up a painted wooden cuckoo clock. 'This'll cheer the place up. I'll get you some batteries.'

At the top of a box of plates, Carol finds a small black radio. Together they unpack the rest, singing along to the music, sometimes chatting, sometimes in comfortable silence. Pauline's friends and colleagues have spared these things for her. Charity, that's what it is. Not that she isn't grateful; just that she wonders if gratitude is ever free from shame, since the two seem much the same to her now.

She fights off this shame as best she can.

In the evening, Tommy brings a collapsible picnic table and four fold-up chairs, two sunloungers, sleeping bags for the kids, two quilts and two pillows for her. The gratitude, the shame makes a knot at the back of her mouth.

'I'm sorry I've no mattress,' he says.

'Don't be silly, I'm fine.'

He loads two bags of shopping into the kitchen cupboards, then sets the timer for the heating so that it will come on in the morning. While Pauline gets her coat, he attaches a piece of cardboard to the letter box with duct tape.

'That should keep out the draught a bit at least.'

It's as if he has to do one last thing to protect Carol against whatever lies outside: the night, those feral kids, those shadows. He nods to Pauline, the sign that it's time to go. It's late, they have a long drive, work in the morning. Their lives to live.

Pauline hugs her tightly. 'Will you be all right tonight? Do you want me to stay?'

'Course not,' Carol manages. 'I'm champion. Thanks again, love.'

She waves them off, locks and bolts the door and slides the chain across. In the kitchen, what she thinks is a crumpled bit of paper turns out to be a twenty-pound note wrapped around a tenner.

'Oh, Pauline.' She picks the money up and puts it in her pocket.

She unlocks and relocks the back door. There's no bolt, no extra locks. The big window bothers her. She shades her eyes with her hand and leans into the glass. Yellow light glows in slices from between other people's curtains. In the gardens, junk lurks in shadowy hulks. Nothing human, though, nothing that looks like a man. From out there, this place must look derelict. No lightshades, just bulbs. No blinds, no curtains. They're alone, her and the kids. They're scared. They're skint. It's like they're advertising it.

Steeling herself, she goes into the lounge and finds Graham sitting cross-legged in the middle of the floor. The main light is off. He's smoking, watching nothing, listening to nothing in the dark. Here is another worry, perhaps the biggest: her son. He's grown quiet, strange. He's never once spoken about his dad since they left, even though she tried to get him to talk; he's never answered her when she asked about his school. Now he's left school and is on the dole, and she wonders what life will show him, whether he can make something of himself, whether this is just a phase or what he has become, who he is now. She hopes not. She should have left Ted sooner or not at all. She should have protected her son. She should show tough love, make him get a job, stop him smoking in the house. Shouldn't let him smoke at all, at seventeen, but you have to pick your battles, and for now, getting him to speak is the biggest.

'Hey up, Confucius,' she says, feigning lightness. 'You meditating or what?'

When he doesn't answer, she tries again.

'My mum used to say, "We could have bacon and eggs if we had some bacon. But we don't have any eggs."'

The tip of Graham's cigarette moves up towards his mouth and glows brighter, fades as it falls.

'I was thinking we could shut the curtains and watch the telly,' she adds, still at the doorway. 'You know, if we had any curtains, but we haven't got a telly, have we?'

'No.' There's no hint of a laugh, but no sign of his voice shaking either. Not crying, then, just wanting to be in the dark, and to be silent.

She steps a bit further in. 'We've got our bums to sit on, anyway, even if it does look like we've had burglars, and there's a sofa coming tomorrow. Is our Nicky asleep, d'you know?'

'I ch-checked on her. Dead to the world.' Few words, but she's grateful for them. He speaks as if he were Nicky's dad.

'I'm off up anyway,' she says.

'I'll l-lock up.' Now he sounds like a husband.

'It's all right, love, I've done it.'

'I'll ch-check.' Like a husband all right – not trusting her to do anything right.

She makes to go but changes her mind, needing to touch him – to scratch his back, squeeze his shoulder, whatever, make physical contact after the day they've had. She crosses the lounge on the pretext of checking the windows, puts her hand flat to the spikes on the top of his head. Gently, just enough to feel the baby hedgehog prickle. Any longer and his hair will start to round off, to be thick and black, like his dad's.

'Pauline said she'll bring her portable,' she says. 'It's only black and white, but it's better than nowt.' She gives his earlobe a pinch. On the edge of her thumb, his stubble is soft, not yet coarse from years of shaving. He's still a boy.

He tips his head back to look at her. 'Have you h-heard? F-f-from him?'

Unease fizzes in her belly. 'Your dad, d'you mean? No. Why? Have you?'

He shakes his head, puts out his cigarette in a saucer on the floor. 'Just thought P-Pauline m-might've said something.'

'He doesn't know where we are,' she says simply.

'No.'

'He doesn't.'

'I know. I j-just …'

'Just what?'

'D-d-dunno.' Graham shrugs.

'Did you want to see him?'

'N-no.'

She wonders whether she should say more, ask him how he feels about it all, but doesn't want to break what counts these days as a long conversation. She'll leave it there. That way he might start talking to her again. It might come trickling out if she doesn't push him. Her silent boy, dark circles under his eyes, eyes that never meet hers anymore. He doesn't have to look at her, doesn't have to say anything for her to know he hated it at that school. He's come out without much in the way of qualifications, but it's not that that worries her. There's something else these days, something darker she can't name. It's too soon to ask him about going to college, about turning his life around. He's not ready to think about any of that. None of them are. So for now he draws the dole. More charity, but here they are, both of them at the bottom of the heap. Pauline would tell her that at least there was only one way, and that was up, but Carol knows better. No matter how low you sink, there's always further to go.

Upstairs, Nicola is flat out, arms up out of her sleeping bag. Carol holds her face a moment against her daughter's slumbering breath, catches the vanilla whiff of Malted Milk biscuits. Her eyelashes, in their thick black arc, look false – an innocent doll-child, ignorant of her father, of what he's capable of, what he's done, could still do. Carol has cut this child off from him with one swipe of an axe, without any real explanation. That her children will never see Ted again is a possibility she didn't reckon on. She only thought as far as getting out. She never thought she'd be this lonely. She never pictured this house, herself checking the locks every five minutes, looking out of the windows like a fugitive. That she'd feel this weight of guilt, like she'd killed him somehow, abandoned him to his misery, robbed the kids of their father. And Graham. That Graham would take it so hard. There are so many things she didn't reckon on.

Cleaning her teeth in the bathroom, she thinks of Jim. He has become her secret habit. She has thought of him every day since that night. Even sent him her new address, like some kind of silly schoolgirl. No word from him, obviously. Just because he's been on her mind doesn't mean she's been on his, does it? Probably won't even remember her name. She's been a daft cow, that's what she's been. Her mum would have killed her. Throwing herself at him, she would have called it. And at that thought, she misses her mum too, despite everything.

She'd meant to try again with her parents once things settled after Graham. But the years went by, as years do. Ted started on her. Nicola came along. It became too difficult to pick up the phone – because she hadn't done it sooner and then later because by then what could she have said? *You were right, Ted's a wrong 'un, my life is a mess?* And then last year, in the refuge, she'd been scanning the obituary pages as she did every day, looking for Ted, and read: *Ralph Green. Died after a short illness. Gone to join his beloved Shirley. Rest in peace.*

She'd had no idea her mother had passed, let alone her father, and so just like that, when she was half expecting to become a widow, she'd become an orphan. All of which reminds her that she should contact Johnny. He would have read about them both, wanted to tell her. But if she tells him where she is, he'd only have to tell one other person and that person might tell another person. And before too long someone would let slip something to someone and on it would go until her whereabouts reached Ted. Not yet then. She'll drop Johnny a line soon. When she's up to it. Like Pauline said, no rush.

She closes the bathroom cabinet. In the rusted mirrored door, the face she's tried to avoid flashes in the cold light: bluey-white, purple bags under red-rimmed eyes. She pinches her nose, pulls it from left to right. It still hurts where Ted held her under the water. He must have broken it. Behind her, the wallpaper curls away from the wall. Mould grows black on the horrid little window frames. This bathroom is like her: wrecked, rotten, bits flaking off. She turns from her reflection and switches off the light.

In her bedroom, she looks out of the window. No one about. Not even a gang of kids. They'll be on the scrubland behind the Spar or sat in the railway sidings smoking funny stuff, sniffing glue or whatever it is they do. Graham will be drawn to them, she knows that much.

She lies down in the bedding Tommy brought. The floor is hard. The quilt smells of Pauline's house. She presses it to her nose and breathes it in. On the bedroom ceiling, the naked bulb grows out of the gloom, hanging on its wire like despair. She must get some shades, even paper ones. Her eyes prickle and she presses her fingertips to them.

Home. She misses her home. Her kitchen, her lounge, her bathroom. Her bathroom was her haven: soft apricot, spotless, clean towels, lovely soaps. And with Ted so often out, she was able to take a bath more or less when she wanted. Ted wasn't bad all the time. It was just the drink and what it did to him. He could still make them all laugh when he was in the right mood, and the kids loved him. The kids loved him and she stole them from him. He would be worse without them, lost. And if they hadn't left, Graham wouldn't have retreated into that terrible silence. A stuttering boy is better than one who doesn't talk at all. She can't remember when he last made a joke. She should face facts, get back home and fix what she had instead of lying here with her shoulder blades knocking against the floor. If she had anything about her, anything at all, she'd pack up and go. Things would be different now that Ted had had the shock of her actually upping and leaving, had had a chance to see what he had to lose. They could get some help for him, have counselling, be a family again, instead of this, this mess.

'Ted,' she whispers, picturing herself walking through the door, Ted all tearful and sorry. *Carol, oh Caz, I'm so sorry. I love you, Caz, come here.*

She sits up, eyes stinging in the fuzzy half-light. With the cash Pauline left, she could go back. While the kids are at school, she could take the bus. If she goes on her own, they could talk things through. He's in a bad way, she knows that from what Pauline won't say. He'll be so sorry now. She's never left him like that, and now he knows that she will, that she can, he'll be different. She'll go to him. They can be a family, start again. She has to try. She owes it to the kids.

CHAPTER FIFTEEN

Richard

1992

The three men Richard speaks to that morning are candid; their stories pour from them like polluted streams. Andrew used to chide him about so many things – his silence, his reticence, his passivity – but he always told him he was a good listener. And listen is what Richard has done, for hours. The men fascinate him. They pain him, fill him with melancholy and hope, disgust, love. Some of them, he knows, are capable of terrible violence. Some of them, it seems, are no more than hapless, daft.

He is about to return to the office when the boy from earlier appears at the door.

'Hello?' Richard says.

The lad gives a perfunctory nod. 'G-Graham G-Green.'

'All right,' Richard replies carefully. 'I have a Graham Watson here. Could that be you?'

He nods again. 'I go by G-Green. I p-p-p-prefer it.'

'Graham Green. Like the author. Does your surname have an e on the end?'

The lad narrows his eyes and shakes his head, as if he has no idea what Richard is talking about. It was a stupid thing to say. Richard resolves to do better.

'Come in,' he says. 'Don't be shy.'

The young man steps inside, stops, seems to wonder about turning away, then appears to change his mind again and shambles across the room. He sits down on the plastic chair opposite Richard. Stands up, moves the chair back a little and sits down again. He coughs, glances at Richard, rubs his hands on his knees as if to wipe the sweat from his palms. His upper lip looks conspicuously bare, as if he has recently shaved off a moustache, and close up, he appears to be somewhere in his twenties. Around ten years younger, give or take, than Richard. There is a scar under his left eye.

Richard holds out his hand. 'Richard,' he says. 'Pleased to meet you, Graham.'

'All right?' His accent is strong Liverpudlian. He doesn't acknowledge Richard's hand, choosing instead to look over to the window, though the blinds are down.

Richard retrieves his hand and wedges his fingers under his Bible. 'I'm well, thanks. How are you?'

Graham gives a mirthless laugh. 'I'm very w-well, thank you f-for asking.' The g on the end of 'asking' is hard, a scathing consonant, if such a thing is possible. He glances at Richard, meeting his eye for a second. The short flash of a smile.

Richard returns the smile. He had planned to ask the usual ice-breaking questions, questions that he learnt on the counselling course and which he has barely needed all day, but as he frames them in his mind – *What brings you here today? What's on your mind?* – they sound inane, his every word and gesture weighed down by the absurdity of the context. An absurdity pointed out moments ago by Graham Green himself.

The room hums, a cocoon of quiet within the larger continuous din of the prison. It is difficult to surrender to the silence after the garrulous men of the morning. Richard tries to get comfortable in his hard chair, to no avail. Seconds pass. He waits for eye contact, which doesn't come. Closing his fingers around the spine of the Bible, he wonders how to proceed. He appears to have met someone who finds talking more difficult even than he himself does. And yet this man has come here to talk.

'Why Green?' he asks, for the sake of asking something. 'Why not Watson?'

Graham stares at his legs, draped in grey prison-issue sweatpants. Richard tries not to think about the irony of inmates dressed in this uniform of leisurewear.

He is about to ask another question when Graham says, 'Green is m-my m-mum's m-maiden n-name. We w-went back to it after my f-f-f … after my f-f-f …' His eyelids hover, almost close. Richard holds his breath, wills the word out of the boy. 'After my d-dad d-died.'

A wave of relief and pity washes over Richard. How much it costs this poor man to speak. The death of his father is the first thing he has mentioned. Richard makes a mental note.

'I'm n-n-not Catholic or n-n-nothin'.' Graham stares at the floor. Beneath the brutal black spikes of hair, his scalp is grey.

'That's OK,' Richard replies. 'God doesn't mind who or what you are.'

Graham looks up, that screwed-up expression again. He stops short of meeting Richard's eye before looking back down to his knees. 'I d-don't b-b-believe in G-God, if you want the truth, like.'

A clanging sound rings through the ceiling. Startled, Richard ducks his head into his shoulders and looks up. Above them, someone whistles tunelessly. The whistle recedes. Richard refocuses his attention on Graham. The uninvited noise seems, oddly, to have settled the young man, but Richard's instinct tells him he must not rush him, not at any cost.

'I've been c-clean f-f-for one and a h-half y-years,' Graham announces to the floor. A non sequitur, but another big statement nonetheless.

'That's a long time,' says Richard. 'Well done.'

Graham pushes his thumb against his teeth and tears off a strip of skin. 'I f-feel b-better.'

'Great. That's great. Good for you.'

'I alw-w-ways do.' He stands up abruptly and paces towards the window where he turns and rests his backside against the sill. He rubs the back of his neck, scowls.

Richard wonders how bad Graham must have looked before he gave up the drugs. His yellowish-grey skin stretches over his face like hour-old chewing gum. And he is so thin. An unnerving presence, fidgeting and glancing around, he makes Richard feel like he's trying to lure an animal out of its lair.

'Do you think you can stay clean?' Richard asks. 'What I mean is, are you feeling, you know, strong?'

Graham lifts the blind with one finger and looks out. Apparently seeing nothing of interest, he lets the blind fall and ambles back to his seat, where he sits down and rests his elbows on his knees. He huffs and puffs. Seconds pass. Richard's confidence begins to drain away. Buoyed up by the conversations of the morning, now he feels his inexperience swamp him. Graham must have come here of his own volition, but he is scanning every corner of the room as if for an escape route.

'I'm up for p-p-parole in s-s-six m-months.' He chews another lump out of his thumb, scratches his forehead. 'D-do you n-n-need to know what I'm in for, like?'

'No,' Richard says, too loudly. 'We talk about what you want to talk about.'

Graham moves forward and perches on the edge of his seat. He raises his right heel. His leg starts to shake. Whatever he has done, Richard has a feeling it isn't petty theft.

He has made his thumb bleed. He presses his tongue to it, replaces his tongue with his fingertip. Looks up, finally. 'Well, I k-killed someone.'

An alarm rings out. Lockdown.

Graham stands abruptly. 'See ya.'

A moment later, Richard is staring at the empty doorway, unsure of what just happened, how Graham managed to leave the chapel so quickly, and whether he will ever see him again.

CHAPTER SIXTEEN

Carol

Runcorn, 1985

Coniston Drive looks exactly the same as when she left it. The lawn at next-door-but-one's is still as manicured as a golf course, the beds dark with freshly turned soil. Across the road, at number 23, there's still a rusty gold Ford Granada with three flat tyres. At the end of her own driveway she stops. Her house is the same but different. All the curtains are closed, which they would never usually be at this time, and the front lawn needs edging and mowing. By contrast, Tommy and Pauline's house is up and ready for the day, curtains pulled, garden all neat. Pauline's Escort is parked out front and the living-room light is on. Carol's stomach churns at the sight. Tommy and Pauline should be at work. If either of them catches her here, they'll be furious. She sighs, tries and fails to stop picking at her cuticles. Tommy and Pauline have been so good to her, but the trouble is, they don't understand all of it.

Slowly she walks up the drive. At the front door, she stops, overtaken by a coughing fit. She's not smoked all week, that's why. It's always worse when she tries to give up, but at least she's saved nearly a fiver on ciggies, which, determined to pay Pauline back, she's put towards the bus fares here.

She reaches up for the doorbell, but her finger hovers over it. Maybe she should just leave the letter she's brought. She takes it out of her bag, out of the envelope she hasn't yet sealed, and reads it one last time.

Dear Ted,

I'm sorry for the way we left but I'm hoping that by now you'll understand. I couldn't have the kids growing up in fear and ending up in a mess themselves so I had to leave and it had to be then. The social worker told me never to contact you, never to come back, but I was hoping now you've had time to think that we can talk things through and work out how we can still be a family.

If you can agree to see someone professional with a view to changing, there's hope. I will be at the café in Widnes market, the Ave-U-Et, remember where we used to go sometimes? Anyway I'll be there at midday this Saturday. I'll wait for an hour. It's up to you.

Yours,
Carol

She puts the letter back in the envelope and seals it. Taps it against her hand, air whistling through her teeth. His car's not here, so that means he's probably at work, not lost his job as she thought. If he's not in, there's no harm ringing, is there? Even if he's in, it's maybe better to do this face to face. She won't go in the house. She'll stay out here where it's safe. It's broad daylight; what's the worst that could happen?

She pushes the doorbell, hears the familiar notes of 'Oranges and Lemons' chime from inside the house. She waits, looks over her shoulder to the empty street, back to Pauline's house. Nothing stirs. She presses the doorbell again. Again, nothing. On the third ring she senses movement from inside. She steps back, looks up just in time to see the bedroom curtain twitch. Her stomach churns. A moment later she hears footsteps thumping down the stairs. Her breath comes fast and shallow. She could run, she could—

The door opens. Ted, in a grubby white vest and baggy Y-fronts, stubble, bloodshot eyes. Pauline did drop hints but even so, the sight of him is a shock.

'Ted,' she says.

'Carol.' He blinks at her. His voice is a croak.

Behind her, the close is silent. In the distance, a train rattles by, the slip road to the M56 hums. She picks at her fingers, bites her lip.

'Ted, I …

'Carol.' His mouth contorts, his eyes fill. His hand flies to his head, pushes back his greasy hair. He starts to cry. 'Come home, Caz.' He is holding on to the door frame, his knuckles white. 'Come home, will you? I'm sorry. I'm so sorry.' He takes a step towards her, sways. Body odour comes off him. Alcohol fumes. His belly is swollen like a pregnancy. She steps back. 'It'll never ever happen again.' His words are slurred. He sounds like it must hurt to talk. 'Caz. I'm sorry. I promise. I promise it won't happen again. Ever. A hundred per cent. A thousand per cent. I mean it this time. I'm … I can't … I need you, Caz. Caz? Come home. Please come home.' He lets go of the door frame, makes a steeple with his hands but almost falls against the wall. He rights himself and give a thick, rattling cough. He looks at her with his wet brown eyes. 'Come in, Caz. I can make us a cup of tea.'

She shakes her head. 'No, love. I'm not stopping. I just wanted to say that if you're ready to talk about it all, then I think we should meet somewhere … somewhere in town, like a café or something.' She holds out the envelope but he doesn't take it. 'Here. I've written you a letter. See what you think.'

His eyes narrow. 'Just come in, will you? Caz? What's the matter? Just come in – come in and we can talk now. Inside, like.' He looks helpless. Lost. He's ill. This is not who he is, not really.

She inhales, feels the breath fill her lungs. 'No, love. I'm not coming in.'

'What d'you mean?' His voice rises. She hears the turn in it. 'I've said I'm sorry, haven't I? I've said it won't happen again, and it won't. What more do you want?' His eyes close for a long second, open again. He lowers his voice. 'Just come in, Caz. Honest to God. What do you think I'm going to do to you?' He pulls a comic scary face, makes claws with his hands, but the joke isn't real – his eyes are too desperate.

'Ted, let's meet up at that café in Widnes market, eh? Saturday, this one coming.' She knows, even now, that she will not go. But she has to get away without the scene her guts tell her is coming. This has been a mistake. 'Where we used to go, do you remember?' she continues, her words fluttering and high. 'How about that?'

'Where are the kids?' he asks, his voice rising once again. 'Where are my kids, Carol? Our Gray, our Nicky? You took them. You *stole* them. I don't deserve that, you know that, don't you? I don't deserve to have my kids taken away, do I? How could you do that? How could you do that to me, Caz, eh? Just … just come home. Bring my kids home.'

'Ted. I'm sorry.' She puts the letter back in her bag. Takes a step back, another. Her movements are slow but her legs have started to shake; her scalp prickles.

Ted steps out of the house. Her shoulders rise instinctively. She takes another step back. But before she can make sense of anything, his hand is round her throat. There's a loud roar. She sees his socks, black and strange on the tarmac drive. And then she's falling, falling backwards. The back of her head hits the ground. He's on top of her, his fingers tight. She tries to call his name, but it's blocked in her throat.

With his full weight, he sits on her belly. The stench of sweat and stale alcohol. She opens her mouth, tries to shout, but there's no breath in her, no voice. He's crushing her. His features blur.

'I don't deserve that.' His spit lands in her eye. 'You took my fucking kids off me. How dare you! How dare you do that to me, you fucking bitch. No one leaves me, no one.'

'Ted.' Her mouth forms his name but she hears nothing above his ranting rage. She closes her eyes. She has been a fool, a bloody fool. There's no hope. There never was. Idiot. Idiot, Carol.

'Oi! Oi!' Pauline. 'Oi! Ted Watson! What the bloody hell d'you think you're doing?'

Carol opens her eyes. Sees Pauline's white teeth gritted in a burgundy mouth. She is swearing, shouting, pulling the back of Ted's stinking vest. 'Get off her, you drunk bastard. Off! Tommy's calling the police right this minute and you've got three seconds to leave her alone, do you hear me, Ted Watson? Tommy's on to them now, he's literally calling them now. Three seconds, Ted, d'you hear me? One. Two. Thr—'

Ted lets go. Carol's hands fly to where his have been. She rolls over, coughs, feels grit press against her cheek. Her lungs inflate, empty, inflate, empty. Insults crackle: Pauline and Ted going at it, hammer and tongues. *You've got a bloody nerve … Don't you tell me to mind my own … Interfering cow … Tommy'll have your guts …*

'Stop it,' she tries to shout to them, but her voice is hoarse, her blood still pounding in her ears. She rolls onto her back, still holding her throat. The sky is blue. Not one cloud. Ted has his face in Pauline's, finger jabbing her shoulder. He's in his pants and vest, on the street in his pants and vest, dear God, his work socks, his face purply-red, his forehead oily. 'Keep your fucking nose out of it, you nosy fucking bitch – it's got nothing to do with you.'

'Ted Watson, if you don't get inside that house now, I swear to God I'll kill you myself and dump the body in the ruddy Mersey. And I tell you something else, you'll be doing time, you'll be locked away and they'll throw away the bloody key, 'cos we've all seen you now. We've seen you, d'you hear me? Whole street has.' Pauline's bosom rises and falls. She points to the house, lowers her voice.

'Get in, Ted. Go on, piss off back in the house before Tommy calls the police, or better still, sorts you out himself.'

Ted laughs, a laugh full of malice. 'Tommy? Bloody Tommy?' He puts up his fists, and at the sight, the fear drains from Carol. He is pathetic. Pathetic. 'I'll have him; I'll have him right now. I'll rip his bloody head off. Go on, come on then.' But he is backing away, towards the house, where he stops, lowers his fists and shouts as if to address the whole street. 'I'll have you, Tommy Wilson! I'll have you right here, right now, soft lad. Outside, now! Come on! I'll have you, I'll have you no bother. I'm Ted Watson – you don't know who you're dealing with, mate.' He beats his chest like an ape. His legs are skinny, his face livid as a bruise; his vest strains over his bulbous gut.

He stops, finally, fixes Carol with his red eyes. 'You.' He levels his finger at her, like a gun. 'Back in this house by the end of the week, yeah? The end of the week or I'll find you and I'll kill you, do you understand me? I'll kill you, Carol. I'll fucking kill you. No one walks away from me, no one.' He staggers, wipes his mouth with the back of his hand.

Still on the ground, Carol is aware of Pauline standing nearby, watching the whole sorry spectacle. Ted stumbles into the house, still throwing out raging threats, but they are quieter now, no more than muttered mad ramblings.

The front door slams.

A silence falls.

Pauline blows at her fringe. After a moment, she scans the street. She must spot one of the neighbours, because she shields her eyes with her hand and calls out, 'Had a good look, have you? Back inside now, go on, off you go, show's over.'

Another silence. She pulls Carol to her feet.

'I'm so sorry,' Carol says, brushing herself down. 'I don't know what to say.'

But Pauline's arm is around her shoulder, leading her towards next door. 'What were you thinking, love? What the hell were you thinking?'

'I thought I could talk to him. I thought that now he'd had time to think … I was going to leave a note. Why isn't he at work?'

'I don't think he goes to work anymore.'

'How come you're here? How come Tommy … Is Tommy here?'

'No, Tommy's not here. I was bluffing. I'm only here because I had a dental appointment. Come on, come in the house. I'll grab my keys and I'm taking you home. You're lucky I was in.'

'You don't need to do that. I can get the bus. You've got the dentist.'

'It was only a check-up. I'm bloody taking you. It's not safe here. Besides, I've got to make sure you get there, haven't I? And I tell you what, I'm bloody well locking you in this time.'

CHAPTER SEVENTEEN

Carol

Rochdale, 1985

It is twelve hours since she saw Ted. Saw the ruin of him, the mess. They're all a mess, all of them. She thought she could reason with him, that time might have shown him what he'd lost. But no.

I'll kill you, Carol.

I'll find you and I'll fucking kill you.

She rolls from under the quilt and gropes her way across the floor, up the wall to the light switch. Her watch says two o'clock. It takes her a second to realise that this means two in the morning. She must have slept for an hour or two after all. Her stomach growls. But even in her sleep haze, she knows it wasn't her stomach that woke her. She's sweating. Her head aches and her mouth is dry and bitter-tasting.

There was a smashing noise. A smashing noise, yes, that's what broke into her dream.

Her ears prick now, awake. A window. One of hers?

She creeps out onto the landing. Checks on the kids, both asleep in their rooms. She edges down the stairs in the dark, listens closely. Listens, listens.

'Hello?' she calls out, her voice little more than a whimper.

No sound. In the kitchen, no smashed window, no sign of a break-in. The back door is still locked. She keeps the light off so as to see out, but there is nothing, no one. The windows in the other houses are all black. In the lounge, same thing, nothing broken. Kids, she thinks. Throwing bricks at street lights for no reason beyond the illegal ecstasy of the noise. She checks the front door: locked, bolted, chain on. In the dark hall, she stretches, feels her ribs separate. She is thin, a bag of bones, an old nag. Under her bare feet, the carpet is waxy. Bits of other people. Dead cells and nail clippings, hair and eyelashes, fallen from other wretches and trampled into the pile. She wonders what it will take to get this house to feel clean.

The kitchen stinks of bleach, but still beneath it she can smell dirt. Unsettled, unsure of what she's looking for, she pulls open the cupboards and drawers, shuts them again one by one. She finds some fig rolls and eats three with a glass of milk. The milk is cold; it soothes her insides. She contemplates her supplies: tins of beans, tins of tomatoes, tins of Heinz chicken soup – store-cupboard food that Tommy brought. Plates, pots, pans, forks, knives, all from Pauline. She plucks a butter knife from the cutlery drawer and turns it over in her hand. Her mum used to own a knife like this, same bone handle, in the days of pantries and coal fires, proper china butter dishes. Her dad used a knife almost identical to this one for stripping wallpaper.

In the weak moonlight, the blunt blade flashes.

'Right,' she mutters. 'Bloody right then.'

She takes the stairs two at a time. Under the fluorescent tube, the bathroom flickers into life. She closes the door.

Woodchip curls away from the walls, its patterns raised like welts. In the mirror is a mad woman holding a knife, teeth bared, eyes red. She laughs at her reflection and stabs the blade hard behind the first flap of wallpaper. A huge piece comes away, thick with paint, dusty in her fingers. Another lunge, another strip of paper drops to the damp nylon carpet. Another, and another: tattered shreds raining onto her feet. It reminds her of when she used to peel the dead skin off Ted's burnt back on summer mornings. She'd sit on his bottom, pulling slowly, carefully, holding strips of skin up to the light, transparent and thin as cling film.

'Carol,' he used to say, muffled by the pillow. 'Give my back a scratch, will you?'

She did everything for that man, everything: washing, ironing, cooking, cleaning, you name it. She believed him over and over when he said he was sorry, made excuses for him when he stopped apologising, and if she didn't know before that it was no good, she does now. Where was he tonight? she wonders. Pissed under a bridge somewhere probably. Rambling at strangers in The Grapes, getting into fights, finding other people to punch. Staggering home in the middle of the road. He's not even in work now. She wonders how the hell he survives. The house will be repossessed. He'll end up on the street. After this morning, he'll be raging. He'll be banging on Pauline's door. Carol's breath quickens. He'll be looking for her and the kids.

Will he find them?

Has he already found them?

Was that smashing sound minutes ago him playing with her, warning her, huffing and puffing before he blows her house down?

She digs in the knife and pulls back another ragged sheet. Working her nails under the surface, she picks at ever smaller scraps before plunging in again and again. Ted was and is a bastard. He ruined her life, ruined it, and there he sits in her house, the house she decorated herself, letting it all go to waste. She jabs and stabs, scraping the paper until it covers her feet. She bashes the blade's end against stubborn patches of glue, grits her teeth until she wins, goes in for a second, a third lunge, prising off long pieces, which she holds up before letting them fall.

After fifteen minutes, she is sweating, down to her vest and knickers, her jogging bottoms in a tripe-like heap on the floor amongst the scraps. The wall too is half stripped. She wipes her face with the back of her arm. Crumbs of wallpaper stick to her forehead. Half the room is the skin beige of bare plaster, crusted with scabs of white paper; the other half still shines with sickly pale blue gloss.

It looks worse than when she began.

This is what she does: makes a mess of things – story of her life.

A low knocking sound comes from downstairs. She checks her watch. It's almost three. It won't be her door, not at this hour. She stands totally still and holds her breath. Again she listens, listens.

Three more knocks, a little louder this time.

She inches along the landing in the dark. She should wake Graham. No. He's seen enough.

She reaches the dark mouth of the stairs. She thought the worst had already happened, but there is worse to come, much worse.

On trembling legs, she goes down the stairs one at a time. The hallway is black. She reaches for the light switch but stops herself. It's better if he doesn't know she's here, behind this door, inches away.

The knock comes again. She purses her lips to stop herself panting but can't prevent the air from escaping in bursts, as if she were blowing out a thousand candles one by one. She has to open the door soon. If she doesn't, he'll start banging and shouting. He'll wake the kids.

The knife slips in her grip. She should call the police. But no, there's no phone. The doorway is a silent mouth. Cold comes through her feet, tracks up her legs. She is shivering from head to toe. The knife is still in her hand. A mewing sound, like a small trapped animal, escapes her. She puts her hand over her lips and tries to get her breathing under control.

The knock comes again, louder – the bang of a fist.

She does not have the guts to open the door. She cannot open it. She stares at the black space of it, shaking, useless.

Ted will not stop until he kills her. She knows it, knows it deep in her guts. The kids will find her cold where she's fallen. Oh God, they will find her. How did she think, how did she dream it was possible to go back to this man? This, this is how it felt, how it always felt. Dread. Unending dread that scrubs her insides raw. She will never get away from him. She's been a fool to think she can.

She reaches out for the catch.

CHAPTER EIGHTEEN

Carol

'Hello? Hello? Carol?'

A man's voice, calling through the letter box. She lets go of the catch, holds the knife in both hands. Finding something, some small reserve within herself, she squats and lifts the cardboard flap by no more than an inch. Sees green, blue and black checks. Tartan. Blue eyes replace the tartan, eyes the colour of Wedgwood.

She falls back, hits the floor with a yelp.

'Carol?' Jim stage-whispers through the letter box. 'Carol? Where'd you go? Are you hiding?'

She pulls herself up, puts her hands over her face, presses herself into the corner by the door.

'Oh God.' Her legs shake. 'Oh God.'

'Carol? Are you OK? Sorry it's so late but I've come straight from the rig. Just let me in, eh? I'm freezing my cohones off out here.'

'I can't … I just … just …'

'Carol?'

She pulls her face from the wall and exhales. Her legs are shaking so much she fears they might collapse under her. After a moment, she closes her hand over the catch and pulls open the door. Outside, the street light casts its soft yellow glow onto his face: ruddy, chubbier than she remembers. His cheeks push up against his eyes as he grins, blinking at her. She is glad to be in the dark.

'Do I feel a numpty in this kilt? It's a wonder I didn't get my head kicked in.' He shields his eyes, squints at the butter knife. 'You planning to stab me? I can do that by myself.' He gestures to his leg. Under the thick wool sock, the handle of the dagger sticks out from its leather pouch.

'I'm armed,' she says, waving the knife. 'Watch it. I might butter you to death.'

He chuckles. He comes into the house with a blast of freezing air, filling the doorway as he passes through it.

She wipes her cheeks with her arm, circling round him as he passes. Her teeth have been clenched so hard her gums ache. The front door is at her back.

'I don't ...' she begins. 'How did you know ... You didn't reply. I thought ... I didn't know if you'd remember me.'

'What? Of course I do. They ... look, they send the post out. That's why I told Tommy to give you my work address. In case you asked for it, like. I was gonna write, but I was due to get off a few days ago, then there was fog, you know? So that was me stuck between a rock and a hard place. Ach, I had all these plans, right enough. I was going to come down on the train, grab a hotel, then surprise you today. I should have called our Tommy, so I should. In the end, I bagged a lift as soon as we got off, got the guys to stop off at mine so's I could grab the kilt. I thought, you know, you'd ... you know ... 'cos I was wearing it when we ...' He looks at her, downcast and sheepish and shy. 'I was trying to be romantic, like. I'm sorry. It was inappropriate. I wasn't—'

'It's all right,' she says.

They are still in the hall. It is cold, and dark, and she is standing here shivering in her underwear. Her heart still hammers in her chest, her breath is still coming short, though the fear has gone; it went the moment she saw him. He is not Ted. Not Ted, thank God.

'Kitchen's straight ahead,' she says, though she doesn't move. 'I'm sorry it's so cold.'

He puts his bag down at the foot of the stairs and raises both hands above his head. He turns to lead the way, and like that they walk towards the kitchen: an intruder held at knifepoint by a madwoman. In the kitchen, she pulls the cord for the strip light. It blinks white, plink-plink-plinks until the light stays on. Jim stops at the table, Carol a little way behind, putting the L of the counter between them. They are both screwing up their eyes against the sudden brightness. She must cover herself, she thinks, eyeing her cardie draped over the back of one of the chairs. She needs to get to it and put it on without making a fuss. She puts down the knife, fills the kettle and forces herself to look back at him. Jim MacKay. A stranger who feels like part of her own body.

'I bet I look a right arse in this get-up.' He pulls at the kilt.

She laughs a little. 'It's me stood here with half the bathroom wall in my hair. I was stripping wallpaper, like you do at three in the morning.'

'That what it is? Thought you had a bad case of dandruff.'

She laughs again, too much, like an idiot. She fusses about, getting cups, milk, opening cupboards, putting the rest of the biscuits on a little plate.

'It's freezing in here.' She turns the heating dial to ON. 'Can you chuck us that cardie?'

'Oh, aye, right.' He throws the cardigan to her and she pulls it around herself, relieved to be warmer and to be halfway decent.

The kettle chatters against the side of the mugs as she pours the hot water. 'You've still got your coat on,' she says as she takes the tea over. 'Looks like you're waiting for a train.'

Beyond the table's edge, the colours of his kilt are bright under the strip light, just as they were in the hospital that night – over a year, a lifetime ago. It seems like a miracle, like something not real – that he is here in her kitchen, splashing whisky from his hip flask first into her tea, then his, without asking, as if it were their own secret and practised ritual. Yes, she thinks. Whisky. She might, after all, need a drop of something. She sits down, folds her arms.

'Here's to you.' He chinks his mug against hers.

A gale blows around inside her. She fights to stop herself from touching his face, to check he isn't a ghost or a dream. He peers at her over the rim of his mug and takes a sip. His eyes and the sense of him, how it feels to be near to him, she remembers.

'You look lovely.' It's out of her mouth before she can stop herself.

He stares down at his hands, apparently fascinated by his own thumbnails. 'I know it's been a long time, Carol. But that was not my average Saturday night. With you, I mean.' He glances up at her and she turns away. 'And I'm guessing … if you bothered to write to me after all this time, it wasn't yours either, was it?'

Her face throbs; she bites down so hard she fears her tooth might pierce her bottom lip. 'No.'

'So you've thought about me?'

Unable to answer, she nods.

'I'm here now, so.'

'Yes.'

'I mean, Tommy told me you'd moved. That you were getting on your feet, like. I just thought things might be a bit tough, you know?'

Tough. It's all been tough. The first days in the refuge, social workers, benefit forms, new schools for the kids, second-hand uniforms from the charity, women who barely became friends before they moved on, more women, bruised as dropped peaches, coming in where others left, Graham's terrible unending silence, the call from the headmistress to say he'd been in another fight, more social workers, more forms, the need to get them housed before Graham turned eighteen, days, long days, watching old detective series on daytime television, the loneliness, the shared kitchen, the battle within herself: go back, don't go back. Go back. Ted in the street, the disgrace. Yes, it's all been tough. It still is.

She pushes at her hair, looks up at the ceiling and tries to tip her tears back into her eyes. Jim has this way of knowing her. When she does manage to look at him, she sees him taking in the dirty walls, the manky worktop, the Artex ceiling, all of it. She knows that expression. It is the same one he wore when he pulled her clothes from her. There is too much to do here, too much to fix.

'I like what you've done with the place,' he says.

She laughs in surprise. 'I had a whatsit, you know, an internal designer.'

'Interior designer.'

'Aye, that's it.'

They smile at each other. The tea is hot. They take little sips. After a moment, he puts his mug back on the table and reaches for her hand, his upturned, expecting hers. She keeps hold of her mug.

'The kids are upstairs,' she says.

'I didn't think you'd leave them behind.' He gets up from his chair and drags it around the table, sits down opposite her, near her. 'Don't worry.'

'What about?' She laughs without knowing why, perhaps at the idea that she could stop worrying, even for a moment. 'You know my eldest is seventeen, don't you? Our Graham. He turned seventeen in the shelter. And our Nicky turns twelve next month.'

'I know.'

He's in front of her, but she can't get the thought of him, from before, out of her head – the hotel room, so far away from everything she knew or had known, him taking off her blouse, his mouth on hers. It seems impossible now that she could ever have done such a thing, impossible to imagine doing anything like it again, finishing what they began that night.

'I mean, it's not like we could go to a hotel or anything,' she says. 'And our Graham's changed. He's … quiet, you know. More than quiet. Sleeps more than he should, and he's left school. Sleeps all the time. Didn't do so well in his exams, which is understandable.' She puts her tea on the table. As she lets go of the mug, he takes her hand and holds it. Another moment and he pulls it to his mouth and kisses her knuckles, keeps them pressed to his lips.

'You've scuffed your hands,' he says. 'I don't need a hotel.'

'They're asleep. The kids.'

'I imagine so.' He lets her hand fall with his onto the table and pushes his fingers through hers, making one big, complicated knot.

His stare becomes too much. She watches their hands instead, locked together.

'I'm just saying they're in the house, like,' she says. 'The kids, you know. That's all. Though our Graham's not a kid.'

Jim moves his head back slowly before nodding it forward again.

'A-ha. I get it. You think I'm going to pounce on you? You think that's what I've come for?'

'No, I …' Her cheeks burn. 'I don't know. No. I don't know.'

He moves his chair closer, until their knees touch. She thinks of her legs, bare beneath the cardie, her vest and knickers, her stomach, her ribs and heart. There's no movement from upstairs. If one of the kids were to wake, she would hear footsteps. She'd have time to move away from him. But even so.

Jim strokes her wrist, the soft inside of her arm, her shoulder. She closes her eyes. He reaches up and squeezes her neck softly. 'I'm just here, that's all.'

She opens her eyes, leans in and kisses him, listening out all the while. He pushes his forehead against hers and sighs. They stay like that, heads pressed together, in the silence.

'It's nice to see you,' he says after a moment.

'To see you – nice.'

'Stupid. Are you warm enough?'

'Yes.'

'Do you want my coat?'

'No. I'm fine.'

She runs her hand up his thigh and takes hold of him. He is already hard, silky in her hand.

Without moving his forehead from hers, he pulls the bobble from her ponytail and strokes her hair. 'You don't have to do that.'

She leans back a little from him, so she can watch his face. 'I can't take you upstairs.'

His breathing changes; his eyes are closed. 'But what about you?'

'What about me?' She keeps a rhythm, keeps her eyes on the door. They are both fully dressed. Well, he is. And she can move away at the slightest sound.

He stays her hand. He moves his chair so that it meet hers, lifts her legs over his. He presses his forehead back to hers and holds both her hands.

They kiss, their hands tightening, until he lets go and reaches between her legs.

'No,' she says, pushing him away.

'But what about you?'

It takes her a moment to understand what he means, what it says about him, about how he sees her, himself. Them.

She pulls her cardigan around her. The kids are so near, separated by sleep alone from the shock of seeing their mother with someone in this way. 'I can't,' she says. 'I'm sorry.'

'No, *I'm* sorry.'

'How much did Tommy tell you?'

Jim shakes his head, just a fraction. 'Bits and pieces. Nothing really. And I saw ... you know.'

She makes herself meet his eye. They stare at each other until, embarrassed, she breaks his gaze.

'I was married to him for a long time,' she says. 'He did —'

'. You don't have to tell me.'

She shakes her head. 'He never thought about me in … you know, in that way. I mean, what I might have wanted. I just don't think it crossed his mind. He just … did what he had to do, like.'

'Carol, he abused you.'

'He thumped me about, you mean.'

'That's not what I meant. I mean, yes, but the other. If he … took advantage. It's supposed to be about two people.'

She laughs. But it isn't funny, what Jim has said.

'Ted was always the star of the show,' she says. 'He had a very strong sense of humour. Once, he locked me in the porch. The kids were in bed and he told me there was a letter for me. He kicked me from behind and locked the door and he didn't let me out until, well, until about four in the morning. I was freezing. I only had my nightie on. He thought it was hilarious, like. And I couldn't shout for help, obviously. You shout for help when there's no one there, don't you? Not when there's someone right there on the other side of the door.'

'Ah, Christ.' Jim rubs at his head.

'I'm sorry,' she says. 'I shouldn't have said owt.'

Jim goes very still. His lips press together. She recognises the look and feels her shoulders rise. He brings the flat of his palm down on the table with a loud bang. She jumps, despite having braced herself.

'Jim, love,' she whispers. 'You'll wake the kids.'

He pushes back his chair. Both his hands are fists now. His colour has changed; his neck and face are red. He's so big. He could kill her, kill anyone. She feels the fury coming off him, feels herself shrink, an old familiar pain in her chest. He brings his fists up to his temples and turns away from her. She can hear him breathing, heavily, as if he's recovering from a race.

'Jim?'

With a noise like a growl, he throws out his arm. She closes her eyes, her shoulders high against the violence, against the crunch

Then silence. When she opens her eyes, he is crouching by the back door, cradling his head. The knuckles on his right hand are bleeding. There is a hole the size of a fist in the wall.

'The world is nuts,' he whispers while she wonders what the hell to think, what to do, whether she should tell him to go or what. 'There's women out there who take all they can get, who want you for your money, for what you can buy them, and then they cheat on you the moment your back's turned.' He looks at her; his mouth is odd, and for a moment she thinks he's going to cry. 'And then there's you,' he says. He shuffles over to her on his knees and takes both her hands. 'This shouldn't have happened. This should never have happened.' He lowers his head into her lap. 'I'm so sorry about your wall. I'll repair it tomorrow. Ach, Christ, it shouldn't have happened to you, my darlin'. Not to you.'

'It shouldn't happen to anyone, love.' She hesitates, before laying her hand on his head.

'I tell you what. If I ever meet him, I'll kill him.'

'Oh, I don't know, love. Killing never helped anyone, did it?'

'It'd help you, though.' He looks up. 'And I tell you what, I'd do the time. Gladly.'

'Don't say things like that.' She shakes her head. She's no idea why he's so upset, not really. But then again, she does know. At the wedding – and after – something passed between them. She doesn't know exactly when it was or what it was or if she felt it at the time or later, but she knows she hasn't stopped thinking about him. And just because she never imagined it would be the same for him doesn't mean it wasn't. His head is on her lap, his hands now on her hips. There's blood on her cardie. She looks at the hole he has made with his bare hands, at the blood on his knuckles. Men and their rage and their damage.

'It's too bright in here.' She shifts so that he'll move his head. 'We're probably giving the neighbours a floor show. And you need something on that hand.'

She crosses over to the kitchen units, wets a tea towel and throws it over to him. 'Put this on it. I've got some candles somewhere.' She opens a drawer, then another. 'I'm sure I saw … Ah, here they are.' She takes three candles out of the box and finds three eggcups in the cupboard. She is moving too fast; one of the eggcups falls and smashes on the floor. 'Jeez Louise,' she says, frozen, listening for the kids. Jim too is caught, eyes white and round, staring up at the ceiling. When she's satisfied they haven't woken anyone, she crouches down to pick up the pieces.

Jim appears beside her. 'Careful. Don't cut yourself. And I'll fix the wall no bother. I'm so sorry about that; must be cheap plasterboard.'

'Here,' she says. 'Make yourself useful and light these. If they won't stand up in these eggcups, I've got all sorts here. Pauline brought it all.'

He takes the candles and eggcups from her and returns to the table.

'And don't worry about the wall,' she adds as she gathers up the last fragments of pottery. 'House is a shithole anyway. One hole in the wall's not going to make any difference, is it?'

'Even so, I'll repair it tomorrow. Christ, that was lousy of me, I just … Just the thought of him doing that, y'know?'

She hears his lighter clicking. His breathing is heavy, as if he's cross with himself, which she thinks he probably is. She puts the broken crockery pieces in the bin, taking her time, waiting for the flames. When they come, she switches off the light and sees bright tear shapes rise from the white wax. Jim has fallen into half shadow. The orange light catches his laughter lines, falls in the hollows under his eyes. She returns to him and strokes his hair. He has become himself, she thinks. He was strange on the doorstep, but now he looks like Jim – her Jim, as she has thought of him.

He pulls her onto his knee, but she feels herself tense.

'Sorry. Let me sit here.' She slides her bottom over to her own seat. He follows her with his mouth, turning her face so he can reach her lips with his, his hands sliding down to her neck. She reaches under the kilt once more, wanting to please him, to give him this reward. It is, she thinks, all she can offer.

'You don't have to do that,' he says again.

'Let me.'

His breath quickens. His hands push inside her cardigan, trace her hips, the dip of her waist, the rise of her ribs. He slides his hand under her vest, his thumbs running back and forth over her breasts until she has to concentrate to keep her mind on him. She holds the rhythm; his pleasure her own, since her own is impossible. He tries to kiss her again, but she turns her face away, feeling that these are his last seconds. He pushes his head into her shoulder.

'Oh God.'

They stay like that a moment; she leaves her hand where it is, enjoying the feeling of him dying away. She's good at this, if nothing else. She did it so many times to Ted in the early days when they had nowhere to go, and later, when it became a chore. An order when she was indisposed.

She jumps up and goes over to the sink.

'Are you OK?' Jim asks.

'Ghost on my grave, that's all.' She shakes her head. Bloody Ted, polluting her thoughts, her actions, dirtying everything. The water warms; she puts her hand under it. She doesn't dare look to see if and how Jim is cleaning himself up.

'Is it the kids?'

'It's everything.' Still with her back to him, she washes with soap and rinses off the suds.

'I shouldn't have let you do that.'

'Maybe I wanted to.'

'I know, and that's lovely, but I came to help you.'

'Don't say that.' She stays where she is, drying her hands on the towel, staring at the last bubbles popping at the brink of the plughole. 'Please don't say that.' She makes herself turn around but can look only at the floor.

Jim crosses over to her and strokes then kisses her hair. 'What's the matter? Don't you want me to help?'

She digs in her cardie pocket and finds her cigarettes, at a loss as to why she feels so furious. 'Light one for me,' she says, opening the packet.

He lights two and passes one to her. 'What's the matter?'

She looks away, anywhere but at him. 'I don't know.' It's her who's ruining everything – bringing Ted into it, taking things the wrong way. 'I just don't want to be a charity case, that's all.'

'Oh, come on, that's not what I meant.' He puts his arm around her. She shrugs him off and moves back to the table to sit down, crosses her legs and arms and draws on her cigarette.

'Carol.' The candles throw their orange light onto his brow, ploughed deep with grooves.

'I'm just sick of feeling grateful,' she says.

'Hey, it's me that's grateful.'

She knows by the way he says it that this is meant to be a joke, that he's referring to what she's just done for him.

'I came because I wanted to see you,' he adds when she doesn't laugh. 'I've wanted to see you since the wedding. I've thought about you every day. All day sometimes. I think about you all the time.'

She's made him gabble. Because she's so bloody difficult – touchy – shattered glass for him to walk on, cuts on his feet.

'Well why didn't you say so?' She tries for the same jokey tone, but the room pools in front of her. 'I'm sorry.' She hears him move around the counter, senses him sitting beside her, feels his arm around her, his hand on her back. 'Take no notice of me,' she says.

'I won't, you daft bastard.' He kneels on the floor in front of her. 'And I won't lift a finger to help, OK? I promise. I'll sit here like a big fat lazy arse while you wait on me hand and foot, OK?'

'OK.' She sniffs, laughs a little and finally is able to look at him. He has come all this way. Perhaps he'll stay. At least until morning.

CHAPTER NINETEEN

Richard

1992

The door of his mother's house brushes against the morning's post. He picks up the envelopes and rifles through. He thought he'd got through all the paperwork after her death, informed the few of her friends who live out of town, but clearly there are still people to write to, bills to change into his name.

The house is chilly. He goes into the sitting room, puts a match to the gas fire, which flares with a hollow blue *woof*. Inches away from the fire, chafing his hands against the cold, he looks about him. His parents' furniture is dark and old, saggy; the patterned carpets old-fashioned, sludgy. The whole place reeks of sadness, frugality, death. If Andrew were here, the house would have been emptied by now. Painted too, probably. Bright furniture would have been ordered from John Lewis or that new Swedish store that sells wardrobes in kits. As it is, his mother's glasses are still on the little table next to her copy of *Reader's Digest*. They have been there for months.

In the kitchen, he empties the flimsy striped carrier bag: a tin of baked beans, a white sliced loaf, a shimmering sleeve of Penguin biscuits. The bottle of cheap white wine appears to be the only warm thing in the house; he pushes it into the small freezer compartment of the fridge. He can have a shower while the wine cools; try to scrub away the stink of institution.

The shower is connected to the taps. Every time, it takes him ages to get the temperature right, shivering on his haunches under the white glare of the bathroom light. There should be hot water enough, but he'll probably have to put the immersion heater on to wash up. Everything in this house is decrepit. It all needs tearing out, burning, replacing. Three months here and he has done nothing, nothing at all. Apart from a few pleasantries, he has hardly spoken to anyone since the funeral. The people on the counselling course. Andrew, twice, on the phone – a poor line from Mexico, the second call possibly the last. Viv and the inmates, today. Part of grief is the loneliness of missing someone. The impossibility of ever seeing his mother again, talking to her. The possibility of never seeing Andrew again. The weight. A weight he doesn't want to give to anyone. It is his to carry, but it is too heavy.

'It's like loving a stone,' Andrew said to him once. 'Why can't you talk?'

Why can't you talk? He said this again, over the phone, two nights ago. Richard didn't argue. His life seems to consist of things not said, regret at not having said them. Things not done either: this house, his life, his mother's glasses on the little table.

The heating has taken the edge off. He puts on his father's flannelette pyjamas, his dressing gown, his own moccasin slippers. A fleeting glance in the mirror reveals an old man who on closer inspection is in fact still young. He returns to the kitchen, pulls out the by-now-almost-chilled bottle of white and pours himself a glass. On the gas hob, he heats up the beans in a pan. Graham is on his mind, more than the others. His silence, his cruel stutter, his palpable discomfort. His colouring is very similar to Richard's own. His height too. Where Graham's hair is buzz-cut, his bony jaw clean-shaven, Richard's hair is longer, in need of a cut, actually, and his beard is a thick black pelt. They are both too thin. It was, he realises, a bit like looking in a mirror that plays with time.

He empties the beans onto the toast and takes his meal through to the sitting room. Here at least, with the fire on, it is warm.

Why won't you talk? Andrew asks from the fog of Richard's thoughts, and for a moment he is not sure if it is Andrew's question for him or his own for Graham.

The following week, Richard finds he can remember most of their names. Craig is a happy soul, possibly because his parole is very near. He has been working out, he tells Richard, and shows off two impressive inked biceps. Daniel is more sombre, though not as brooding as Graham. He is serving two life sentences. Richard has not asked him why. Both these men are Catholics. Both have requested confession, and Richard has had to explain, politely, that he cannot take confession but that he can hear them and that they are always in the presence of God.

To Richard's delight, Graham's name is on the sheet. And at 11.45, he drifts in. Richard wonders if this is a safety measure – leaving only fifteen minutes until lockdown.

'All right?' Graham smirks a little.

'Yes thanks, Graham. Good to see you.'

He doesn't sit but walks instead along by the bookshelf, head thrown back, looking down his nose like an old man peering through bifocals. 'D-d-d'you ever r-read any of these?'

'I haven't, no.' Richard considers the books a moment, wondering which titles, if any, Graham is particularly interested in. 'But I've not been here long.'

'Oh aye, yeah.'

Richard averts his gaze, trying to leave Graham the necessary space to come and sit down. Hearing a crack of knuckles, he looks up to find Graham beside him, staring darkly at his chair. Both chairs have a clear view of the door; there is nothing to favour one above the other.

Eventually he sits, plunges his hands between his knees and exhales heavily.

'How are you?' Richard asks.

'All right, th-thank you for asking.'

Thank you for asking. The manners of a child that has had politeness drummed into him.

Moments pass. Richard steels himself against the silence. Graham is here, at least, rubbing at his face and the scant stubble of his hair.

'So, d-d-d'you go to church every Sunday and that, yeah?'

'Most Sundays, yes,' Richard answers, thankful for the opener.

Graham nods and looks at his thumb. He pushes one side of it with his forefinger, bites at the skin, then inspects it again. The ends of his fingers have swollen over the tiny nails. He folds his arms, as if to put his hands out of temptation's way.

Unsettled by the continuing silence, Richard feels with one hand for his Bible, tucks the other under his thigh. He shifts in his chair and puts his feet flat to the floor. It feels like the most monumental effort just to stay still and quiet. It is a little like attending Mass as a child, the feeling he used to get of wanting desperately to jump up and run amongst the pews shouting nonsense.

Graham gives a short, scornful laugh.

'Is something funny?' Richard asks.

'Nah. I was just th-thinking about … s-s-somethin.' He leans forward and looks up towards the corner of the ceiling. He seems about to say something else when there is a noise at the door. Another inmate – Richard recognises him: Damien. In for assault. Damien transfers his weight from one foot to the other, looks up from under his furrowed, apologetic brow. Like Craig, he has been in and out of prison more times than, as he put it, most people have had hot dinners. And like Craig, he should get out next week. Again.

'Hello, Damien.' Richard raises his hand. 'Do you want to come back in a bit?'

'All right, sir.' With a nod, Damien vanishes from the doorway.

Richard refocuses on Graham, who claps his hands, rubs them together.

'Listen, I'll g-g-g-g …' He half closes his eyes with the effort. 'I'll get off, yeah?'

'You don't have to. We have plenty of time.'

'Aw, you look b-b-busy. And them others are p-proper C-C-Catholics and that.'

'You really don't have to go, you know. Damien's left now. If you go I'll simply be here on my own.' Richard is aware of sounding desperate.

Graham stands up. 'D-don't w-worry about it. I'll see you next week.'

'OK, if that's what you want. See you then. Thursday or Friday, any time.'

Graham walks out with an exaggerated swagger, as if he has won some sort of battle. Down the corridor he whistles a slow tune. It echoes against the thick stone walls, melancholy as lost love, lonely as birdsong.

CHAPTER TWENTY

Carol

1985

The sun is already high and shining in through the bare window. Unable to doze, she tries to sit up without using her arms, stupidly, to see if her muscles will stand it. She fails and laughs at herself there on the floor, a dying fly. Her eyes sting. Her back and ribs are stiff. Jim might be awake, she thinks, there in the lounge, wrapped up in his big coat. She could creep in and check that he's really there.

She heaves herself up and looks about her. Jim's holdall is on the floor. He put it in her room last night, out of the way. She grabs it now and pulls it towards her. It's heavy, too heavy. She knows she shouldn't look inside, but she can't help herself. Besides, the bag is open.

The way he's rolled up his clothes makes her smile: like a little lad on a school trip, not quite sure how to fold them. She checks the door, listening for any sounds. When she's satisfied everyone's still asleep, she rifles through his clothes: T-shirts and socks, a couple of jumpers, underpants, some with holes in. She rolls them up again, taking care to leave them as before. A stripy toilet bag is wedged at the end of the bag, flecked with dried toothpaste. She figures she may as well put it in the bathroom; that way she can go for a pee while she's at it. She grabs the pouch and pulls it out of the bag.

Underneath, nestled amongst the clothes, is a gun.

She springs back, hands flying up to her cheeks. Jim has a gun. Why would he … How could …

She throws the toilet bag back, returns the holdall to where it was, adjusts it so it looks the same. Her heart is banging in her chest, her breath shallow. He seemed so nice. He seems so nice. She'd never have thought such a thing of him. And for the life of her, she can't think why, why on earth, he'd have a gun. Unless by offering help, he meant something more than lending a hand getting things straight in the house. Maybe he meant something bigger, something darker. Last night he punched clean through a wall. Did he mean to finish Ted off? Is that the kind of help he meant? *I'd gladly do the time.*

By now desperate for the loo, she totters to the bathroom, only to find the shocking results of last night's anxious frenzy: shredded walls in the unforgiving morning light.

She claps her hand over her mouth. 'Oh, Jesus.'

'I prefer plain Jim, but good morning to you too.'

She turns to see him behind her, at the mouth of the stairs, his hair a windswept, grassy tuft.

'Morning,' he whispers, as if he's just remembered they aren't alone.

'Morning,' she whispers back and feels herself blush. She can barely look at him. 'I'm just popping to the loo.'

In the bathroom, she sits and pees and listens. She hears the creak of a floorboard, a low, stifled cough. Her gut tells her the gun is not meant for her, but whoever it's meant for, it needs to be out in the open. Men and their bloody violence. Thinking it's the answer to everything when it's not, and never will be.

Steeling herself, she unlocks the bathroom door and goes out to face him. He is still on the landing, waiting. She notices now that he has two mugs of tea in one hand – his knuckles have scabbed over – and a folded copy of the *Mirror* in the other. He looks fresher for a few hours' sleep. The hair on his forearms is the colour of wheat.

'You've been for a paper?' she says.

He nods. 'Popped to that Spar shop down the road. Got bacon and eggs and stuff for a fry-up.'

'You've been for food? For us?'

He nods again, gestures with the mugs towards the bedroom door. Understanding, she leads the way into her room.

'How d'you get back in?' she asks him.

'Found the key on the side in the kitchen.' He hands her a tea.

'You've made me a cup of tea as well?'

'Aye.' He looks at her blankly, as if he hasn't understood the question. She pictures him in the kitchen, opening cupboards to find mugs, tea bags, sugar, trying different drawers to locate the teaspoons. And that's nothing compared to going all the way to the shop. All for her.

'Jim, listen,' she says, glancing towards the bag, back to him.

He is leaning against the window ledge, looking out of the window. He has on a white T-shirt that has seen better days, grey jogging bottoms and pinkish woolly socks. She realises she's never seen him in trousers until now. He doesn't look like a man who would have a gun. And if she asks him about it, he will know she's been rummaging in his bag. He's so kind, so open. But then, just like anyone, he could turn. She doesn't know him. She doesn't know him at all.

'Where's your kilt?' she says.

He turns to her and leans on the radiator. 'Didn't fancy waltzing through this place in it, like. Not in broad daylight.'

'I can see that.' It's chilly. She sits on the floor and pulls the duvet over her legs. It's strange, after their time in the hotel, after last night, to feel self-conscious, but now that the day has dawned, she does. 'When did you get your jogging bottoms then?'

'I came in before …'

'You came in here?'

'Yeah, sorry. Is that OK?'

'Yes. So – what? Was I asleep?' Had he watched her? Had her mouth been open, dribble running down her chin?

'Dead to the world.' He taps the radiator. 'Heating's coming on – did you set the timer?'

'Tommy did it for us.'

'Good man.' He joins her on the floor. Both of them sit with their tea, propped up by the wall – an imitation of being in a proper bed.

'I put one sugar in,' he says. 'Just guessed. Hope that's OK.'

'Thanks. I seem to like it better with a bit of sugar since … these days.'

'Well, it's good for shock.'

She blows on the tea and draws the top layer into her mouth. 'What time is it?'

'Half nine.'

'You're joking!' She makes to get up.

'Carol, relax, man. It's Saturday.' He pulls her gently back. 'Christ, you're like a hen in a hot girdle.' Under the covers, his hand looks for hers and finds it, holds it tight. 'You're all shattered, I bet.'

Here was a man who made tea, who did not expect it to be made for him, brought to him. Here was a man who bought food, which he seemed intent on cooking. Here was a man who saw tiredness that wasn't his own.

'I'm fine,' she manages.

'You can't get that shite past me, so don't even try.'

She rests her head against the wall for support. It's true, she is not fine, but she is better with him here. If only she hadn't looked, hadn't seen inside his bag.

Jim blows on his tea and tries to sip it. 'Jesus-arse, how can you drink it so hot?'

'Asbestos gob.' She takes a slurp to prove it, then worries she's drunk it like a man.

He rests his head against the wall, like her. She waits for him to speak again.

'Do you want me to stay for a bit?' he says. 'Help you get straight. Or not?'

Help you get straight. She will have to tell him she wants no violence, not in her name. Tears prick her eyes. She nods briskly, unable to talk.

'A day or two, then? We don't need to think beyond that. I've even brought my power tool.' He nods towards his kitbag, then wiggles his eyebrows at her. 'And not the one under the kilt.'

Two fat tears roll down her cheeks.

'Hey,' he says softly. 'I know it wasn't the best joke in the world, but there's no need to cry.' He squeezes her hand.

She sips her tea. His words sink in.

'What d'you mean, your power tool?' she asks, after a moment.

He hands her his mug and reaches over to his bag. As he does so, some foggy understanding of what she saw in there begins to dawn. But he is already holding up what she thought was a—

'Oh for crying out loud,' she says. 'I thought that was a gun.'

His face breaks into an expression of childlike joy. 'You're joking? It's a drill. Black and Decker don't make guns, you numpty.'

A minute ago, she was almost crying. Now she's laughing. She is all over the shop. She's halfway to crackers. A gun. Wait until Pauline hears that one. *He's from Scotland, not the piggin' Bronx,* Carol hears her say. *Who did you think he was, Al friggin' Capone?*

'I'll get started on that bathroom today,' Jim is saying. 'You've made a right arse of it.'

'That's two arses I've counted,' she replies, recovering. 'There's a lady present, you know.'

'Oh aye? Where's she, then?'

He puts the drill on the floor, crouches down in one swift move and pushes his head under the covers. Her belly tenses as he pulls up her vest and stretches it over his head.

'There's definitely a lady here.' His lips tickle her skin. He burrows his face in her stomach, his stubble the sweetest scratch.

A scuffling sound comes from the next bedroom.

'Jim,' she whispers, lifting the duvet. 'The kids.'

The door opens.

'Mum?' Nicola, bleary as a guinea pig.

Shit. Carol pulls the quilt up to her chest while Jim struggles to get his head out of her top. His breath comes in warm bursts on her abdomen; he grips her thighs as he pulls himself free. This is not how she wanted to do the introductions; it isn't right. Why else has she bothered to make him sleep in the lounge? All she's done is forget herself for five sodding seconds.

'Mum,' says Nicola. 'Whose are them feet?'

Two fluffy heels stick out of the end of the bed: Jim's stupid pink socks.

'Mummy, who's that?'

It's a man with his hand between my legs, she thinks, trying to get his head out of my top. Jim moves his hand. She almost squeals. He lets his forehead drop onto her belly and she can tell he is giggling. Nicola is still looking at her, twirling from side to side. Bugger, bugger, bugger. Jim's head appears, his shoulders. His arm shoots out.

'Found it,' he says. 'My watch.'

She meets his eye, sees mischief. 'Oh good. Thanks heavens for that, eh.' She turns to her daughter. 'This is Tommy's cousin Jim.'

Jim smiles and rolls out from under the covers. Thank God he is dressed. 'Hello,' he says, grinning quite naturally. 'You must be Nicola.'

'Hello.' Nicola looks at them both for a long while. 'Were you doing sex?'

If there'd been tea left to spit, she would have hit the wardrobe with the spray. 'Don't be silly.' Her mind flails. 'Jim's Tommy's cousin.' Oh, she's just said that, and it's not like it explains anything. 'He had to sleep in the lounge, what with us having no spare room yet, and he just brought me a cuppa and then he lost his watch.' She straightens her back. 'Anyway, miss, what do you mean, sex?'

Jim is by the window. He snorts into his tea and takes a gulp.

'OK to drink now, is it?' she says under her breath.

'Just right.'

'Come on,' she says to Nicola, bolder. 'What do you mean, missy?'

Nicola sways from side to side, smacks her lips and looks at the floor. When she finally speaks, it's with her bottom teeth hooked over her top lip.

'It's when you kiss and cuddle and stuff.'

'Is it now?' Carol stands up and puts her cardigan around her shoulders.

'Jim's Tommy's cousin.' Bugger. Change the record, Carol. 'He's brought us some bacon and eggs from the Spar. How do you fancy that for breakfast? Eh? Bit of a treat? Bacon and eggs?'

'Yeah!' Nicola runs out and down the landing. 'Gray!' they hear her call out, exchanging a glance. 'We're having cooked breakfast. There's a man called Jim here. He's Tommy's cousin. He talks funny.'

This last is delivered quietly, but they hear it all the same and it makes them both smile.

Carol pulls on her jeans and heads out onto the landing, where she almost crashes into Graham. She has to grab him by the arm to prevent a full collision.

'Who's here?' He strains to look over her shoulder.

'No one, love.' Why did she say that?

He pushes past and continues into her room.

'Wh-who are y-you?' He's standing, hands on hips, at the doorway. Beyond the black shape of his head, Jim runs a hand through his messy hair.

'Graham, love. Hold your horses.' She lays her hand on his shoulder, grips his waist so she can make her way round the side of him and back into the bedroom. If she can just get where he can see her, she can speak to him. 'Jim's come to give us a hand.'

Graham is not looking at her. He is staring at Jim. 'We d-d-don't need a h-hand.'

'Love.' She grabs for his arm, but he shakes her off.

'Graham.' Jim lifts his palms, spreads his fingers.

'It's OK, Jim.' She puts her hand up to shush him. 'Graham, look at me, love.' Her son is too tall. Has he grown in the night? He won't look at her. She has to get him to look at her. 'Graham.'

He looks at her at last, but just as quickly to the floor.

'Jim's here to help us, love.'

'I c-can look after us.'

She fights to find words. 'You've done a brilliant job, you're doing a brilliant job and I need you to carry on. I didn't know Jim was coming; it's not like I phoned him.'

'S-s-so wh-why's he h-here?' He is still talking to the floor, tracing arcs back and forth across the carpet with his bare feet. His toenails want cutting.

'I met him at Tommy and Pauline's wedding. He's from Scotland.'

Slowly Graham looks up, his head at an odd slant, like he's cricked his neck. Come on, son, she thinks. Meet me halfway.

'He was at the wedding,' she carries on. 'This is the chap who cut his leg, d'you remember me telling you? And I had to take him to hospital 'cos everyone else was plastered. I told you. And then when I got home, that was when your dad … that was when we, you know, left.'

Her cheeks burn. She's using what happened to try to win her son round. No matter what she tries to say or do, the spectre of Ted invades it somehow. But there's nothing to do but press on, cover her tracks. 'I know you've not met Jim before, but that's because he works on the rigs up in the North Sea. He only came down because of the wedding, and then I helped him with his leg, and so when he heard we were, you know, struggling a bit, he very kindly thought he could return the favour, like. When he's not on the rig, he's free, aren't you, Jim?'

'Graham,' says Jim. 'I'll go right now if that's what you want. It's your house.' He holds out his hand to shake. 'But we can at least introduce ourselves properly, as men.'

'H-how d-did he know we were h-here?' Graham asks, ignoring Jim.

'I don't know,' she lies. 'Probably through Tommy and Pauline.'

'I th-thought this was supposed to be a s-s-secret address.'

'It is. But Tommy and Pauline know, don't they? And Jim lives a long way from here and he doesn't know your dad, so there's no harm done.'

'Tommy was only trying to help,' Jim adds, joining her in the lie.

Her son unwinds by one microscopic turn. He raises his gaze as far as her chin. His neck straightens a bit, his hands drop to his sides, shift, find his pockets. Carol rubs his arm, dips her head to try to get him to look at her.

'Eh? Love?'

He flicks his eyes up to hers.

Jim coughs into his arm, then shoots out his hand once more. 'I'm Jim MacKay, anyway,' he says. 'Pleased to meet you, Graham.'

Even Jim's friendliness confuses her now. She doesn't know why, but it feels like he's browbeating Graham in some way, forcing him to accept something he doesn't want, forcing him to be a man, almost, when he is just a boy.

Still ignoring him, Graham raises his eyes again to hers. His dark stare bores through her, as if he's speaking without words, sharing everything they both know, every covered bruise, every failure, every lie. No one knows her like he does – this is what he seems to be saying to her now. Will he know she's just lied to him, covered up the truth as she has his whole life? Probably.

He takes his hands from his pockets, squares his shoulders and slowly turns away from her.

'All right?' He shakes Jim's hand. He is no longer looking at her, but even from the side, it seems his face has hardened: his jaw clenched, his eyes smaller.

'Now then.' She claps her hands. 'Shall I get some breakfast for us all? Jim's been and fetched some bacon and eggs.'

Graham shakes his head. 'Not hungry.'

'Come on. Surely you can manage a bacon butty?'

'Nah.' He wrinkles his nose. She wants to pull him to her and hold him, but knows that, in front of Jim, he'll push her away.

'You love bacon butties,' she coaxes, glancing at Jim, smiling an apology before turning back to her son. 'Come on, love. They're your favourite.'

Without a word, Graham walks out of the room. Instinct tells her to leave him, but she follows him down the landing. 'Graham?'

He goes into his room and shuts the door. She wants to open it but instead stands with her fingers clasped over the door handle.

Something bad has just happened, she feels sure of it. But she doesn't know what.

CHAPTER TWENTY-ONE

Nicola

2019

I remember Jim coming to that house. He was not there when I went to bed, and in the morning, there he was. Mum told me I found them in bed together but that they weren't up to anything, as she put it. I have no memory of that. I remember him from that time as a stranger who spoke in a funny voice, a big man with reddish-blonde hair, a man who was not our dad. His presence in the house made my mother happy but made my stomach hurt. I realise now that kids don't like a lack of clarity. I had no idea who this person was nor what he meant to my mother. She said he was her friend. That didn't make sense to me, but I was not sophisticated enough to know why. My mother had never had a male friend. Her one friend at the time was Pauline. I knew she hadn't met a man or had a boyfriend while we'd been in the refuge, and I could not fathom how she could have met someone while she was married to my dad. My dad was so suspicious of her, so constantly malevolent, that she would never have dared have a male friend, let alone an affair. I only found out about what happened with Jim later, when I was an adult, and at that moment another small piece of my life fell into place along with the others.

While Jim was staying at the house, Graham came into my room to say goodnight and instead of going away immediately, like he usually did, he stayed. He had stopped talking by then, even to me. But perhaps Jim's presence forced him back to me, however temporarily. Perhaps he, like me, was wondering what was going on. What is certain is that whatever the reason, I was thrilled. I idolised my brother, of course I did – he was six years older than me and had always been kind, not to mention fiercely protective. That night, with the muffled bass notes of my mum and Jim talking downstairs, Graham lay next to me on the sunlounger that was my bed, the two of us squashed up, spooning, me in a sleeping bag that smelled of Tommy and Pauline's house.

'You're never at home anymore,' I said to my brother in the dark. It was easy to say it because he was behind me. I didn't have to look into his eyes.

He reached over and held my hand.

'This isn't my home,' he said.

'I know, but …'

'Do you like Jim?' he asked.

I shrugged. 'I dunno. I don't know him. He seems nice. And he does jobs. Dad never did jobs.'

Graham was silent.

'D-do you miss Dad?' he asked after a minute, squeezing my hand.

I nodded. 'But I didn't like it when he shouted. And … I didn't like it when he hit her.'

Graham's body tensed against mine. 'How d-do you know about that?'

'I just … I just know. And once, when I went in the bathroom, I saw Mum in the bath and she had this massive bruise on her leg and when I asked her how she'd done it she went all funny and said she'd bumped it on the sideboard and I could tell she wasn't telling the truth.'

Again my brother fell silent.

'He never hit you, though,' he said after a moment. 'He never hurt you, did he?'

'No,' I whispered, hot and tense with an urgent need to keep my brother with me as long as I could. 'But he shouted. And he shouted at you. He was scary.'

'He was.' Graham held me tight. I wanted to ask him to play Name That Tune. I thought that maybe if I hummed a few notes, he might join in, try to guess the song. I knew I couldn't, that he wouldn't, but I hoped that we might be able to do it the next night or the next or one day soon like we used to before, when we lived at home. For now, it was enough that he was my big brother again, the one I could chat to about secret things all snuggled up in the dark.

I was happy, in that moment. I was wildly, precariously and – whilst I did not realise it at the time – dangerously happy. And even though I was only a child, what I said next to hold on to that happiness, I still regret.

CHAPTER TWENTY-TWO

Richard

1992

It is four minutes past three on Friday afternoon. Graham did not come last week or the week before. He did not come yesterday; he has not come so far today. He has not put in an application to come, so far as Richard knows, and it is hard not to feel a sense of loss and failure. He of all people should have known how to coax the boy out of himself without frightening him away. But then who is Richard to advise anyone on how to talk?

He can listen, though. And the other men here have spoken in their sessions; good Lord, they haven't stopped. Lost boys, stories to make your hair stand on end. Hopelessness, educational failure, chaotic home lives, drugs, generations of unemployment, poverty, boredom, absence of love to make a stone heart break … Richard has heard everything in the hush of this chapel whilst all around the constant noise reigns – industrial cleaning machines, chatter and shouts, the jangle of keys, and always, always the tuneless whistling.

Compared to the rest of the prison, the chapel is almost too quiet sometimes, he thinks. Maybe it is the silence that stifles Graham, puts too much pressure on him, like the blank canvas terrorises the painter. If he can miss weeks, it's more than likely that he won't come back at all. It's frustrating, because Richard believes he can help him. He has even wondered whether God has sent Graham to him for some greater purpose, though as yet he doesn't know what this might be. Graham did say he'd come back. But he hasn't. These boys are full of broken promises, resolutions unfulfilled. It isn't personal, Richard tells himself. It's just the way it is.

At ten minutes past three, Graham walks into the chapel, whistling with almost comedic nonchalance.

'All right?' he says with that low-key swagger of his.

'Yes, thanks,' Richard replies carefully, determined not to appear too pleased. 'How're you getting on?'

'Not bad, thank you for asking.' Graham rubs his hands together, as if he were cold. The room is, as always, stuffy. 'What shall we t-talk about t-today, then? The w-w-weather?'

Richard ignores the sarcasm. 'It's raining.'

'Is it? I always remember the weather as s-s-sunny, for s-s-some reason.'

Richard digests the fact that for Graham, weather is a memory. It's true, now he thinks about it: after a day enclosed within these six-foot-thick walls, these permanently sealed windows, trapped in the stale smell that sticks to his clothes and hair, in the evenings, the weather always takes him by surprise.

'It's p-probably just my s-s-sunny d-disposition, like.' Graham wraps his tongue and teeth around the word 'disposition', saying it oddly, as if it belongs in inverted commas.

'Undoubtedly,' says Richard, and smiles.

Graham points at him briefly, almost returns the smile. Perhaps this is what he wants: a bit of banter. Richard isn't sure he can manage that – he's never been particularly witty.

'What have you been up to?' he asks.

'Oh, you know, went to the p-piccies, the p-pub, hired a s-s-sailing boat, that t-type of thing, like.'

Richard folds his arms, leans back in his chair and waits.

Graham rolls his eyes and moves his head from side to side. 'I'm working on a design for a t-tattoo.'

Richard doesn't know much about tattoos, but this is the only nugget of information Graham appears willing to give up, and progress by millimetres is still progress.

'A tattoo. Sounds interesting. What of? Are you allowed to bring it to show me?'

Graham's neck looks like he might have cricked it. 'You're not arsed about s-s-some p-poxy t-tat.' There's nothing wrong with his neck; it's twisted only by suspicion, the wariness of a cat.

'I tell you what.' Richard meets his eye. 'I'll make you a promise. How does that sound?'

'What do you mean, a promise?' Graham's neck rights itself, but his eyes are screwed up and ancient-looking.

'A promise. My promise is this: I won't lie to you. I swear it before God.'

'But I don't believe in G-God.'

'I know. But I do. And it's my promise.'

Graham sits back, his legs apart – recalcitrant, as if to say, so what? 'Are you a priest then, are you?'

'I'm a chaplain,' Richard says. 'I'm Catholic, though if anything, my faith is a personal interpretation. It has to be. But in an emergency, I could make the sign of the cross on your head with water, you know, to prevent you from going to hell, for example.'

'I think it m-might be a bit l-late for that, to be honest with you.' Graham addresses the words to the floor before standing up.

'Graham?'

But he has already turned away. Without looking back, he raises a hand and begins to amble out. This can't be it. It can't be. They've only just started!

'Graham.' It is all Richard can do to stop himself from shouting. 'Don't feel you have to go. If I've said something wrong, I apologise.'

No answer. Richard feels his jaw clench. He wants to ask if Graham will be here next week. More than that, he wants to tell him off, tell him to stop all this obfuscation. But he does neither. Instead, he watches him fill then empty the stark rectangle of the doorway and finds himself, moments later, shockingly alone. With no idea what to do next and fearing he might let out a great roar of frustration, he locks his hands together and bows his head.

Oh God, why won't he speak? Why, when he comes here out of choice? Is silence the only way he can assert himself in a place where all control has been lost? Does he feel unworthy of absolution, if that's what he's even looking for? Help me to understand him. Help me to make him understand that he is worthy, and that it's never too late. Help me to help him, Amen.

On his way out, Richard stops by the office to say goodnight. Frank and Viv are chatting, so he simply waves and says, 'See you,' before heading away down the stone steps.

'Night, Richard love,' Viv calls after him.

He is about to take the second flight when he notices that his trainer lace has come undone. He sits down on the step to tie it.

'Tell you what, he's hard work, isn't he? Old Bible-basher?'

Richard's ears prick. It's Frank's voice, travelling from the office to the stairwell. The prison is suspended in a rare moment of silence. Frank's penetrating timbre makes its way down to where Richard sits perfectly still, a shoelace pinched between each thumb and forefinger. 'Christ, it's like pulling bloody teeth. I tell you what, I wouldn't want to get stuck at a party with him. Jesus. Talk about torture.'

Richard finishes tying his lace but cannot bring himself to stand. *Torture*. There it is, another man's verdict on his character.

'Oh, don't be like that,' Viv replies, though not without giggling. 'He can't help being shy.'

'I know, but I'm just saying, that's all. I mean, the other day I asked him if he lived nearby, and d'you know what he said?'

'What?'

'"No."' Frank laughs. 'Literally – no. Not even "no, I don't". 'Cos that'd be too bloody chatty obviously.'

'Don't be horrible,' says Viv, but she chuckles. Chuckles. At his expense.

Richard pulls himself to his feet. Holding on to the handrail, he runs down the rest of the steps, two, three at a time, stumbles into the courtyard and towards the gates. Fumbles for his keys and scrabbles through them, plucking out the key for the first gate. It doesn't fit. The locking mechanism must be bent. He'll have to go back to the office. This is not a possibility. He tries the key again, realises it's the wrong one. Forcing himself to slow down, he picks through the bunch and finds the right key. It fits. The lock bangs. The gate squeals. He locks it before continuing to the next gate, and the next and the next. The guard ushers him out of the black door, onto the cobbles, into the air, where he puts his hands to his knees and recovers his breath.

Viv was laughing at him. He'd thought she was kinder than that, thought they were becoming friends. But he can't blame her. The criticism is not new – his quietness, his failure to make something as simple as words fall from his mouth following him like a bad smell. Andrew was patient but his teasing would have turned to criticism eventually. Andrew, who did not fly home with him in the end. Richard, who promised he'd go back.

Andrew is still in San Cristóbal de las Casas. They haven't spoken for weeks now. Richard wonders if he's still making his students fall for him with talk of grey skies, English pubs and tea.

He should go back up to the office right now. He should face Viv and Frank and ask them how, how does someone avoid being 'torture'? What do people find to talk about at parties? Perhaps Frank could tell him how he does it, what subjects he covers, how he maintains that jocular lightness people like him seem to manage. It all seems like such hard work. Counselling is easier. There's legitimacy to the asking of questions, a demand for real exchange, for a kind of endorsed intimacy. You don't have to be funny or clever; you just have to listen. In the chapel, even with Graham, Richard can be of use. At a party, he doesn't know which questions to ask, nor which answers to give.

CHAPTER TWENTY-THREE

Carol

1985

Carol is halfway down her third cuppa of the morning when Graham puts on his jacket, picks up his toast and leaves the kitchen.

'Where are you going?' she calls after him.

'Out,' he calls back, from the hallway.

'Where to?'

'Friend's.'

She knows it will be one of the hooligans from that school. One came round for tea once, nasty piece of work – skinhead, tracksuit, not that you should judge a book by its cover. 'What friend? Whereabouts?'

'Oh my God, just a f-friend, Mum. Lay off, w-will you?'

'I'm not laying on, love, I'm just asking where you're going, that's all. Do you know what time you'll be back?'

No answer. The front door slams.

Jim is upstairs painting the bathroom; she's glad he didn't witness the way her son spoke to her just now. Humiliated, that's how she feels. She wonders whether to follow Graham out into the street, try again to have a reasonable conversation.

It is Sunday. Jim's only been here two days. Dumbfounded, she stares at the kitchen doorway before shaking herself back to reality. A cigarette, smoked on the back step while she searches the estate for signs of Ted, always Ted, doesn't help calm her nerves. In the end, leaving Nicola to tidy the breakfast things, she goes upstairs to find Jim, who's rolling white paint onto the bathroom walls after spending most of yesterday stripping the paper and filling the cracks. He has a strip of cloth tied across one hand because he keeps knocking it and making the knuckles bleed, poor sod.

'He needs space, that's all,' he says when she tells him about Graham's behaviour. 'Needs to be a lad about town for a wee bit, sow his oats. He'll work it out, don't worry.'

She sighs. 'Of all the things I thought my son would become, a stranger wasn't one of them. Not after … not after everything.'

'He's not a stranger. He's just young. He's had a lot to deal with.'

'I know. That's what worries me. How's he dealing with it?'

That afternoon, Pauline and Tommy come over for a couple of hours and Jim takes a break from painting. The house fills with chatter, even laughter – it's amazing how quickly it happens. As they sit together, Carol can't help watching the street. But there is no one sinister, no one watching from the shadows.

'Seen anything of Ted since … you know?' she asks Pauline when there's just the two of them in the kitchen.

Pauline shakes her head, busies herself getting two tins of lager from the fridge for the men. 'You need to put him out of your mind, love. You'll drive yourself mad if you're not careful. He's made his bed, hasn't he?'

'What d'you mean?'

'Just that. It's not up to you to look after him now. What he does is his responsibility.' She presses her lips tight and goes back to the table. Ted is in a bad way, then. Worse. Carol knows it by what Pauline's not saying, by the fact that she didn't look at her, the way she cut the conversation short. There is a hardness to her that is new.

At the table, the men do most of the talking: Thatcher, the miners, the usual daft jokes. No one mentions Ted, nor the fact that Jim is here where Ted might once have been. If anyone were to pass by and look in the window of this house, she thinks, they'd see two couples sharing a drink on a Sunday afternoon. They wouldn't see a woman whose eyes sting from lack of sleep and wide stares, a woman unable to stop fretting about her boy and wondering how he has floated so far away from her and how on earth she can get him to come back. So much is hidden away, under the surface of things, in some dark place where silence lives. So much never makes it into the light, never finds its shape in words.

She knows it's not right to think it, but it feels wrong being together like this, without Ted. She knows Ted will kill her if she goes back; he's proved it, yes, he has, he has, but he looked so wretched, making his false promises, asking after the kids, begging her to come home. He looked destroyed. Has she destroyed him; is that what's she's done? Where is he now? God knows where with God knows who doing God knows what. Killing himself slowly, alone and miserable. It was always Pauline and Tommy, her and Ted. In the old days, he didn't always get so drunk. Even later on, while he was still only a few drinks in, he was all right. He was good company, a laugh. Impossible to put it all together in her mind and hold on to it. His hand round her neck, his spit in her face. *I'll kill you, Carol.*

The afternoon cools, darkens. She walks Tommy and Pauline to the door. Tommy goes out to start the car, leaving Pauline to say goodbye.

Pauline takes both her hands. 'Look at me, Carol Watson.'

'It's Morrison now. They gave me a new name, remember?'

'Stop mucking about, you know what I mean. No more silly buggers, all right? I'm not going to find you being strangled on my front lawn again, am I?' She is smiling, but even through the black make-up, her eyes are serious.

Carol can't hold her gaze. She glances down, at their hands locked together. On Pauline's wrist there are blackish-blue marks. Finger marks.

'What's that on your wrist?' she asks, her chest filling immediately with white heat.

As if electrocuted, Pauline pulls her hands away. Her sleeves fall back over her wrists. 'Nothing. Nothing at all. Right, I'd better run. See you next week.' She bends forward, kisses Carol on the cheek. A moment later, she is waving from the car, Tommy beep-beep-beeping his way out of the close.

Carol waves after them. Her legs feel wobbly, but something inside her takes shape, solidifies, calcifies. Whatever last shred of doubt she had leaves her.

'That's it,' she whispers, to the memory of a man she vows never to see again. 'That is it.'

Graham arrives home five minutes later. The moment he steps in, the atmosphere tightens. He looks exhausted, red-eyed, his complexion spotty and pale, paler than this morning. He lets Nicola hug him but does not come near Jim or Carol. And of course, he doesn't speak. He is in that place, the silent place, where everything he needs to say won't come out of him. He is in the dark.

'Are you hungry?' she asks him, to be met with his back as he puts two slices of bread on the grill. Several silent minutes later comes the thin scrape of margarine on white toast, the slam of the kitchen door and the dull batter of trainers on the wooden stairs.

'Let it go,' says Jim, who is reading the paper at the kitchen table, and looking at him she wonders if this is her choice now: Jim or Graham. She cannot, it seems to her then, have both, even if Jim is sleeping on the sofa, even if he is simply Tommy's cousin, come to help. Anything physical they began that first night has stopped completely. It has had to. He hasn't pushed her. She hasn't invited anything. It isn't that she hasn't wanted to – quite the opposite, when she thinks of the comfort of his arms around her – but it has felt impossible, complicated, wrong. Now, even the fact of Jim being in the house is beginning to feel wrong too. It is over a year since she left Ted.

Today it feels like less than a week.

CHAPTER TWENTY-FOUR

Carol

Monday morning comes. Nicola goes to school. Graham leaves mid-morning, muttering something about signing on. And like that, she and Jim are alone for the first time, and around them the air shifts as if it doesn't know where to go. Perhaps he feels it too, since he disappears with his paintbrush into the bathroom, as if to hide. With nothing urgent to do and no one to talk to, Carol busies herself cleaning and sorting, a trip to the launderette, to the Spar. Jim doesn't break for lunch, surviving on the coffee and biscuits she takes up to him at intervals, snatching them from her with a dusty white hand. In the afternoon, she forces herself to get on with benefit forms until, bored, frustrated and in need of company, she takes Jim yet another hot drink.

'Refreshments,' she says, pushing open the door with her foot. 'Are you allowed to stop for a second? I've not seen you all day.'

Through the crack of the door he smiles and takes a mug from her. His face is comically white, like a clown's. 'Want to get the last coat on the woodwork before the kids get home,' he says as the door opens wider. He must sense her loneliness, though, because then he asks, 'How did you get on with the forms?'

'Oh God, I think they get the devil himself to write them, just to confuse folk.'

'The very folk they're meant to help. Looked like a Bible.'

A shallow laugh escapes her. 'The holy book of benefits. Thou shalt not claim money from our lady Mrs Thatcher who art in Downing Street. And you, Mr MacKay, might have to put your things back in your bag, 'cos if they come snooping, they'll say we're living as a couple and cut it off altogether.'

Jim crosses his legs and covers his privates. 'Ouch.'

'Not that, you soft thing. The money.'

'I know what you mean. Don't worry so much.'

In silence, they sip their coffee. Jim puts a Bourbon cream whole into his mouth. She's glad to see him eat, although he tells her it's she who needs building up. He's right. She can't look at herself naked anymore – reminds her of those poor dogs on the RSPCA adverts. It's a good thing Jim is still sleeping on the couch – she can't imagine anyone would want a bag of bones like her.

He drains his coffee. 'Let's get fish and chips tonight, eh?'

He makes it sound like a joint decision, like they have some sort of kitty, when in reality he is offering to pay because he knows she can't. Debt ties knots inside her: debt to him, to Pauline and Tommy, to the kids: debts of money, of time, of kindness. She took limited cash to the shop earlier but forgot herself, filling her basket before remembering she couldn't pay, retracing her steps, cheeks burning, unloading the contents back onto the shelves one by one.

'I'll do bread and butter,' she offers, 'then we won't need so many portions.'

'OK. Do you like mushy peas?'

'God, no. Can't be doing with them.'

'No mushy peas then.'

And now she's said the wrong thing. 'I mean, you get some if you want. It's not like I can't be in the same room as them or anything.'

'Ach, they make me fart like a lawnmower anyway. I'll get on, eh? See you in a bit.'

'See you then.' She's still worried that she sounded rude, ungrateful.

'Not if I see you first.'

'See you in a bit.'

'That's what I just said.' He keeps his face to the edge of the door as it closes. She waits a second. He's put out, she knows it. Then it opens again and his head pokes out for a kiss. She leans in, then back, wiping dust off her nose, silly with relief.

'Come here,' he says, pulling her into the bathroom and holding her tight.

'Jim, I'll get paint on me.'

'So?'

He shuts the door behind her. They are kissing, their hands running over each other. She pulls back and meets his eyes and sees there that, with the house empty, he knows what this means. She is filled with terror and thrill. But he checks his watch and frowns.

'Shit. It's quarter to four.'

'It's not, is it? Our Nicky will be back any second.'

They've had all day to take their chance. But it has been difficult to find each other. She moves towards him and he kisses her again. They hold each other and he rocks her from side to side. Frustration, friendship, consolation – there are so many types of hug.

A bang sounds, followed by heavy footsteps on the stairs. Not Nicola, but Graham. She jumps away from Jim and grabs for the door handle. As she does so, the door swings open and there is her son, red-eyed and sullen, smelling of cigarettes and something else, something cloying and sweet she can't identify.

He looks her up and down, then stares pointedly at Jim.

'Hiya, love.' She glances down at her black T-shirt – it is covered in white dust. 'I was just bringing Jim a cuppa, well, a coffee actually, 'cos he gets thirsty, you know, all that sweating and toiling, and hungry too – we've had a chocolate biscuit, haven't we, Jim? There's some downstairs if you want one – I bought a packet for a treat. Anyway, you know, I thought I should check his handiwork.' She makes herself stop talking.

Graham nods, but his face is sour. 'His h-h-handiwork.'

'Not bad, eh?' She looks to Jim, whose nervous eyes are pink against his whitened face. The bathroom, too, is pure white, the brown between the tiles and the bath edge gone, replaced by fresh silicon, gooey and gleaming as toothpaste. 'You'd never have known an avocado suite could look so nice, would you? What's an avocado anyway, when it's at home?'

The room is too small for the three of them, the air grown hot. She realises that both she and Jim are staring at Graham, waiting for judgement. Something in his expression seems to switch, or is it her imagination? He gives a slow, unreadable nod.

'L-looks all r-right.'

What is happening in that head of his? The thunderous expression on his face when he burst in, and now he's looking at the ceiling and the walls like some sort of foreman to Jim's labourer. It would be better, she thinks, if he made a scene, called her a name, accused her of something.

Jim smiles, and she wonders if he, like her, is hiding his confusion. 'I'm glad you think so, because you'll be painting the kitchen, mate.'

'F-fine with me.' Graham crosses his arms and sets his feet a little further apart. 'M-m-mate.' The word is a slow drip.

Jim hands his mug to Carol. 'I'll get this finished then, eh? Then I'll grab us a fish supper.'

'Smashing. Jim's going to treat us to fish and chips, Graham.'

But Graham has left. A moment later, she hears the click of his bedroom door.

*

That night, Graham appears as they are putting out the fish and chips. He's wearing his jacket and doesn't come further than the doorway before muttering something that sounds like *bye*.

'Graham?' she calls after him. 'There's fish and chips for you here. Love? Where are you going?'

The front door slams.

Her eyes meet Jim's. 'I'm sorry,' she says.

'Don't worry about it. More for us.'

At the table, Nicola chatters away, oblivious or compensating, it's hard to tell. She loves school, can't get enough of it. She shows Carol her exercise book, her work beautifully presented, scribbled with red ten-out-of-tens and A pluses. She's coming top in everything, she tells Carol.

'And guess what?' she adds. 'Miss said I'm going to get a prize for the most merit points this term.'

Carol feels her face glow with pride. She smiles at her daughter, sees the shine in her eyes, a shine that by some miracle has not dulled.

'Well, aren't you my too-clever-for-me girl?' she says, kissing her on the forehead. 'God knows where you get your brains from, 'cos I know it's not from me.'

Nicola grins, turning pink. She and her brother could not be more different. But Graham is her son, her family, her blood. Both kids, both of them, are the reason she left. That Graham isn't here with them is wrong. That Jim is here instead is wrong. Jim is the most wonderful man she has ever known. She can see that he is her chance as plain as her own hands. But he cannot stay.

CHAPTER TWENTY-FIVE

Richard

1992

Richard sits back and blows on his steepled hands. Graham has applied for an appointment at 11.30. It is now 11.31. Too apprehensive to read, Richard studies the room: the books on their shelves, the table-cum-altar, the crucifix – arms out, as if ready for an embrace. The cross is small, made of pale new wood. There is nothing fancy about it; it is not gilded or bejewelled or embellished in any way, and yet here it waits: humble and steadfast. As must he.

'I've b-been reading.' Graham is at the door. Without any kind of greeting, he comes to sit down, claps his hands together and holds them in his lap.

'Reading can be a comfort,' Richard replies. 'It can help us to realise that we are not alone in our frailty and doubt.'

'A c-comfort.' Graham appears to be mulling this over.

'One could even say an escape.'

'I'd prefer a ladder and a d-decent hacksaw, to be honest with you.' Graham shoots him a wry glance, suppressing obvious delight at his own wit.

Richard curses himself inwardly. Seconds pass.

'I meant more that reading can take you to another place, you know, in your mind,' he tries.

Graham huffs and stretches his neck to reveal the soft pink fin of his Adam's apple. He shakes his head, as if returning to his physical body, then rubs at his hair and looks back at the floor. It is possible that more serious reflection has caught him off guard. In here, jokes can do that sometimes: leave a sharp, melancholy aftermath.

'You're doing English A level, aren't you?' Richard prompts.

'Yeah.' Graham looks out of the window, to the small grey strip of sky. In profile, the set of his chin and eyebrows reveals a yearning so private that Richard has to avert his eyes.

'Is it one of the texts? That you're reading?'

'Nah.' Graham sighs, returns. 'It's this b-book called *Jonathan Livingston Seagull*. Do you know it?'

Of all the books he could have chosen, Richard cannot believe he has picked this particular one. It is so … spiritual.

'Yes.' His scalp tingles with anticipation.

Graham rubs his face. Continues the washing gesture by pushing his hands to the back of his neck. 'My s-s-sister made me promise to talk to someone. I didn't see the point, but then I read this b-book …'

Richard holds his breath, but nothing more comes.

'OK,' he says after a moment. 'So why the chaplain?'

Graham ignores him. 'And m-maybe it's because I'm twenty-four years old and I'm fucking sick of playing hangman in English lessons with a b-bunch of d-dickheads, do you know what I mean?' He gives a hollow laugh. 'Maybe I thought coming here would be more interesting.' His mouth distorts, exaggerating the last word, undercutting it with something – rage, perhaps. Sarcasm. He is so afraid, so very afraid of saying anything straightforward, as if revealing one small thing about his true self will strip him to the bone, leave him humiliated and defenceless. Aggression is a carapace worn by so many in here, and often, the harder the shell, the softer what lies beneath.

'Are you enjoying the book?' Richard asks.

Graham brightens. 'I did, y-yeah. I finished it. It s-s-seems really simple on the surface – but it's not.'

'What's it about?'

'Thought you said you'd read it.' Graham looks back at the floor – a wary child playing hide-and-seek, too scared to stay in the dark, too proud to come into the light.

'I have read it,' Richard says carefully. 'But it was a very long time ago – fifteen years, there or thereabouts. I meant, what do *you* think it's about?'

Graham doesn't look up.

Richard tries something else. 'My friend Alexis gave me a copy when I was eighteen, as a gift. She was my girlfriend, actually, until things … until I ended it.' He is divulging his personal life. How ironic, that outside these walls, talking about himself has been so impossible, and here, where he is meant only to listen, he is bringing up one of the most painful moments of his life. He shouldn't do this. There are boundaries. But there is also a difficult and fragile relationship here, one in which trust must be won at a higher cost than the others, and consolidated. 'I let her down, badly,' he continues. 'But she forgave me.' He tries to read Graham's reaction, but his face is inscrutable. 'We made … the usual vows. Pledges of love, you know, which I … broke … inevitably.' He stops. Alexis could not save him. It took Andrew to make him see that there was nothing to be saved from.

Graham pushes out his bottom lip and appears to be considering what Richard has told him. Richard wonders what effect, if any, his words have had; what, if anything, Graham has understood.

Graham puts his hands on his knees, like a storyteller. 'It's about this seagull who wants to fly a b-bit higher than the others, that's all.' He is still looking at the floor. 'Not because he's a snob or anythin' like that; he just wants to, you know, see what's up there.' Finally, he looks up.

'That's right, I remember now.' Richard's suspicions are confirmed. In offering up a piece of himself, freely, he has managed to strip off at least one thin layer of shell from this troubled, reticent man.

'My pad-mate, Dave, he reckons reading's for poofs.' Graham coughs, raises a hand. 'Sorry. No offence to poofs and that.'

Richard dismisses the apology with a wave. It is Dave's prejudice, not Graham's, although the fact that Graham should say this now is perhaps an indication that he has understood what Richard has not quite told him.

'It must be difficult to concentrate in here,' Richard says quickly. 'I know how noisy this place can be.'

'You're not wrong. The nights are terrible.' Graham shakes his head. 'Sometimes the screaming and that is so loud you think someone m-must be getting m-murdered or something. And if you're j-just trying to have a little read, you get so much stick, it's like, *oh, who d'you think you are, f-f-f ... '* He glances up, corrects himself. *'Think you're effing Jeffrey Archer?* D'you know what I mean?'

'Mm-hm.'

Graham is talking. He is talking of his own free will. For the second time this session, Richard holds his breath.

'S-sometimes, y-you're just knackered. And t-t-tense, like, you know? Nervous, jittery. I mean, Dave's all right and everything, but I wouldn't want to get on the wrong side of him, d'you know what I mean? He's got tats all the way up his neck with stuff from the Bible and he can be scary as hell when he wants to be.' He frowns. 'C-Corinthians, does that ring a bell?'

Richard smiles. '"Love is patient, love is kind. It does not envy, it does not boast, it is not proud. It is not rude, it is not self-seeking, it is not easily angered, it keeps no record of wrongs. Love does not delight in evil but rejoices with the truth. It always protects, always trusts, always hopes, always perseveres." It's one of my favourite passages.'

'Bloody hell.' Graham's face lights up momentarily before clouding over again. 'But that's not what he's got on his neck.'

'"Love never fails"?'

He smiles. 'That's it. You're a brainy get, you, aren't you?'

'Not particularly. I was lucky enough to get a good education, that's all.'

'S'pose.' Graham puts his teeth to his thumb and tears a strip of skin, which he spits across the room. 'Anyway, Dave's all right. Hard as fuck, but all right. Listen, I'll stop swearing. It's out of order with you being religious and everything. I k-keep forgetting, sorry.'

'Don't worry about it.'

Graham stands up. 'No offence and that, R-Rich, but I've had enough.'

'That's all right.'

His eyebrows shoot up, lending his face an expression of near enthusiasm. 'But thanks, yeah?'

In the office, Viv is sorting through papers. She gives Richard a wide smile that takes with it the corners of her eyes, her whole face. But he can't shake the sound of her treacherous laughter reaching him on the stairs.

'How you diddlin'?' she asks.

'OK, thanks. Slow progress. I try to get them to talk about their lives, how they came to do what they did. I suppose the aim is to lead them towards forgiveness so that they can move on. There's one in particular who's been very resistant but I think I'm finally getting somewhere now. Starting to get somewhere anyway.'

'Aye, well. Some of them've got plenty of time.' She chuckles, bangs a stack of documents on the desk.

'One of them mentioned a particular book today, which I think might be the key to the lock.'

'Oh aye?' She goes over to the filing cabinet and, after flipping through the tabs, slots the papers inside. Her hair is swept up onto the top of her head and is held there with a pencil.

'Yes, I'm pretty sure I've still got a copy in the loft somewhere.' The fact that she isn't really listening spurs him on, as if he were talking to himself. 'I think if I could just read it again, I might be able to get him to open up a bit more, you know?'

Viv is silent, engrossed in a new task. She must have tuned out. There is a greasy black lump, no bigger than a ladybird, stuck to the desk. He worries it with his thumbnail, thinks it might be old Blu Tack. When he looks back at Viv, she is standing before him, hands on hips.

'Sounds like you need a trip to that loft.' She raises her eyebrows at him. She was listening all along.

'D'you know, I've been meaning to go up there for months and I just haven't got round to it.' He hesitates. 'There's a lot of things I've been meaning to do, to be honest. I've been a bit stuck lately. It's strange, it almost feels like ... No, it's silly, forget it.'

'Come on, out with it. You can't get me all excited then leave me danglin' like that.' She restrains her customary laughter to a brisk nasal exhalation; it is Richard who laughs.

'No, I just ... It feels like this chap ... Graham, his name is ... it feels like he's sending me up to my own loft, if that makes sense. Not just for the book, but for this other thing – it's a film, a film of my parents' wedding. I've been meaning to see if it could be converted to VHS, you know? I promised my mother I would. But typically, I never got around to it. And now that I have to go to the loft, I will. I'll do it because it's not for me but for Graham. But at the same time, it is for me, it will be, do you see what I mean? Forget I said it. It's a silly thought.'

'I don't know if it's as daft as all that. I mean, these poor buggers might have a funny way of doing it, but they do give something back, you know, if you let them.'

CHAPTER TWENTY-SIX

Carol

1985

Jim is sitting by the open back door, sipping from a can of lager and holding his cigar outside. He has finished fixing and painting for the day, including making good the hole in the kitchen wall, and has had a bath and changed into a blue shirt and jeans. Nicola is upstairs doing homework and Graham is out, as usual.

For a moment, Carol says nothing, wanting only to look at Jim for a second longer before he sees her looking and changes that tiny bit. Just the sight of him brings her a feeling of peace. She forgets for a moment about Graham and Ted and all the rest. Jim has been here for five precious days and what she is about to say makes her chest hurt. It will spoil everything they've had but she has to say it, she knows that. Because while Jim is here, her son is lost. She cannot lose her son. She cannot. And so … this will be her last evening with a man who has shown her something so simple: that love can be kind and slow and free from fear. That he doesn't know what she's about to say, that he is held in this quiet calm before she says it, makes her feel terrible, but it's nothing compared to the thought of actually telling him. He must know they have to talk, that things have been difficult, but he will not expect to be told to go and not to come back, not after all his kindness. It isn't fair. Of all the punches she has taken, this is the hardest. And she's the one giving it.

He must sense her standing there, because he turns to her and smiles lazily. That smile. She could drink a pint of him and still be thirsty.

She sits on the chair nearest his. 'Not exactly Butlin's round here, is it?'

'Believe it or not, darlin', it's actually worse on the rig.'

The house will be so empty after he's gone, emptier than before. And less safe.

'At least you won't have to put up with us band of gypsies on there.' Out of the corner of her eye, she searches his face for a reaction. She can't seem to get to what she needs to say.

'It's the peace at night I'm looking forward to.' He squeezes her hand and winks at her. 'I'm starting to feel violated, to be honest with you.'

'Give over.' She laughs, reassured that he can joke about their lack of love life. He has waited for her, has not minded that she's had nothing to give him. And soon he will know that his patience has been for nothing. Her eyes fill.

'I'm sorry,' she says, wiping at her cheeks. 'I'm a bloody wet weekend.'

'Don't be daft.' She hears him take a swig from the can. 'You might be a wet weekend now – which you're not, more of a very nice weekend with a few showers – but it'll be clearing up by Tuesday, and before you know it, you'll have sunny spells on Friday … Oh, for fuck's sake, what am I talking about?'

She makes herself face him, sniffing, laughing. 'But you could have anybody.'

'Oh aye, that'll be right. Wanted: hairy divorced roughneck with beer belly, available only half the time for DIY and dodgy romantic gestures involving kilts.' He stands up, does a muscle-man pose and pushes out his stomach until he looks pregnant.

She smiles. He always tries to make her smile, as if that's his main aim in life.

'But I've got no job,' she says. 'And two kids. And our Graham ...'

'Well, having a job isn't everything. Mine's already ended one marriage for me.'

'I can't ask you to take us on. It's too much.'

'Oh, come on.' He pulls her up from her chair and holds her. 'I mean, don't let it go to your head or anything, but don't forget how beautiful you are either, OK?'

She sobs into his chest. Her shoulders shake. Jim keeps her close, says nothing.

'I'm sorry,' she says finally. 'But it won't work, love. I think you know it too.'

'What?' He pushes back. His blue eyes are broken glass.

'I'm so sorry. I can't ... This can't work with our Graham as he is. He's only just had to leave his dad. I can't ask him to accept another.'

'I'm not trying to be his dad, Carol. I would never do that.'

'I know. You're lovely. You're too lovely, I'm not used to it. Sometimes I don't know how to be with it. But we're not just friends, are we, even if we haven't ... and Graham's not stupid.'

'But you said he was out of sorts before I even got here.'

'He was. But he's got worse, much worse. There's something else; I can't put my finger on it. Something not right. He won't look at me, he won't speak and now he's not coming home nights. It's all too soon.'

Jim rips off a piece of kitchen roll, hands it to her and sighs.

She presses the tissue flat to her eyes and hides there. After a moment, he takes her hand and leads her through to the lounge. With his arm around her shoulders, he sits with her on the sofa.

'Shh,' he says. 'Come on, now.'

She sniffs. 'It's just that Ted was ... I mean, what I've told you is only a small bit of it. It was every day. I was scared stiff every day for years. This … with you, I mean, it isn't what I'm used to. It's too much … it's too much kindness and it's not that I don't trust you, I do, but I don't trust *it*, do you know what I mean? The kindness. I keep waiting for you to turn nasty, which is terrible, I know, and it's not your fault. I keep thinking I'll say or do something wrong.'

'What could you possibly do wrong?'

'I don't know! I never did know. One minute it'd be all smiles and the next he'd have his hands round my throat.' She thinks of Jim punching the wall, the hole he made, the violence that's in him too. 'You're too kind, love,' she says.

'No such thing.' He strokes her hair. She moves her nose under his arm and smells washing powder, men's deodorant and sweat. She inhales it, holds it in her chest like smoke. He pulls his arms tighter and rests his lips on the top of her head. Together they slide, in little surrenders, until they are lying down.

'I'll go in the morning,' he says softly. He is still stroking her hair.

Carol wakes to the creak of the living-room door. Graham is standing over her, eyes flashing with accusation.

She sits bolt upright, still groggy with sleep. Behind her, she hears Jim stir, groan as he too wakes.

'Hiya, love,' she says to her son, who shakes his head and disappears.

She jumps up, follows him through to the kitchen. Wiping her cheeks, she grabs for the kettle, fills it. 'Must have fallen asleep,' she says. 'What've you been up to?' There is nothing she can do but this: start again from scratch every time she sees him, hoping that eventually he will want to start again too.

But he shrugs, eyes glued to the floor. 'Out.' He looks up, glares at her, a lip curl worthy of Billy Fury.

She's about to tell him off about the hours he's keeping, point out that looking at her like that gets none of them anywhere. But Jim is in the lounge, and besides, she doesn't want to put any more aggro between herself and her boy, not now. You have to pick your battles, and he is almost a grown-up. Oh, but he is still a child, a child who has been through too much.

She is about to speak when she hears Jim's shoeless tread on the stairs. Graham is still looking at the floor.

'Jim's off tomorrow,' she says.

'So?'

'So, that's it. He's helped us and now he's going. He won't be back. It'd be nice if you could shake his hand and at least say thanks, seeing as we won't see him again.'

Graham looks up, meets her eye. His curled lip becomes a sneer. It tightens the barbed wire already in knots around her heart.

'Nice,' he scoffs, and shakes his head.

She knows better than to respond. And anyway, her son has already turned his back on her. He is already heading up the stairs. A moment later, she hears him go into Nicky's room – to check on her, she thinks. She has no idea what comes next, other than that by tomorrow evening, she will be facing all of it, all of it, alone again.

CHAPTER TWENTY-SEVEN

Carol

Jim is on the doorstep, his kitbag over his shoulder. The sun is not yet up. Behind him, a black cab rattles. This is not real, she thinks. This is not fair. This can't be it.

'I'm so sorry,' she says.

'Don't be. I'm gonna stay with our Tommy a few days. Be good to catch up.' He touches her arm lightly. 'We'll keep in touch, eh? Never know how things are going to work out.'

He should be angry, she thinks. He should be shouting at her, telling her she's a time-waster.

'I can't ask you to wait,' she says. 'It's not fair.'

'I won't. I just won't put too much energy into looking else-where.' He puts down his bag and takes both her hands in his. 'I've left my number. Give us a call when you get a phone, OK? When you get straight. No crime in talking, is there?'

'You're too good, Jim MacKay. Too kind.'

'Told you, no such thing.' He kisses first one hand, then the other. 'Maybe I'm just like you. Maybe we're both just held together with tape, eh?'

She nods. 'You'll miss your train.'

He lifts her chin and kisses her on the mouth. She doesn't stop him. Not like Graham will see; it'll be hours before he gets out of bed. And even if he did by chance look out of the window, he's already broken into pieces. She'll pick them up later, try to put him back together. This moment is all she asks.

'Tell Nicola,' Jim says, 'if she doesn't get that merit prize, I'll be down to the school to bang some heads. And tell Graham ... tell him to look after his mum for me, OK?'

She wipes at her eyes. Sadness is usually mixed up with something else. Not today. She wonders if she's ever felt it as purely as she does now.

He picks up his bag, draws his finger down her cheek. 'Look after yourself, Carol.'

As if to prove a point, that evening, and the next, Graham stays home. When they cross in the kitchen, he doesn't talk but at least he's there, where she can see him. He's eaten his tea two nights straight, and tonight he's even come down to watch a bit of telly with her, albeit in silence. She misses Jim, misses him terribly, but she doesn't try to talk to Graham. For now, it's enough that he'll sit in the same room as her. She'll try in a few days, when she feels him thawing out a bit. Besides, she hasn't the strength to try to get inside his head. Not just yet.

'Listen, it's getting after eleven,' she says. 'I might head up the wooden hills, eh?'

Graham shrugs, puts his cigarette to his lips.

'Night then,' she tries, fighting the sadness in her chest. She's about to ask him if he's OK when a banging sound comes from the front door. Her heart leaps into her throat.

'Who can that be?' She meets Graham's wild brown eyes. He is already standing up.

'I'll go,' he says. 'You s-stay in h-here.' He makes for the living-room door. The material of his T-shirt and jogging pants seems suddenly very thin.

'It's probably some neighbour or other,' she calls after him. 'Look through the letter box before you open the door.'

The banging comes again, louder. It couldn't be Jim, could it? But even as she has the thought, she knows it cannot. Jim is at Tommy's. Or halfway back to Scotland by now.

She follows her son into the hall, watches him crouch, peer out of the letter box. He stands and, without looking at her, opens up. The loud click of the door latch. Low voices. Graham in the door frame, gesturing as if to show someone in. A flash of silver. Black. Chequerboard-striped cap. The bark of a police radio.

A uniformed policeman is stepping into her house. Behind him, in a dark overcoat, another man.

'Mum,' Graham says, all trace of meanness gone. 'They w-want to t-talk to you.'

'Come in,' she says simply, pulling her cardie tight around her.

Graham heads for the kitchen. The black uniform follows, then the dark overcoat. She lets them go ahead of her, their dark hulks filling the hallway. A second later, the strip light blinks into life. She steps into the kitchen after them, hand to her forehead to shade her eyes. Black uniform, peaked cap, big black shoes. Dark overcoat, balding head, hangdog face. They fill the room. Outside, the sky too is black. They are all reflected in the curtainless windows: her, Graham and two coppers in her kitchen. Like a picture.

'This is Carol Morrison,' says Graham.

They all have their eyes screwed up against the white glare of the light.

She takes a step further into the kitchen, relief coursing through her. 'No, love. I think you might have got the wrong house. I'm Watson. Carol Watson.'

The dark overcoat checks his notes.

Morrison. Black and silver uniform. Carol Morrison. Morrison. My God, it *is* her. That's her name now. The one they gave her. That's her name here, in this life.

'I beg your pardon, love,' she says quickly. 'I am Carol Morrison. I'm not thinking, sorry.'

'That's quite all right.' Dark overcoat speaks whilst the uniform moves from foot to foot, as if the floor is hot beneath his big black kicking shoes. 'Your former neighbour, Pauline Wilson, was able to provide an address.' He checks his notepad. 'Can I confirm that your married name is Carol Watson? Formerly of 22 Coniston Drive, The Lakes Estate?'

She feels for the worktop. 'Is it Ted? Has he done something? Is he in trouble?' The policemen are both looking at her as if they're waiting for something. 'I'm sorry, yes, I am. I mean, that was my address. They gave me a new name, you know. We had to … Call me Carol, anyway; I can't be doing with Mrs.'

'I'm DC McGann,' the overcoat continues. 'And this is PC Price.' The uniform clasps his hands in front of him and looks at the floor. 'Would you like to sit down?'

She lowers herself into a chair. Graham stands behind her. His hands are warm on her shoulders. She pushes the ball of her thumb to her chest, to try to ease the pain that has started there. She smiles at the policemen. She has a peculiar feeling – like she's about to go under anaesthetic.

'Mrs Watson? Carol?' DC McGann is talking to her. He's sat down too and is resting his hands flat on the table. She doesn't recognise him for a moment. He looks up, meets her eye. 'I'm afraid I have to inform you that in the early hours of this morning, the body of a man was found outside The Grapes Inn on Halton Road, Runcorn.'

'The Grapes.' She studies her hands spread out on the table: chapped skin, chipped nail varnish, raised veins running like tree roots. 'That's Ted's pub. Was he drunk?' She looks up at DC McGann. His eyes are shiny and dark, like the peat puddles she saw once on a walk, she can't think where. 'You can tell me, you know. He was drunk, wasn't he? Been fighting? Wouldn't be the first time.'

DC McGann shakes his head. 'Mrs Watson. Carol. The man we believe to be Mr Watson ... your husband ... is deceased. We cannot confirm the identity or cause of death at this stage, but if you could answer a few questions, it would be very helpful to our inquiries.'

'Deceased?' She puts her shaking hand to her mouth. 'Dead, d'you mean? D'you mean dead?'

Graham's hands leave her shoulders, though she senses he's still behind her.

'We apologise for the delay in notifying you but it took us some time to trace you.' DC McGann moves on his chair. It scrapes on the floor, loud in the silence. His eyes are lighter, now that she looks at them properly – chestnut, kind eyes, animal eyes. 'Carol, we believe you're separated from your husband, is that correct?'

She nods.

'This is difficult, I know, but did your husband have any particular distinguishing features that would help us to establish his identity?'

She clears her throat. 'He's got an appendix scar on his belly and another scar on his knee from a cartilage operation.'

He writes down everything she says on a notepad. She watches his upside-down handwriting grow across the page. 'Left or right?'

'Right,' she says. 'Delamere Forest. That's where we saw peat puddles. With my dad, when I was a girl.' She laughs. 'God, I haven't thought about that in years and of course my dad's no longer ...' The table blurs into a single shade of beige.

'M-Mum, wh-what are you g-going on about?'

'Sorry, love, I—'

Graham makes a strange noise. She knows she'll remember it for the rest of her life, this noise, like the howl of a wild beast. She knows she'll remember it and remember that she knew immediately that it was coming from her son. She turns on her chair and holds him around the waist, presses her head into his stomach.

'Wh-what have we d-done?' he says, his stomach muscles tense against her ear. 'What have we f-f-fucking done?'

'At this stage, we don't have a formal identification.' DC McGann's soft Scouse accent. 'I need to ask you to come with us to identify the body. We can do it now, or in the morning if you prefer.'

She finds herself to be in a kitchen in the middle of the night. Graham is striding towards the back door. The chairs slow him. He shoves them under the table as he passes.

'Graham, love,' she says. 'Where are you going?'

The tips of his ears are red. He won't look at her. 'Out.'

But the uniformed officer is by the back door. He's somehow showing Graham back to the table.

'I'm afraid you'll have to stay here, son.' He pulls out a chair. Graham sits down, beaten, and so quickly, as if he never wanted to go in the first place. He covers his face with his hands.

'Graham,' she says gently.

He draws his hands from his face and looks into her eyes with disgust. 'We did this. If we hadn't left him …'

'All right, lad.' DC McGann's pencil hovers over his notepad. 'You're in shock. That's understandable. But let's wait until we have more information, eh? Can you tell us where you were last night?'

'He was here,' Carol says. 'With me.'

DC McGann says nothing. He is looking at Graham.

'I-I w-was here.' Graham glances towards the door, his mouth wet and ugly with pain. She knows she should speak to him, offer him something, but no words come.

'We'll take some fingerprints anyway. It's procedure, nothing to worry about, just to eliminate you from our inquiries. Mrs Watson, you have other children?'

'Yes, my daughter. She's eleven. She was here an' all.'

'And where is your daughter now?'

'Sorry? Oh, upstairs, asleep. We didn't realise it was so late. We were watching telly but I'd just this minute said we should be getting to bed. We haven't got a decent telly at the moment, just the little black-and-white portable my friend Pauline gave us—'

'Mum?' Graham's eyes are black. 'S-stop t-talking. Just ... f-f ... stop.' He stands, sends the chair into the wall behind him. Head down, he marches out of the kitchen. A second later, his footsteps hammer up the stairs.

'I need a cigarette,' Carol says.

'Of course,' DC McGann replies.

'I'll come with you now. To the hospital. I just need a minute.' She stumbles towards the back door, fumbling in her pocket for her fags.

Outside, the houses are dark and flat against the bruised sky. The silence hits her – its rareness. The air is as cool as water. She turns in a slow circle. Here and there, in other houses, strips of light shine. Her own kitchen window makes a clean white mouth in the wall. She stands still and alone, a damp chill on her arms. She wills it to penetrate her bones, this chill, to harm her in some way, bring her down. Ted, Jim, Graham, Nicola, coat, bag and shoes, hospital, morgue, husband, death, her little girl, innocent, brainy, stuck in the wrong life, waking up to what? She will have to leave Graham here. She has to go and see Ted. It is her fault he's died. It's all her fault. She has known this since the moment they got to this house. By leaving him, she's killed him – that's what Graham meant, and he is right. Her son will hate her for ever.

Darkness is all around, pushing in towards the house. The street lamp is broken, smashed by bloody wolf-kids. Her neighbour's garden still has a radiator in it. Somebody should call the council. Somebody should report it. Somebody ... somebody should do something.

CHAPTER TWENTY-EIGHT

Richard

1992

In the loft, Richard studies the labels scrawled in marker pen on the sides of the boxes. *Christmas decorations; Books – Richard; Books – Richard; Books – Richard; Camping equipment, smaller pieces.* The tent and sleeping bags will be up here too somewhere. And here: *Photographs and reels.* This last box he pulls towards him. Inside are photo albums with padded covers, which he forbids himself to look at now but carries to the edge of the hatch to take downstairs with him. An old cine camera in its original box is there too, and a tray of films in round tins: *Wedding 1956; Richard 1959–1965; Richard 1966–1968.* The other labels are indistinct or blank. 1968. He was ten or so. He can't remember his father using the cine camera when he was a teenager. It was around then that Dad became the head teacher at the grammar school, a fact kept quiet by both of them once Richard went there the following year from St Peter's primary.

But he's supposed to be looking for the book. And after another ten minutes and much fighting against the temptation to thumb through the old texts he studied as a sixth-former, he finds *Jonathan Livingston Seagull* in the second of the book boxes. The dust on his hands is beginning to irk, but he opens the cover eagerly.

My darling Richard, I love you, always will. I know you can't love me, but that is not your fault. Your friend always, Alexis.

She was so gracious. He will never forget her face when he told her, visibly working through her shock, confusion, embarrassment, all the while trying not to let it show in case *she* hurt *him*. Oh, Alexis.

'It's got nothing to do with you,' he said, adding quickly: 'You're as beautiful as any girl could be. And I've loved you since we were six; I have and still do. But I can't love you like that. I can't love any girl like that. I can't love girls, you see. So we can't be married. It isn't fair to either of us. I'm so sorry.'

It seems to him, remembering that he did say all this, that with her, talking was not so difficult as it went on to become. He misses her. Misses the version of himself he was when he was with her – open, talkative. They used to talk for hours! He needs to find his way back to how he was then. He needs to return to himself, just as Graham does. He needs to move forward, just as Graham does. Maybe this is why Graham consumes his thoughts more than the others. All the lads are looking for the light of forgiveness. But he and Graham are still scared to come out of the dark.

The following Thursday at three p.m., Graham fills the doorway – the haunted outline that Richard holds ready-sketched in his mind. He sits down, looks at the floor and brushes imaginary dust off his right leg.

'All right,' he says.

'Well, thanks. How are you?'

'Very well, thank you for asking.'

'Do you always say that?'

'What?'

'"Very well, thank you for asking"?'

'D-dunno. My mum always says it. She t-taught us to be p-p-polite, you know?' Graham looks towards the window. 'So we could speak nice to the prison officers when we grew up.' He smirks at his own flippant remark, shifts in his seat, moves as far back into it as he can. He looks a little better: still thin, of course, but muscular, with an athlete's sprung potential for physicality, for violence.

'Last week you began telling me about *Jonathan Livingston Seagull*,' Richard begins. 'Did you say you'd read the whole thing?'

'Even I can read a book that short.'

They both smile at each other.

'I dug out my old copy,' Richard says. 'It was in the loft with my university bits and pieces.'

'Sound.' Graham's smile fades. He looks at his thumb, worries the skin around the nail until he's made a tiny ridge. He puts his teeth to it, pulls a shaving of white skin away into his mouth. 'What did you think – of the b-book? Did you still l-like it or what?'

Richard has made a loose plan of what to say, and for the first time since he met Graham, he feels prepared. 'I thought to myself, I bet Graham knows this isn't just a story about a seagull. And I also thought I should give a copy to all the lads who come and see me from now on.' This is the truth. Reading the book, he remembered his younger self and the impact it had at the time. Although Graham is twenty-four he is, like most of the inmates, held in a kind of stasis, pinned, perhaps, to the moment when his life outside came to an end, to late adolescence and all its intensity and questing, flippancy and lunacy. 'So I wanted to thank you for putting me on to it.'

'Ha.' Graham folds his hands together and tucks them between his legs. He looks directly at Richard for the second time, albeit fleetingly, with those dark and soulful eyes. Richard remembers him, weeks ago, at the door to this chapel, and it seems there is less fear there than that first day. He imagines him now with longer hair, with skin that has seen the sun, exercise in his blood.

'I mean,' Graham says, interrupting his thoughts, 'it's all about breaking out, isn't it?'

'I think so, partly.'

'I really liked the way, though, that even though he went higher up than the other seagulls, he didn't f-forget his m-mates, did he? I mean, getting out of the crowd was one thing, but he was like, "Hey, lads, it's great up here, c-come on up."'

'That's right. And—'

'And,' Graham interrupts him; he actually interrupts him, 'I like the way it's written. I mean, some of the sentences, about the sun on the water and the flying and that.'

'You're right. I'd forgotten that. If you hadn't mentioned it last week, my copy would still be in the loft and I'd never have rediscovered it. And what about Jonathan? Do you identify with him?'

Graham pushes out his bottom lip and raises his eyebrows as if to suggest either that he doesn't have a clue or that he isn't going to be caught that easily.

'Nah. Well, yeah. Well, I mean …' He hugs himself. 'I mean, it's something I've been thinking about for a long time. Not necessarily flying off, more … when I was reading the book, I did think about flying off. I mean, I'm doing English A level and I suppose that's me learning to fly sort of thing, isn't it?'

'Education can give you wings.' Richard can barely contain himself. 'Who gave you the book?'

'I nicked it. From here, like. I was going to ask Tracy to get it for us, but it was quicker just to nick it.'

Richard's mouth drops open in shock.

'Don't panic.' Graham spreads his hands. 'I put it back.'

Richard covers his mouth to hide his … his what? Not shock, not now. Amusement would be more accurate. It's not funny, of course, but the thought of a prisoner stealing from inside a prison tickles him. 'Who's Tracy?'

'She's …' Graham looks at the floor and sighs. 'We're … we've got a kid together. A girl. Jade, her name is.'

'Right.' Graham has a child. Many of the lads have children – and what of them? Where do they end up?

Graham is looking at him blankly.

'How old is she, your daughter?'

'Five.'

Richard wonders how old Graham must have been when Jade was born but can't calculate and talk at the same time. 'You must miss her.'

'Jade? She was only six months, not even that, when I came inside. I miss Tracy. Mind you, I couldn't even tell you how many sugars she takes in her tea anymore.' He scratches his head. 'You lose touch, like.'

'Memory fades.' Richard has a clear vision of his mother, sitting on her armchair with a home-made buttered scone on a plate on her knee. She could make a batch of scones in under half an hour – used to get the giggles rising to the challenge for Richard and Alexis when they arrived home, starving, from school. Perhaps the memories of his mother will fade eventually, or perhaps, like today, they will be just as clear, but happier.

'Most of all,' Graham continues, 'more than missing anyone, I mean, I feel like there's all this w-w-wasted time. Wasted, you know? In here. What's it called when you can't settle an argument, and you tell your story and you say – right, that's it, ladies and gentlemen, what am I then?'

'Judgement?'

'That's not the word I was thinking of, but yeah. Wait a minute.' He bites his thumb again, holds the bit of skin between his teeth and clicks his fingers. He picks the bit out from his teeth and flicks it across the room. 'Arbitration, that's it. But maybe your word is better.'

'Not at all, I—'

'I mean, I just … and it gets stronger – no, it gets heavier, that's it; it gets heavier when I stop the drugs. It always does; that's why I end up starting them again.' Words are tumbling from him, fast, his voice urgent. 'Since I read that book, it's still heavy but I feel like I can carry it, d'you know what I mean? I d-don't want to go back to the drugs. I want … I want to find another way, I really … Wh-what with me coming up for parole and that, I mean. I c-can't go back out there in this state, can I? I can barely walk for the weight. It's not like I need to get it off my chest; it's more like I need to get it off my back, d'you know what I mean? In court, you don't set it all down, not really. It's just the stupid details.' His whole face screws up.

'What do you mean, the details? Isn't that the truth?'

'Well, yeah. But you're judged on the facts of the crime, not whether your dad was a bastard or whatever. The truth is some-where … between … Oh, I don't know what I'm going on about.'

He is talking about context, Richard thinks. Of an act taken in isolation rather than in the framework of a life. 'That's OK,' he says. 'You're doing—'

'So there's this seagull, and I'm thinking, that's all very well, mate, but I couldn't fly anywhere anyway. I'm too heavy with it all, do you know what I mean? Even if I learn all there is to learn in the world …' He leans forward and points both thumbs at his back. 'I still need to get rid of this lot before I can fly.'

Richard holds his breath and nods.

'I mean, just now, you asked me who Tracy was, and honest to God, I didn't know what to say. Tracy was my girlfriend. But that's not the whole story, is it? She's the mother of my child but I can't expect her to wait for me, not this version of me. I need to be better. I need to be better, Richard. And every time I think about some other twat, you know, being with her, I can feel myself losing it. But it's still just the tip of the iceberg, isn't it? I mean, you can't say you're a robber just because you stole something, can you? I mean you can, but you might be, say, a teacher or something else as well. Like you, Rich. You can't say you're perfect just because you're religious. You can't say you've never done anything wrong, can you?'

Richard isn't sure what Graham is asking him for. 'I would never say that.'

'And I'm not just a murderer, am I? That's not all I am. Or does that one thing just f-f-f … obliterate everything else, for ever?' Graham sways in his chair, purses his lips and blows out a jet of air. 'M-m-my dad. He … h-he p-p-passed away and that, about a year after we moved out of the refuge.' He looks as if he's been kicked in the shin but doesn't want to admit how much it hurts.

'Was he ill?'

He pushes both hands under his thighs. He nods steadily, ten, perhaps twenty times, flaring his nostrils, leaning back then forward, almost bucking. 'He … h-he got m-mugged. B-beaten up, like, you know? They k-k-killed him.'

'Who did?'

Graham shrugs. 'Just thugs. Probably druggies. Irony's ironic.'

'So they never found his killers?'

'They never looked, not really. I mean, they went through the motions, but he was a skank. No stranger to a night in the cell, like, d'you know what I mean? It was par for the c-course with him, getting drunk, getting into fights, just … that time he didn't make it to the morning. But I think about it a lot, like. I think about it all the time sometimes.'

'I can imagine.' It must be indelible, a death like that – the kind of event one reads about in the papers. Richard thinks of his own guilt. He wasn't with his mother when she died, but he can see now that her passing was at least natural, and peaceful, and private. The thought provides strange comfort for him, set against this squalid public end.

Unprompted, Graham continues. 'If I'd stepped in a bit more, y-you know? If I'd had the balls to stand up to him, she'd … my mum would've been able to put up with it. But I didn't. So we left. And he couldn't cope. I helped her leave him. I helped k-kill him.' He sighs and stands up, walks over to the window and pulls up the blind. He looks out and talks to the glass pane, to the courtyard beyond. 'So I just wanted someone to hear it all together, like, you know, instead of just one bit of it, do you know what I mean?' He turns to Richard and lowers his voice. 'I want someone not perfect exactly, but g-good, like, to hear it p-properly.' He returns to his chair and slumps in it. 'I need arbitration. I need someone to take the weight off my back.'

For a moment, Richard is too stunned to speak.

'Talking will help you lift that weight,' he says finally. 'It's why so many people find comfort in God.'

'God.' Graham presses his lips tight. 'I don't know if I'm up to Him yet, m-mate. N-not someone like me. I was thinking I could start with you.'

CHAPTER TWENTY-NINE

Carol

1985

The morgue is cold. Carol pulls her cardigan across her chest and folds her arms. Still the icy air comes at the hollow of her collarbone. The smell of disinfectant hits the back of her throat. She screws up her eyes against the bright white light. Here they are, down in the basement of a hospital, halfway to being buried, and the light is too bloody bright.

Behind the glass, white contours on a table rise and fall. She stands next to DC McGann and looks in, thinking about what is under the sheet. The last time she was in this hospital was with Jim.

'I'd expected him to be in a drawer,' she says. 'You know, like on the television.' She can make out Ted's feet under the sheet, his gut, the peaks and troughs of him, hills and valleys, the whole rolling landscape. 'It's him, though,' she says. 'I can tell.'

DC McGann glances at her. 'Ready?'

She nods. This copper is no more than a boy; poor bugger, having to do this.

'Now as I explained in the car, Mrs Watson, you need to prepare for the fact that there has been considerable damage to the face, OK?' He walks away and through a door at the far end of the glass divide.

She holds her breath. He disappears for a moment before reappearing on the other side of the glass. Slowly he peels back the sheet. Some TV series, she thinks. Some murder victim. Ted emerges inch by inch. His black hair is matted, crusted with dried blood, his face a pulp, save for one shiny bulge, hard and round and split: his eye. She steps away from the glass and puts her hands to her knees while the bouncing blackness clears.

'My God.'

Taking in what she hopes is enough breath, she rolls her body slowly into a standing position, leaving her head until last. She looks in again, hand over her mouth. Ted's head is still a mess.

'Can you take the whole sheet off?' She mouths the words, mimes the action with one hand.

The DC hesitates. He shakes his head but looks unsure. She feels suddenly old, old enough to be his mother.

She holds up her hands in prayer. 'Please.'

DC McGann frowns, pulling back the sheet from Ted's skin, which is yellowish and shot through with mouldy patterns. His swollen body is dead, so dead. Grey fogs his ribs. There is his appendix scar; his shrivelled penis nestling in the dark frizz; his legs, bluish, hairy, bald patches on his shins. She can't stop looking. DC McGann is already pulling the sheet back into place. The sheet. The shroud.

Carol turns away from the window and presses her hands to her face. Nausea rises in her chest. She wanted to see all of him. To see that it was all of him. And it was him and not him, familiar and strange: slack and bare, skinny limbs, gigantic belly, no vanity left now in death.

Behind her, DC McGann sniffs. She didn't notice him come back out.

'Bruises killed him,' she says. 'And here's me, covered in bruises all my life and still alive.'

'He took quite a beating.'

'He'd have hated to be seen like that. Always pulled his stomach in for photos.' She steps back and bends over, crosses her arms over her belly against another rush of nausea. What was she expecting? To feel nothing? That she could pretend he was someone else, someone else's, not as much a part of her as her own bones? She presses her fingertips to the glass, stares at her fingers, splayed and white around the tips. Her engagement and wedding bands shine yellow – looser now than when she ran away. She left them on out of some sense of loyalty, as if taking off two silly rings would amount to betrayal after she'd abandoned him without so much as a note.

She twists the rings around her finger. 'I should take these off. The diamond keeps dropping underneath. It bangs on the surfaces, you know? I'm terrified of scratching everything.'

'Mrs Watson.'

'Thirty-five. Beaten to death outside his local, silly bloody bugger. Drunk, I assume.'

'Mrs Watson?'

'He'll be somewhere even whisky can't take him now, won't he?'

'I knew it was him,' says the copper, touching her lightly on the elbow. 'Recognised him myself. We've had a few … dealings with your husband these last few months.'

'What do you mean, dealings?'

'Trouble, you know. He was lucky he hadn't been locked up before now. Or unlucky, I suppose. All I'm saying is, this wasn't the first time, like.'

'It'll be the last, though, won't it?'

He looks at his shoes, then back at her. 'Listen, there's some papers to sign, some personal effects, et cetera.'

Head thrumming, she lets herself be steered away.

From the patrol-car window, the grand houses in the old part of town slide away, one after the other. Iron gates protect them; mature shrubs skirt their long front gardens. Further back, chimney pots float in a sky slowly bleaching now to pale pink. Here the golf course, there the church, now a housing estate so familiar – the place she ran from – cul-de-sacs coming off the main road like lungs off a windpipe, supporting life, living, breathing: Solway Grove, Ullswater Place, Coniston Drive. Coniston Drive, her old address, her home. Her home once more, she supposes, but not tonight.

'I used to live on this estate,' she says to McGann, who drives in silence while she sits in the darkness of the back seat. 'I always liked the trees. The grass, you know? And the little lanes and that.' She wants him to know that she once lived in this nice place. It seems important.

'I've got a mate lives here. It's friendly, he says.'

She's pleased that he doesn't sound surprised, hasn't taken her for rougher than she is, just because of the house he found her in.

'Our Graham was two when we moved in,' she says. 'But then it took ages for our Nicky to come along. Funny really, with Graham happening so quick.' She remembers when they first moved from their flat in the old town to the new housing estate, the house they'd bought from the plans. The garden, how big it seemed, how posh. *Our own piece of England*, Ted said.

'I tell you what,' she continues. 'That lawn was Ted's pride and joy. He used to try to make stripes with the lawnmower to get it like Anfield, you know? And his legs were that white they used to glow in the summer when he wore his shorts. He used to make the kids laugh so much sometimes they were nearly sick. Used to do Max Wall impressions in his long johns, used to have them in hysterics.' She draws a face with one finger on the window pane. 'He was skinny too. All the drink went to his belly till he looked like a boiled egg, you know, a boiled egg in a cup. Well, a dinosaur egg.' She chuckles. How easy it is to talk, in the dark, to the back of a stranger's head. There's hardly another vehicle on the road. Inside the car, only silence.

'I left him to protect the kids,' she says, into that silence. 'I thought he was going to kill me.'

'I'm sorry,' the copper replies.

Ted's bruises, how like her own they were. Perhaps death was what happened if they came all together instead of one by one. Perhaps Ted had always been killing her – slowly, over years.

The copper drives on, turns onto the expressway.

'He had this rage in him, you know? It was what made him fun in the early days. Exciting, like, you know? I didn't realise he'd turn it on himself. Because that's what he did in the end, didn't he? It wasn't me he was punishing. It was himself.'

CHAPTER THIRTY

Nicola

2019

My father was murdered in the street. It's not a phrase that falls easily from anyone's mouth. There's always a moment's hesitation, a small gasp before the words can be formed and expelled. They change my relationship with whoever hears them. They are usually arrived at only after a certain measure of intimacy, of trust, and after all attempts at avoiding the subject have been exhausted. Sometimes I leave it there. Sometimes I add that my father was an alcoholic who was beaten to death by a gang outside his local pub. A brainless crime with no motive, no reason other than drunken fists raised in the dead of night, a pack mentality, bored boys with insufficient medical awareness to know that head injuries can be fatal. If I were to tour schools, talking to kids, this is one of the things that I would tell those boys, floundering in their male insecurities, their confusion, their hormones and their rage. The appeal of violence is so strong; it is a life force as old as time. Men have always murdered, baited each other in packs. From Shakespeare to the latest gritty TV drama – gangs, senseless rivalries, war. Knives and guns, chains and baseball bats. Whatever. Not the head, I would tell these boys. Never the head. Their intention is rarely to kill. It is their ignorance that makes murderers of them.

I wasn't awake when the police came. I woke to the sound of a car engine starting and looked out to see a blue flashing light driving away from the house. I crept downstairs to find Graham sitting at the picnic table we were using for a kitchen table at the time, head in his hands. When he looked up at me, his eyes were red. But back then, his eyes were often red. At eleven years old, I had no clue that this meant he was using. To me back then, red eyes meant only that he'd been crying.

'Gray?' I said. 'Are you all right?'

He sniffed loudly and wiped his nose with the back of his hand.

'Yeah,' he said. 'Do you w-want some ch-cheese on t-t-toast?'

'Where's Mum?'

'She's had to g-go out for s-something.'

'What?'

He shrugged. 'Do you want cheese on toast? I'm having some.'

'Are we allowed?' I will have asked – always the goody two shoes.

Graham stood, ruffled my hair as he passed me to get to the grill. 'Yes, we're allowed. Mum said. Do you want Branston?'

We ate our cheese on toast there at the table in the middle of the night. I can't remember what we talked about – it was probably television or my friends – but I was filled with the hot thrill of my older brother deigning to talk to me like he had a couple of nights before. He didn't say much about himself, didn't speak about his friends. I didn't know if they were from the school he had gone to briefly or from round the estate – only that his eyes were often red like they were now when he had been out with them. It was exciting, there with my big brother in the middle of the night, eating toast. It was like it had been when I was very little, when my parents were happier, and they would get in late from the pub and the smell of Chinese takeaway would come drifting up the stairs.

My dad would stage-whisper, 'If anyone's still awake there's some chicken chow mein going spare.'

My eyes would pop open. Graham would invariably be on the floor by my bed. He used to sleep there when my parents went out because I was always afraid of the dark. I would sit up and find his eyes glinting at me.

'Yesss!' we would say at the same time, punching the air, scrambling out of our covers to go and share the illicit late-night treat.

These were the nights my father was nice.

That night, when we finished our cheese on toast, Graham said he had to go out.

'Mum'll be back soon,' he said.

I didn't want him to go, but he said he had to do something, that it was urgent. I was far too scared to go back to bed, so he fetched my bedding for me and brought it downstairs. Jim had rigged up a VCR to the television and Graham put a video on for me, switched on the big light, as we called it, since we didn't have a lamp or anything, and told me to lie on the sofa till Mum got back. I was miserable, desperate for him to stay. But I didn't want to let him down. I feared that if I protested and made him stay, he would think I was stupid and little and stop talking to me again.

'She'll only be half an hour,' he said. And he left.

I hated being alone. I lay on the sofa, ears pricked for every sound, eyes on stalks. A vague need to pee I ignored, not daring to go to the loo. I knew that something was wrong, of course I did. I just had no idea what. I stayed under my covers and watched some stupid film or other, fretting. I must have fallen asleep through sheer exhaustion, because the next thing I remember was the sound of the key in the door.

'Graham?' It was my mother's voice. I jumped up off the sofa. 'Graham?'

'Mum,' I said.

My mother appeared at the living-room door. Her eyes were as red as Graham's had been. She took off her coat and threw it on the armchair. 'Everything OK?'

I nodded, still half asleep. I wasn't OK but I didn't want to land my brother in it.

'Nicky, love. Where's Graham?'

I shrugged. I knew now that wherever he was, he was not running an errand. 'Dunno.'

'What d'you mean, you don't know? Did he say where he was going?'

I shook my head. Everything had turned strange. Wrongness shimmered in the air like heat. Did I know it had something to do with my father? I don't think so, not in any concrete way.

'Nicky,' my mum insisted. 'Where is he?'

'He hasn't been out long,' I lied, yawned, shivered.

Mum put her arms around me. She was warm, but she didn't smell like herself. 'Come on, let's get you back to bed, eh?' She guided me upstairs, settled me in my makeshift bed and tucked me in. 'Can you remember what time he went out?'

'I heard noises,' I said, eyelids drooping. 'Were the police here?'

'The police? What makes you say that, love?'

'I saw blue lights. I saw a police car driving away.'

And she, Carol, had been in it. How difficult it must have been for her in that moment, knowing that my father was dead, wrestling with whether to tell me or let me sleep. And the truth is, I can't remember what she found to say. She may have mumbled something about it being one of the neighbours, up to no good. What I do recall is that I wanted to stay awake and feel her arms around me for a little longer, but that sleep was pulling me under, away from her.

'Nicola?'

'Yeah.' I tried to open my eyes but couldn't.

'When did your brother go, can you remember?'

'He made me some cheese on toast,' I said, my words slurred with exhaustion. 'He said you said we could. I fell asleep on the sofa and then you were back.'

'Did you look for him? Nicky? Did you leave the house?'

I shook my head.

'Good girl. That's my clever girl. Sleep tight, love.'

I felt her lips on my cheek. I was safe, safe now that she was here. Sleep took me.

CHAPTER THIRTY-ONE

Carol

1985

In the lounge, the television screen snows. The overhead light is still on. The sick feeling returns. For a moment Carol thinks she is going to throw up, but she stands very still and it passes. Graham has left his sister alone in the house – on this night of all nights. Poor girl won't have dared leave the lounge. She will have been stuck there, rigid with fear. Selfish boy. Stupid, selfish child. Thinks he's a man but he's not. He's a child, a baby. He's all over the place. She should call the police, she should call …

A click comes from the back of the house. In the short time she's lived here, she has come to know the sound the back door makes when it closes. A sniff. Graham's sniff – she's had his whole life to learn that noise. Has he been watching the house, waiting for her to come back? She checks her watch. It is after three.

Sure enough, Graham is in the kitchen, rustling in the bread bin. He has not put on the light. In the dull yellow glow from outside, he looks different. She opens her mouth to say something, but nothing comes. Instead, she pulls the cord for the light, which buzzes and flickers and flashes, fighting with itself before giving up and staying on.

Without turning to look at her, without saying hello or asking about his dad, Graham pulls two floppy slices of Mother's Pride from the packet. She checks him all over, for damage, and sees that his ear has been pierced with a gold stud. Even in the dull half-light, his ear lobe is as red as raw steak. He looks up at her for a second, as if daring her to say something about the earring. His expression is hateful, arrogant. He turns to the fridge and pulls out the margarine and a jar of apricot jam. He opens the cutlery drawer so fast the knives and forks crash against the side of the tray. All she can do is watch him spread the margarine thick on the bread, then the jam. He presses the second slice onto the eggy-looking mess and lifts the white wedge to his mouth. His eyes are bloodshot and strange, pushed up by putty half-moons. He has left his sister in the middle of the night, the night he has found out his dad has died, to go and get his ear pierced. She knows this is so, and yet part of her cannot accept or believe it.

'Did you leave the back door open?' she asks.

He grunts, picks up the key from the worktop, dangles it at her like she's stupid. He is chewing noisily.

'So?' he says.

She nods. 'Yes.' There is no hug for her here, no warmth or kindness from her son, this boy who has been her friend, her ally, her cheeky monkey. Where he has gone, she has no idea.

He sits at the table, spreads his legs wide apart. Takes another bite of the sandwich.

'You'll want another butty,' she says. 'That one won't touch the sides.'

He nods, coughs into his hand.

'Cup of tea an' all?'

She makes the sandwich, wonders who on earth has pierced his ear in the dead of night, which one of these wolf-kids. Who has he been with? Where? And what's with all the mystery? She takes the second sandwich to him, on a plate, with the tea, and sits down, leaving a chair between them.

'So,' she says.

He doesn't look at her. 'So, he's dead then, yeah?'

She swallows down the overwhelming need to cry, an ache lodged in her throat, sharp as tonsillitis. She reaches into her bag and pulls out the small plastic bag that the copper gave her. Out of it she takes Ted's signet ring – the letters EW engraved on the oval top – and slides it across the table. He never wore a wedding ring, only this.

'This is yours now.'

Silently Graham picks up the ring and puts it on his middle finger. He spreads his fingers, makes a fist, then stretches them out again. The ring fits him. She reaches for his hand, but he takes hold of his mug. The tea, she knows, is still too hot to drink.

'J-Jim c-coming back now, is he?' He spits the words, his eyes small and mean.

'Jim didn't kill your dad.'

He shrugs. 'Never said he did.'

Something knots in her belly. Jim left two days ago. Said he was going to see Tommy. And now Ted is dead.

Graham stands, stuffs the rest of the sandwich into his mouth and picks up the tea.

She makes her voice as loving as she can. 'Get your head down for a bit, eh? See you in the morning.'

His feet thud, taking the stairs two at a time. He's probably spilling tea. She doesn't care. It's a shitty, horrible stairwell in a shitty, horrible house. But now they can get out of here. Ted had life insurance, she's pretty sure. He was always terrified of the machines at work, always scared of hurting himself, made a fuss of any little scratch. She can move back, be next door to Pauline and Tommy again, like old times. Except now she won't have to face Pauline over the fence wearing sunglasses at seven in the morning, pretending she can feel a migraine coming on. They can start again, her and the kids, properly this time. There'll be no one to stop her chatting to other people, no one to stand over her while she plants vegetables in the garden, saying she's an idiot, that it's not worth it, that they'll get eaten by pests. There'll be no one to stop her dancing.

She gets up, switches off the light and returns to the table. Shame burns her face. Ted is barely cold and she's planning her future. She is a bloody monster.

But surely Graham can settle now. And wanting that isn't a bad thing, is it? Graham isn't lost. He's in shock, that's all. Didn't the detective chap say that, before? But there's a gnawing mouth murmuring at her that there's something else here, something darker. Where was he just now, leaving his little sister all on her own in the middle of the night? And why does she feel more than ever that her own son, who has been at her shoulder through all of it, is a stranger to her? Now, when they can all finally step forward, it's as if a shutter has been pulled down, one she'll never be able to pull back up.

The weight of her head rests on her hands and she wonders how much longer she can bear it, this weight, too heavy for her spindly wrists.

'Carol,' Jim whispers to her. 'You've had a terrible shock.'

She looks up. There is no one there; of course there's not. Only the dirty amber light from the street lamp. No feral kids, no smashing of milk bottles on front steps, no sirens. She can't separate anything out in her mind, only exhaustion: warm, almost hot. The sight of him, Ted. Like a smashed plum.

She rests her forehead against the cool, hard table. What now? What now? Jim strokes her hair. Grainy stubble on the back of her neck. *Don't forget how beautiful you are either, OK?* Her eyes close. Ted's hair had been going grey at the sides. Salt and pepper, they said, though she always thought it looked more like oatmeal. She thinks of porridge oats and the man on the packet – the chap in the white vest and kilt, holding the ball at arm's length. She thinks of the blood on Jim's knuckles. The sound of his fist punching through the flimsy wall.

'Ach, come on, darlin,' he says through her dream. 'Don't think bad thoughts, now.'

'Sorry, love,' she whispers. 'I'm sorry for all the mess.'

Jim. Here only days ago, days ago when it was still possible to lie in each other's arms. He told her his story then and it comes back to her now, his words pooling beneath her, pushing her slowly out to sea. She tries to open her eyes, but her eyelids are too heavy.

'She did go with other men, Moira.' His remembered words come at her through the fog. 'She didn't just threaten to do it. Used to do it on purpose, bringing men back to my house while I was away, to spite me. Everyone knew.'

Humiliation, then, she thought. She'd begun to understand why he might have fallen for someone like her. You could break someone without laying a hand on them; you could find recovery in another broken soul. The warmth of him was all around her that night as he asked for nothing, nothing at all except for her to lie still with him and hear what lay beneath the proud, funny life and soul of the party, the raucous man who had sliced his own leg with a knife.

'My own fault, I suppose,' he said. 'I could've retrained. But the money was good offshore and I've no Highers or anything like that. Christ, I was so unhappy, Carol. I know how unhappy one person can make another. Trust me, I know.'

'Best off out of it, love. We both are. I'd never do that to you.'

'I know.'

Beneath her the sea of whispered words ebbs. Flows. She owes it to Jim to hear out this sweet memory of him, but every time she tries to stir herself awake, his voice rocks her, sweetly, gently.

'Carol, I know you might feel like you did that to Ted.' The words reach her, words he never said but which she has given to him now, in her despair, when she needs him to say them. 'I know you're thinking of me. I know you're thinking about me punching a hole in your wall and thinking that I might have used that same fist on Ted. Don't think about that. Think about us together. Think about us talking and still in the candlelight. It's different with us, you know that, don't you? Carol? Listen to me. We're different. I'm different. You know that, don't you? We're …

His voice bubbles away, no more than sound now, sending her to where the sea is flat and wide and still.

CHAPTER THIRTY-TWO

Richard

1993

'All right, Richy-Rich?'

Graham's new nickname for him is like a friendly punch on the shoulder. Almost five months into their time and he is, Richard realises, becoming cheeky.

'I'm fine, Graham,' he answers in a level tone. 'How're you getting on?'

'Not b-bad, thank you for asking. But you look a bit on the fidgety side if you don't mind me sayin'.' Graham nods at the pen that Richard is banging on the small table he's managed to procure from the library. A newspaper lies on this table, folded, unread. Graham is right: he was brooding.

'Sorry, yes,' he half sighs. 'I've just found out that Craig's back inside. He only got out, what, a few months ago?'

Graham grins and rolls his eyes. 'S-stupid get broke his licence. Did they tell you he got c-c-caught in a car?'

'What do you mean, in a car?'

'Didn't you know he wasn't allowed to go anywhere near cars? It was one of his conditions.'

'So he wasn't even driving?'

'Well, he reckons he was g-gettin' a lift to a wedding. But you know Craig.' Another mischievous grin spreads across Graham's face. 'Aw, he's a nice guy and everythin', b-but he's not the sharpest tool in the box. Nothin' against him or anything, but, I mean, he was probably getting a lift with himself in the driving seat of a stolen Mondeo.'

'Graham, you don't know that.'

'F-fair enough. You've g-got to see the f-funny side though. I mean, you do know who he used to work for, don't you?'

Richard shakes his head. 'I've a feeling you're going to tell me.'

'V-V-Vauxhall.' Graham laughs, slaps his knee. 'Used to make cars, gets sent down for stealing 'em. Oh, come on, Richard, don't look like that. It's classic.'

But Richard cannot laugh. In the weeks before Craig left prison, he saw God move within him as surely as he sees his own hands clench into fists now. The lad is ruining his life, and all Graham can do is laugh.

Richard tells himself to concentrate on the positive, to be in the present. This is Graham's time; he can reflect on Craig later. One good thing is Graham's joyful mood, as irritating as it is.

'So, Graham,' he says, his voice sterner than he intended. 'Recently, we've really begun to cover some ground.'

Graham pushes out his bottom lip. It's hard to tell if he's even taking this seriously.

Richard pushes on. 'You've told me about your childhood, your neighbours, the night your mother left. We've touched on your father's death and your feelings of responsibility.' He stops, tries to gauge how this remark has gone down.

Graham adopts a frustratingly inscrutable expression – neither smile nor frown.

'It's all part of getting to the bottom of things,' Richard continues. 'We have to mine the rock face to discover who we are, what we've done, how we can move on from that.'

Graham frowns. 'Excavate the past sort of thing.'

'Exactly.' Richard smiles. Only at the required depth will Graham find peace through the Lord. Not that Richard can couch it in such terms – Graham would run a mile – but he has to lead him to some kind of light. Rewriting the past is impossible for anyone – all the more difficult for those who have taken a life. 'You can't change what happened. But reframing it, taking responsibility for it, can help create a place from which to go forward and live. And that's what you want, isn't it? To live?' He waits for Graham to stop fidgeting.

'S'pose,' Graham says, retreating.

'You mentioned someone called Jim,' Richard tries. 'Do you want to talk about him?'

Graham studies his thumb. He has bitten the nail so far down he has to turn the thumb upside down to get his teeth to the raggedy edge. 'Let's talk about you for a change. It's boring talking about me all the time.'

Richard acknowledges the chess move with a nod. He knows Graham too well to think he can get away without giving him anything. He'll keep it brief.

'There's really not much to tell,' he says. 'I live alone. I come here two days a week on a voluntary basis. I've recently inherited some money – not much, but enough to tide me over while I decide what comes next. Erm, that's it. Oh, I'm thirty-three.'

'No way, man! Th-thirty th-three? I thought you were much older. I thought you were, like, forty-odd. No offence, like.'

Richard does not feel offended. His appearance is not something he thinks about much.

Graham pinches at his grey sweatshirt, holds it out like pointed bosoms. 'I mean, I d-dress like this because I have to. Wh-what's your excuse?'

Richard looks down at his tweed jacket, his olive-green corduroys. He can't remember buying the trousers. Perhaps his mum bought them for him – yes, she did, for university. That must have been thirteen, fourteen years ago. He hasn't noticed them wearing out, and yet here they are, bald at the knee. It's as if the cotton cords have dropped off individually. He half expects he will find them when he gets home, in the bottom of the wardrobe or on the kitchen floor, like so many etiolated worms.

'I mean, what's with the big Jesus beard, for a start?'

Richard brushes his hand across his jaw, tries to think when he last looked in a mirror. 'Um. I suppose it saves having to shave.'

'I mean, the trainers are all right,' Graham goes on, as if he hasn't heard. 'What are they, Nike? They're OK, but the rest, Richard my man, seriously. What's that tie? Looks like a school tie or something.' His face shows no sign of malice. If anything, shaking his head like that, he looks concerned.

'I bought the trainers because I was told the prison floors were hard. And that there were a lot of steps. I'm afraid I'm not much of a shopper.'

'No shit.' Graham throws up his hand. 'Sorry. But you want to get yourself down the high street and go into … well, I don't know what's good now, but try B-Burton's or Next or something. I mean, I'm not saying go down JD Sports and get a trackie and a baseball cap and start rappin' like the Beastie Boys, but try Marks if you like that fuddy-duddy gear, like. At least it'll be new fuddy-duddy gear. Cardies and that old-get shit – they've got all that.'

'I'll bear it in mind.' Richard meets Graham's eye, sees the guile-less twinkle of a schoolboy playing up to a teacher. A rogue giggle escapes him, shocking and unbidden as a belch. He can't remember the last time this happened. Graham laughs then. And the next minute, they're both laughing: at Richard and his old-man clothes.

After a moment, they sigh, take a deep breath and stop.

Graham shakes his head. 'You're as square as a biscuit tin, you, aren't you?'

Richard smiles. 'I think you might have a point, Graham.'

'What about?'

'About seeing the funny side. Perhaps, in here, it's the only way to survive.'

'Comes from playing hangman all friggin' day.' Graham smiles. Melancholy fills the silence that follows.

'You said your father was violent,' Richard says. 'Do you recognise him in yourself?'

'I try not to. That's why I shave my head, like. My dad had hair like yours. Except his was in a quiff. But I'd never hit a girl. I've had loads of fights, but I don't like it; I never liked it. And it wasn't just my dad that made me like I was; it was all of it. What he was like, what I was like, how we left, where we ended up. I hated all of it. But … one thing. When my dad died, it meant we could move back to our old house. A nice house, like. A nice estate. My dad's work gave my mum a bit of dough; I think she inherited some from her parents even though they weren't in touch. And she got her job back, so she had her wages and that. It was still pretty tight, though.'

'That must have been better for everyone – a nice house in a nice place?'

'Yeah, well, but I was too far gone. I can see that now, like. I was too messed up. I was on the dole. I met this lad called Barry and he had a flat and I started going there. I'd got in with a hard crowd before my dad died, and basically, when we moved back home I just replaced one set of head cases with another. I was looking for it, d'you know what I mean? I wanted it. Wanted aggro, like. Used to carry a rounders bat up the sleeve of my jacket and that. It was like my signature. Hard-man sort of thing. I'm n-not sure what I was looking for n-now. D-destruction, probably. Self-destruction, like.'

'And this Barry, he was your friend?'

Graham shrugs. 'If you can call it that. He sort of took me in. At least I thought that's what he was doing. He was older than me and that, y-you know? Used to wear this red b-baseball jacket with white leather sleeves that I thought was the business and he had this tattoo on his wrist that said *Work hard, play hard*. It went round, like.' He draws an imaginary circle round his own wrist with his finger. 'I thought he was the bees. Obviously now I realise he was well dodgy, like, but at the time I thought he was sound, you know. S-s-sympathetic, like.'

'So you found a friend, or you thought you'd found a friend.'

Graham doesn't appear to have heard him. 'I mean, you don't think going to school is a good idea when you're seventeen, do you? Getting qualifications and that. It's all just boring.'

'You played truant?'

'Ch-Christ, Richard, you sound like someone from the p-past sometimes. Sorry for saying Christ by the way, that's d-disrespectful.' Graham leans back in his seat and crosses his right foot over his left knee. 'No, I'd left school ages b-before. L-left as soon as I could. Our N-N-Nicola never missed a day of school. H-hundred per cent attendance, pretty much. Never gave my mum a day's worry. She's at uni now, p-p-posh twat.' He smiles, to show he means it affectionately. 'Our Nicky got all the good.' He stares at the floor, bites at his red-raw thumb. 'She's an angel, like my mum. I'm … well, I'm like him, aren't I?' He looks up, his eyes flashing. 'The devil.'

CHAPTER THIRTY-THREE

Nicola

2019

After my father's death, I had dreams in which he would come and sit on the end of my bed. They were so real that my mother would find me sitting up, talking. She would ask me who I was talking to, but I wouldn't answer. I don't remember her doing this, but I do remember the dreams. In them, my father never shouted. Some were specific to real memory. A time when he took me to see *Jaws* at the pictures, bought me sweets from the corner shop, cuddled me to sleep when the film gave me terrible nightmares. But whatever dream it was, he was always gentle, and he spoke in a quiet voice.

'Look after your mother, won't you, kid?' he said sometimes – not a memory, but my own invention.

I would nod. 'I will, Daddy.'

I didn't, of course. I was a child, and was ignorant of so much. Now I think those dreams were my subconscious instructing me to take care of my mother. But it never instructed me to do the same for my brother. In my child's eyes, it was my brother's job to take care of me. The time for me to look after him came later. And that was not a subconscious decision. What pushed me into law is tied up with that. My drive to, as I saw it, put things right.

Once we returned to our old house, we were caught up in the day-to-day business of survival – the net that catches what it can, leaving so much to run through and away. It amazes me sometimes how slowly I understood what was happening. The foggy truth sharpened as I grew up. Details came into new and ever-changing focus only in the light of retrospect. In later conversations, I had to slot each new revelation into place, construct the story of my childhood for myself. Even now, faced with clients just like my brother, like my mother, there are small moments of illumination; their lives mirror my own past. They would never know, never think that I was once part of their world. But I was, and their world is part of me. It formed me.

I know how quickly one apparently functioning family can be jettisoned into disarray. I know how quickly one young person can lose their way, turn to find the breadcrumbs eaten by birds, themselves utterly unable to retrace their steps. I make no apology for the life that made me, made my values, informed what I believe and what I believe in. And when, in my disguise, robe billowing behind me as I stride through chambers, I catch some scathing remark muttered from beneath the yellowed wigs of my entitled peers, I know that while I no longer belong to the world I left, I will never belong to this one either. I don't mind. I have no desire to belong. My own brother took a life. Had I been a barrister back then, I would have defended him to the best of my ability, all the while believing that he deserved to go to prison. If I belong to anything, it is to the law, the same law that found my brother guilty and sent him to jail.

PART THREE

CHAPTER THIRTY-FOUR

Carol

Runcorn, 1985

As Tommy turns into Coniston Drive, Carol's stomach lurches at the memory of Ted, here in this street, shouting and roaring in his pants, his hand round her neck, the look of confusion as he staggered backwards in a kind of defeat. Seeing the close now, it's like she's never been away. But at the same time, it's like she's lived a thousand years between times and nothing will ever be the same.

'Will Pauline be in?' she asks.

'Of course she will. Only reason she didn't come was because we were worried there wouldn't be enough room with all the gear.'

'Well I've left most of it behind, as it happens.'

Tommy parks up. The kids tumble out almost before he switches off the engine. Nicola runs up the drive like a mad thing; Graham strolls slowly, his head down. Tommy makes to get out, but she rests her hand on his forearm.

'Tom,' she says.

He settles back into his seat and looks at her.

'Can I ask you something? While the kids aren't earwigging, like.'

His brow furrows. 'What's up?'

'It's nothing bad, don't worry. I was just wondering about the night Ted ... you know, died. I mean, obviously they fingerprinted our Graham, interviewed him and that, but he was at home that night and I … I didn't mention Jim.'

Tommy's bottom lip pushes out. 'No. Why would you?'

'Well, they asked if I knew anyone who'd want to, you know, duff Ted up or whatever, whether he had any enemies and that.'

'Jim wasn't Ted's enemy, Carol. He never met the man. Booze was Ted's enemy. Honest to God, he had a black eye more often than not the last six months or so.'

'I know, but …' She glances out of the windscreen, up to the house that was hers, then not, now hers again, and for a moment wonders if she'll even be able to get through the front door. She should have sold it, started again. But money doesn't grow on trees.

'What?' Tommy says.

'Oh, nothing. Just, Jim said he was coming to yours the night I … the night he left. And I just wanted to ask if you definitely saw him. Only the night after would've been the night Ted died.' She meets Tommy's eyes, holds them. 'And Jim would've still been at yours.'

Tommy's face breaks open. 'Oh for God's sake, woman. Jim'd never do owt like that. Gentle giant, isn't he, Jim? Softest bloody bugger I've met, and I've met some bloody soft buggers.' He shakes his head. 'Nah. No way. Not Jim. He did come here, we went out for a few pints, he slept on the couch. He was heartbroken more than anything. He's bloody mad on you; you know that, don't you?'

Over Tommy's shoulder, Carol glimpses Pauline running down the driveway wafting a tea towel in front of her and crying.

'I told him not to give up too quick, like,' says Tommy. 'You need time, that's all. And that's what you've got now, isn't it? Me and P are here. We'll see you right.'

She nods. 'Thanks, Tommy.'

'Oi!' Pauline's flushed face appears in the frame of the car door. 'Are you two going to sit here all day or what? Kettle's boiled three times since you've parked this car, and I'm bloody parched.'

Carol laughs. She opens the passenger-side door, aware of Pauline running round the front of the car. By the time she has stood up, Pauline has folded her into her bosom and is crying again into her hair.

'Oh love,' she says. 'You're back.' On the doorstep, she hugs the kids, squeezes Nicola's hand and keeps hold of it. Looking at their bags, she adds, 'Is this all you've got?'

'Left the rest for the Oxfam,' Carol replies. 'Someone else can have it now. Didn't want anything from that place, to be honest.'

'Right you are.' Pauline holds Carol's hand now too as they step over the threshold. The house smells of lemon Flash and Mr Sheen polish.

'Have you been cleaning?' Carol asks as Nicola breaks away to claim back her home.

Pauline shakes her head, her eyes half closing. 'No heroics. Just popped a cloth round.'

The hall carpet is striped where a Hoover has just this minute passed. The skirting boards have not one speck of dust on them. Pauline is fooling no one. The kitchen is spotless too, in a way Carol could never get that last one. Her kitchen. It's lovely. She runs her fingers along the table, the vinyl-covered bench seats. The floor is wet. The whole place is immaculate.

'Sorry, P,' she says. 'I've made footprints.'

Pauline has bustled ahead. 'Cuppa?' she says, opening the cupboards, which are full of tins. 'I've got some Garibaldi in somewhere. I'm allowed three with my points.'

Points. Carol's not heard of the points diet. Hopefully it's kinder than the cabbage one, which almost sent Pauline psychotic. She has her head in the fridge now, pulls out a full pint of milk. Carol sees cheese, some tomatoes, a cauliflower, all fresh.

'Have you been shopping an' all?'

'Few bits.'

Carol sits at the kitchen table. Above her, she can hear Nicola's voice, high to Graham's low, but can't make out the sense. They sound excited. She hopes it's less complicated for them, being back.

'It was a mess, wasn't it?' she says. 'The house. Was it filthy? Eh, was it?'

Pauline puts a mug of tea in front of her. 'I tell you what – it's good to have you back, love. No fun smoking on my own. I had no one to tell when Tommy was doing my head in.'

'Pauline.' Carol waits until her friend looks at her. 'Tell me. Was it a state?'

Pauline looks out of the back window. 'Tommy gave the lawn a quick mow.'

'Pauline.' Carol lays her hand over her friend's. 'Come on.'

But Pauline only shakes her head. 'It just needed a cloth running over, that's all. Windows opening. And we couldn't expect you to come home to an empty fridge. Besides which, you're at ours tonight for tea, all right? No arguments. I've made chilli con carne. It's Mexican, apparently, get me, *caramba*. Got a recipe from this woman at work; she says it's smashing with baked spuds, and she puts fresh cream with it, but I have to say, I'm not sure about that.'

'Thanks, love.' But Carol is imagining the house. Stinking. Foul. Her best friend having to face that. It's too much – she closes her eyes against the thought of it.

'How much do I owe you?' she asks. 'For the groceries.'

'Now you're being pathetic, Carol Watson. It's only bread and milk and a few tins. Come on, let's have a ciggie in the garden. Tell you what, you can give me one of yours for a change, you tight bastard.'

Carol waves Pauline off from the lounge window, even though she only lives next door and they'll be seeing each other again in a few hours. Pauline seems to be doing some sort of dance down the drive, fake maracas, swinging hips. Carol can hear her singing 'La Cucaracha' and supposes this has something to do with tonight's tea. It's a funny sight. Hilarious, really. Which is why she can't understand why she's not able to laugh, nor leave the window for fear of falling into the empty room behind her.

She makes herself turn but rests her back against the ledge. Her ornaments have that same strangeness as the kitchen did: like looking at an old photo of a place you knew but never thought you'd see again. Her house is a memory, one she's blocked for the painful longing it threw up in her. How she's wanted to come back, to feel safe. But not like this. Not like this. Her breath shudders in her chest. *Ted is gone, Carol. Try not to think about how he went. Imagine him somewhere far away but alive and well. On a beach, that's it. Sand in his toes, warm sea. Peace. The house is yours now, that's all there is to it. The kids are safe. You are safe.*

You'll still get your benefits, the social worker said. And there's a cheque coming for Ted's life insurance. There's food in and Pauline can tide them over if needs be. Think about the practicalities, Carol; that's all you need to do.

Slowly she pulls herself from the ledge and walks into the room. She dare not sit on the couch. Wonders how and when she'll go into the bathroom. Decides. Now.

Pauline's done the stair carpet and dusted down the sides. She must have been here all morning. Maybe yesterday as well. A job, that's what comes next. Tommy mentioned something about the Spar on the estate looking for a cashier. She'll go tomorrow, ask around if not. She reaches the top of the stairs. There's music coming from Nicky's room – Duran Duran, she thinks. Every so often either Nicola or Graham speaks, and she remembers the lazy way they used to have, only talking when one of them had something to say, comfortable together in silence.

Her bedroom is as she expected: the smell of polish, fresh sheets, vacuumed carpet, a posy of freesias on her bedside table. She covers her mouth and sighs.

'Oh, Pauline. Love.'

Backs out of the room. Finds herself once again on the dark landing.

The bathroom door is upon her now. She turns on the landing light to help her. She wishes the door was open; that way she could see it by degrees instead of all at once in a big rush. She stands for a moment outside the door, fingers over the handle. Her breathing has gone shallow again; she catches it, hot, in the palm of her hand. Her forehead prickles. The roar of the bathwater, his hand on her face, the back of her head against the base of the bath. Her children, walking away along the white sand – a bad dream wrapped inside a memory she must try to forget.

She pushes open the door and steps inside. The room rushes at her. The bath, the shower curtain. Pauline has left it lovely. She's even folded the loo roll into a point. Carol sits on the loo, and this time when the tears come, she feels the draining down of all of it, down into her feet. Her shoulders loosen; she is able to stretch out her neck. It's not too bad. She's all right. It might be months before she can take a bath, but that's all right. It's all all right. Like Tommy said, she has time. She has not known how to feel, or even what she feels half the time, but there's something now in the mix she identifies at last: relief.

Sniffing, she looks up. Next to the towel rail there is a bald patch on the wallpaper. She stands, bends over to inspect it. The wall has been scrubbed, the woodchip completely gone. Her stomach flips. What was here? What stain? It's opposite the loo. She sees Ted, eyes half closed and bloodshot, staggering, trying to pee. She sees him miss, as he often did, sees him spray all over the floor. The times she had to put the bath mat through the wash. He sways, loses his footing, falls backwards, crashes against the wall, hits his head. Blood, then. Blood.

CHAPTER THIRTY-FIVE

Richard

1993

'Remember that boy I told you about, the one who wouldn't speak?'

Viv is at her desk, writing a report. She nods. 'Graham.'

'Well, he doesn't stop talking these days. I can't tell you what he says, obviously, but he's pretty much stopped stammering too. I'm becoming quite hopeful. It's since I found my copy of that book.'

'The one you were going to look for in the loft that time? That was months ago, wasn't it? Didn't you have something else you were looking for?'

'I can't believe you remembered. Thank you. It was my parents' wedding film. I found the reel, along with a load of others, so I finally got round to converting it to VHS.'

And there they'd been, on the television screen: his parents, in their heyday, moving about as if alive. Old Fords, black suits, heavy-framed glasses. Just to see them had brought an ache to his throat.

'Aw,' says Viv. 'Did she love it?'

'Who?'

'Your mum.'

'Ah, no.' Richard falters, momentarily stunned by this crossing of wires. 'My mum … my mum … well, she passed on. Recently, in fact. Well, a few months before I started here.'

Viv's face falls. 'Sorry to hear that, love. You must have been a bit sad then, watching that film.'

'I wasn't, actually.' He had expected to be. But he was not. He had felt … happy. Curled up in his mother's chair, he'd watched, quite dry-eyed, while his parents and relatives made their jerky black-and-white way into St Joseph's. His mother's veil blowing up and back from her face, her smile, her laughter then as she couldn't control the crazy cloud of white netting. His maternal grandfather, walking towards the camera, pointing at someone out of shot, grinning. A big day. His only daughter getting married. A happy day. Richard's parents had been happy. Quiet people. No fuss. No sentimentality. No need to say every last thing out loud like everyone seems to want to do these days. Richard was their late blessing, his mother always said. Just when they had given up hope, along he had come. The well-worn story of his existence, told to him over and over by his mother when he was little. The miracle of him, the late-falling fruit in the autumn of their lives.

The wedding film had finished to a scratchy roll of white bands on black. Richard had just been about to press stop when another image bloomed: himself, aged one or so, toddling towards the camera. Hand-knitted jacket and hat, chubby knees, all of three teeth in his head. His mother's voice: 'That's it. Walking nicely, that's it, my love. Clever boy.'

Richard had felt a smile spread across his face, watching himself, no older than two. Stumbling, falling. A kerfuffle then. Grass. Himself, wailing from somewhere off screen. His mother had obviously put the camera down so she could pick him up and comfort him.

'Oopsy daisy,' came her voice. 'Don't cry, my love. Don't cry. Mummy's here.'

And Richard had found himself sitting in his mother's chair, tears falling thick down his cheeks. He'd let them come. Glad of them at last.

'So yes,' he finishes telling Viv, aware that he's been talking to her for a fair while. 'I hadn't cried since she died, you see. I was beginning to think I was made of stone. And there I was, weeping like a baby – at her telling me not to cry. Ironically.'

'You've set me off now.' Viv is blinking furiously and Richard realises that his own face is wet. 'That's made me go all funny. Do you think … do you think that's a message? You know, from the other side? You know, do you think she might be telling you not to be upset, that she's OK?'

Richard brushes his cheeks with his hands. 'I hadn't thought of it like that. All depends how you look at these things, I suppose. But I suppose you could be right. It's a nice thought.'

CHAPTER THIRTY-SIX

Carol

1986

Carol carries her new trowel and gardening gloves over to the raised bed she's built at the top right-hand corner of the garden. To be back in her old garden, in her old home, is like a dream, so much so that sometimes she has to remind herself that this is her life now – something like the life she had before, but without Ted. Kneeling on the lawn, she begins to jab at the soil. The surface is hard and doesn't seem up to much. She'll give it an hour, she decides, then have a Mellow Bird's and a ciggie on the sunlounger, if it hasn't started raining again by then.

The soil gives up its weeds. The weeds give up their roots: white and spindly and shedding black crumbs into her hand. Weeds are no different from flowers, she thinks. The soil plays a big part in whether they wither or thrive; the plants themselves wilt almost the moment you pull them from their home.

Hidden stones clank on the trowel's edge, making her shudder. She winkles the blade under what she thinks is yet another stone, and out comes a doll's arm, reaching out of the brown like something from a zombie film. She yelps with shock, sits back. Ted in the ground flashes into her mind – the same image she often sees before falling asleep at night. Except at night she only sees it; now she senses it: how the trowel would hit against his rigid body, how the handle would push back into the palm of her hand, how the blade would scrape the black earth from his marbled corpse.

She shivers, pushes her hands against her thighs and shakes her head against her thoughts. There is no escaping the fact: Ted being cold in the ground is the only reason she is here digging in the garden they once shared. He never let her grow vegetables when he was alive, as if they threatened his existence or something.

Drizzle soaks through the back of her shirt. She steels herself and works on, uncovering a pink plaster, a Matchbox car, more pebbles. By three p.m. her back has gone cold and she makes herself stop. A few stones are good for the soil, to ventilate it; her dad told her that so many years ago now.

'You have to know when to accept the way the earth is,' he said as she knelt beside him, thrilled to be allowed to help, 'and just go ahead and plant your seeds.'

She showers and dresses, then sits with a cigarette and a coffee on the armchair by the French windows. Dirt and hard work bring their own pleasures – you get lost in the graft, and then once you're all clean again, your whole body tingles. Outside, rain still hangs in the spring air. April's steady showers have given way to May's constantly shifting spells of summer heat and winter chill. She takes a swig of coffee and rubs at the soles of her feet.

'Mum.'

It's Nicola, home from school. 'Coo-ee,' Carol calls, staring out at her beloved pansies.

'Don't be shocked.'

'What d'you mean, don't be shocked?' Carol makes to get up, but Nicola is there in the doorway. Before she has time to take in what her daughter is telling her, she sees that her eyes are ringed with black. They've all but disappeared, in fact, into little holes. Her nose, wide and bluish, splays strangely across her face. Carol's coffee spills all over the newspaper on her lap.

'God in heaven, Nicola love, what've you done?' She flings down the newspaper and the mug. Rushes across the room and holds her daughter by the arms. 'Oh my God, Nicola. Nicky, love!'

'Mum, it's all right.'

Nicola's beautiful hair, her lovely plaits. They're too neat for her swollen, blackening face.

'Love? Did you fall?'

Nicola's cheery bluster disappears, and she sits down on the settee and bursts into tears. Carol lowers herself next to her, puts her arm around her bony shoulders. It takes all her force of will to leave her daughter the space to cry.

'Oh, my love,' she says, her knee jiggling like a jackhammer. 'Let it all out.'

'They were calling me names.'

'Hang on. Somebody ... someone did this on purpose?'

Nicola whines softly.

'Who, love? Who did this?'

'Vonny Brewer.'

'Vonny who? She did this to you on purpose? Are you sure? Who's this Vonny when she's at home?' This causes a wave of noisy sobbing. 'Sorry, love. I just want to know what happened, that's all.'

Nicola leans against her. Carol strokes her cheek, swaying her from side to side. After a moment, she gives her plait a little tug. 'What happened?'

'They were saying stuff about Dad. Calling him a tramp.'

'How do they know about your dad?' She sits back, bites at her lip. They do, of course. Nicola's back at her old school now. And despite Carol and the kids taking her maiden name, everyone knows who they are and the rumours still run beneath: half-truths, inflated stories; God only knows what they say. 'He's not a tramp,' she continues. 'I mean, he wasn't. Bloody gossips, they want shooting. What's it got to do with anyone anyway?'

'I don't know.'

Carol tries to think it through clearly – a girl hitting another girl for no reason. She can't think it through; it's beyond thinking about.

'Where did this happen?' she asks.

'In the girls' toilets.'

'What? When?'

'They were all smoking in there and I didn't even say anything. All I did was try to wash my hands and Vonny started saying I was a goody two shoes for using soap and that you wouldn't think I had a tramp for a dad. And her friends were all laughing and she asked me if I liked boys and I didn't know what the answer was so I …' She wails, plunges her face into her hands.

Carol presses her lips tight and waits. A fat tear, round as a globe, plops onto Nicola's school skirt. Carol jumps up and fetches the box of tissues from the hall table.

'I didn't know, Mum,' Nicky sobs. 'I didn't know what the answer was. I just said I didn't know and they all laughed and then she got hold of my hair and sort of pulled my head down and punched me in the face.'

'On purpose?'

'Loads of times.'

'She … what … she carried on hitting you? In the face? Did you hit her back?'

'I tried to grab her but I could only get hold of her jumper.' Nicola's back is a curve. Her shoulders shake; her face is still in her hands. Poor thing. This poor, poor girl who wouldn't hurt a fly.

Carol's chest swells. If she leaves now, she'll surely catch the headmaster.

'Right,' she says, rubbing Nicola's back. 'I'm going up that school right now.'

'Mum, don't! You'll make it worse.'

She feels her ribcage deflate, her belly fold in on itself. Her daughter is right. Things haven't changed that much since her own schooldays.

Nicola blows her nose and groans. 'Ow.'

'Does it hurt to blow?'

She nods. Unable to sit, Carol lights a cigarette, stands and begins to pace in front of the fireplace.

'Mum?'

'Yes?'

'Our Graham saw me.'

'How d'you mean?'

'He saw me, you know, like this.'

'Oh Christ.' That's all she needs. Graham has taken to meeting his little sister from school. It's given him something to do with his day. And it's been a good thing, up until today. She's even dared to think he's on the mend. 'Did you tell him what happened?'

'Yes.'

'Oh, Christ in heaven.'

Nicola bursts into tears again. 'I'm sorry.'

'Don't be silly, love. It's not your fault.'

Carol tries again to sit still, buttocks barely on the seat. She rubs her daughter's shoulders while she thinks. Nicola's nose is surely broken. Graham knows she's been hit, and who did it. What will he do? Carol knows what he'll do. Or she has a bloody good idea.

A few minutes later, she's running along the lane, pushing past the slowcoach schoolkids dawdling home. Her breath is short. A bloody, metallic taste fills her mouth. She has to stop smoking – definitely – it's doing her no good. Down towards the school field she takes a left and half runs, half walks towards the path that leads to the chip shop. She is panting like a bloody racehorse. That's it, no more fags after this packet. How could a girl thump another girl like that? There were rough girls at her own secondary modern, of course there were, but they were all dark threats, backcombed hair and waspy belts; nothing of any substance. Why was it every time she thought she was out of the woods there was something else? And Graham, who knew where he was now?

If Jim was here, he could help, she thinks. But he isn't. He isn't likely to be either – another thing she's made a bloody mess of.

She takes the first right off Field Road and sees the school up ahead. There's every chance that Graham has already been and gone, done what he had to do, but she hurries all the same.

'Graham,' she calls out, heart in her mouth, looking through the faces of the thinning crowd. These are the real go-slows, the drifters. The skirts on the girls stick out stupidly from having been rolled up too many times; their eye make-up is thick, slutty. The boys' ties hang loose, their jumpers knotted around their waists; their bags trail on the ground. Graham isn't with them.

Up towards the school, she sees three girls clutching at each other, standing over a scene that makes her blood run cold.

A lad dressed in a tracksuit, with a black crew cut, is kneeling on top of a girl whose legs are kicking madly. The lad has pinned her arms down and is leaning into her face. Her friends look on, apparently too frightened to help. It is Graham. She knows him as surely as she knows her own hands.

'Graham!' She runs, pain in her chest, blood in her lungs. 'Graham!'

He's heard her, she can tell by the twitch of his head. A mother knows when her child has heard. And when her child has chosen to take no notice.

'Graham!'

He bends forward and … Did he just kiss her? Is that what this is? Carol slows, thinking she's got the wrong end of the stick. This is some bit of flirting, some teenage horseplay, and she has no business here, making a scene like this.

But Graham stands, wipes his mouth with the back of his hand. His head jerks forward and the girl on the ground shrieks, the back of her hand flying across her eyes. Did he just spit on her – is that what Carol has seen?

'Graham!'

This time he does turn and gives her a look to freeze boiling water. He makes his way towards her, shoulders rolling, rubbing at his hair. The girl she presumes is this Vonny gets up off the grass, is helped up by her friends, who close around her, cooing with outrage.

'Wh-what are you d-doing here?' His expression is so mean, his face harder to recognise than the back of his head.

'I might ask you the same question, son.' Carol stands her ground, hands on hips. She is not, will not be, afraid of him.

'I'm t-taking care of things, th-that's what I'm d-d-doing.'

'That's what you call it, is it?'

He screws up his face. 'She twatted our Nicky – what do you want me to do? Just leave it? That'd be m-more your style, w-wouldn't it?'

Carol closes her eyes. She should have stayed at home. There is no talking to her son anymore. She's drilled right and wrong into him, table manners, politeness, and at one time it stuck. But his dad's death has blown a hole in him, and all that good has gone trickling out.

Graham is striding off ahead of her. She tries to keep up, but she's too puffed out, and with every step he pulls further away. He lights a cigarette; the smoke rises in a wisp over his shoulder. She runs a bit to catch up, but he is too far ahead.

'Graham,' she shouts after him.

That twitch again, the set of the ears. He's heard her, he can easily hear her from here, but she raises her voice anyway, just to be sure. 'You can't go hitting girls, son. Do you hear me? You can't hit girls.'

Without bothering to stop, without taking the time to look at her, not caring if the whole world hears him, he shouts over his shoulder: 'I n-never h-hit her, all right? So g-g-get your f-f-f-facts straight before you say them.'

The street is empty, but shame burns in her cheeks all the same. He carries on down towards the main road with his stupid, stupid swagger. He looks like a madman, jabbering away, shouting out his own mangled version of events. He looks like a lunatic, a man other people avoid, stare at, fear.

He looks like his father.

CHAPTER THIRTY-SEVEN

Carol

Two in the morning, the front door bangs. Still awake and listening out, Carol throws back the covers and half runs down the stairs. The smell of toast wafts from the dark kitchen, where Graham is swinging on the fridge door, his face white in the light.

'Graham?'

He turns, and she sees he's holding an open packet of ham. A huge bite is missing from one corner. It takes her another second to realise he's bitten through all four slices at once. He looks her up and down, as if to ask her what she wants, what she's doing there, in her own house. His face is grey, his eyes still red and bruised-looking. He's not getting any sleep. How long has it been since he's looked properly well?

Months.

'You hungry?'

He nods and sniffs.

Toast pops out of the toaster. She jumps. He turns away to butter it, taking another bite of the ham.

'I know you're hungry, love, and I don't really want to have to say this again, but you can't come in and eat all the ham. I don't mind you having toast, but I can't afford ham, not a whole packet, not as a midnight snack, all right?'

'Mm-hm.'

'Do you hear?'

'I said yes.' He pushes half a round of toast into his mouth.

'Your sister's nose is broken. I took her to the hospital to get it fixed, but it's just a hairline fracture. She's in bed now. Obviously.'

He turns around and folds his arms. There's something in his eyes that she can't read. *I was right and you were wrong*, perhaps. That's what it looks like, anyway. She has to look away.

'I don't know what you did to that girl—'

'I d-didn't hit her.'

But did he force his mouth onto hers? Did he spit on her? She can't ask. She is too afraid of the answer. And in the dark, at this hour, she is too afraid of him.

He tears another bite from the toast, the packet of ham empty on the counter beside him. She wants to shake him; she wants to kiss his forehead and hold him to her, to love him back to sense, but she can't move from the door.

'Switch the light off when you come up, won't you?'

'Mm-hm.'

'Night, then.'

She climbs the stairs with concrete feet. From nowhere, she pictures Graham's toothless dunce's grin as she fastened the endless poppers on his Babygro; his skinny little legs poking out from his school shorts as he told her one day after school, all serious, that he had some sad, sad news: did she know that Jesus had died on the cross? His arm thrown across his belly when he laughed, how he used to point at whoever had made the joke – his dad, usually – unable to speak for giggling.

She pushes open the door to his room. Staggers back onto the landing, overpowered by the smell of stale fags, beer, unwashed clothes and God knows what. On his chest of drawers an ashtray bulges with hollowed-out cigarettes and other makeshift fag ends made out of little rolls of card. In an effort to have him here at home a bit more, to keep a better eye on him, to stop him smoking so much wacky baccy, she's told him his friends can come over sometimes. There's a lad called Barry he seems to idolise. He came over a few nights ago to listen to records, but looking at the evidence in here, this has far from kept Graham away from trouble. Barry seems to have turned her son's bedroom into a drug den. She doesn't like him, this Barry. Doesn't trust him. His manners are sickly sweet. Fake. *Hello, Mrs Green, how are you today? That's a lovely cup of tea, Mrs Green, thank you very much.* He doesn't fool her, not for a minute. With his brash American-style jacket. The way he dips his head and laughs under his breath if she says anything. The influence he has on Graham bothers her. But the only idea she has for now is to keep him close. Like the enemy.

She closes her son's bedroom door, her heart heavy. All she wanted was to have him home safe. Now, she doesn't know. At home, this is who he is, or has become: this disgusting mess. Out, his absences worry her sick. When he says nothing, she wonders at the thoughts running riot in his head; when he speaks, his broken words fill her only with the deepest sadness. Every day he looks more like his father. She has never thought him capable of the things his father did – there is too much kindness in him. But that kindness has gone into hiding, and sometimes, when he gets that murderous look in his eye, she no longer knows what he's capable of. And she, she has taken to creeping about in her own home, her belly knotted with a feeling she recognises all too well: dread.

CHAPTER THIRTY-EIGHT

Richard

1993

Graham claps his hands, striding into the chapel like he owns the place. 'New jeans, Richy-Rich! Talk me through it, talk me through it.'

Richard waits.

Graham sits down, still grinning like a chimp, then flattens his smile and raises his eyebrows as if to say, *go on*.

'I went to Marks and Spencer,' Richard begins, 'like you suggested. Viv, my friend, came with me actually. My mother left me some money, I think I mentioned.' He pulls his new navy blazer from the back of the chair. 'I got this too. It's wool.'

'That's as smart as, that is. Put it on – let's see it.'

Richard stands up and puts on the jacket.

Graham nods gravely and whistles. 'I like the way you've got it with the tie and everything, very smooth. You could present the footy on the telly in that. Is the tie new an' all?'

'Yes.' Richard is hit by the absurdity of himself modelling clothes for Graham and makes to take off the jacket. Though he knows it to be the right size, it seems too tight; he feels like he has to dislocate his shoulders to remove it. He gets it off and, sweating slightly, shakes it out and puts it back over the chair. Now that he is standing above Graham, he notices that his hair looks longer, thicker.

'Graham, your hair's grown.' He sits down. 'How can it have grown in a week?'

Graham rubs his head. 'It was always growing – you just haven't noticed before now.'

'I guess this week it looks longer all of a sudden.'

'Yeah, well. Yours needs a cut, like. You're starting to look more like Jesus than Jesus does.'

Richard gives a brief laugh. 'One step at a time. Rome wasn't built in a day.'

A pause follows.

'Last time,' Richard begins after a moment, 'we talked about you moving back to the family home. I thought we might look at that, see where it takes us.'

'F-fair play.' Graham puffs out his cheeks and limbers up his neck like an athlete preparing to compete. 'I was already a nightmare before I got there, to be honest.'

'In what way?'

'At the school I went to when we lived in the refuge, I'd already started to get into ... well, let's be honest, I did start a lot of fights. I was good at it. You had to be hard in that place otherwise you'd be finished, do you know what I mean? And I never said much because of my stammer, like. I pretty much never opened my mouth after we left my dad. I was too ... I was too s-scared.'

Scared. This is a big thing for Graham to say. Richard meets it with a slow nod. 'What were you scared of, do you think?'

The frown is back. 'Getting my head kicked in, Richard. Literally. Nothing mysterious. Didn't you have that at school? At ours, there was always someone getting twatted. Every lunchtime someone would shout, "Scrap!" and everyone would start legging it so they could have a look. There'd be these massive crowds of kids all shouting and egging them on, like.'

'No, I have to say. That never happened at my school.'

Graham doesn't appear to have heard or seen the shock Richard knows must have shown on his face. To be educated amidst such violence. He can't imagine it.

'One lad I punched,' he continues, 'his tooth ended up coming through his lip. I'm not proud of that now, but at the time, if I'm putting my cards on the table here, I was made up with myself.'

'Made up?'

'Pleased, you know? I suppose I thought if I was the hardest, you know, the baddest, I wouldn't get beat up by anyone else. I couldn't talk. So my f-fists did my talking for me sort of thing.'

'Right.'

'But the problem is, when you're cock of the school, like, you end up like—'

'I'm sorry, *cock* of the school?'

'The hardest. The hardest lad, yeah? You end up like Muhammad Ali or something and then everyone wants to have a go, and pretty soon you can't stop even if you're, like, Gandhi or someone.' He scratches his head, folds his arms and leans back in his chair. 'The school was going to expel me.'

'And did they?'

'Nah. I just about made it till the end. But it didn't change anything. As I said, when we got back to our old house, I started hanging out at the flats, met Barry and ended up getting into fights up there and that. I used to meet our Nicky from school sometimes ... This girl beat her up, so I went after her too.'

'You went after the girl who hit your sister?'

'Yeah. Well, I mean, she broke her nose, like, you know? But I didn't hit her or anything. I kind of pushed her to the ground and knelt on her and then I ... I put my ciggie up to her face and I told her if she ever came near our kid again, I'd burn her, like.' He looks up, his eyes doleful.

'You told her you'd *burn* her?'

He nods. 'I said, "If you touch our Nick again, I'll burn your … f-f-f."' He looks up, frowns. 'You know, I said "your effing face, you effing b-b-b …" Well, you know. You know what I mean.'

Richard appreciates Graham's effort not to swear but still he has to fight to hide his fresh shock as he imagines how terrified the young girl must have been. It is not comfortable to imagine Graham doing such a thing.

'How did you feel about that?' he asks.

'I didn't feel anything while I was saying it. I was angry, like. For my sister. And then this girl was crying a bit and I … I sort of kissed her on the mouth, just a peck, like. But she was well freaked out. And I feel bad about that.' He scratches his forehead, bites a strip of skin from his finger.

Richard doesn't know what to think. If he had to describe how he felt right now, the best he could say would be grim. There is a feeling of urgency too, as if there is still time to stop the young Graham on this path of destruction, knowing as Richard does that it leads here, to prison, the most soul-achingly depressing place he has ever been. The abuse Graham has just described is so at odds with the person Richard has come to know – the by turns shy, teasing, funny boy who knows he needs to rewire himself. And yet, violence *is* part of him, and to leave it unacknowledged would be foolish.

'Are you shocked?' Graham asks.

'Are you?'

'No. But my mum saw me do it. I mean, I don't know how much she saw, but that wasn't good, like.'

'And how did you feel about that?'

'Well, at first I felt all right, because I hadn't hit the girl, you know? I thought I'd found a way round it. I was like, *clever me*, sort of thing. But then when I saw my mum, I felt bad, like. Yeah, I felt well bad then. I was ashamed.' He puts his hands flat over his eyes and inhales deeply, pushes his fingers to the end of his nose and keeps them there, as if in prayer.

It is a relief to see him so contrite. His sense of right and wrong is intact. Perhaps it is this very sense that has fuelled the hate and self-hate. Shame is a terrible force; it circles endlessly, gets no one anywhere.

He huffs. 'I think when I saw my mum I just thought about my dad and how sometimes he could be so scary just by the way he spoke. He didn't just use his hands, do you know what I mean? I mean, one minute you'd be having a laugh and the next he'd put his face really close to yours and say "What are you laughing at?" or "What did you say?" that kind of thing, and you'd shit yourself, do you know what I mean?

'And so after that girl, I was like, *that's it.*' He puts up his hands in a stop sign. 'I gave up drinking then. Just stuck to weed after that, used to smoke a lot with Barry and them. I tried to settle down, honest. Barry even came over to ours, to my mum's, like, but he always wanted to get stoned and my mum wasn't having that, so we cleared off back to his most of the time.'

Graham has paused but is nodding slowly to himself, as if building up to something else. Richard holds his breath and waits.

'I thought the weed was OK,' he resumes. 'More mellow, like. I thought I'd be fine. Thought that would put some distance between us, like.'

'Between you and the person you became when you drank?'

'No. Between me and … him, like. My d-dad.' He looks up, narrows his eyes. 'I was wrong.'

CHAPTER THIRTY-NINE

Nicola

2019

I have returned to my mother's bedroom. I know I shouldn't, but I open the second drawer of her bedside cabinet. There are letters in here. Some are from me, sent to her in hospital. I can't read those, not now. I flick through the rest: get-well cards from her friends, one from Pauline with the message *Soon have you back on the Blue Nun*, *cock*; and a postcard with four photos on the front, a rose in the centre and the words *City of Roses*. I turn it over, see that it's from Jim. I don't feel too bad reading it, because after the first few words, I realise I've read it before. I remember my mother handing it to me, her eyes round as saucers.

Dear Carol,

I thought a card would be better, but I didn't want it dropping on your welcome mat unannounced, so excuse the roundabout postal service and the crap postcard, which I'll admit I just grabbed at the airport. I wanted Pauline to give this to you by hand, to make sure you got it. How are you doing, anyway? I'm OK. Thought of you at Xmas. If you'd seen us in our paper hats out on the rig, you'd have laughed. I was sorry to hear about Ted, but

Tommy tells me things are working out for you. I'll put my number at the bottom just in case you've lost it. It'd be nice to have a wee blether. I think about you often.

Love, Jim

'What do you think?' she asked me, giddy as a schoolgirl. 'Do you think I should ring him or what?'

'Yes,' I'd said. I didn't see why not, unburdened as I was by any romantic past of my own. And I like to think that at twelve, I was mature enough to realise that she deserved someone in her life. Perhaps having a brother who caused so many problems made me grow up faster than I would normally have done. In families, we assume roles without even knowing we're doing it. We fill in the blanks.

I lie on my mother's bed and stare at the ceiling. The bedding smells of the detergent she used, but not of her, not anymore. She spent her last weeks in a hospice in Halton. When I first heard, I felt her death without me as a kind of betrayal. How could she? I thought. How could she leave me out? But when you've loved someone all your life, when you've never fallen out, when you harbour no resentment for them and in your heart there is only love, well, what is there left to say? There was never going to be a last-minute dash to tell her I was sorry, or that I forgave her, or that I loved her. She knew I loved her and I know she loved me. We didn't say it much; hardly ever, in fact. My mother never threw out the words *I love you* in any kind of casual way. She was not brought up like that. I tell my own children that I love them all the time, but things are different now, and even I'm not sure if the words have been cheapened through overuse. My mum would think so. *I can't be doing with all this 'I love you' business every five minutes*, she would undoubtedly say. And she'd have a point. Where do we go to when what we want to say is that very deepest thing?

Perhaps there are no words for that anymore. Perhaps no words are needed for those who know it of one another: a hand on an arm, a meeting of eyes, a smile.

My mother died in peace. After all the pain and turmoil, she was free, had been free for many years, and happy. It was Graham who was with her at the end. My brother, so lovely and so beloved, and the cause of so much angst. Of course it was him. He will have wanted to say sorry, though he was forgiven long ago.

I think my mother hoped that our return to our home after we'd left the safe house would mean we could really start again. It was our second chance. But the thing about second chances is that they drag with them the scars of the first fucked-up attempt, scars that infiltrate and derail our best attempts at redemption. What happened the first time round can take so much longer to eradicate than we anticipated. It is only really possible to start again once the decks are cleared. With my father dead, perhaps my mother thought this was so. But it was not. Graham, red-eyed and stumbling blind through life, was a stranger to both of us. My mother told me later that she was afraid of him. As for me, I didn't know him, not anymore. After our brief and precious return to closeness, he had once again vanished from my side. And perhaps I had lost hope that he would ever come back.

But with the passing of summer came a breakthrough. My brother turned eighteen. There was a sense of things looking up. Graham announced that he had got a part-time job, cash in hand, at the Esso garage up on Clifton Road. I was in the living room with my mother when he told us, his face brighter than I had seen it in years. As autumn progressed, he came home at night more often, seemed to mention his friend Barry less, was less black around the eyes. I can remember my mother still complaining that he had left all the lights on, the electric ring glowing orange on the hob, the smell of burnt toast up the hall. But at least he wasn't as aggressive and seemed at last to want to work, to live well. The year turned. A little after, we found out he had a girlfriend. Her name was Tracy. She was quiet, with brown hair, as unremarkable as it gets. That sounds uncharitable, but she was so young – she had not left school – was not, in fact, that much older than me, and like me, she had not grown into herself. She was an ordinary girl, but with her, Graham appeared to finally be settling and my mother could not, would not argue with that. And I think because of that, she finally found the confidence to call Jim.

She was not to know that whatever peace Graham had found, it would not last.

CHAPTER FORTY

Carol

1987

After a few faint ticks, the phone rings loudly in her ear, and then quietly in Scotland: near and far, near and far, over the hills and far away. She runs her nail down the frame of the mirror and sucks her teeth. *Come on, Jim, answer.* Near and far. A click. She inhales deeply, pulls in her stomach.

It's a woman's voice. Another woman; she should have known. She's about to put the phone down when she hears what the woman is saying. 'Please leave a message and your number after the beep.' The voice is electronic-sounding. A machine, not another woman at all.

Beep.

'Oh.' Her own voice is high, startled. 'Hello. Erm, this is Carol Green … I mean, you know me as Watson … I mean Carol, anyway, leaving a message for James MacKay, sorry, Jim MacKay, I mean Jim. My number is one five one, seven two nine, three five six. Thank you. That's the message. Thank you now.' She hesitates, puts down the phone and feels the heat of a blush spread to the roots of her hair.

Her hand is still on the receiver. She picks it up again and dials Pauline's work number.

'ICI Human Resources, Pauline speaking, can I help you?'

'Hiya. Can you talk?'

'Aye, go on. Make it quick, though, I've got a BO case in five minutes. Last warning, smelly bastard's killing us by stealth.'

Carol giggles. 'I called him. Jim, I mean.'

'You never?'

'I did.'

Pauline gives a squeak. 'Get you, scarlet woman.'

'Don't.'

'So what did he say?'

'It was one of them answering machines. I nearly died.'

'Did you leave a message?'

'Yes.'

'Well bloody good for you, love. Well done. I hate them things.'

Carol smiles to herself. 'Well, I mean, I was thinking, you know, our Graham's been so settled recently. I mean, he's almost cheerful sometimes. And Nicky's busy with exams and that.' She gives a little excited chuckle. 'And so I just thought – what the hey-ho, you know?'

'About bloody time. Listen, love, I have to go. Niffy Nigel's here and I've got to tell him how to use a bar of soap. Thirty-bloody-two, you'd think he'd've figured it out by now.'

'Righto – off you go, love.' Carol laughs, though she's disappointed not to be able to chat. 'Ta-ra.'

'Ta-ra, temptress.'

'Give over.'

The following Saturday morning, Carol is halfway through spring-cleaning the kitchen cupboards and thinking about a quick cup of coffee and a cigarette. Five minutes later, she's sitting in the armchair by the window with a cup of Mellow Bird's and a B&H.

Bliss.

She pushes her bottom back into the chair, closes her eyes and tries not to think about Jim. He hasn't called back. She's been a fool to think he would. He's kind, that's all. She waited too long. If only she hadn't left that stupid message.

'Mum.'

She opens her eyes. Graham and Tracy are looming over her, holding hands like a torn-out paper chain.

She jumps up and plumps up the cushion. 'I didn't hear you come in.'

'Mum. Sit down, you're all right.' They're standing a little apart in front of the gas fire.

Carol perches, then moves her bottom properly onto the chair.

'I've only been here a minute,' she says. 'I've literally just this minute sat down.' She looks into Graham's face and sees something she doesn't like. 'What's the matter?'

As if in answer, he puts his arm around Tracy's shoulders. 'We love each other, me and Trace, right? We really do.' He sounds strange, like he's rehearsed it or something. 'I've calmed down loads, I really have, so this could be the icing on the cake, like.' His knuckles whiten on Tracy's shoulder. He grins. Tracy looks like she's faking a smile for the camera.

Carol moves back to the edge of her seat but realises she doesn't trust her legs to stand. Her chest has tightened. 'What could be the icing on the cake?'

'We're … we're going to have a b-baby. We reckon it m-m-must be d-due in about August. Tracy'll be out of s-school by then and she'll get a flat on the c-c-council. I'm going to ask Mr Weston if h-he'll take me on as t-t-trainee m-manager.' He raises his eyebrows, giving her a flat, hopeful smile.

'You're having a baby?' Carol hauls herself to her feet but sees black. She bends over, rests her hands on her knees.

'Mum, are you all right?'

She straightens up slowly, her vision clearing, and meets Graham's gaze.

'Listen while I tell you something.' She reaches for her cigarettes, to give her fingers something to do whilst she tries to control the temper she can feel bubbling up the walls of her, hot as oil in a vat. She lights up, trying to stall, but still her blood rises. 'You think you've got it all worked out, do you? Think this baby will be different? Different from all the other millions and trillions of babies?' Her voice trembles. 'Look at you! You've barely been together five minutes. Kids, the pair of you.'

'C-c-come on, Mum, I'm not a kid, d-don't be like that.' Graham takes his arm from around Tracy and spreads his hands.

'Like what, Graham? Knackered?' She is shouting now. She can't help it. 'Is that what you mean? Like that? Worrying you're going to punch some customer in the face if he speaks to you wrong? Choking half to death from the fumes in your disgusting midden of a bedroom – worrying all the time, *all the time*, about how much of that stuff you're smoking. Is that what you want, is it? Hassle, grief, trouble, fighting, money worries, tiptoeing around your moods, explaining to some kid's parents that no, he doesn't come from a broken home, he just can't control his bloody temper? You think you're a hard knock, don't you? Cock of the walk? You think because you've stayed calm for all of two months you're ideal father material? What're you going to live on, son? Two pound fifty an hour won't feed it! Christ, how the hell do you expect to look after a child when you're still one yourself? You're still living with your mother, for pity's sake.' She takes a drag of her cigarette and blows the smoke up, away from them.

'You can f-frigging talk.' Graham spits the words. Typical – nought to belligerence in two seconds. 'You didn't exactly w-wait, d-did you? Eh?'

'No, love. No, I didn't. And that's how I know how hard it is.' She looks at Tracy, who has shrunk away from her. 'And you, love? I tell you something, my girl, I hope you know what you're taking on with him. He's a piece of work, I tell you that. And don't expect me to come and play babysitter; I've got enough on my plate without bloody grandchildren.'

Graham's face darkens. 'Well if h-having me was so b-b-bad, I'll get out of your w-way. All I ever d-did was try to look after you. Who h-helped you get away from D-Dad? Eh? F-f-forgotten that, have you? I've done everything for you, everything. Wasn't enough, was it? Nothing's ever enough for you.' He drags his bewildered girlfriend out of the room. 'Come on, Trace.'

'I don't want to be a grandmother,' Carol shouts after them. 'I'm only thirty-eight.'

'Well don't worry,' he shouts back. 'We won't be bothering you with your own fucking flesh and blood.'

CHAPTER FORTY-ONE

Carol

The house howls with silence. Graham and Tracy have been gone an hour. Carol has no idea what to do with herself. She could ring Pauline, but decides not to, not yet. Her son's stupidity feels, for the moment, private.

A moment later, she hears Nicola's music start upstairs. Another moment and the banging of her feet comes through the ceiling. The sooner this aerobics craze is over, the better. And on top of that, the phone is ringing.

'Can you turn the music down?' Carol shouts up the stairs. 'I said, can you turn it down? Oi!' The music drops. Still irritated, still furious with her stupid son and his stupid girlfriend, she picks up the phone.

'What?' she shouts into the receiver.

'Carol?' The roll of the R, the swallowed L. Jim. He has called – just when she'd given up hope. And she's just yelled into the phone like a madwoman. Buggeration. She puts her hand over the receiver. A deep breath shudders out of her. Once she's sure her voice won't betray her, she takes her hand away and speaks.

'Jim.'

'That's me.' His voice carries the hint of a croak. 'Long time no speak. How're you doing, anyway?' He sounds so normal, not tragic like the women at work when they ask that question, heads to one side, biting their lips at the imagined tragedy of the newly widowed woman. It dawns on her how much she misses people speaking normally to her. There's only Pauline. And Tommy. And now Jim. His voice, deep with cigars, rattles away, seems nothing but glad to be talking to her, and now she too feels glad and clear and uncomplicated. 'Finally come to your senses?' he is saying. 'Can't live without me?'

She tells herself to keep her voice steady, to ask how he's been and for that to be that. But he speaks again before she has a chance to ask him anything.

'So what's new?'

'I've been gardening.' She smacks her forehead with her hand. Idiot. 'And I'm redecorating. I've got the paint – it's a Dulux one: magnolia. I've told Graham I'll pay him if he gives us a hand. Could do with some shelves putting up too, except the car's falling to pieces, obviously.'

'That an invite?'

'Oh. I didn't mean. I …' Stupid woman. She needed bloody duct tape putting over her mouth.

'I'm just teasing.'

Down the line comes a smack-smack-smacking – Jim lighting a cigar, probably. Just the sound makes her feel less angry inside; he doesn't even have to speak. She imagines him in his kilt, in an armchair with old-fashioned rounded arms in some country hotel, the head of a deer on the wall, cut-glass tumbler of whisky on the coffee table. She imagines him on the doorstep, right now, suitcase in hand and no other home save hers.

'Graham's got his girlfriend pregnant,' she says.

Smack, blow. 'You're joking.'

'I wish I was. I don't know where he is, where either of them are. He left in a rage.'

'He always comes back, though, doesn't he? He'll be knocking on the door by the end of today, I guarantee it.'

'He'll be nineteen by the time it's born, but she's still at school. It's no age, is it? I should know. And it's raining outside, it's pouring down, and I just can't stop thinking about where they might be, the two of them. Oh God, listen to me. I don't know why I'm telling you all this.'

'Just trying to cheer me up? I mean, I've got a few funnies myself, but I can't top that. Carol? Are you crying or laughing?'

'Bit of both. Can't tell. You have to laugh, though, don't you? Listen, Jim, it was nice of you to keep asking after us with Pauline and Tommy. It's good, you know, to hear you.'

'You too. How is he? Graham, I mean. Tommy told me he'd been on the old weed, like.'

Carol closes her eyes and sighs. Thanks, Tommy. 'He's not smoking as much now, not since he found Tracy.' She laughs. 'I don't know, most women get a chance to pretend things are hunky-dory, at least for a bit. They get taken to restaurants in their best clothes.' She fumbles for her cigarettes. 'Me, I get bits of wallpaper in my hair, a dope-head son and a murdered husband.'

'Aye, well. I don't like restaurants that much. Bit stuffy for me, all that, bit fake. Listen, I'm sorry. I shouldn't have mentioned it.'

'It's OK, love,' she manages. 'But this girl, this Tracy, she's all right, you know? Not exactly the sharpest tool in the box, like – I mean, you ask her how she is and she looks at you like a monkey doing long division – but she's lovely. And he's better with her, and that's all that matters. He's got a job at the garage. He's getting there, Jim, he really is. He's a good kid.'

'I know that, darlin'.'

Darlin'. She ignores it, the fact that it makes her stomach flip. 'But she's still at school. I mean, they're just kids.' She lights her ciggie. The line is quiet, but she knows he's there. 'I just wish he'd given himself longer, do you know what I mean? After everything. Anyway, you don't want to hear about my troubles.'

'I do.'

She doesn't know what to say to this. Wonders if he can hear her heart knocking on her ribs. 'It was nice to hear from you, anyway. I mean, I've got your number now, so …'

'So?'

'So, we can, you know, have a natter sometimes. If you want.'

'A natter? I'd like that.'

'Right then, I'll let you go. You must be busy.'

'Right.'

She waits for him to hang up.

'Carol?'

'Yes, love?'

'Can I call you again soon?'

Surely he can hear how much she wants him to. How could he not hear it? She makes her voice friendly and light. 'Course you can, love. Any time. It'd be nice to have someone to talk to. Bye then.'

'Bye.'

An hour later, they ring off. Both the receiver and her ear are damp with sweat.

He didn't mention a girlfriend.

The phone rings the moment it touches the cradle. Typical Jim, just his sense of humour. She picks up, smiling stupidly, twirling so the cord wraps around her waist. 'I know I said any time, but I didn't mean straight away, you daft bugger.'

'Mum?'

Slowly she disentangles herself from the cord and sits down on the phone stool. 'Graham.'

'Mum? I've been trying to get through. Who were you talking to?'

'Me? Oh, just Pauline, love.'

'Isn't she at work?'

'Thrown a sickie. Anyway, what is this? The Spanish Inquisitive? Where are you?'

'It's Inquisition.' A sigh. 'I'm in a phone box.'

'Well, that narrows it down.'

'I mean, near the house.' He sounds flat, suspicious, frightened. 'Tracy's parents have thrown her out.'

'Oh. Are you all right?'

The line goes quiet. Men and their bloody silences. She hears a sniff.

'Graham? Love?' Her heart fills for her son. He's doing his best.

'C-c-can I c-come home?'

'Of course you bloody can. You can always come home, you know that.' The line is silent, but she knows he is getting himself together to speak. 'Hey, come on,' she coaxes. 'This is your home and I'm your mum, even when you're a total pain in the bum, and that's all there is to it. I was just cross, that's all. I don't want you ruining your life.'

'I'm s-s-sorry I shouted.' His voice is hoarse. 'I shouldn't have shouted at you. I know I've shouted a lot, b-but that's over now, I p-p-promise. It wasn't me. It's n-n-not who I am. And we won't s-stay long. As s-soon as we get a flat, I'll t-take care of everything. I c-can do it, Mum, I know I can.'

CHAPTER FORTY-TWO

Richard

1993

'When I was a kid, I used to listen for him coming home.' Graham tears a strip of fingernail with his teeth. 'I could tell just from hearing him on the street what was going to happen. If he was singing, it was all right. Elvis songs he used to sing, all the time. But if he was muttering away to himself, different story.'

Richard holds his breath for fear that any noise he might make will break Graham's flow.

'I knew he'd have it in for her, like. If I was still downstairs, I'd try to get in between them, because he never hit me. Don't know why, but he never. Strange or what?' He changes his voice to an affected over-pronunciation: 'Bizarre moral distinction.' Then returns to his normal speech. 'Listen to me, I've got the words to describe it now. A prison A level will do that for you. But back then I was just shit-scared, and when I met Tracy, I was determined never to do to her what my dad did to my mum.'

Richard says nothing, merely nods, to show he is listening, that he is here.

'I can't stand the thought of her outside, you know?' Graham looks about him, as if for something to tear apart. 'I feel like I'm handcuffed to the wall.'

'Do you think that's to do with your parole coming up?'

Graham squints at him. 'What d'you mean, like?'

'Well, maybe your feelings are beginning to stir. Once we glimpse the possibility of change, we come alive to all that we cannot bear in our current situation. You couldn't afford to think of yourself as chained to the wall while you were facing years incarcerated; it would have been too hard. Sometimes you have to block things out to survive. But now that the door might soon open, your mind is accepting how unacceptable your situation really is. And the possibility of becoming close to someone again might be frightening now that it's imminent. The possibility of freedom itself might be frightening. Freedom *is* frightening, I think. It's so … vast.' Richard cannot help but think of Andrew. Andrew set him free. *Go home*, he said. *Go and make peace with yourself. I'm not going anywhere.* Richard has done precisely nothing with that freedom, only stare into its light and let it blind him.

Graham is nodding slowly. 'This is why I come to you – you make sense. You make *me* make sense.'

'I'm glad you feel that way. I like talking to you, Graham.'

Graham smiles; his face pinks a little. 'Aw, cheers, mate,' he says. 'That's very nice, that is. You too, mate. You too.'

'So you met Tracy,' Richard says after a moment. 'And you … fell in love?'

Graham turns his thumb upside down and nibbles at the nail, ragged and embedded in the swollen flesh. 'I don't know if I loved her straight away. But at the same time I think I did, from that first night, because I felt like I wanted to be with her all the time. She didn't get on my nerves or anything.'

'That's a great definition of love.' Richard smiles. 'Someone who doesn't get on your nerves.'

Graham returns the smile. 'Except if you're a girl. I think fellas get on girls' nerves all the time. Anyway, that was that. But she got pregnant.'

'Right,' Richard says, stalling while he takes in the lightning summary of the relationship. 'And how old were you when that happened?'

'Eighteen. She was sixteen, like.'

'That must have been very frightening.'

Graham pulls a thread of white skin from his thumb and swallows it. 'Not that I would've admitted it, but yeah. I shat myself, to be honest with you, but I kept it together – for pride more than anything. Mum went ape. Tracy's folks didn't want to know. To be fair, they didn't want to know her before; she was practically living at ours by then anyway.' He takes a deep breath. 'So then we all calmed down and Mum let us stay at hers until we got a flat sorted.'

'You stood by her.'

'Who? Tracy? It never crossed my mind not to, like. I was working at the garage, I'd cut down on the weed. I was still not drinking. I reckoned I could look after her and the baby OK.'

'That was brave.'

'Nah.' Graham's thumb begins to bleed. He licks it and keeps it on his tongue, then takes it out and inspects it. 'Anyway, Barry put a word in for us and we got a flat up at the Globe.'

'That was a housing estate?'

'Yeah, the flats where I was hanging out. You know the estate we went to after we left my old man? That was shitty, right? Well this one was a fucking sewer. Sorry. No more swearing, I promise.'

'Do you know there's a theatre called the Globe?'

Graham makes a face. 'I'm not completely stupid, you know. The flats were named after it.'

'A block of flats named after a Shakespeare theatre?' Richard hears his mother say, *Eeh, I've heard everything now.* He feels the same way. The patronising pretension is mind-boggling.

'You might well grin, Richy-Rich. You can laugh out loud if you want. It was called that because they built it in a circle with a kiddies' playground in the middle – the stage, like, you know – which lasted about ten minutes. The floors were meant to be like the audience, do you know what I mean? "All the world's a stage" and all that bollocks? You couldn't make it up, could you?' Graham rubs violently at his face and pushes his hands back through his hair. 'It p-pisses me off thinking about that place.'

'Because of the architecture?'

'Yeah. No. Yeah and no. I suppose because of what ended up happening there.'

There is a pit in Richard's stomach. He has tried for months to get Graham to move towards whatever it was that sent him here, and now that this moment seems near, he is filled with a sense of doom, as if it is all about to unfold again for real.

Graham stands up and walks over to the window. He rests his back against the ledge and crosses his feet. Richard does not move.

'I suppose when me and Trace moved there I thought, oh well, it's not for ever, you know? I thought I'd save up for a house and that. I thought, we won't be here long. Well, I mean, I wasn't there long in the end, was I? I ended up here pretty quick. Left Tracy alone with our little girl. Good work, Graham. Nice one.' He batters his hands rhythmically on the window ledge, and then, like a street magician who's collected enough coins to pack up his box of tricks and head home, he closes himself up. Closes himself up and walks out.

CHAPTER FORTY-THREE

Carol

1987

Jim calls often, once a day when he is onshore, which makes her happier than she can remember being in a long time. Nicola knows about the phone calls, but Carol says nothing to Graham. Her son's relative calm, his apparent resolve to sort himself out, is new. Carol doesn't trust it, not yet, is still tiptoeing around him, eggshells at her feet. She is desperate for Jim to visit, to see what they have, what they might have together, but mentioning his name could break whatever fragile stability Graham has managed to achieve.

Tracy begins to show towards Easter, and since her parents have disowned her, Carol goes with her on her visits to the midwife. The months clock up on the calendar. Tracy's belly gets rounder. She complains about feeling like a space hopper when she sits her CSEs. Carol meanwhile knits her new hopes into two matinee jackets and a white crocheted shawl.

One evening in early August, Carol is lying on the sofa watching *Coronation Street* with her eyes closed. When the phone rings, it wakes her.

'Mum?'

'Graham? You at work, love?'

'No, Mum. No.' A pause, a choking sound.

'Graham?' Her heart leaps to her mouth. 'Graham, love, are you all right?'

'Mum, I'm at the hospital. Trace was amazing. Just amazing. The baby, she's all pink and she's p-p-perfect and she's got these little fingers with these little nails, oh my God, the nails …'

'A little girl,' she says, eyes filling.

'She's called Jade. Like the jewel. Precious Jade. What do you think?'

'I think it's perfect,' she manages. 'New life, new start. This'll be the making of you, son. The making of you. Congratulations to you both.'

A month later, Graham, Tracy and Jade move into a flat at the Globe. Carol tries not to remember that this is where Barry lives, nor think about the fact that it is Barry who is somehow involved in this deal, someone at the council, something she won't ask about. When they leave with the baby, she feels the silence in the house like never before. Nicola is so studious. Carol will not disturb her, not at any cost. Her life's aim is to get that girl off to university, out of here. And so records play quietly, radio and television mumble, there are no arguments, there is no baby noise to fill the rooms, no smell of burp cloths, no talc, no nappies. And when Jim is offshore, there isn't even a daily phone call to look forward to. For once, she is glad of her shifts at Safeway and the company they give her. But none of the women there can put their arms around her and tell her it's going to be all right.

Tracy comes over with the baby at least twice a week. Jade is bonny and dark, by turns furious and placid. Graham comes for a roast dinner on Sundays, but as winter gets a grip of the year once more, he grows quieter, stranger, and Carol feels her guts tie into knots once again. Tracy seems on edge, seems to be cross with Graham for little things that shouldn't matter. On two consecutive Mondays after Graham has been to the house, Carol finds less money in her purse than she remembers having there. Both times she tells herself she must have spent it and forgotten.

On the last Sunday in November, Graham and his family come around once again. The moment Graham arrives, Carol can see that his eyes are puffy, red and small. He hasn't been as bad as this since around the time Ted died. He isn't aggressive, but he has returned to silence. He is smoking again, it is obvious, and it is getting the better of him. And now that Carol thinks about it, there is something about the way Tracy speaks and moves that is duller than usual, lifeless. Cautious, perhaps. She checks the girl's face for bruises but finds none.

Doesn't mean there aren't any. Carol of all people knows that.

After the meal, which he barely touches, Graham excuses himself from the table. Carol realises she has to act. She has to speak to him now before it's too late.

'Are you two all right clearing away?' she says to Tracy and Nicola, standing up.

'Yep.' Nicola is already collecting the plates. Sometimes Carol thinks she has a sixth sense, always seems to know when not to make any kind of fuss. Tracy is feeding Jade with mushed-up banana custard. Carol strokes the baby's head as she passes and gives Tracy a flat smile. 'Won't be a tick.'

Graham is on the patio, staring into space. She notices straight away that his cigarette is hand-rolled, in the shape of a Cornetto ice cream. A year or so ago she'd have been none the wiser. Now she knows exactly what this is. Here in her garden, brazen as you like, her son is smoking pot, and at the sight, she feels the familiar burn of shame.

'Aren't you cold?' She pulls her cardie tight and shivers.

Graham is in his shirtsleeves. 'I'm all right.'

Even outdoors, the smell of his smoke is sickly, sweet and heavy. This smell too, if you'd asked her last winter, she'd have said was a make of tobacco she didn't know, or perhaps an incense stick from one of those hippy shops.

'Are you all right?' He doesn't reply. 'I said, are you all right, Graham?'

'I s-said I'm all right, d-didn't I?'

She lights her own cigarette while she thinks what to say next. 'Things OK at home?'

'Yeah.' He pulls again on the roll-up, closing his eyes.

'What about work?'

'Wh-what is this?' His face flashes with an anger she knows of old.

She takes a step back. She is frightened of him, there is no getting around it. She is afraid of making him cross, of his temper, just like she was with Ted.

'I'm just asking if things are OK at work, that's all.'

'N-no you're n-n-not.'

'I am.'

'You're not. You're asking if I c-can h-hold my job down. Very d-different, Mum, very different. Just 'cos I smoke a b-bit at the weekend. Had a good chat about it with Jim, have you?'

A pain thumps at her chest. He knows.

'I haven't, actually,' she manages to say.

'Our Nicky told us. If you're wondering.'

'I was going to tell you, but I don't see that much of you, do I?'

'Oh that's right, t-turn it into a g-guilt trip.'

Every word she chooses is wrong. But for the life of her she can't figure out which are the right words, let alone how to say them. 'I just … I should've told you. I'm sorry. I didn't know how you'd take it, that's all.'

Graham sucks hard on the joint, screws up his eyes. 'I don't give a t-t-toss. That's how I t-take it.' His voice is reedy, like he doesn't have enough air to finish the sentence. The words sting.

'All right.' She tries to make her voice soft. 'But Graham, love, you're smoking that stuff in my garden as if that's a normal thing to do. And it's not. The food is barely cleared away, your daughter's still eating and the neighbours'll smell it a mile away.'

His face creases in what looks like disgust; something superior and full of hate. 'I'm sure Tom and Pauline have w-witnessed much worse c-c-coming through these walls. Don't think a bit of w-weed is gonna shock 'em, do you?'

'Son. When you had this baby, you said you weren't a kid, didn't you? So stop acting like one.'

Her cheek blazes. Instinctively she puts her hand to it.

Graham's mouth has dropped open, his eyes shining and sinking and sorry. His arrogance has vanished. In its place, there is only horror. Her face burns. Her cheek is wet. She brings her hand away. There is blood on her fingertips. Understanding seeps in. Graham, her son, has slapped her. Her son has slapped her hard, across the face, and drawn blood.

'Oh my God, Mum.' He steps towards her, reaching for her. She backs away. 'Mum … it was the ring … it was Dad's signet ring.'

No words come. She isn't angry. She isn't scared. She isn't anything. Her son has hit her. There is blood on her hand. Blood. It's all in the blood. It's in his blood. It's in him. Her son is standing in front of her and all is clear.

'Get out.' Everything stalls. She realises that she can say these words again if she has to, and she does. 'Get out. Take Tracy and the baby and don't come back until I say you can. Do you understand? Not until I say.'

All his swagger is gone. He is crying, his mouth gaping, miserable. 'Mum, I'm sorry. I'll never do it again.'

'No, you won't. Now off you go. Go on. Get out of my house. Now, please.'

He sobs into his hands, the joint burnt out between his fingers. She watches him as if through glass. He throws the filthy stub onto the wet grass and, still crying, stumbles into the house. She waits in the garden, listens to the commotion inside, feels nothing. How funny it is, she thinks. When all ability to cope with another human being leaves you – a human being you love more than your own life – how funny that calmness should come into you and fill you up, replacing all that worry, all that dread, all that waiting anxiety. Calm. Calm is all she feels. 'No more,' she says softly. 'No more.'

When the front door shuts, the house is silent. Wherever Nicola is, she is keeping her distance. Carol lights another cigarette and stares at the brown leaves mulching in the flower bed. Today her son has pushed her to a limit they both know is final. What he needs is tough love, the kind she never showed his dad. Telling him to go is the only way to help him. He will not murder Tracy over years the way Ted murdered Carol, not on her watch.

Her son will not become his father.

He will not become a murderer.

CHAPTER FORTY-FOUR

Carol

The Globe flats rise from the concrete. Porthole windows like shocked mouths gape from its brightly coloured walls. It is nearly three weeks since Carol has seen Graham, Tracy and the baby. She has tried to resist, but with Christmas just over a week away the need to make peace with her son and to see her grandchild has begun to make her feel ill. She has come up to the flats with the excuse of bringing a cottage pie but has decided to call in when she knows Graham will be at work. She can leave the dinner with Tracy, see the baby and go. Graham will know she has been, that she has not disowned him. One step at a time.

The plastic handles on the carrier bag have cut into her hands all the way from the bus stop. At the bottom of the flats, she puts down the bag and puts on her gloves. She walks down Macbeth Way, up the steps to Othello Crescent, then up again to Hamlet Walk. At the top, she turns right, relieved to be out of the stench of the stairwell.

Out over the chest-high wall, clouds hang above the white hulk of the Shopping City. It looks like an enormous Airfix spaceship has landed on the scrub, just missing the expressway that loops around it. Scalextric, she thinks. The world is cheap as plastic.

Up ahead, a man appears from the doorway of what looks like Graham's flat. Head cocked to one side, he begins to walk towards her, whistling a tuneless jumble of notes. A red baseball jacket with white leather sleeves hangs off one shoulder. She recognises the jacket before the face. Barry. She recognises the walk now, the swagger, like he's won the pools. She adjusts her handbag on her shoulder, rehearsing the piece of her mind she will give him once he's in range. She can see him quite well now. Not just the jacket and the walk, but the face starts to appear – smug, ferrety, pleased with itself.

She is grabbing him by the scruff of the neck as he passes. She is putting her hands around his neck, strangling him. She hears the choking sound he makes.

Nearer he comes, in all his horrible detail: low-slung jeans, pricey trainers, sovereign rings on all but one of his fingers. He sucks at his ciggie like it's a straw in a carton of juice, wincing as he draws back the nicotine and showing a big gap on the right side of his teeth. She doesn't remember that. Two, maybe three teeth missing now. She hopes someone punched them out. Her footsteps echo, bounce around the concrete walkway. His rubber soles make no sound. She feels her guts fold, and under her ribs a burning pain like a poker end pushed into her sternum. He is almost level now, almost passing by.

'All righ'?' He nods to her from down to up.

He does know her, then, as she knows him. His small green eyes she remembers, his sickly sweet manners – *Is Graham in, Mrs Green? How are you today, Mrs Green?*

Just as quickly, there's the back of his head, dark and spiky, a scar to the right of his crown. She has not grabbed him by the scruff of the neck, not strangled him. She's done nothing.

She stops, puts down the bag. The burn from her chest moves into her throat.

'Oi!' she shouts after him. He doesn't turn around, doesn't break his stride. 'Barry, I'm talking to you.' Still he doesn't turn or slow. 'Whatever it is you're giving our Graham, stop it, all right? Leave him alone or I'll call the police, d'you hear me? I'll call the police.'

He reaches the stairwell. He is still whistling. Without so much as glancing at her, he disappears from view.

She runs to the mouth of the stinking stone steps. He heard her, she knows it. The top of his head goes first one way, then the other, down and down. Whistling away, trying to pretend he's in no rush, but his miserable, scurrying feet give him away.

'Barry!' she shouts down. 'You're a coward, love. Did you hear me? You don't know right from wrong. I'm warning you. Leave our Graham alone. He's got a kid.'

The whistling fades. She clatters down the stairwell and onto the ground floor, just in time to see a door bang shut. Bastard. Weasel. Coward.

She trudges back upstairs to her bag and heads to Graham's flat. Never, she thinks, never ever did she imagine she'd end up walking through a place like this, let alone to visit family. Never ever did she imagine she'd shout in public like that, like she was as common as muck.

The doorbell crunches under her finger. She isn't sure whether it has rung inside and is about to press again when Tracy opens the door, but only wide enough to show half of her face. She looks frightened, but it is just a flash, a moment, before she smiles.

'Hiya, Carol,' she almost shouts.

'Blimey, Tracy, no need to yell, love, I'm only here.' Carol laughs, nerves jangling.

'Sorry,' Tracy says, though her voice is no quieter. 'It's just a surprise to see yer, that's all.'

'Are you going to let me in, then, or what?' Carol falters, no longer sure whether she is welcome, why Tracy won't open the door. Barry has something to do with this, she feels sure. 'Peace offering.' She holds up the cottage pie. Gravy has spilt thick and brown against the inside of the carrier bag; she curses at it.

Tracy retreats into the flat, still gripping the door handle. Carol edges inside and finds herself up against the girl in the gloom.

'Sorry.' She pulls at her sleeves, but there seems to be hardly enough room for her to take off her coat.

Tracy shifts but stays between Carol and the rest of the flat. 'Can I get you a cup of tea?' Christ, the volume. As if she's calling across a football pitch.

'Stop shouting, love, you'll wake the baby.' As the words leave her, Carol senses a strangeness in the air. She isn't imagining it. Yes, she's fallen out with Graham, but she's not had words with Tracy. Tracy, who usually gives her a hug, who tells her she loves her every five minutes. As Carol hangs her coat up on one of the hooks behind the door, it dawns on her: Barry has been here. Barry has been here while Graham is at work.

'Oh, I see,' she says, her heart quickening. 'I get it.'

She steps over the cottage pie and nudges Tracy to one side.

'Carol?' Tracy calls after her, her voice quavering with worry.

Round the L of the hallway Carol marches, past doors closed to her, cramped together, like something from *Alice in Wonderland*. There is only one door she needs: the bedroom.

'Carol, Carol.' Tracy is scuttling behind her, though Carol can hardly hear the girl for the humming in her ears. 'Don't go in there. Please, Carol—'

'That's exactly where I'm going, love.' She grabs hold of the door handle. Tracy has given her the right to do this. Cheating. On Graham. With Barry, of all people. She opens the door.

Graham. Graham lying on his back, fully clothed, legs wide apart, still as a dead man. The air is thick and grey, sweet and strange. Graham.

'Graham?' She approaches the bed, not understanding. She was expecting crumpled sheets, the smell of sex, but not this, not her son. 'Graham?' His belly pushes his T-shirt into a dome. 'Graham.'

He opens his eyes. His eyelids are slabs, gravestones. He rolls his head towards her and gives the start of a laugh through his nose. His eyelids give up, close.

Carol staggers backwards, ears roaring, eyes clouding. On Graham's bedside table is the black Casio watch he's had since he was thirteen, some foil, some odd bits and pieces. The room rises up in front of her – what should be dark is light, what should be light, dark. She blinks and waves at the air, feels herself falling, falling, fall …

'Carol?' Tracy crouches in front of her. She is holding out a glass of water.

There is pain on the top of Carol's head. She finds she is half lying, half propped up against the bedside table.

'You fainted.'

Carol sits herself up, sips the water.

'It's since last month,' Tracy says. 'When we saw you that day, he'd already lost his job. He just missed work too many times. He couldn't tell you. He was too ashamed, like.'

Carol's head aches. Her eyes sting, her eyelids are heavy. It's the thick air; it's making her stoned. 'Hang on, slow down. I thought he wasn't too bad.'

'He got worse. Barry's always round here and … he scares me. He gives Gray the stuff but I can't say owt to him – I wouldn't dare. And Gray's got a lot worse since … since he lost his job.' She frowns. She looks miserable, lost, like a child. She is a child. 'He told us not to tell you, like.'

Carol lets herself be helped up, then led into the lounge. The sight of Jade in the basket on the floor makes her want to yell, but instead the tears come silently.

'He just about got it together to collect his dole this week,' Tracy says. 'But I can't see him keeping it up if he gets any worse.' She reaches for Carol's hand. Together they sit down on the sofa.

'What's happened to his stomach?'

'What?' Tracy is biting her thumbnail.

'It's all swollen.'

'Oh, yeah. He eats. In the night, like. Clears the fridge out. He ate all the beef mince the other night, and I'd only browned it. I don't know how he didn't chuck it up. He eats jam out of the jar. I find the spoon on the side. He eats crisps and that, Frosties, Jammy Dodgers, you name it.'

'Why didn't you tell me?'

Tracy sniffs, looks away. 'He kept saying he'd stop.' She starts to cry.

Jade snuffles in her wicker basket. Her head and feet touch the ends. They need a proper cot.

'Carol?'

'What, love?'

'I'm so sorry.' Tracy bows her head. Her shoulders shake and she hides her face in her hands. It is not her who should be sorry. Graham has knocked her up and now he's not standing by her, not rising to his responsibilities. Just like his bloody father.

'Come here.' Carol puts her arm around the girl and pulls her close. Gently she rocks with her back and forth, kisses the top of her head. After a while, Tracy calms down enough to break away and sit back. Carol stays perched on the edge of the sofa.

'Carol?'

'You don't need to be sorry, love.'

'No. I mean, thanks. But I think … I think he's stealing.' Tracy hunches her back as she speaks, flinches almost. Why would she do that? Why would she flinch?

'What d'you mean? When?'

'It's just that, with Barry and that, you know, at night. They go out. They go down the new estate.' She folds her arms. 'It's just that sometimes there's money on the table and I don't know where it's from and he won't tell me. He tells me to keep out of it.'

'And you think he's stealing?'

'I don't know. Or dealing. I'm too scared to ask.'

'Why scared, love?'

She shrugs. 'He's just – weird, like. I feel like I don't know him sometimes. He turns.'

Turns. Carol reaches for her cigarettes, pulls out two and hands one to Tracy. What a mess, she thinks. Her own fault, letting them move here; she should've made them stay with her. They're kids, the pair of them, nothing but kids. Too much too soon. She lights Tracy's ciggie, then her own. 'I'll bloody kill him.'

'I shouldn't have said anything. I'm sorry, I just don't know what to do.' Tracy begins to cry again, holding a tissue to her nose.

'Is it just the pot he's on?'

'No … no, it's not. It's just got so much worse since … well, since before we came to yours last time, you know, when … Whatever he's on, he just can't seem to get enough of it. I can't not let Barry in – he scares me half to death. I've heard he killed some lad who grassed on him. It's supposed to be a secret but everyone knows. Except the police, like.'

Carol takes a drag of her ciggie. Another. It isn't like he's injecting, hopefully. Or is he? What is he doing? That foil, that's something to do with needles, she thinks now. And the state of him, like he can't be bothered even to live. Is that what this is about? The weight of life too much for him after everything? He looks so like Ted when the whisky had finished him off for the night and he'd collapsed, dead to the world, on the sofa. He's even getting fat the same as Ted, all belly, legs still skinny, a boiled egg in a cup. What is she supposed to do now? Leave them here? No. Impossible. They're family.

In her mind's eye, her thumbs press down on Barry's throat; she watches his eyes bulge and blacken, his stupid grin give way to a blue, lolling tongue. She should have killed him while she had the chance. She should have chucked his horrid little ferrety face over the balcony.

She stands up and holds out her hand to Tracy. 'Go and wash your face and get your coat on, love. Let's get Jade in the pram.'

'Are you going to call the police?'

'No, I'm not going to call the police. I'm going to order you a cot bed from Argos before our Jade's toes start poking out through that basket.'

CHAPTER FORTY-FIVE

Carol

Carol leaves Tracy at five and takes the bus home. Outside, it is pitch dark and bitterly cold. At the lights, another bus pulls up alongside. In the window, she sees only her own face, staggered and ugly, with two sets of eyes. The bus lurches forward. The seat shudders beneath her. She thinks about the mountain that lies ahead. Graham is not well. Ted never got the help he needed. Graham must. She just has to work out how to give him that help, how to get him to let her.

She will call Jim, she decides. She will call him and ask him to come. She will admit to him that she thinks about him all the time, that she can't do another day without at least knowing that he is, in some way, a real part of her life. He's been part of her life since she saw him at Pauline and Tommy's wedding. Part of her. She doesn't even know what she's keeping him away for anymore. Some guilt she's decided to make herself feel, some loyalty – to what? To the past? To the memory of her kids when they were little? Something, anyway, that helps no one. As Pauline said to her the other day, what is Jim if not her other half? He knows as much about her as if he'd been living under her roof, and here she is, rushing home with no thought other than to tell him what has happened.

Making the decision only makes her more desperate to act on it. Meanwhile, the thought of getting through the next few hours makes her wish she could tuck up her arms, lie on a grassy bank and roll away down the longest of hills.

Later, when Nicola asks why she's not eating her cottage pie, Carol says she's got a dicky tummy. Nicola doesn't ask after her brother. Carol can't remember when she stopped. She's lonely, Carol thinks, watching her load the meat and mash into her mouth as if it were a task she had to get through. It's as if she's grieving for a brother she's lost. Whatever happens in all of this, her daughter, her too-clever-for-me girl must at all costs get away. She must have her education. She must fly.

After tea, Nicola goes upstairs to her books. At least this house is at peace for her to do her studying. Although if Carol brings Graham here, all that will be lost. A groan escapes her. It's so bloody difficult. Can't do right for doing wrong. In the hallway, she sits down at the little table and picks up the phone. Immediately she puts it back in its cradle.

'Bugger.'

Jim is offshore. She can't call him, not until next week. Next week might be too late. By next week, Graham could be …

The phone rings, sending her shooting out of her chair. One hand to her chest, she picks up.

'Hello?'

'Carol? That was quick.'

'Jim? I was just about to phone you. I'd literally just this minute sat down.'

'Why didn't you then?'

'Because I remembered you were on the rig.'

'True. The supervisor let me use his office phone, but I don't have long.'

'You better hurry up then.'

He laughs, as he always does, as she does too whenever he says the slightest not quite funny thing. Should she just go for it, she wonders, ask him to come? Or wait and see how the conversation goes? She puts her hand over the receiver to hide her sharp intake of breath. Her head spins. It's impossible to ask him to come. How could she ask *anyone* to come down to all this, let alone a lovely man like Jim? She would be asking him to step into hell. And just because she knows by now that he would, that he wouldn't hesitate, doesn't make it right.

Jim is talking. She realises she's missed the first bit of what he's saying.

'I mean,' he says, 'it's the twenty-third by the time I get off, you know? Practically Christmas Eve. So how would that be? Just for a day or two.'

'Sorry, love, what're you saying?'

'Me coming down next week? Just for a day or two, like. For Christmas.'

A grin spreads across her face, a grin she can't shift despite the horror of the day. It pushes at her eyes, at her ears; her jaw begins to hurt, but she has no control over it.

'I mean, I could go back on Boxing Day; I don't want to ruffle any feathers.'

'Jim. I was going to ask you, but …' She's not even thought about Christmas. But yes, he's right, it's nearly here.

'That's great. That's magic.'

'Jim, stop.' She feels her face slacken as the grin leaves it. 'It's not great or magic. I mean, it is. You are. You're … But things are not … I was at our Graham's flat today. I need to tell you; it wouldn't be fair not to … You might feel different once I've finished.'

An hour later, she hangs up and presses her fists to her cheeks. Jim is coming. Despite everything – because of everything – and after all this time, he is coming back to her. *Sounds like you need a wee bit of backup*, he said. That way he has of giving so much, all the while making it seem like it's nothing. He asked her to dance that first night because he knew about her situation. But *you cannae be sitting here on your own all night* were the words he used, as if her problems began and ended there. What's heavy with him becomes light.

But she won't wait for him to sort this out for her. She will go to Graham's tomorrow. Hopefully she can get him home, get him into bed. She'll buy a lock for his bedroom door and nurse him through the heebie-jeebies. Yes, she'll nurse him as she did when he was little. Tracy can look after the little one, Nicola can go to one of her friends' houses to get on with her swotting, and her and Tracy and Jim – Pauline and Tommy as well if needed – between them they'll get Graham back on track.

It's a plan.

The only thing she can't figure out is how to physically get him home. But she'll cross that bridge when she gets there.

She leans her head back against the chair, half of her lost smile returning. Jim coming makes all the difference. He gives her faith, confidence, and she knows she does the same for him. His life was nothing, he has told her. His life means nothing without her. He loves her, has done from the moment he met her. She never thought she could offer him anything at all; she thought he wanted her only as something to fix, but she sees now that it is loyalty that he needs, someone who will never do to him what his ex-wife did, who isn't capable of such a thing. But still, even with proof, she almost daren't believe it, this love – the surprise of it, the way it came from nowhere at all at the darkest point of her life. It is a miracle, that someone like Jim would love someone like her. Ted did, had. It was just that his love was a different kind. Maybe love comes in different flavours, like ice cream. And maybe she, Carol Green, is allowed a second scoop.

CHAPTER FORTY-SIX

Nicola

2019

Some memories are harder than others. You can push the harder ones aside, over and over, like bogeymen in nightmares, but they are insistent, there at the periphery of your vision. Tonight, the bogeymen are here. They are edging in and will not be refused.

It was a little before Christmas that my mum muttered something about my brother not being well and that she was going up to see him – 1987, this must have been. I would have been about fourteen.

'Will you be all right on your own?' she said, head round my bedroom door, as ever not wanting to disturb.

'Course,' I said.

'There's Kit Kats in the cupboard if you want one.'

'Hmm.'

Hmm, like that. *Hmm.* Barely noticing her. I knew she and Graham had argued at Sunday lunch a week or two earlier. He and Tracy and baby Jade hadn't been to our house since, though I knew my mum had taken a cottage pie up to their flat the day before, but honestly? I didn't take too much notice. As usual, my schoolwork took what remained of my attention after the latest U2 album or Andy Curtis, fourth year's answer to Brad Pitt. I was lost in a world of boys, discos, fledgling gossip about who did what to whom behind the community centre, who was a bastard, who was a slag. Like any normal teenager, I was self-obsessed, oblivious, almost, to what was going on behind the scenes. Graham was simply no longer on my radar. He wasn't very friendly, he wasn't very nice. He had been my lovely brother, but he wasn't lovely anymore. I had not yet pieced together the details, was not yet able to shine the light of maturity on my own part in his decline. He had moved out, he had a family. These were the basic terms I'd have used if anyone had asked. If I had thought harder, I would have missed the old him too much. And so I didn't think of him.

My mother protected me from the reality of Graham as she had from my father. Later, she said only that she was absolutely dead set on me getting to university, or *college*, as she called it.

'You had your bedroom all done out,' she said later – one of those boxed-wine evenings, stolen cigarettes in the back garden. 'You had your desk and your lamp and that. All I had to do was keep that door closed and let you get on.'

She kept so much hidden from me, as she had from her family and friends when Ted was alive. Keeping things bottled up becomes a habit, I think. You reach the stage where even if you want to tell someone something, you can't. Did she long to tell me how difficult things were, I wonder? Did she ache to get that weight off her shoulders and at least share it with her daughter, now that her daughter was almost a young woman? Did she hover in her loneliness outside my door, wanting to knock but not wanting to disturb? My studies were sacred to her, my exit from her world her life's aim. Education was the ticket.

And so she waited on me hand and foot, kept the television low in the evenings, brought cups of hot chocolate to my room, silent as a servant.

I took it all as my due, of course. Now, I wish I could thank her one last time for shielding me from the truth while she still could. Over the years, I have thanked her with words, with gifts, but I wish I could thank her with time itself, an hour spent together, a day in Liverpool trying on clothes, going for lunch at Casa Italia on Matthew Street, the only restaurant I know that still has a dessert trolley. Without her, I would not have excelled in my GCSEs, later my A levels when Graham was in prison. I would not have reached university. Without my heritage, I would not have become interested in family law. Without my guilt-fuelled determination, I would not have become a barrister. A girl like me has much stacked against her; it takes sheer bloody-mindedness to make it through. What she did, what she gave, every day of her life, formed me every bit as much as my education did. I did not know that then, growing up.

I did not know the half of it.

I was in bed when she got home from Graham's. I heard her downstairs in the kitchen, the roar of water in the kettle. A little later, the shush of my bedroom door opening over the carpet, the amber light from the landing.

'Nicky, love?'

'Hmm.' I kept my eyes closed in the half-light.

'You in bed, then?'

Any of my friends would have answered, *Er no, Mum, I'm at the zoo*, or given out some equally crap teenage sarcasm. Where I come from, it was simply the way we spoke. But whilst I never acknowledged or even saw my mother's devotion to me, at least I can hold on to the fact that I never spoke to her with disdain. Something about our life before prevented me. Perhaps it's because, as a child, I had known in a real way the fear of losing her. I think I knew that my father might kill her, if only on some subconscious level, through processing what I heard through the walls, saw in marks on her skin, intuited from her cowed demeanour. I was always, again subconsciously, grateful to have her there.

'How's our Gray?' I asked simply, mouth thick with sleep.

'Couldn't find him, love. Out on the randan, I expect.'

'Thought he was ill?'

'Aye, well. Must be better, mustn't he? See you in the morning anyway, all right? Just off for a bath.'

The shush of the door, the landing light narrowing to a thin line, her footsteps, the bathroom door closing, the clatter of the lock, the thunder of the water. Sleep. Oblivion.

Until a little before three a.m. I can remember checking my digital alarm, the red glow of the numbers – 02.57. I can remember the pit in my stomach. No one calls with good news at three a.m.

By the time I'd pulled on my dressing gown and gone out onto the landing, my mother was running down the stairs.

'Mum,' I called after her, following her down. 'Don't open up.'

'Hello,' she said, ear cocked to the door.

Behind the bevelled glass, two figures in black. I knew it was the police. And on an instinctive level, I think I probably knew it was to do with Graham.

'Mrs Watson? It's the police, love. Can you open the door for us, please?'

My mother opened the door. The rest followed so quickly, so slowly. In they came: a man and a woman whose faces I can no longer bring to mind. I can remember sitting down on the sofa next to my mother, the warmth of her body next to mine. I can remember taking her hand as they told us.

'Mrs Watson, your son Graham's at the station. Has he called you yet at all?'

My mother shook her head.

'I need to tell you that your son has confessed to a murder. He says he stabbed Mr Barry Simmons at approximately ten p.m. A body believed to be that of Mr Simmons has since been found in Mr Simmons' residence at the Globe flats. His injuries were consistent with Mr Watson's story. Pending fingerprints and identification of the body, they'll be charging him.'

My mother was still shaking her head. Her hand trembled as she raised it to her mouth.

'Our Graham would never kill anyone,' I said. 'Our Gray wouldn't hurt a fly.' But even as I said it, I knew it wasn't true. I knew in my guts that he'd done it.

'No,' my mum said. 'It was me. I killed him, this Barry chap. It was me.' She held up her hands. 'Go on, put the cuffs on. I did it. It wasn't our Graham.'

The policewoman shook her head. She crouched down in front of my mother and spoke to her softly.

'Mrs Watson, we have the murder weapon. Your son's prints are all over it. The victim's blood was all over his clothes. I know you're his mum, but he's turned himself in and that'll count for him. I understand where you're coming from, love, but you can't help him this time, all right?'

'I did it.' My mother's voice was quiet and high and trembling. She turned to me, her eyes desperate. 'Tell them, Nicky. I was out, wasn't I, at that time? I don't have a whatsit, an alibi, do I? Tell them.'

I was crying so much I couldn't speak. I collapsed against her, sobbing into her chest.

'We've spoken to his partner, Tracy Adams,' the policewoman went on. 'She said you went to see your son, but that when he wasn't there, you came home. She says that was around nine p.m. Can you confirm that for us, Mrs Watson?'

My mother nodded. 'Yes. But then after that I killed Barry. You can't take my son. He's just a boy. He's had a lot to deal with. He's … he's not well.'

The policewoman was still on her haunches. She nodded, her brow set in sympathy. 'If you'll just come with us, we'll take a statement. Do you think you can do that, Mrs Watson?'

'Can you wait a moment? I need to make a phone call.'

The policewoman helped my mother up. I watched her stagger into the hallway.

'Please,' I said to the policeman. 'Sit down.'

'Hello.' My mother's voice came from the hallway. 'I need to put in an emergency call. To Jim MacKay. He's offshore.'

We waited. Minutes passed.

'You can come to the station with your mum,' the policewoman said.

The carriage clock on the mantelpiece struck quarter past. I met the policewoman's eye and she smiled her sympathy at me.

'Won't be long,' my mother called through, then an urgent 'Hello? Hello, yes. Jim, yes.' Her voice lowered to a whisper, but still we heard everything she said. 'No, I'm OK, I'm all right, I'm … It's our Graham. Jim, listen. Graham's been arrested. They're saying he's killed someone. Can you come? Can you come, please?'

It was no use. My mother could not protect Graham from justice. The evidence against him was overwhelming. It seems to me now that my brother was always heading for that moment, that his tumbling towards it was unstoppable from the moment we left my father. It was my father's legacy: damage, seen and unseen, bruises and broken bones, physical pain and mental chaos.

I visited him in prison, but he was taciturn and I always left discouraged. The third or fourth time I went to see him inside, he told me not to come back.

'I'll see you when I get out,' he said, realising that he'd upset me. 'G-go and s-study, will you? That's all I want you to do, all right? You have to. Otherwise there's no p-point in any of this. I d-don't want you to be c-coming here all the time. I've got nothing to t-tell you.'

'But that doesn't mean—'

'N-Nick, listen. L-listen to me.' He took both my hands in his. His grip was tight. 'Y-you better make something of yourself, all right? Otherwise, it's all just ...' He looked about him, his mouth strange with anxiety. 'P-promise me. Promise me you'll g-get a g-good job, yeah? Make p-plenty of m-money. Make shitloads. Look after Mum.'

I nodded, blew my nose. 'All right.'

'I'll see you when I get out, yeah?'

'Will you talk to someone?'

He shook his head. 'I've g-got n-nothing to say.'

'Well if you won't talk to me or Mum, talk to someone in here. There must be a counsellor or someone. There must be someone who can help you. If you don't come out a ...' I almost said *better* but caught the word just in time, 'a more peaceful person, then this has all been for nothing, hasn't it? So I'll keep up my side if you keep up yours.'

He shrugged. 'Up yours.'

'Don't joke, Graham. You can't joke your way out of everything in life. Just talk to someone. Or I ... I won't stop visiting. I'll make this trip every week and I'll probably fail everything.' I forced him to meet my eye. 'Gray? Promise me. Then it's fair.'

He rolled his eyes. 'All right. P-promise.'

CHAPTER FORTY-SEVEN

Richard

1993

Graham rubs his face, scrubbing at an imaginary mark that, it seems, will never come off. His eyes shine, but he rubs at them too with the same gruff sweeping motion. 'Have you ever done anything you really regret?'

Richard feels for his Bible. 'Yes.' He wonders whether he should tell Graham how he let a girl believe in him for years, didn't tell her what he knew to be true. How, so caught up in his infatuation with Andrew, he didn't get on a plane until it was too late. But actually, it occurs to him, he's not done anything he regrets. His regrets come from all that he did *not* do, all that he did *not* say.

Graham continues, leaving him feeling strangely interrupted. 'W-we were just so skint, you know? I promised Tracy I'd look after her and the baby, but I didn't. But it wasn't my fault.' He shakes his head, stands up and goes over to the window. He leans back against the sill and begins to scratch his forearms with opposite hands. Richard has never seen him do this before. 'I'd finish a shift and I'd say to myself, "Look, Graham, lad, go straight home." And I always thought I would. I'd even get as far as our front door sometimes. Then I'd just carry on past, back down the other stairs to the ground floor to Barry's, like. I couldn't help it.'

'So you became addicted?'

'Everyone was on something in them flats. Barry gave me everything – meth, crack, coke, temazies, you name it, other stuff. I thought I had it all under control, even when I lost my job, because Barry told me I could make loads more selling for him.' His arms are tracked with red where he has rubbed them with his blunt, bitten fingers; other marks too, faded dots that Richard hasn't noticed before.

'You sold drugs?' It's a tale by now familiar to Richard.

'I did.' Graham presses his face into his hands, then pulls them away to the sides, stretching his features into a grotesque mask. He walks across the room like this, like a ghoul. He sits down and lets go of his face, which thankfully returns to normal. Richard wishes Graham could be still, at peace. He fights the urge to lay a hand on his arm, to try to calm him, but Graham's leg begins to jiggle about. 'I did something terrible.'

Richard leans forward, but says nothing.

'I hit her.'

'Tracy?'

He shakes his head. 'I never laid a hand on Trace. It was my mum. I hit her. I cut her face with my dad's ring. And that's when the bottom dropped out of my world, d'you know what I mean? Everything was black like ... like an abyss, you know? A black hole. That's when I got into everything, really got into it, like. I just lost it. I was a right mess. I'd lost my job, so I suppose I lost my mind ... lost everything.' He bites his nail, spits it. 'What really gets me is that it was just a few weeks, like. I never even sold much in the end. Barry was still showing us the ropes when we ... when I ... He stands up again, strides over to the bookshelves and paces up and down, studying the titles. He picks up a tatty paperback, *Beyond Bars: How to Get Out and Stay Out*; puts it back. With his crew cut grown out, his hands clasped behind his back, he could be a regular guy, a father or a brother, browsing in the local library, choosing a book to take home. He could, Richard thinks, be anybody.

Graham turns to him, frowns. 'Sorry, mate,' he says. 'I can't do this today.'

CHAPTER FORTY-EIGHT

Carol

1987

Carol places her shaking hands on the front-door catch. She has been expecting Jim all day. She can see his outline now through the glass, hear him clear his throat, brush his feet on the mat outside. He is here. He is here, he is here, he is here.

She opens the door. 'Jim.' His name is a half sob into the damp palm of her hand.

He drops his bag, takes one huge step towards her and smiles. His grey-blue eyes sink at the edges in the exact way she remembers. 'My darlin'.'

His arms are around her. She is crying into his shoulder. He smells of smoke and oil and the damp wool of his donkey jacket. She told herself she would not cry. All day she has done nothing but fret about Graham and wonder how she would feel once Jim got here, but now she realises she had a very good idea how she would feel and it is this, exactly this: relief. Love, this love, feels like relief.

After a moment, she pushes back against his chest, so she can see him.

'It's you,' she says.

'It is.'

'Your hair's longer.'

'Aye well, I need a shave too. There was no time to go to the barber.'

She leads him inside, to where Nicola and Tracy are fussing with the baby. The police brought Tracy and Jade to the house after Graham was charged. The flat is now sealed off, Graham's clothes taken as evidence. Along with the knife, she imagines. It doesn't bear thinking about. She can't think about it.

'Hello, ladies.' Jim breaks into her thoughts, raising his hand in a shy wave.

'Hello, Jim,' they reply, smiling, natural, as if he's one of the neighbours popped round for a coffee.

They are all smiling, she thinks, smiling away as if none of them were in this thick smog of disaster. Thing about disaster, it occurs to her then, is that life has a way of carrying on. Doesn't she already know that? The baby still kicks on her little mat. Tracy still feeds her and changes her. Nicola still does her schoolwork. She, Carol, will still make the dinner and put the hoover round. She will still go to work, swallow down guilt in place of the food she can't eat, only to vomit it out in empty bile, in secret, in the staff toilets. They, all of them, have to carry on. There is nothing else any of them can do.

'Sit down, love,' she says to Jim.

Jim sits heavily in the armchair. He looks so much bigger, but then she's never seen him in this house before. She is not used to him. She never got the chance to get used to him, never had long enough. And yet his being here brings her such peace, as if all the time he hasn't been here she has felt his absence as something not right.

'How's he holding up?' Jim asks when she brings him some tea.

'Hasn't said much. Doesn't say anything, really. I think he's lost faith in words altogether, to be honest. Not like they got him anywhere fast, I suppose. Or anywhere at all.'

'Have they set a date?'

'First hearing will be after Christmas now. The trial will be a month or so after. They've told him to plead guilty to manslaughter. They reckon he's got a good chance, what with Barry coming at him and that. They took photos of his neck. Well, both their necks, I suppose. Graham's had finger marks on it. Barry's neck was …' Her eyes fill. The sight of her son, in that place. She tried one more time to persuade him to let her do the time. *I'll convince them it was me*, she said. But there were coppers all around and he wouldn't even look at her. He wouldn't let her.

He will go down, she knows it. They both do.

CHAPTER FORTY-NINE

Richard

1993

Viv has just taken Richard to visit the decorating area, where he watched an inmate wallpaper a room only to have to strip it and wallpaper the whole thing again. And again. And again. Now, waiting in the chapel, it strikes him as some specially designed metaphor for the hopelessness of prison existence.

'Why can't they go out and decorate real homes for those who need help?' he asked Viv. 'You know, with supervision?'

She shook her head and replied only, 'Oh, Richard.'

All of this has been compounded by his route back to the chapel: flight after flight of the stone steps that sometimes feel like torture to him now – Escher's optical illusion of the endless ascending staircase.

'Rickie Lee Jones!' Graham thuds onto his chair, his energy palpable.

'Graham, hello, yes, sorry. I'm great, thank you. Yes. Really well. Good to see you on such good form.'

Seeing Graham has begun to feel like seeing an old friend, albeit a very different kind of friend than he's used to.

Seconds pass, reminding Richard that unless Graham digs deep and finds what he needs to talk about, then they have nothing to say to one another. He and Graham are not friends. They are here for one reason only, to help Graham pick his way through what led him to do what he did, to acknowledge what he did, to take responsibility. This task is all they have in common. To think of Graham as a friend is a mistake. And yet ...

'How come you never talk about yourself?' Graham is looking at him intently, making him wonder how long he's been silent.

'I do. But these sessions are for your benefit, not mine.'

'S'pose. But don't you ever feel like saying something? About a problem or something?' Graham squints at him, his head to one side.

'Sometimes.'

'So go on then, what's your b-biggest problem?'

'I'm not here to talk about myself.' Richard cannot hold Graham's gaze, but even when he looks away, he can still feel it, boring into him. 'I lost my mum recently. I can tell you that.'

'Was she ill?'

'Oh, frail but steady, you know? A creaking gate.'

'So, what, like, old age?'

'A heart attack, apparently. She was ill, but not, I thought, seriously. It appears she tried to do too much too soon. Collapsed on the way to the post office.' Richard stands up, exhales heavily. He wanders to the window and looks out over the courtyard. The courtyard, the only external space in the place, is way too small. Cruelly so. This place! His fist lands on the sill with a bang. What would he do in here, unable to run other than on a treadmill, to enjoy a pint of bitter, to ever feel at home, breathe the air? Praying would be all he had – but then, hasn't praying been all he's had anyway, recently?

'I was in Mexico,' he says, still at the window. 'For a couple of years. Teaching English with my ... my partner. I got a call from my mother's neighbour to say she'd been ... she'd been taken ill and was in hospital. I got the first flight I could. An— my partner was going to come with me, but ... but I went alone, in the end. When I got home, my mother was already ... she'd already passed on.'

'Oh, mate. Oh, mate, that's terrible. You should have said something, you know, before, like.'

'What is there to say?' Richard turns back from the window and makes his way back to Graham.

'Do you miss her then, yeah?'

He knows he shouldn't be talking like this, but now he's started, he can't help but carry on. Something about the sweetness of Graham's expression lodged in his scrappy, grey appearance.

'I've hardly told anyone. I haven't really seen anyone since she … since I came back. I've been a bit isolated, I suppose. Can't seem to face doing anything other than come here. I run. I pray. I keep meaning to paint my mother's house, fix it up, but I …' He is aware of rattling out sentences. His speech feels disjointed, odd, as if he's lost fluency in his own language. Graham is breathing with an almost sleep-like regularity, waiting, as Richard himself has done many times. And so he continues, to fill the void. 'I guess I wish she hadn't died alone. I think … I wish I could've had one last conversation with her, you know? And known it was important.'

Graham is silent, pensive.

'It's all important, though, isn't it?' he says, after a moment, one eye half shut. 'I mean, you don't think it is until it's taken away, but let me tell you, it is. Even buying milk is important, bread, whatever, sitting on the sofa watching telly with someone, having a laugh.'

'I suppose so.'

'I mean, if she was here now, what would you say to her?'

'I don't know. I've had conversations with her in my head, I suppose. I ask God for help. There's nothing major. She knew who I was, I think, although we never said anything out loud. I think I've realised that. My parents weren't ones for saying things out loud.' He looks up at Graham, who is nodding steadily, his mouth pushed into a solemn pout. Richard tries to read his expression but can't tell what he's thinking, what he has understood, whether he is judging. If he were to guess, he would say not. This violent man is one of the kindest people he's ever known.

'Come 'ead, though, mate – what would you say?' Graham sits up in his seat and grips his knees with his hands. 'Come on, let's hear it. Pretend I'm her, like. Close your eyes and pretend she's sitting here. Talk to me. Tell me.'

Richard closes his eyes and thinks. Say goodbye. Embrace freedom. Live. Perhaps this is what has tied him to Graham all along. Both of them must face their respective liberties. They must get to a place where they can live.

'Richard,' Graham says. 'What is it you want to say to me, son?'

Richard's eyes prickle.

'Just "Hello, Mum", I suppose. "How're you getting on?" Just that. That's all I want to say to you.' His voice falters. He opens his eyes and coughs into his hand. 'And goodbye. Bye, Mum. That's all I'd say.'

Ten years his junior, Graham is wearing a face full of parental pride.

'Well, she knows that now, doesn't she?' His brow furrows with sincerity. 'You know, in your world? She'd have been listening, wouldn't she? Upstairs, like? If you said it to me, you said it to her, didn't you?'

Richard takes a deep breath. His chest feels looser. 'Yes. Thank you.'

'No biggie.'

The clock on the wall clicks. Outside, the constant cacophony of voices and machinery, the noise that has always been there, returns.

'And what would *you* say?' Richard asks.

Graham wrinkles his nose. 'Who to?'

'Your father?'

He sighs, sits back in his chair.

'I can remember one time,' he says after a moment. 'I was in bed. I was supposed to be asleep, like. It'll have been late, you know, one in the morning, or two, even. He'd've stayed for the usual lock-in at The Grapes. I could hear him through my bedroom window, swearing at lamp posts, stupid get. And then the front door opens and it was my mum opening it – she knew he'd take half an hour to get his key in; he used to scratch the paintwork, like, you know? And I heard him call her the usual, like, you know – *bitch*, that was the word he used, *stupid bitch*. And I was just lying there looking up at the ceiling and closing my eyes tight then opening them again, making stars. It was more scary being upstairs, if that makes sense, than it was being in the thick of it, like.

'And I can remember just lying there thinking what a frigging coward I was, how I should go down there and kill him, you know, get a spanner and twat him on the back of the head or wait for him to pass out and do him with a pillow, you know, just smother him while he slept. But I did fuck all. I just lay there blinking my eyes open and closed like a … like a c-coward.

'I haven't even told you why I'm here, have I? Not properly. I mean, my dad was a bastard and everything, but he was ill. He was ill. He wasn't a coward, or a junkie, or a criminal. He worked his bollocks off for us. He "functioned", as they say – held down his job in the jelly works, crushing bones. Crushing bones.' Graham gives a brief laugh, shakes his head. 'Irony's ironic, I keep telling you. I mean. Crushed bones at work, broke them at home. You should have smelt it, though, the factory. You had to wind up the car window when you drove past. I can't even think what it must've been like inside – a big smelly prison.' He presses his fingers to his eyes, mutters something that sounds like *irony*.

'And what would you say to him?' Richard asks. 'If he were sitting here, where I'm sitting. Are you strong enough to imagine that I'm him, do you think? Can you talk to me? Can you talk to me, son?'

Graham rips a strip of fingernail with his teeth and closes his eyes. His lips press together, relax, and he places a hand on each knee. The room shrinks, becomes preternaturally still. Time hovers.

'I'm sorry,' he half whispers into the quietness. 'I'm sorry, Dad.'

CHAPTER FIFTY

Nicola

2019

I wake to the sound of the key rattling in the lock. Four a.m. I have fallen asleep on Mum's bed. Hazily I pull myself up. The key scrabbles. It has lost the lock and is searching it out once more. This house is so small, I can hear every scratch and blunder. How did we ever all live here? How did I ever think it was big?

'Fuck,' I hear as I step onto the landing and smile to myself.

That'll be Jim, back from the lock-in at the Traveller's Rest. The stragglers went on there after the wake – Tommy and Pauline, of course, Uncle Johnny and his partner Bernie, and the hard core of hard drinkers, red of nose and cheek now, clothes straining against their bellies. They asked me to come, but I wanted to be here, in my mother's house, to be alone with her things. Jim went with them, one arm flung around Tommy's shoulders, the other around Graham's. A strong man broken is a hard thing to see. And like most truly strong men, Jim is kinder than any man I have known, including my own husband.

'Will you be all right here on your own, love?' Pauline had asked as they got themselves together to leave, a rolling, raucous shambles if ever there was one. Her eye make-up was smudged, all but gone from her eyes. At seventy-odd, her black hair is harsh against her pale face, but without it she wouldn't be herself.

'I'll be fine.' I'd taken her hands in mine. 'I just want to be on my own now.'

'Right you are, love.' She'd raised her shoulders briefly and given me a sad smile. 'Come here.'

I am small-boned, like my mother, and to be hugged by Pauline is to be swaddled in warmth, soaked in perfume, bathed in soft flesh. My love for her is old. It is the love of the child who called her Auntie P, that child become woman, become mother in her turn. My love for Pauline has matured with each stage of my life, a companion to the love I have for my mother, a love that has redefined itself and deepened with each new nuance of understanding of my mother's past, the past before me and the past I shared with her. When I was little, Auntie P was mad and funny and always dressed up to the nines. She was the woman whose tidy house we went to for tea sometimes, who bought a SodaStream machine so she could make us dandelion and burdock in the summer and pass it over the fence. She is the friend who never needed to ask, who understood without words, who gave my mother the number for the women's refuge, who helped move us into what we all called 'the terrible house', who made dinner for us the day we moved back home, sandwiches the night Graham went to prison. *She's a bloody rock, is Pauline*, my mother used to say. And the more I think of that everyday phrase, the truer it is; the geology of Pauline lies in strata laid down over years beneath my mother's life and the life of her family.

'Hey,' Pauline had said, rubbing my arm once the monumental hug had finished. 'No more tears, eh? I've told Tommy we're coming down to London to see you. He said he'd book us a Travelodge, flash get. Trump's got nothing on him, has he? En suite and everything.' She was trying to make me laugh and I loved her for it. 'So, you figure us out a restaurant, all right? None of your rubbish, somewhere decent. Somewhere that makes them Kir royales you made us last Christmas, eh? Our treat. What d'you say?'

I'd nodded. 'Yes. Yes, let's do that. Let's do it soon.'

Another hug and she was on her way, off to drown the sorrow of her best friend's passing, to give her the send-off she deserved in the pub they all used to go to.

And now here's Jim, at four a.m. A shuffle, a bump – the phone table possibly – another expletive, and he's at the foot of the stairs. I see his shoes, his cream woollen socks. There was no way he would have forgone the kilt. This was Carol's funeral, after all, and her fondness for him in traditional dress is the stuff of family legend. These days, he's more careful with his skean-dhu.

'Jim,' I whisper, though there are only two of us here.

He looks up, sees me. Grins. His hair is almost white now, infused with the merest blush, the colour of certain rosé wines.

'You OK?' he says.

I nod. 'You?'

He nods, but his mouth crumples. He meets me at the bottom of the stairs and pulls me into his arms. 'Ach, Nicky.'

We dissolve into each other's shoulders. This loss is too big, I think. We will never get over it.

He takes my hand and leads me to the kitchen. We sit at the table and he pours us a tumbler of whisky each. I marvel at his capacity for drink. He is, let's face it, a functioning alcoholic in medical terms, but how different he is from my father. I'm not sure if drink unleashes one's true nature, or if it is simply the case that we all have demons and it's just that some demons are more sensitive to booze than others. Whatever, Jim's drunk is this: a little clumsy, a little more affectionate, a little more philosophical.

'What a day,' he says, swirling the whisky in his glass.

'She would have loved us all being together.'

'Aye.' He takes a swig. He knows I mostly mean him and Graham. Their relationship is a credit to both of them. And perhaps to Richard Crown.

CHAPTER FIFTY-ONE

Richard

1993

On Thursday morning, Richard approaches the prison gates with trepidation. Graham comes up for parole in two weeks, a fact that only now registers in all its vital clarity. It's possible they have only two sessions left, if the decision goes the right way. Graham's parole, Richard realises, has become, in a sense, a deadline they both share. Graham must reach the end of what he has to say next week; Richard has to find a way to help him do that. After that, it is time for both of them to step into their lives and, finally, live.

These days, he's used to the feel of so many keys in his hands. The task of unlocking and locking the doors and gates is oddly soothing. The keys, once heavy, cold, a little intimidating, are now comfortable, practical, warm.

He thinks about how time has passed, for him and for Graham. For all the lads in here. He thinks about how all the phrases relating to time change its meaning so dramatically. To spend time, he thinks, means to use time in some way for some discernible purpose – leisure, industry, work. People waste time, or believe they have, after an hour or two lost in front of the television, when in here time wasted can mean months, years, a life. Time is money for those in business, for whom every second counts in dollars or pounds. In here, they *do* time – such a contradictory phrase, holding as it does the idea of asserting oneself in some way over that vast, uncontrollable force, when the reality is that there is no control to be had, or very little, in here. When these boys do time, it's more a case of passively grinning and bearing it.

He arrives at the education office with no memory whatsoever of performing his infinite security rituals, only of the thoughts that accompanied them.

Vivian is at her desk.

'Hello, chucky egg,' she says. 'How're you diddlin'?'

'Good morning, Viv. I was just thinking about time, actually. About how our context changes our relationship with it in the most mundane yet massive way.'

'Bloody hell, Richard, that's enough with the small talk – can't we go a bit deeper?' She chuckles, shakes her head and gives him a wry look. In that moment, it hits him: her laughter doesn't always signify amusement; it is an integral part of how she manages the world. Why has he not understood this before? Months ago, when Frank was criticising him as Richard listened cringing in the corridor, Viv had laughed. But it was not out of disloyalty, he thinks now; rather discomfort. He sees now that she stifles laughter almost every time she speaks, as if the gravity of her workplace has her teetering on a brink between hilarity and madness. She is, he realises, quite possibly as shy as he is. With a sense of shame, he sees that she is, and always has been, a friend to him, more than he has to her, and he watches with almost overwhelming fondness as she bustles past him and out of the office.

'Sorry,' he says, meaning more.

'Don't be sorry, love; it's only me mucking about. At least you think about things. What conclusions did you reach anyway, Professor Hawking?' She heads into the kitchen, which is no more than a broom cupboard with a small sink and a power point. Richard stops at the doorway, as there isn't space for two.

'Well,' he says.

As he tells her his thoughts, Viv busies herself at the sink, rinsing mugs and teaspoons, wiping down the draining board. He finds her way of listening, always whilst doing something else, oddly comforting, and it occurs to him that his mother was always busy whenever he told her anything, and that too always gave him the freedom to talk.

Viv has finished washing up and is putting the kettle on to boil. She puts her hands on her hips and fixes him with a stare. 'I tell you what, love. You need to get out more.'

Richard feels himself blush, but he does laugh.

'You for coffee?' She points at him, raises her eyebrows and giggles.

Richard is still laughing. 'Me fuckoffee, yes please, thanks.'

'You're trying to tell me you've heard that one before?'

Richard arrives late at the chapel, fearing that Graham won't turn up, or worse, that he already has, only to find an empty room. If this is so, they will only have one session to conclude their time together, and at the moment, that doesn't feel like enough. But when he turns the last corner, Graham is ahead of him, heading towards the door, shambling in his usual way in the baggy prison sweatpants and a T-shirt.

'You beat me to it today, Graham.'

He turns and grins. He is unshaven, the ghost of a beard blackening his jaw. This shading makes his face appear even thinner, and Richard feels a stab of concern. But Graham's eyes are clear; a glance at his forearms – they are unmarked.

'Good to see you,' Richard says as they take their seats. 'Are you growing a beard?'

Graham rubs his chin. 'I'm hoping for the full grizzly like yours.' He stands up, adjusts his chair, sits down again.

Richard waits for him to stop fidgeting and focuses on what he should say.

'Graham,' he says once Graham is sitting still. 'Listen to me. I want you to listen.'

'All right.'

'We've talked a lot these last months, and I think you've managed to lift some of the weight we talked about. But we've got a little way to go yet, and I guess, now that your parole is upon us, time is of the essence.'

Graham grins. 'Oh man, the way you speak.' He pinches his nose and shakes his head.

But Richard has no time for this. He must find a way to pin Graham down. Perhaps he should tell him something more about himself; Graham seems to respond better when it is a conversation rather than a confession. He tries again. 'I wanted to tell you today that I've been flailing around a bit lately too, not knowing what I was doing, that kind of thing. Since my mother died, I've been kind of stuck. I haven't done anything with her house, haven't decided whether to sell it or decorate it and live in it. And through my conversations with you, I think I've realised that what I was blaming on grief is in fact down to fear. I'm afraid, Graham. I'm afraid of going out there and living. So you see, we both need to fight our fear and find a way to embrace the future. What do you think? Do you think we're similar?'

'Especially now I've got the beard.' Graham grins idiotically. 'We're like twins.'

'Yes.' Richard humours him. 'But what I meant is in the sense of not really making the decision to live, to embrace life rather than hiding from it.'

'What do you mean?'

'I think you need to start thinking about your parole.'

'Think about my parole? What for?'

'Are you going to stay out, Graham? That's what I mean. Or are you going to be coming straight back in like Craig and some, well, many of the others? What I'm saying is, are you going to use the revolving door or the permanent exit? Can you be the one who gets out and stays out?'

Graham exhales loudly and folds his arms. 'It's hard out there, Richard. You don't know what it's like.'

'Don't I?' Richard raises his eyebrows in challenge.

Graham looks away and then back. To Richard's relief, there is a slight upturn at the corners of his mouth. 'OK, OK, you do know what it's like outside. It's me that doesn't, but you know what I mean.'

'Yes. And I know that sharing the moments that have scarred us brings intimacy. And intimacy can be as frightening as freedom.'

Graham looks up, meets his eye, holds it, and Richard feels the intensity of them both, together, in the now, the right now.

'You became tired last week,' he says, 'but you're here today. You always come back, and I think this is because you know that there's more to do and that you can only do it here. With me. And very soon you won't be able to come here, do you understand what I'm saying?'

Graham nods.

'I'm not asking you to find God or anything like that. I would never do that. But you need to think about how you might go forward once you get out, and I believe you can't quite do that at the moment. You're almost ready, but you're not … you're not ready.'

'You mean I need to tell you what I did?'

Richard sighs. There is truth in what Graham says, but the right spirit is missing. If Graham is to unburden himself, he has to do it freely. 'The weight you talked about, remember, when we talked about flying? That weight, whatever is left of it, needs to go. You don't need to tell me specifically but if you can talk about it, it might help lift it.'

'I know. I know.' Graham clasps his hands in his lap and bows his head. 'I can't go anywhere with all that, can I?'

'If you leave here still carrying … all that … my fear is that it will prove too heavy and you'll be back inside within months.'

Graham looks at him but says nothing. After a moment, he nods and pushes his hands between his knees.

Richard tries a more specific tack. 'Graham, your dad died a long time ago. You've spent years of your life in here; you have a child. How much longer are you going to blame your father, or anyone else for that matter? Blame yourself? How can blame help you? How will it help you when you get out?'

Graham's skin flushes red and he bows his head. Tears, Richard suspects, for the first time in five months, are being blinked back furiously beneath that thick black fleece of hair. But all he can see are Graham's hands, knotted between his knees.

'Graham,' he whispers. 'It's time. If you can brave it today, we can chat about nothing at all next week. We can simply say goodbye and good luck, can't we?'

Graham lifts his head. His eyes shine. 'He was such a good laugh, like. My dad. I never told you that. He was hilarious when he wanted to be. Used to do Max Wall impressions in the lounge in his long johns and stuff like that. He used to make jokes. It was the way he said them, you know, quick-fire, he had us all in hysterics. It's just that when he was nice, he was wicked, you know?'

'No one's a hundred per cent evil.'

'He wasn't evil. I've spent a lifetime blaming him for everything, but it was me who put myself here. That's what you want me to say, isn't it?'

'I only want you to say what you feel. I like talking to you, Graham. You have so much to give. And … you've had a real impact on me.'

'Get lost.'

'You have!' Richard pauses. 'You said in one of our sessions, very bravely, that you were addicted to drugs. Do you blame drugs?'

'No. But yeah, I was an addict. Barry had this gear.' Graham begins to scratch at his forearms.

'You were dealing,' Richard prompts.

Graham seems not to hear. 'Barry was training us. Taking the money, dropping off the orders. It wasn't rocket science, like. We went round to this lad's. Cornflake, he was called – he had ginger hair – to collect the dough. And he wasn't in, Cornflake, I mean. I can remember her, Leanne, his missus. I can remember Barry pushing the door in on her and slamming her with it, into the wall, like. The kids were running about inside the flat and this Leanne was shouting from behind the door, "Get in Mummy and Daddy's room!" Like that. It was horrible. It made me feel sick, but I was a bit out of it. Anyway, Barry went inside, banging on the wall all the way down the hall shouting, "Cornflake! Cornflake! You ginger get." I'm telling you this, like, but I don't know whether I remember it or whether I've thought of it so many times I've kind of practised it in my mind, d'you know what I mean?'

Richard tries to slow his breath as he inhales, to keep it quiet, but it rattles on the way out, as if his windpipe were full of stones.

'So Barry made her, Leanne, he made her leave the bedroom door open so she wouldn't try anything. Her and the kids were on the bed. She had these massive slippers on – they were huge white fluffy things.'

'When was this?'

Graham looks up, meets his eye. 'It was the seventeenth of December 1987.'

Chilled by the precision, about where it might lead, Richard presses his mouth closed.

'It was about ten in the evening, apparently. According to the autopsy.'

'OK.' Richard puts his hand over his mouth and nods. He has a grim feeling in his belly, anxiety lodged like a rock.

'So, yeah, so Barry, right.' Graham looks away and down. 'He was asking for the money, hassling Leanne. She said she didn't know anything about it. The kids were crying, she was crying. It was horrible, horrible. I was looking in the kitchen but I sort of lost track of what I was supposed to be doing and I started eating chocolate from the fridge. It was a big bar of Cadbury's Dairy Milk. I put too much in my mouth and it went all thick, you know? I felt like I was choking, so I went to the sink to get a glass of water. I mean, when I think about that, I realise I was off my head. Not the screaming abdabs or anything, just not properly there, doing low-key weird stuff like eating someone else's choccy. And I could hear Barry getting lairy, nasty, like. Next thing, he'd smashed something. I went into the hall to see what was going on, and he had this pottery dog thing, an ornament, like. It had no head because he'd smashed it off and its neck was all smooth, but it had like a point sticking up – the edge, you know?'

'Mm-hm.' Richard can think only of this sharp porcelain edge, can see it in his mind's eye: raised, blade-like.

'Anyway, it was chaos. Leanne was shouting, the kids were crying. She was holding them in the bed; she'd got them under the duvet with her, you know, maybe to protect them or something, and then Cornflake arrives – her fella, like, you know. He had ginger hair, did I say that?' Graham puts his face in his hands. 'Fuck, this is hard.'

'You're doing great,' Richard says gently.

Graham drops his hands to his lap and laces his fingers together. 'So this guy, I mean, I knew him from round about, he was a hard case, like, he starts shouting "What's going on?" and that. And Barry kind of pushes past him and does one.'

'Barry ran away?'

'Yeah. He didn't think Flakey'd be there. He used to collect when he thought the fellas weren't in. The women were easier to scare, like, get the money off and that. So then I was left with this ginger get and he goes for us. Next thing I'm on the floor and I'm trying to push him off and I'm thinking about how I need another glass of water and how I need to get out of there. I get on top of him, anyway. And I ... I just knew I had to get out, like.' He stops.

'And then what happened?'

'Well, I get him off us and I'm flying out of there and ... It all happened at once. I get round the hall, I get as far as the door, and he starts shouting at her, at Leanne, like, calling her a bitch, a stupid bitch for letting us in, and I heard something. I mean, I'll say now that I heard a slap, a punch, whatever, but God knows what I heard. Anyway, that was it.' He rubs his face and sighs. 'I went back.'

Richard's heart tightens. His brain races – to Graham, to this red-haired man, to the glinting porcelain edge. 'And then?'

'The china dog thing was there on the floor and I grabbed it and I jumped him and he fell. I put the point to his neck and I could feel where it was snagging against his skin and I felt like I was tripping a bit, you know? I mean, I wasn't, but I think I was in state of panic or something. I threw the pottery thing down, anyway, I don't know why, and just sort of had my hands round his neck, like, telling him never to call his girlfriend ... that word, telling him he was a disgrace and that, hitting a woman. He was making this sound, coughing, and I was pushing, and it was like he was a doll and he was all pink, like plastic. And then I think I must have realised I was choking him.' He sits back in his chair and crosses his legs. 'So I left.'

Richard shakes his head, confused. 'So you didn't kill him, this Cornflake chap?'

'No. I ran after Barry. He was in his flat. I went tearing in there, all fired up, like, and I was like, what the hell? I was furious with him. Doing his rounds, intimidating girls when their boyfriends weren't home, and he'd almost made me kill someone, like.'

Richard holds his breath.

'Barry must've been scared I was gonna do something to him. I must've looked mad or something 'cos he took us into his kitchen and he was all chatty, like, and then he opened a drawer, all smiles, and just … he just goes for us with this big knife, you know, like a carving knife? I dodged it. I told him to calm down, but he was all pumped up. We both were. I mean, I knew he'd killed some lad on the estate – that was the rumour anyway, so I was pretty scared. So, we … we fought. And I … I …' He puts his hand over his face; his mouth contorts.

'Graham, I'm here. I'm listening. You can do this.'

Graham is crying. He plunges his face into his hands. 'I killed a man. I killed a man, Richard. I took a life and I can't give it back.'

Richard lets the words settle around them. He is about to speak when Graham sits up, wiping at his face with the backs of his hands. Richard digs in his jacket pocket, finds a tissue, hands it to Graham.

'Ta,' he says, and blows his nose. 'I called the busies. The police. My hands were covered in blood; his blood was all over me, all over the phone. That's all I can remember. I was in the lounge, they said, on the floor, when they got there. I was in a state of shock, crying and that. They could hardly get a word out of us.' Graham sits up straight, finally, and spreads his hands. He stops fidgeting and becomes very still. 'I confessed straight off. I didn't try to duck out of it. But today I want to say properly that it was my fault. It was me. Not drugs, not my dad, me.' He pauses, to control his shaking voice. 'And that's why I'm here.'

Richard's chest contracts slowly. He'd thought himself ready to hear Graham's confession, but now the truth of it is out, he feels a suspended sense of shock, as though his body is aware, overhead, but is preparing to deal with it later. At the same time, everything falls into place. It is possible to know someone, he thinks, to know them well, and still, after one more conversation, to have the solution to the whole puzzle of them in so far as anyone can fathom another human being. Graham has confessed – not to God, no, but he has got the words out before Richard and before Richard's God, and that is enough. This is how Graham's unburdening has gone, how it always had to go.

Seconds pass.

Richard senses that Graham is waiting for him. 'How do you feel?' he says.

Graham puffs, shakes his head.

'Are you sorry?'

'Of course I am. Fucking hell, Richard.' Graham rubs at his hair, blinks repeatedly, but tears win out and run down his face. 'It's like, my whole life, everything good I tried to do, I messed up, you know? And everything bad I tried not to do, I ended up doing. I mean, it's so f-f-final. Life is the last thing you can take from someone, and you can't give it back and there's nothing you can do to change it. There's nothing *I* can do to change it. And I get eight poxy years. Why? Because Barry attacked me. But he didn't kill me, did he? He didn't take my life. I *wanted* to come here, do you know that? I turned myself in. I should stay in here for ever for what I did. They should throw away the key.' He blows his nose again, wipes at his eyes.

'It strikes me,' Richard says after a moment, 'that your sentence began more than six years ago. You were suffering long before you ever came here, weren't you?'

Graham bows his head and sniffs. 'S'pose.'

'But like you say,' Richard continues, 'no one else did what you did; it was you. And it takes a lot of strength to talk about something like that, to accept responsibility. I guess now the important thing here is to say sorry and put it behind you.'

'I *am* sorry.' Graham covers his face with his hands again. 'I'm so sorry and I'm so ashamed. I'm sorry.'

Richard crosses himself and moves his chair alongside Graham's. He hesitates a moment before placing his hand on Graham's shoulder. This is not permitted, but in all humanity, in all faith, in all conscience, Richard cannot leave him in his loneliness. 'Graham. You've served your time. Nothing in the past can be improved or changed by you staying here, and yet nothing can be gained in the future by you leaving under the weight of what you did. Guilt is not helpful. It is there to tell us when we have behaved badly and when we need to make amends, but other than that, it has no purpose. You have taken responsibility. You have paid. What you have done is irreversible, but your journey is not. It's not. Your family has suffered enough. You have suffered enough. Your daughter misses her father; your girlfriend wants you home. Your mother wants you home. Your sister wants you home. You have to forgive yourself as God forgives you, otherwise nothing good can ever come of what happened. Do you understand that? Without forgiveness there is no freedom, inside or outside, not in any real sense. You have to forgive yourself as others forgive you. Do you remember I promised never to lie to you all those months ago? Well, I can tell you now, in all truth, that God does forgive you.'

Graham pulls at his face. 'Do you forgive me?'

'Of course. Yes, I do.'

CHAPTER FIFTY-TWO

Carol

1993

Carol sits back and checks her foundation. Hard to tell if it's blended properly without daylight, but her reflection's not bad, she decides; not for forty-odd, for a woman who isn't a film star or anything, and who's had three kids. She decides she looks like an old Snow White, if Snow White had actually given birth to all seven dwarves. The thought makes her laugh; it's like something Pauline would say. She likes the dress she's wearing too, although she worries it's a bit young for her, the pink a bit bright. Jim made her buy it when she passed her Grade 1 accountancy. She wore it when he took her to the Casa Italia in Liverpool to celebrate. She got tipsy on red wine and Jim had to give her a piggyback to the train station.

'Carol!' Jim shouts in a whisper, so as not to wake the others. Tracy and Jade are staying, so Tracy can look after Katy and take her and Jade to school.

'Coming!'

Lipstick. Inside the drawer of the dressing table, the little compartments are lined with red velvet. She waves her finger over the top, looking for the newest and finding it: Fuchsia Frenzy. A change from Red Tulip, but it's a perfect match for her dress. She smooths it over her lips, almost rubs it off, worried she's making too much effort.

'Carol!'

'Coming now, love.'

She stands and picks up her cardie, slips her lipstick and mascara into her bag, just in case she gets upset once she's there and makes it run. She's been in and out of tears for the last three days.

She stops at Katy's room. Still asleep, with that expression of peace she always has, this funny, fair child, so like Jim when he sleeps, except much prettier, and with a much smaller nose. And she doesn't snore. Or fart for that matter. Not loudly, at least. Carol lets her cheek hover millimetres from her daughter's mouth, almost touching, so that she can feel the regular soft, warm bursts of breath. After a moment, she kisses her little girl on the forehead, making her stir and roll over with a groan. She tucks the covers over her, kisses her again and pulls the door to behind her.

She thinks about checking on Tracy and Jade in the spare room but decides to let them sleep. They'll all be up for school soon enough. Funny to think that Katy's a couple of years younger than Jade, what with her being Jade's auntie. Still, a higgledy-piggledy family is better than a broken family, and by tonight, once Nicky gets home, they'll be a whole higgledy-piggledy family once again. Graham sounded bright on the phone. Said he'd sorted himself out, just like he'd promised, that it had taken him almost until the end of his sentence but that this Richard chap he'd been talking to had really helped him.

'Mum,' he'd said. 'I'm ready.'

Fingers crossed.

Jim is in the hall with his coat already on.

'About ti— Wow!' He smiles up at her, making her feel self-conscious. He hands her a lukewarm cup of tea. 'It was hot when I made it. You look beautiful, by the way.'

Carol downs the tea in one go.

'Are we right?' she says.

'You're a cheeky bastard, you are. I've been waiting for half an hour.'

She chuckles and puts on her coat, opens the front door. 'This is it,' she says, something like hope fluttering in her chest. She waits for Jim to pull the door shut. 'Seems strange going without our Katy.'

'She'll be fine. She's got Tracy to look after her. Did you eat something?'

'Couldn't face breakfast.' Carol looks back at the house. 'Did you hear me tell Tracy where to find the fish fingers?'

'Look,' says Jim, 'she might not be the sharpest tool in the box but she can find a packet of fish fingers in a three-drawer freezer.'

'What about the heating? Can she work our gas fire?'

'She'll be fine. Stop worrying.'

'I'm not.' Carol gets into the car.

Jim is laughing. What's he laughing at?

CHAPTER FIFTY-THREE

Richard

1993

Richard sits on a camping chair, sipping tea in front of the fire. There is white paint on his old cord trousers, on his hands, on his socks and, he suspects, in his hair. There's white paint on the carpet too, where it escaped the ground sheet, but he doesn't care. The carpet is destined for the tip anyway, and actually, thinking about it, he will have to pull it up tomorrow if he wants to freshen up the skirting boards. Why didn't he think of that before? He's done it in the wrong order. Ah well, it's a learning curve.

The hot tea washes down his dry throat. It tastes absolutely delicious – almost shockingly so. Like nectar, as the saying goes, and he realises it's because he's been painting for over three hours without a break. He's worked up a labourer's thirst. He wonders if this is the first time he's ever tasted tea as good as this, ever worked so hard for it. It seems worth it. And he's enjoyed stretching his arms, clambering up and down the stepladder, the physical effort, the concentration that stills the mind, the earning of the break. He's enjoying sitting here now, feeling the ache after the stretch, thrilled to bits with how transformed the room is and by the hot, sweet taste of this magnificent tea. But most of all he is enjoying the buzz of finally doing something, something that isn't perhaps the most dramatic thing in the world but that to him feels seismic, life-changing. As if to reward him with its heartfelt agreement, the sun drifts out from behind a cloud, bathing the room in warm yellow light.

The house clearance people came yesterday. They took everything. *Everything.* Richard has only this camping chair and a blow-up camp bed upstairs. It is all he needs until he has finished painting the house, and, frankly, it is utterly liberating to be without any real material possessions. The once brown and beige floral living room, now so bright in the morning sun, adds to his feeling of lightness. He chose soft cream for the walls, white for the ceiling. He wasn't up to stripping the wallpaper – he didn't know where to begin – so he has contented himself with painting over it. It might not be what you're meant to do, but it looks brilliant, just brilliant, and it's his house now. Maybe he'll lay a wooden floor, throw on a rug, like that picture he saw in the magazine Viv showed him. Viv will have some ideas. She said she'd come over at the weekend and help him decide. She has some catalogues, she said, one from the new Swedish place, which she says has the nicest, freshest-looking things she's ever seen, and great prices. When the time comes, she said she might even come with him and help him choose. The idea warms him.

He drains his tea. One more coat on the back wall and he can move on to the kitchen. By next Thursday he hopes to have the whole of the downstairs gleaming like a grin.

'Come on, Richy-Rich,' he says to himself, standing and rolling out his shoulders. 'Time to crack on, you lazy get.'

The following Thursday, on his way into the castle, Richard strokes his chin. It is still strange to feel bare skin where his beard used to be, where it was until yesterday afternoon, when Raymond, the same barber his father used to take him to as a kid, shaved the whole lot off with a cut-throat razor and clouds of white foam. After which, delighted with his new youthful appearance, Richard called in at the pub. He only meant to have one for the road but ended up in conversation with a man called Doug, who turned out to be a primary school teacher on his way home from work and who insisted on buying him a pint. And then, of course, Richard knew it would be rude not to buy him one back. By the time he left, at almost nine p.m., he had made a loose arrangement to see Doug there the following week, the thought of which makes him smile now as he makes his way through the myriad doors and locks of the prison.

At the top of the stairs, he steels himself. His appearance has changed dramatically; it will not go unnoticed. Sure enough, as he steps into the office, there are whoops of appreciation from Viv and the gang. Someone wolf-whistles. He thinks he hears relief in the mix.

'That's right swish, is that, like a film star,' Viv says, looking about her. 'Who does he look like?'

'I know,' says the woman with the black hair whose name Richard has forgotten. 'That one off *ER*.'

'That's it,' says Viv, clicking her fingers. 'Whatsisname. Thingio. Him.' She smiles, as if satisfied at getting to the bottom of it. 'He's got two eyes and one nose, hasn't he?' At this, she laughs so much she has to hold her own nose to stop herself from choking.

Richard laughs along but doesn't try to think of a comeback. It will doubtless fall flat, and it's enough that they know he can take a joke. He rolls his eyes, waves and takes his leave.

On the stairs, Viv shouts after him. He waits while she catches up, surprisingly nimble in her little white pumps.

'I've got to go to D Wing anyway,' she says. 'I may as well chum you along. Still on for Saturday?'

'Absolutely.' As they continue down the stairs together, he tells her of his decorating progress. 'It's not perfect,' he says, 'but it looks so much better and now I can't wait to get it all done.'

They reach the bottom of the stairs, where Viv must cross the courtyard and he must turn back to head down the corridor and up another flight of stairs.

'Well, I'll love you and leave you,' she says. She makes to go but hesitates. 'Are you all right, chuck? You seem a bit …'

'Yes. Yes, I'm fine. Do you remember Graham?'

Viv nods; her eyes widen a fraction. 'Of course. Seagull man.'

Richard smiles. 'The very one. Yes, so this'll be the last time I see him.'

'You hope.' She chuckles.

'Quite. I don't know, I guess it seems strange that they're just released like that – you know – like … well, like seagulls.'

'I know. And some of them have got nothing, you know, absolutely nothing. And no one.'

Richard frowns. 'I guess I'm just thinking it's a shame we can't bring anything in with us – you know, by way of a parting gift.' He'd wanted to buy Graham his own copy of *Jonathan Livingston Seagull* to take home, but it's against regulations to bring anything into the prison. He could, he supposes, send him one in the post.

Viv places a hand on the door handle. 'They don't expect anything. Anyway, your new look is present enough.' She punches him lightly on the arm. 'It'll give him a laugh, if nothing else.' She unlocks the door and is still mugging when she steps out. 'Seriously, though, you look really great. Ten years younger, at least.'

'Thanks.' He raises a hand in a wave. 'Viv?'

She pops her head back round the door. 'Yeah?'

'I was thinking of going into town after work for some new shoes.' He is thinking of next week, of Doug.

Viv looks lost for a moment, before she slaps her own forehead. 'And you need a personal shopper?'

'I don't want to impose. But I'd buy you dinner afterwards.'

Her face breaks into a wide smile.

'Or not,' he says. 'If you have to rush home, it's not a problem, forget I said it.'

'Richard, shut up, will you? Bloody hell, I can't get a word in edgeways with you sometimes, you gabby bastard. I'll see you in the office when you finish and we'll wander down together, all right? They've got some nice ones in Dolcis. Pink cowboys boots … Just kidding. And you don't need to buy me dinner – we can go halves.' With that, her head disappears behind the door and she is well and truly gone.

In the chapel, Richard takes his seat and waits, stroking his naked chin. He has the impression of touching someone else's face. It is warm, slightly oily, with the merest abrasion of growth beneath. It would be good to touch someone else's face, he thinks, and have someone touch his.

Graham's whistling reaches him from the corridor. After a second or two, he appears at the doorway and makes an exaggerated show of stopping, holding the door frame as if for support.

'Fuck me,' he says loudly. 'It's Clark fucking Kent.'

Richard laughs – a proper laugh that requires a small recovery afterwards. 'Graham, I'm going to miss your sense of humour.'

'Nothing humorous about it. Jesus – sorry – Christ – sorry – but God – ah, shit, sorry – you look young.'

Richard ignores the trio of blasphemy. 'Try not to sound quite so surprised.'

'I knew you were young underneath.' Graham sits down, eyes still wide.

'What about you then?' Richard asks, keen to divert the glare. 'You're the one with the old-man beard now. Not tempted to shave?'

Like his hair, Graham's beard is thick and black, although his beard is flecked with a lighter, nutty brown.

'Too right,' he says. 'I'm shaving it next Thursday morning.'

'Shaven for release, like a lamb to the ... to the summer.' Richard winces at his almost faux pas. 'Good idea.'

Graham is still grinning, his shoulders wide and straight against the back of the chair. He looks away and back again. 'I can't get over it, like. I keep expecting you to pull your shirt off and fly out the window in your blue tights. You look so different.'

'I feel different. Free somehow – I can't explain it. But we're not here to talk about me, so stop trying to distract me. Are you ready for next week?'

Graham glances at the floor. 'S'pose.' He looks up, smiles. 'No, yeah. Yeah, I am.'

'Who's coming to meet you, do you know?'

'Spoke to my mum; she's coming with Jim in the car, like.' He mentions Jim casually and seems cheerful. Richard is glad they're coming. He feels connected to them, through Graham. He trusts them to look after him, this precious, precarious man.

'I'll probably see them on my way in,' he says. 'I always see the crowd waiting outside on a Thursday morning.'

'You should say hello, like. My mum'd be made up. She knows about you. I've told her about you, like.'

He can see that Graham is serious and perhaps more – that he is asking him to do this.

'I will,' he promises.

'She's got dark hair, going grey, sort of shoulder-length and really straight. She's skinny. Well, she's got a bit of a pot now, but she's thin on her arms and legs, and she's small height-wise. Erm, she often wears nail varnish for special occasions and she'll deffo be wearing lippy. I mean, I've not seen her without lippy for years, 'cos I s'pose, coming here, she was always in her best togs, like – always done up nice. And Jim is massive. He's a mountain. I can't really describe him any more than that. He's quite Scottish-looking, if you know what I mean. Not totally ginger but kind of a weird colour, like tomato ketchup and mayo mixed together. Oh, and they've got a Mondeo now, I think. She said it was a greeny colour, like a seaweed colour, she said. Look out for it.'

'I will. And how do you feel about Jim coming along?'

'It's cool. I mean, fair play to him. He's a good bloke. That's all in the past anyway, with the drugs.' He smiles. 'I think Tracy and Jade are staying with our Katy.'

'Who's Katy?'

'What do you mean, who's Katy? Didn't I tell you they had a kid?'

'Your mum and Jim had a child?'

'Yeah.' He puts his thumbnail to his mouth and worries the edge with his bottom teeth. 'She's like a cousin for Jade, except she's her auntie. It's like that country and western song, "I'm My Own Grandpa" – do you know it?'

Richard shakes his head and laughs. 'And how do you feel about Katy?'

'What do you mean, how do I feel? I can't wait to get to know her properly. I can't wait to spend time with Jade and get to know her an' all. I'm going to do everything I can to make it up to her. When I'm clean, I'm actually quite a nice person, you know.'

'Well, you know what my answer to that is.'

'S-stay c-clean, then, yeah?' Despite the good-natured replies, Graham seems suddenly jittery. The pressure of freedom must be disconcerting, terrifying, even. Seeing him so tense, Richard realises that he himself has passed this moment. That tension is behind him. Something mysterious has happened here, something that has tied him irreversibly to Graham Watson, that has to do with love and forgiveness and the transformative nature of acceptance. He has passed through something. He can feel it. He wonders if Graham has yet to make that final step.

'What about Tracy?' he asks.

'Tracy – well, we'll see how it goes, like.' Graham grins again, briefly, but continues to chew at his thumb.

A silence falls. Richard knows he'll miss Graham more than he can ever put into words.

'So,' he says. 'What about Graham in all this? Do you forgive yourself?'

Graham sighs. After a moment, he says, 'I suppose the trouble is, the old seagull never killed anybody.'

'What do you mean?'

'Just that. I can't ever fly away from what I did, can I?'

'But you know God forgives you?'

'Whatever that means.'

'I think it means you could try to accept that, if you can. And I forgive you. Think of that, if it's easier. And forgive yourself. There are people outside this place who need you to be the person you really are.'

'Jade.' Graham looks out of the window. 'I'll get there. I have to, for her – she's kept me going in here, I can tell you. It's just fighting the guilt, isn't it?'

'It is. But like I said before, guilt is not helpful.'

Graham smiles and raises his eyebrows. There is something final about his expression. This lad, who has helped Richard in so many ways he will never know. Who has been on his mind throughout, who was on his mind this week, when he finally called Alexis's home number, heard her mother answer in the warmest possible tones, thanked her when she gave him Alexis's address. She is living in Morecambe now, has two children and is working as a GP. She will be thrilled to hear from him, will be desperate to see him again. Richard will write to her. He will. Friendship is part of his future. Love is part of his future. And love will be part of Graham's future too.

Graham is still silent. There seems to be nothing left to say.

Richard leans forward a little. 'Do you mind if I say one prayer before you go?'

Graham shrugs. 'Go for it.'

Richard clasps his hands together in his lap and closes his eyes.

'O my Jesus, forgive us our sins, save us from the fires of hell and lead all souls to heaven, especially those most in need of your mercy. Amen.'

'Amen,' says Graham, colouring. 'That was shorter than I thought it was going to be.' He looks relieved. 'I suppose that's it then.'

The conversation is faltering as it draws to a close. Richard realises he was expecting far too much. He wanted to cement everything they'd achieved in the last six months. He wanted to send Graham out unburdened. But Graham is not St Paul; he will not head out of here bathed in light, nor will he embrace God's love as Richard wishes he would. The most Richard can hope for is that he is cleaner and lighter for their time together, and that outside these walls, this will be enough.

Graham is chewing his fingers. 'I mean, the thing is, sometimes I think it'd be easier to stay. Everything's taken care of in here, do you know what I mean?'

Richard's heart sinks. They have only minutes left together. He has to find something, a last word of comfort.

'I remember once,' he says after a moment. 'I was going on a long drive. It was winter. My mother gave me a candle and a box of matches to take with me. She'd heard on the radio that in an emergency, a candle could be the difference between life and death. You know, for the warmth. A small candle can give enough heat to keep you alive.' He can't tell what Graham is thinking; his face is impassive. 'I'm not explaining this very well. I guess that's what I want to give you now – a candle, for your journey, to keep you safe.'

'Aw, you're a good bloke,' Graham says.

'I once thought about becoming a priest,' Richard adds after a moment. 'A long time ago. There were things about myself, about the world, that I couldn't face.'

'Why didn't you then?'

'Well, I decided that it was better to live in the world, to be a part of it, no matter how difficult that might be. When my mum died, I lost my ability to be in the world, but now I'm ready again. I'm ready to step out. And so are you, Graham – so are you.'

Graham rubs his hands together as if he's about to start clearing a garage of junk. Richard half expects him to push up his sleeves.

'You've just got to get out there and get on with it,' he says. 'Haven't you?'

'The last time I saw my mum, she wished me a nice trip,' Richard says.

'Now I don't know what you're talking about.'

'Just that that was the last thing she ever said to me, but I didn't know it at the time so I guess I didn't lend it too much importance. But we once talked, you and me, about the things we say to each other and about what's important, do you remember? And you said it's all important. All those little things. I've thought about that a lot and now I think that what my mother said that last time was very important. "Have a nice trip." It was normal. It was normality.'

'It was love,' Graham says. 'Just as much as anyone saying they love you.'

'It was the candle,' Richard replies, blinking fast. 'The warmth that helps us survive.'

Graham stands up abruptly, making his chair scrape, and rubs his hands on the sides of his sweatshirt. 'Listen, mate, anyway, I just wanted to say ta, like, for everything you've d-done for us.' He hands Richard a white envelope. His face is pink and he cannot hold Richard's eye. 'You can open this once I've gone, 'cos I'm too embarrassed for you to read it now, all right? It's well mushy.'

'All right.' Richard shakes Graham's hand and meets his eye once, twice. For the moment, he is too choked to speak.

'See you later then, yeah?' Graham's voice cracks. He takes a step back.

'Good luck.' Richard gets the words out before they shatter. 'Goodbye, Graham. Be free.'

Still backing away, Graham points at Richard. 'Pray for us, yeah? It seems to work when you do it.' He makes two thumbs-up signs, turns, and like that, he is gone.

The doorway is empty. Surrounded by the shouts and bangs from elsewhere, the chapel is quiet and still. Richard turns the envelope over in his hand, his throat thick. *Richy-Rich*, it says on the front, and this makes him smile. He puts it in his pocket but almost immediately brings it out again. Half of him wants to save it until he finds the perfect moment, but the other half knows that waiting for the perfect moment is a dangerous, dangerous game.

He walks over to the window and opens the envelope. On the small white sheet of paper, words are arranged in what looks like a poem. The handwriting is painstakingly neat. There is evidence of pencil lines that have been rubbed out after the ink has dried. All of this moves him, and steeling himself, he reads.

> I had a friend in front of me,
> If I would only dare
> To talk, to find the hardest words,
> While he was waiting there.
>
> He listened while I got it out
> And now I'm going home.
> I will not see him anymore
> So I'm leaving him this poem.
>
> It's you, the friend, old Richy-Rich!
> You'll always be my mate!
> You helped me fly like the seagull.
> Like you said, it's never too late.

Told you it was embarrassing. Cheers, mate, seriously.
Take care, all right? See you sometime.

Gray

Richard puts the letter in his pocket and wipes his eyes, hoping
that the chapel will remain empty while he composes himself.
What was it Viv said? *These poor buggers might have a funny way of
doing it, but they do give something back, you know, if you let them.*

Outside, in the courtyard, the small patch of yellow sunlight
makes its way around the yard. The men stand huddled in it for
warmth. They will follow this light, as the day grows old and dies,
down to the far corner. They will reappear tomorrow, back where
they started, pulling at cigarettes and following the imperceptible
progress of the sun. In another wing, men paint and strip walls,
walls they will paint and strip again tomorrow, and the next day,
over and over again. In the classrooms, men of thirty will disrupt
English lessons with bravado and buffoonery, stuck in a teenage
that never ends. And here in the chapel, troubled souls will pour
out their stories while Richard listens. That they will leave him a
little lighter is all he can hope for, though of course he hopes for
much more.

Beyond the yard, the metal gates, the curling barbed wire
looping overhead. The tall towers and the saw teeth of the gatehouse
cast their long shadows. Walls and wire, locks upon locks. And
men, hunched and smoking, following the yellow patch of light.

CHAPTER FIFTY-FOUR

Carol

1993

Carol stands on tiptoes. The door hasn't opened yet, but she can't help looking for Graham, as if he might be out here already, through a security mistake or something. The air has warmed up since six, but it's still chilly, still early. There's quite a crowd. Some of them look rough, not like any families she knows, not anymore.

Oh, and there he is! From the far side of the cobbles, there's Graham walking towards her.

No, it's not Graham, of course it's not – how could it be? He's slim like Graham, though; too thin for his bones, with the same black hair, clean-shaven. His cheekbones jut – even from here you can see the slicing shadow of them. Definitely not Graham – wrong walk, not cocky enough – but he looks like he's heading towards her. She can smell Jim's cigar but turns to check he's there anyway, and he is, in the driver's seat, one ear to the radio, one leg out of the car. This thin fellow coming towards her looks like he needs a good bowl of soup; he must be nine stone wet through. He's holding out his hand now – to her.

'Carol MacKay?' he says. 'Hello. I'm Richard Crown. The chaplain at the prison.'

The chaplain. So this is the chap that Graham mentioned.

'Hello, love,' she says, shaking his hand. He's almost bowing now, what lovely manners. 'I'm very grateful to you, love. For all you've done for our Graham. He said you've really helped him, like.'

'I did nothing. He did all the work.' Oh, and he speaks so nicely. His nails are lovely – clean and cut neat.

'Well, thank you anyway.'

Richard chafes his hands together and looks towards the prison for a moment before turning back to her. 'I just wanted to say hello. And good luck. Give Graham my best, won't you? I'll miss him; really I will. But he'll be in my prayers.' He digs in his pocket, pulls out a funny little candle. 'If … if you could give him this?'

'Will do.' She takes the candle from him. She thinks it's called a tea light. There were bags of them for sale in that new furniture place when she went with Jim, but why this Richard chap wants Graham to have one is anyone's guess.

Jim has got up out of the car. He's shaking Richard's hand. 'Pleased to meet you, Richard. Thanks for everything, like.'

'I'd better get inside,' Richard says.

'Right you are, love.' Carol says as he shakes her hand a second time. 'You look after yourself, all right?'

He smiles and waves, already turning to go. She wishes he'd put on some weight and wonders if he has anyone to look after him; whether she should invite him to come for Sunday lunch sometime. But he's walking away, up to the prison, getting smaller and smaller. A moment later, he disappears through the little door in the big black gate.

Behind her now, Jim puts his arm round her shoulder. 'You're cold.'

She is shaking, but it isn't the cold. She glances up at him, shielding her eyes with her hand. 'Eh. You don't think he's con-verted him, do you?'

'Shouldn't think so.'

She's about to reply, but there is movement at the prison door. From the blackened sandstone castle, men begin to spill out. She strains her eyes, steps forward. Her heart hammers. But Graham isn't there. Doubt stalks her. She's maybe got it all muddled, got the wrong day.

But at last, there he is. Definitely this time. She didn't recognise him before. But it is him, it's her son, coming towards her. She'd know that walk anywhere. His hair is thick and black – thank goodness, he's grown out that horrid crew cut. Oh, but he could be his father. He's the image of him, the bloody image, and the sight makes her gasp. But he's not Ted. And nor will he ever be. Ted would never have done what Graham has done for her, for the family.

She is running. The soles of her shoes clack on the cobbles. But she runs. She runs to him.

Graham's features come into focus. He's grinning. He's right in front of her. His brown eyes, his cheeky face. He drops his bag and holds out his arms. 'F-fancy seeing you here.'

She is hugging him. She is holding her son in her arms. His ribs press against hers, his head falls onto her shoulder. He smells of that awful prison soap, but he smells clean. All this time waiting for this moment, wondering how it would go, worrying about it, and now it's here and this is all there is: she just has to hold on to him.

He gives her shoulder a squeeze. She lets go, holds on to his fingers.

'All right?' he says.

'Let's get you into the car,' she says. 'Into the warm.'

'Sounds good.'

He puts his arm around her. Together they walk the last few yards to the car, her feet in step with his, her heart full of fragile hope.

CHAPTER FIFTY-FIVE

Nicola

2019

It is after five a.m. Jim's done in, headed for bed, but I am still wide awake, eyes on stalks. I pick up my phone and text Graham.

U said you had stuff to tell me. Can't you tell me now?

I put the kettle on. May as well pull an all-nighter, though not for a case this time. As I stir in the milk, my phone buzzes.

I'll come over now then.

OK. Text when you get here. Jim in bed don't want to wake him.

Nothing to do but wait for my brother and whatever it is he has to tell me. Restlessness has me stalking through the rooms like a ghost. It's too early in the morning to call Seb and the girls. Perhaps it was wrong of me to come alone. I felt that at six, the twins were too young for a funeral – at least, that's the reason I gave myself. Right now, I wonder if I simply wanted to keep death away from them for as long as possible. Motivations are mysterious things; what we do and why.

In the bathroom, I unscrew my mother's peach bath foam and inhale its familiar synthetic smell. Back in my own room, the weak pre-dawn light filters through curtains my mother made from thin floral fabric from Widnes market. She made the quilt cover too, from the same fabric. Must have got it cheap. On the landing window ledge, there is a glossy porcelain Victorian lady holding a parasol over one shoulder. My colleagues would scoff at such an ornament. They would see tat. But I see her. My mother. This house is full of her, the loving attentions of her life, the touchstones of my life, of my brother's life.

In the spare room, there is a double bed and a travel cot. Graham's daughter Jade and her husband stay here sometimes with their little boy, Connor. That Graham is a grandfather is something I still have to bend my mind around. He had his daughter so early, I had kids so late – another difference in our dramatically different lives. It doesn't escape either of us that we ended up on opposite sides of the law. But what went wrong came right in the end. Carol lived to know five grandchildren – Katy has twin boys, sandy-haired terrors with the cutest freckles. She doted on all her grandchildren, of course, followed their every swimming certificate and qualification, was the first to hold Connor after Jade, up to that hospital before you could say great-grandchild, and the thought brings a small note of happiness to me now. A woman keeps her daughters but loses her sons, they say. A wise woman befriends her son's wife – not sure who said that, if anyone, but it strikes me as true. The fact that Tracy and her family are in our lives at all is down to my mother. When Graham got Tracy pregnant, she must have seen history repeating itself in the worst possible way. She could have abandoned them, as her parents had done to her. But when Graham went to prison, she took Tracy and Jade into her home. She and Jim looked after them, helped them find a flat close by. And when Graham got out, he doted on his daughter with a devotion that was almost unbearably moving to witness. And now, with his grandson, there is such tenderness in the way he is with him that it brings tears to my eyes if I think about it too much. My brother's only ambition, I sometimes think, was to not become his father. For years, he could not escape that legacy, but eventually he did. Much of that is down to Richard Crown, and to my mother, of course.

I pad downstairs and wait in the living room, staring out of the front window, unease in my belly. Graham has something to tell me. This something must relate to my mother's death. It is something he has not been free to tell me until now.

The street is deserted, the sky a muted navy, the street lights still on. I am glad Graham is coming. Jim got him a job on the rigs when he left prison, and for a while they worked opposite rotations. But Jim missed my mother too much, and once he'd saved some money, he gave up the roughneck life and set himself up as a handyman and decorator. He can turn his hand to electrics, plumbing, anything practical, and he's never been short of work. A certain bearish bulk, the accent and an easy smile can't have hurt. Graham stayed on the rigs for a while but left once he had the money together to train as a youth worker. He runs a centre now, specialising in keeping kids off the streets, educating them about drugs, knives and life choices in general, and providing sports facilities. He manages the football team too, and tells me they are the best in the county.

My mother moved into office work and eventually became an account manager, a job she did until she retired eight years ago. A few people who didn't know her so well said that it was a shame she didn't have much time to enjoy her retirement, but I know she loved her job and that she was as happy as anyone, happier than most from the moment Graham came out of prison. Happier for having lost it all and got it back. She used to say that all she wanted was for me to escape, to make it to college, but I know that all she really wanted was a family. It was what she got in the end: a huge higgledy-piggledy family.

Graham's semi-electric car whistles up the drive. I wonder for a second, madly, if Tracy is home with the kids, before remembering that Jade is in her thirties now, that I have nieces and great-nephews that, in my forties, I don't feel old enough to have.

Graham gets out of the car and raises his hand. I dart towards the front door, my insides heating with anxiety. I thought he had told me everything. But he had not. There is one last thing.

I open the door.

CHAPTER FIFTY-SIX

Nicola

Graham is sitting on the sofa, a little apart from me. His spread hands are on his knees.

'Nicky,' he says, my name almost a sigh. 'So, me and Mum, right, we knew we ... we thought we would never ...' He stops, appears to gather himself. 'You know, when things were bad. We were ... broken, back then. After Dad. She was a wreck and I was ... well, I was hell. I was in hell, anyway.'

'It's OK.' I lean forward, stroke his arm, lean back.

He glances up at me, meets my eye with a wary gaze. 'The first thing you need to know is that I d-didn't kill Barry.'

'What?' My body stiffens. I sit tall, rigid on the couch, as if the violent removal of this long-held truth has stripped out the very skeleton of me. I have to concentrate just to sit straight, to not collapse. 'What do you mean, you didn't kill Barry?'

'I didn't kill him, Nick.'

'You didn't kill him? What? But—'

He holds up his hand – wait. 'After I'd had that fight with that lad and Barry had legged it and all that stuff you know about, I ran down to Barry's, like I said, to deck him or at least give him a mouthful, like.'

I bite my lip. I know all this. But I can see that he needs a run-up to whatever it is he has to say.

'I didn't know this, but while all that was going on, Mum had come up to ours to persuade me to come home.'

My throat tightens. A nasty taste fills my mouth. It is the taste of my childhood, the taste of dread.

'So Barry says to come through to the kitchen like nothing has happened. And I follow him and he's joking around and that, asking me if I want anything, like if I *need* anything, you know?'

I nod.

'So I ask him what he thinks he's playing at, intimidating girls and that.'

Graham stops, rubs his head, exhales. He looks out of the front window and then back at me. I don't know what he sees in my eyes, but whatever it is makes him falter. He looks down at his knees and begins to talk again. 'And next thing he's got this kitchen knife … well, it was *the* knife, you know, from the trial … and he picks it up and he's waving it around at us, trying to frighten us or something. And he sort of lunges and cuts my arm, and he lunges again and cuts my cheek.'

Again I nod. There is still a pink line, no bigger than the imprint of a fingernail now, under his left eye.

'Which, obviously, I'm glad he did 'cos just by doing that he got me less time inside, ironically.'

'Irony's ironic.'

'Yeah. So. I mean, I thought I was hard, Nick. I'd always been hard, like, you know, at school and that.'

'I know. My big brother was *the* Graham Green.' I smile at him, remembering the surprise on the other kids' faces, the ill-disguised shock in the eyes of the teachers when they put our surnames together.

'Well, we fought, as you know, me and Barry,' Graham continues. 'Every bruise he laid on me was one year less in jail – well, figure of speech. He had me on the ground. And he still had the

knife. I was squeezing his wrist, trying to get it off him, and …
I can't remember if I did get it off him or if he threw it down,
but next thing he's strangling me, he's f-f-f … he's strangling me,
Nick – well, you know that.'

'Yes.' These too I remember, the strange red finger marks on
Graham's thin neck when we went to visit him in custody. 'And
then you grabbed the knife.'

He shakes his head. 'No,' he says. 'Just … just let me …'

'Sorry. Go on.'

'I thought I'd had it, Nick. Seriously felt myself going, do you
know what I mean?'

I nod. I have no idea what it feels like to almost have the life
choked out of you – that is an experience he and my mother share
– but my focus is not on how he felt then but on how I feel now,
listening. Over the years, my job has given me a spider sense for
lies. But there are no lies here. And the urgency with which my
brother is speaking is that of a certain kind of truth, a final truth
that rushes out when all impediment is removed.

My mother was that impediment.

And at that thought, another dawns. My mother.

I clap my hand over my mouth.

'Mum,' I whisper between my fingers.

Graham nods slowly, his eyes dark and on mine. 'Yeah.' He
shakes his head, as if to right himself. 'She'd been up to ours. But
I wasn't there, obviously, so she ran down to Barry's. I must've
left his door open when I went in, because next thing she's there.
I saw her over his shoulder. She said afterwards that my face had
gone blue.' He stops, meets my eye again.

'She grabbed the knife,' I say slowly.

He nods. 'And she … she sort of lashed out at him. She was
clumsy with it, like.'

We are holding hands. I can't remember when this happened
or who reached out to whom.

'It's OK,' I say. 'It's all right.'

The little brass clock on the mantel strikes six. There's only us here, my brother and me. We are the only people who exist.

'And I think in the panic, she shoved it in his neck. The tip went right in. Well, you know what the injury was. The main artery. The knife was sticking out of his neck. She jumped back and Barry started screaming. He let go of me. I just ... I pulled it out. The knife. It was all so fast, I can't remember exactly how it went, but next thing I had it in my hand and then there was blood everywhere. He went to get off me but I pushed him; I pushed him over and pinned him down on the floor. There was blood gushing out of his neck. I told Mum to run. I was like, *get out, get out*. The blood had sprayed all over me but there was nothing on her. Nothing on her, like. Barry was on the floor and he was screaming. I was shouting at her to get out. I told her I'd sort it. She wouldn't go. She wouldn't go, Nick. She was crying. We were both panicking. She was going to call the police. Barry was bleeding out. Well, you know that. There was loads of blood, Nick, and it was all on me. All on me and on him and on the floor. But it wasn't on her.

'I just kept shouting *go home*, like. "You can't go down for this," I said. "What about our Nicky?"'

'What about me?' I ask. 'What has this got to do with me?'

He traces his thumb across my knuckles. 'It's all about you, Nick. Don't you get it? All of it. That's why I didn't want you visiting me inside. I wanted you to get out. Me and Mum, we had to get you to uni. You had to do well. It was the only way for you to ... for you to fly, do you see what I mean?'

I am blinking, but I cannot see. For so long I thought I understood, but I had not grasped the facts of the case. My brother, my mother. Their conspiracy. For me, all for me.

'She went in the end,' he says. 'I told her she had to look after Tracy and Jade, that I couldn't, but she was still like, "I can't let you go to prison for me. I can't let you do that."'

'So I promised her I'd get clean. Inside, like. I told her it was what I needed, some time out. It was the only way. I promised I'd sort myself out and come back.' He lets go of one of my hands and wipes his eyes before returning his hand to mine. 'She didn't want me to go down, obviously. But she knew that of the two of us, she was the only one who could get you on to better things. And she knew she was the only one who could look after the family; well, she knew I couldn't. I promised her, Nick. I promised her I'd sort myself out inside. I almost didn't do it, but then you wouldn't stay away until I'd promised to get help. Do you remember? I had to practically tell you to piss off.' He glances up, meets my eye. A sheepish grin. 'I found Richard. And he helped me sort it. Myself, I mean.'

In his eyes, I see him pleading: believe me, accept what I have told you, it is the truth. He is my big brother. He has looked after me in ways I cannot even imagine. It never occurred to me to look after him.

Without Graham, my mother would have gone to prison. Without my mother, all would have been lost. My brother took the hit. He was innocent, but he served a prison sentence. He did this for Mum, for me. For our family. I always thought that it was my mother's determination that got me to where I am now, but I see now that my life, the way it has gone, is down to both of them.

'You sorted it,' I say softly. 'You both did.'

'You didn't waste it.' His voice is choked. 'You didn't let us down.'

'I hope not.'

'What d'you mean, soft girl? Of course you didn't. You made it. You're a posh twat now.' A laugh escapes him; he wipes his face. 'You made it, Nick, and we were so proud, like, you know? It was … it was everything.'

We don't hug, not then. We hug later at the door, when he leaves.

'Don't be a stranger,' he says into my ear. 'Posh bird.'

'Bird?' I say. 'Upgrade.'

He waves into the rear-view mirror as he pulls out of the driveway. After he has gone, I stare at the street on this housing estate where I grew up. My mother raised us, mostly here, under the most difficult circumstances, circumstances I have only now come to understand completely. That night when she returned from Graham's flat, the torment she must have been in. All I remember was her checking in on me, her feet on the landing, the run of the bath. And of course, she tried to protest to the police officers – *It was me. I killed him.* The officers, myself, all of us seeing only a mother desperate to protect her son, to take the rap for him out of love. I took her turmoil for despair at what Graham had done. A kind of grief, regret, even a sense of failure. But she could tell no one the truth, not even Jim. To do so would have destroyed the ragged remains of the family she had risked everything to save. My God, to have held that secret, to have borne that guilt. And yet she did it, silently. My mother.

Opposite the living-room window, beyond the driveway, is a bank of grass, the grey kerb that borders the road. Graham used to stand on the far side when we played kerby. He made me stand on the pavement nearest the house so that I didn't have to cross the street. The fact that it might be dangerous to throw the ball into the road and run after it didn't occur to us. We were just kids. I was a little girl, caught in the specific wonder that came whenever my big brother chose to spend time with me.

I lost him, that big brother. From the moment we left my father, he receded, became every day a paler ghost. I was only eleven when he came into my room late one night and lay spooned against me in the dark. That's the only reason, the only justification I can give for what I told him, what has lain at the dark heart of me all these years. What I did is my bogeyman, my guilt, my regret.

My big brother had come back to me that night. And I had to find a way to keep him. In that exquisite darkness, the bedroom floor rumbling with the dull notes of my mother talking with Jim MacKay, this man we didn't know, had never heard of, and who had appeared from nowhere, Graham and I spoke of my father. I told him I knew about the violence. It made me feel grown up to tell him that. It made me feel included. And he held my hand and asked if my father had ever hurt me.

'No,' I said. 'But he shouted. He was scary.'

'He was.' Graham squeezed me tight. He was mine again. I could chat to him and feel safe and loved and protected. I was happy. I could not let go of that happiness, could not let go of him. I had missed him; I missed the old him who would sleep on the floor and play Name That Tune until we fell asleep because I was afraid of the dark. I'm justifying it, I know, but I was only a child. So when my brother asked, 'And Dad never ... he never touched you or anything, did he?' I nodded and said, 'Yes.'

I said yes.

I remember Graham sitting bolt upright in the dark, the loss of his warmth, the air cold at my back.

'What?' he said. 'Where?'

'In my private place,' I whispered into the delicious darkness. 'Don't tell anyone.'

I was so young, too young to understand the potency of words. I understood it years later, but by then, admitting to it was impossible. I will never know what part I played in helping Graham in his descent. By the time disaster struck, it was too late to tell the truth. How do you admit to someone, someone you love, that you told a lie that may well have contributed to their wretched fate? It's possible that it made no difference, that he was already on that path, but it's possible that it made all the difference, and that's what haunts me still.

Looking back, and with a vast experience of dealing with troubled families, I realise that this was a terrible time, the worst – those months after we left. I can see that the trauma of it was not apparent to me as a child. On the surface, I was happy. I worked hard at school, I washed my face and braided my hair and folded my school uniform at night. I took pride in all of that. It was my role as I understood it, my place in the family. If you'd asked me how I was back then, I would have said, 'Fine, thank you for asking' like my mother told me to. I have held this darker memory at the edge of my consciousness whilst all the while being fuelled by the force of it. My lurking shadow.

I have no clue where I got the idea from. Maybe from a kid at the shelter, maybe from television, I don't know. My father had never done anything of the kind. He was scary, yes. He shouted, he beat my mother. He was sick on the floor sometimes. He would stagger around like a wounded bull, too big for the house, his mouth slack and wet, and yes, that was terrifying for a child. But he didn't touch me, not like that.

I know I must forgive the little girl that I was. I know it was no doubt a bid for attention beneath the construct I had made of my mother's too-clever-for-me daughter, a deeper need for sympathy or love or something like that from my beloved but lost older brother, who was stroking my hair and shushing me to sleep as he held me tight. I know that I can never tell him; that if it was too late before, it is certainly too late now.

CHAPTER FIFTY-SEVEN

Graham

2019

Graham can still remember the day Nicky qualified, how he answered the door to his mother, whose eyes were wet with joy.

'She's done it,' she'd said. 'Our Nicky's going to be a lawyer down in London.' She'd held his eye. In hers he'd seen everything they'd fought for, everything they'd agreed in panic and terror that night long ago.

'She'd never have done it without you,' he'd said, holding her tiny frame in his arms.

'You're the one who went to prison.'

'I'm the one who messed everything up.'

She'd taken a step back and gave him a soft punch on the shoulder. 'How about we say we both helped get her there, eh? That do? We did it, kid. We bloody did it.'

At the end, when she could no longer speak, he thought about that conversation. She'd given him something that day – acknowledgement, perhaps. Redemption. Whatever, he had felt something in him shift. He had felt better.

He hopes he's done the right thing, telling his sister. It's selfish, he knows, but part of him needs for her to think well of him. Now their mother has gone, he wants to keep her close. She lives in a world so different from his own. She has never consciously made him feel that difference, but her way of speaking, the clothes she wears, her offhand references to theatres and bars and friends who come for dinner make him feel it nonetheless. She is part of another class now, that's the bottom line. He doesn't resent this or her. It just is what it is. Education is a journey. That you end up in a different place is and always was the whole point. Hasn't he done the same?

But there is one truth Nicola cannot ever know. It would risk the deep bond they have fought so hard for and won despite everything.

He drives past the town hall, grand and white in its green gardens. He and Tracy were married here; it was the day he truly felt his new life begin. He passes under the expressway, turns right after the corner shop into Latham Avenue, left again into Picton Avenue. Tracy will probably have left by the time he gets back, for her early shift in the maternity unit. But the house won't be empty. Jade and Connor are staying the night, and he is grateful.

Because his mind is filling with an old, old weight.

I killed a man, he said to Richard all those years ago, in a makeshift chapel in a castle that was once a prison.

Sometimes words are enough to tie a weight around your soul and drown it. Graham has come to believe in souls. Not that he'd ever tell anyone that.

And nor will he ever speak about the night Nicky told him about his father's sick perversion. There are some things that must remain unsaid. That his father had violated his sister before she was even ten years old is one of those things. That night, Graham had stroked Nicky's hair until she fell asleep, forced himself to lie still though his blood was high and fast with a fury that threatened to send him raging into the street. But he'd waited, made himself wait. The next day, he went to see his boys, to talk business.

'Lads,' he had said. 'I've got a job for us.'

The timing is hazier than the facts. But it was a day, maybe a couple of days after, that Jim left. That night, Graham watched television with his mother, tried hard to be normal, went to bed early. She would be glad, he knew, to have her boy home for a change. She was filled with sadness; he could see it hanging on her face. But he couldn't reach her, not then. He had other things on his mind.

By ten, exhausted, she was asleep. And out he slipped, into the murderous night. It was easy, nothing out of the ordinary. Clothes rolled under his bedding, shimmy down the drainpipe.

His friends were at the bus stop, where he'd told them to be. His crew: the meatheads, the dead-eyed boys, bristling with disappointment and the deep desire for damage. And as he walked towards them that night, from the sleeve of his jacket Graham pulled the rounders bat he'd stolen from school months before.

'B-boys,' he said as the street light caught in their shining eyes. 'Let's do this.'

His knuckles whiten now on the steering wheel. It is a different Graham, that boy, a person he can't believe he ever was. He parks the car outside his house and rests his forehead in his hands. Richard wanted him to talk about it, so he told him another tale. To speak about this was never on the table, even to a man as good and true as Richard. Speak about it? Graham can't even think about it without the palpitations starting, the sickening churning of his guts and an old, old desire for narcotic oblivion. But he makes himself think about it now, as punishment. That night. That dark night, like all dark nights, when a car is easy enough to steal if your crew have been joyriding since they were twelve. When a town you were supposed to have left for ever is easy enough to find your way back to if you can read the road signs. Your father's drinking hole? Well, that's elementary, my dear Watson, if you'll pardon the pun.

You just follow your nose to the stench.

At midnight Graham and his friends were waiting for Ted. Five of them in all. Half past, quarter to one, ten to … his father finally, staggering out of the lock-in, the shine of spit on his lips, piss dark on the crotch of his trousers. Ted Watson, under the painted sign: a flaking, discoloured bunch of grapes on a damp brick wall.

That's him.

Sometimes words are enough to tie a weight around your soul and drown it. Sometimes they are enough to kill a man. *That's him* were the only words Graham needed to send his boys into action. A raining-down of blows, one for each one the bastard had given his mother over the years, let out in a single fatal battering. There was so much blood. In shock and fascination, he watched it spread through the pale fabric of his father's shirt. Stood at a distance, unable to look away. Who is the victim now? Who will step in to protect you tonight?

The blood had a strange, familiar metallic smell. He can remember how thick it was, how dark. A last grunt, and the body was still. He can remember the others telling him to go, to run back to the car, but he couldn't move his feet, couldn't break his own rapt disgust, couldn't tear his eyes from the sight of that black lake.

A body left in an empty car park, found in the early hours of the morning in a pool of dried blood. Old Teddy Watson, got himself into another fight. Handy with his fists, that one. Trouble. A piss'ead. Used to beat his missus, you know. But still, what a shame. A motiveless crime. Thugs these days, what is the world coming to? Bring back National Service. Bring back hanging.

Graham never raised a finger. Stood back and watched, arms folded, mouth tight. He did not lay a hand on his father. The next day, his mother vouched for him.

'He was here. With me.'

'I was here all night.'

There was not a mark on him. They took his fingerprints, found nothing. Asked him questions; some he answered with lies, some with the truth. The facts of it were that he did not lay a hand on his father, but the bones and blood and flesh of him know the deeper truth. The deeper truth he carries with him every day of his life. Sucks it in with nicotine and pummels it out at the gym, speaks it in silent prayers in the night and atones for it in each daily act of kindness, with the kids in the community centre he helped set up to keep them off the streets. His whole life is kindness these days. He clings to it. People say he's the nicest guy they know. Friends of his mother's would shake their heads and smile. *Your Graham*, they'd say. *He's a bloody saint.* And he has to be. Because he knows more than anyone that just as you don't have to hit a woman to make her afraid, so you don't have to lay a hand on a man to take his life. You can serve time for a crime you didn't commit and still know that justice has been done. You can put yourself in prison for killing your father long after you watched him fall, broken, to the ground. You can find a way to reframe what you did and learn to live with it so that you can finally stop the suffering of those who need you most. And you can watch your father's blood pool on the tarmac and know that it is yours, that no matter what you do, no matter how many prayers you say, that same blood will flow through your veins for all time, until the very last beat of your troubled, broken heart.

He gets out of the car. Fumbles with his keys. But the front door opens; Tracy is there and she is smiling.

'I was just off,' she half laughs, her face rearranging itself then into concern. 'Are you all right, love? You look sad.'

'I am sad,' he says. 'But better for seeing you.' He leans in, kisses her on the lips. 'See you later, yeah. What d'you want for tea?'

'Oh, anything,' She is halfway down the drive. A click on the key fob and her little Nissan flashes and beeps.

'Have a good shift.'

'Ta. See you later.'

This is normality. This is the candle in the car.

His chest swells. He goes into the house, is greeted by the sight of Jade and Connor sitting close together on the living-room floor. Jade is reading her son a story from the iPad.

'Looks who's here,' she says, looking up. 'It's Grandad!'

But Connor is already on his feet, is already toddling towards him. He throws his arms around Graham's knees, plants his face in his legs.

'Dan-da,' he says.

'All right, little one.' Graham tousles the boy's fine hair and is filled with something new, something light, something clean. His blood runs here too. Into the future it runs, into his family – in peace, in hope, in love.

A LETTER FROM
S.E. LYNES

Dear Reader,

Thank you so much for reading *The Lies We Hide*. If you enjoyed it, and want to keep up to date with all my latest releases, just sign up at the following link. Your email address will never be shared and you can unsubscribe at any time.

www.bookouture.com/se-lynes

This book began back in the late eighties when I was a reporter for the BBC. The programme I was working on was covering the topic of domestic violence, and I was sent to a refuge to interview two women who had been abused by their husbands. One of them had been held under the bathwater. She truly believed she was going to die, leaving her two sons motherless, and she vowed that if she lived through the experience, she would leave that same night and take her boys with her. As you will now realise, that became the inspiration for Carol's story.

Interviewing those women had a profound impact on me. I was in my twenties and reasonably naïve; I was happily married and my childhood had been warm and safe. What struck me most was that although these women's narratives could be said to be over – they'd done it, they'd got away – what I saw was another terrifying beginning. They were badly scarred, physically and emotionally; they were destitute, jobless, homeless, with children to feed, clothe, bring up alone. They were refugees from war-torn homes. I could not get my head around how any woman could even begin to make a new life for herself under these circumstances. So what perhaps should have been the end of a story became for me the start: Carol leaves her husband in the opening section of the novel; it then focuses on how such a violent past might consistently hamper a present, how it might make a successful future almost impossible. As Nicola says, 'The thing about second chances is that they drag with them the scars of the first fucked-up attempt, scars that infiltrate and derail our best attempts at redemption.'

It is said that reading makes people more empathic. In this story, I have tried to explore with empathy how easily a family can fall apart but how, with enough love, it can eventually heal. I am above all delighted that Bookouture have published Carol's story. For me this book is about so many things: family, fear, the legacy of abuse, violence, politics, compassion, friendship, grief, redemption, kindness and, mainly, love. It is not the first time I have felt the responsibility for the subject matter very keenly. Whilst this is not a true story, it is based on a truth all too common. I hope with Carol that I have managed to represent at least some women who have been through something similar and to have told her story and that of her family authentically and compassionately.

The day spent at Lancaster Castle, back when it was a prison, marked me too. The visit, along with many conversations with a close and much-loved relative who worked as a prison chaplain, made me aware of how very difficult it is for offenders to stay out of prison. The psychological and emotional conditions as well as the often-challenging external factors make it almost impossible for some not to reoffend. One inmate I spoke to told me he preferred it inside; the responsibilities that came with life outside were too much for him to cope with. Graham's story too has to do with second chances and why they are sometimes foiled by the past. I wanted to explore how someone so haunted might conceivably arrive at a point where he could come to terms with the huge existentialist crisis inherent in having taken a life, and begin to build a positive life of his own.

I could go on and on as this book means a great deal to me, but if you wish to get in touch, I am always happy to chat via Twitter, Facebook or Instagram. Writing can be a lonely business, so when a reader reaches out and tells me that my work has moved them, stayed with them or that they simply loved it, I am beyond delighted. I have enjoyed making new friends online through my psychological thrillers *Valentina, Mother, The Pact, The Proposal* and *The Women*, and hope to make more with this somewhat different offering.

Thanks again for reading *The Lies We Hide*. If you enjoyed it, I would be very grateful if you could spare a couple of minutes to write a review. It only needs to be a line or two and I would really appreciate it.

Best wishes,
Susie

@selynesauthor
SE LynesAuthor

ACKNOWLEDGEMENTS

Firstly, I'd like to thank my publisher, Jenny Geras, for believing in this book and wanting to publish it even though it isn't strictly speaking a psychological thriller. Really, this is much appreciated because this book has been a labour of love. Huge thanks to Emily Gowers for some great editorial advice that really helped improve the story whilst keeping it completely true to the original. Thanks to Jane Selley for her eagle-eye fine-edit expertise; to everyone who works so hard at Bookouture to turn these books around as quickly as they do; and to the amazing publicity team, Kim Nash and Noelle Holten, whose frantic social-media skills make my head ache just thinking about them.

I'd like to thank my agent, Veronique Baxter at David Higham Associates, for loving Carol's story and being so moved by it that she made me believe it in all over again.

I'd also like to thank my first agent, Teresa Chris. Teresa was the first person from the publishing industry ever to read my work, when I was a shaking hopeful at the Winchester Writers' Festival many years ago. She read Carol and Ted's opening scene back when the book was called *Full Sentences*, and asked for the manuscript. She believed in this book and in me right at the start of my writer's journey, and without people who believe in us, where would we be? In this spirit, I would also like to thank Stephane Zia at Blackbird Digital Books, my first ever publisher, who believed in me too, who allowed me to fly (like Jonathan Livingston Seagull) and who effectively bought me some much-needed time to finish what I felt was an important story.

A huge thank you to Christine Townson, who gave me the inside track on prison chaplaincy over many conversations and who made it possible for me to spend the day inside Lancaster Castle back in the nineties when it was a prison. Thank you to all the staff at the prison at that time, to the lads who talked to me so frankly about their routines, their fears and their hopes, and to the guard who let me out again at the end of the day. Thank you to Sumaira Wilson for answering my queries, to Heather Geddes, and for checking for psychological plausibility, to Patsy Bolton, who talked me through how Graham's struggles would conceivably manifest themselves. Thank you to those brave women all those years ago in a refuge somewhere in the UK who spoke to me so honestly about their experience of domestic violence and how they escaped. It was a humbling moment in my life that I still remember vividly almost thirty years later, and that I wanted so much to give voice to here. I hope they all went on to live in safety and peace.

Thank you to my first ever writing teacher, Sara Bailey; to my first ever writing group: Zoe Antoniades, John Rogers, Callie Langridge, Sam Hanson; to my MA writing group: Hope Caton, Robin Bell, Andrew Baird, Catherine Morris and Sam Hanson (again), who have known Carol and helped me develop her story over many years. Thanks to the MA tutors at Kingston University who advised on those very early drafts – fragments, really: David Rogers, Rachel Cusk, David Bailey and Maree Giles.

Thank you to all my wonderful readers, too numerous to mention, to those who have written to me and spoken to me at bookish events and who have reviewed my books and been so active in waving the S.E. Lynes author flag – without you lot, these stories simply don't exist. To all the bloggers, a mahooossive shout – you know who you are and I know who you are, so thank you so much for your incredible support.

Love and thanks to my beta-reader daughter, Maddie Lynes, who gave me some super-insightful comments; to my dad, Steven Ball, for not being at all like Ted apart from the jokes; and to my mum, Cath Ball, for information on Blackpool Pleasure Beach as it was in the late sixties and, as always, for reading and rereading and telling me when something rings true and when it doesn't. Lastly, as always, to the kind, funny Mr Susie himself, Paul, who even though I sometimes drive him bats is always gentle and always on my side, as well as sorting out all the technical stuff, taking the bins out and dealing with big spiders.

Cheers all, and big love. XXX

Lightning Source UK Ltd.
Milton Keynes UK
UKHW011142271219
355982UK00001B/97/P